KT-483-352

# PRAISE FOR MONICA MCINERNEY'S BESTSELLERS

'Monica McInerney is at the very top of her game . . . if you've yet to read her books, treat yourselves IMMEDIATELY!'
PATRICIA SCANLAN, BESTSELLING AUTHOR OF A TIME FOR FRIENDS

'You'll be laughing out loud one minute and crying the next'
COSMOPOLITAN

'Heart-warming . . . a lovely read'
HELLO! MAGAZINE

'McInerney is becoming a must-read author for women's fiction fans around the world'
HUFFINGTON POST

'The sort of feel-good read you long to get back to'
HILARY BOYD, BESTSELLING AUTHOR OF THURSDAYS IN THE PARK

'Exploring universal family issues of loss, rivalry, ageing and grief, this is a warm, witty and moving novel'
WOMAN'S DAY

'McInerney's bewitching multigenerational saga lavishly and lovingly explores the resiliency and fragility of family bonds'
BOOKLIST

'A world of family, love, warmth and heartbreaking secrets that will sweep you up . . . superb'
BOOKS OF ALL KINDS

'If you haven't discovered McInerney yet, now is the time to do so'
BETTER READING

Also by Monica McInerney

*A Taste for It*
*Upside Down Inside Out*
*Spin the Bottle*
*The Alphabet Sisters*
*Family Baggage*
*Those Faraday Girls*
*All Together Now*
*At Home with the Templetons*
*Lola's Secret*
*The House of Memories*
*Hello from the Gillespies*
*The Trip of a Lifetime*

# *The*
# Godmothers
# Monica McInerney

WELBECK

Published in 2021 by Welbeck Fiction Limited,
part of Welbeck Publishing Group
20 Mortimer Street London W1T 3JW

Copyright © Aibrean Limited, 2020
Cover design by www.headdesign.co.uk
Illustration by Dean Proudfoot at Watermark Creative

The moral right of Monica McInerney to be identified as the author of this
Work has been asserted by her in accordance with the Copyright,
Designs & Patents Act 1988

*All characters and events in this publication, other than those clearly in
the public domain, are fictitious and any resemblance to real persons,
living or dead, is purely coincidental.*

First published by Random House Australia in 2020

All rights reserved. No part of this publication may be reproduced, stored
in a retrieval system, or transmitted in any form or by any means,
electronically, mechanical, photocopying, recording or otherwise, without
the prior permission of the copyright owners and the publishers.

A CIP catalogue record for this book is available from the British Library

Hardback: 978-1-78739-524-4
Trade Paperback: 978-1-78739-577-0
E-book: 978-1-78739-525-1

Printed and bound by CPI Group (UK) Ltd., Croydon, CR0 4YY

10 9 8 7 6 5 4 3 2 1

*For John Neville of St Patrick's Road
and Limerick, with love and thanks.*

# CHAPTER ONE

By the time Eliza Maxine Olivia Miller was eleven, she had lived in eight different country towns. Her mother liked to move a lot.

It was a hot November afternoon. Eliza and her mother Jeannie were currently living in Morwell, two hours from Melbourne. Eliza's class was rehearsing Christmas carols for the end-of-year concert. She was thrilled to have been picked to stand near the front, holding up a tinfoil star. Tall for her age, she was usually asked to keep to the back of school groups.

After the rehearsal, her classmates talked about who'd be coming to watch their performance. Eliza just listened, still not quite part of the class. She often arrived at new schools in the middle of term, when most of the friendships were already formed.

One girl was the youngest of six, born and bred in the town. She announced that her whole family and all four grandparents were coming. They'd fill an entire row of seats. One boy had invited all nine of his cousins.

'What about you, Eliza?' another girl eventually asked.

'Just my mum,' she said, trying not to blush at the rare attention.

'Your dad can't make it?'

Eliza shook her head.

One of the other girls asked Eliza where her father was. Eliza told her she didn't know.

'But you must know,' the girl said. 'Everyone knows where their father is.'

Eliza went red, wishing the bell would ring, hoping the girl wouldn't ask for her father's name. She didn't know that either.

'You do actually have a father, Eliza, I promise,' her mother had said once, smiling. 'I'm not making him up. He just doesn't live with us.'

'Can I please meet him one day?' She regularly asked that.

'I hope so. One day.' Her mother always gave that answer.

'Why not now?'

'Because he doesn't live in Australia at the moment.'

'Where does he live?'

Her mum leaned forward and whispered. 'On the moon.'

Eliza's mother had once told her that her father lived in a pyramid in Egypt. Another time she told her he was a spy for the Russians, working undercover – 'that means in secret' – and it would be dangerous for them to contact him. Once, she said he was a stunt double for a famous actor in Hollywood.

'When will you tell me the truth?' Eliza often asked.

'The day you turn eighteen,' her mother would say. 'As I've promised you many times.'

After school that day, Eliza followed her usual routine, walking home alone and using a key hanging on a ribbon around her neck to let herself in. She hung up her schoolbag and changed into what her mum called her 'casually casual' clothes: brightly coloured, all from op shops. She took a shop-bought chicken pie out of the freezer and set the table for two. Her mum wouldn't be home from her job at the supermarket until eight p.m., so it didn't need to go in the oven yet. She washed out her mother's wineglass and put the two empty bottles with the others by the back door. Then she found the latest list her mother had left her and started to work her way through it.

Lists were one of her favourite things. Her mum loved them too. They often wrote to each other in list form.

*Hello*
*Mum*
*How*
*Are*
*You?*

*Very*
*Well*
*Thank*
*You*
*Eliza.*

Her mum always used lists when she gave Eliza tasks to do around the house. Those lists didn't just keep Eliza busy. They kept her company, in a funny way. The nights waiting for her mum to come home from her shelf-stacking job were sometimes lonely. Jeannie often worked weekend shifts too. She had explained that they needed money to pay for their rent, food and clothes. So while her having to work made their life harder in some ways, it made it easier in others. Her mum was always good at explaining what she called 'both sides of the story'.

That afternoon after school, she did all her mum had asked.

*Do me one of your lovely paintings. (Possible subjects – my pot plants? The green vase?)*

*Sweep the kitchen floor.*

*Watch two cartoons.*

Eliza added other things herself. She played her favourite song on the recorder, trying to ignore the screeched notes. She went out to the verandah and filled up the bird feeder. She picked up her book and curled up on the worn couch to read. She must have fallen asleep. She woke when she felt the weight of her mother sitting beside her, felt her hand gently stroke her dark hair, heard her whisper.

'Eliza? Sweetheart?'

She sat upright. Oh no, the pie! It needed to go in the oven!

Her mother soothed her. 'I've done it, don't worry. It won't take long.'

As it warmed up, her mother asked her how her day had

been. It was mostly good, Eliza said. Except in the last lesson one of the boys in her class had pinched her. It had hurt.

'Do you want me to come to your school tomorrow and kill that boy?'

It was such a naughty thing to say that Eliza found herself giggling. She shook her head.

'Could I hurt him badly?' her mum said. 'Blind him? Break his pencils in two? Set his books on fire?'

Another giggle, another shake of her head.

'Spoilsport.' Her mother smoothed her hair back in the way Eliza loved and kissed her again.

After dinner, they did the dishes together. Eliza was on the way to her bedroom to change into her pyjamas when the phone rang. She heard her mum talking and laughing. She guessed it was one of her two godmothers.

Eliza loved Maxie and Olivia. She only got to see them once or twice a year, with Maxie being so busy acting in her TV show in Sydney, and Olivia now living in a hotel filled with art in Edinburgh with her new husband and stepsons, but it was always great fun when they came to stay. Her mother was always so happy to see them too.

She was in bed reading when she heard her mum finish the phone call. Jeannie appeared at her bedroom door shortly after, with a glass of wine in her hand, a big smile on her face.

'Eliza Maxine Olivia, I have major news.'

Eliza liked it when her mother made these kinds of announcements.

She came over and sat on the edge of the bed. 'Tomorrow I will be phoning your school. I will say it is in regard to the forthcoming school concert. I will be asking the relevant person to reserve three tickets for me.'

'Three?'

'One for me. And one for each of your godmothers.'

Eliza's eyes widened. 'Both of them are coming? At the same time?'

'Both. Alive and dangerous,' her mother said.

That concert was one of Eliza's happiest childhood memories.

The school hall was packed by six p.m., every seat filled, people lining the walls too. Eliza kept peeking out from behind the stage curtains. She started to worry that they'd be late, or not get there at all. Something made her look just before the concert began. The back door of the hall opened. Her mother came in first, so pretty in a red dress, smiling widely, her black curls so shiny. Somehow, she spotted Eliza and blew her a kiss. Olivia was next, tall and slender with wavy brown hair. Then Maxie, curvy, with dyed-red hair. They were wearing colourful dresses too.

They looked so amazing that the photographer from the local paper came up afterwards and took a photo of them with Eliza. It appeared on the front page the following week. Of course, the headline was about Maxine Hill, the famous soap actress, being in town, but Eliza was still named, and so were her mum and Olivia.

In the photo, Eliza was standing in front, beaming, her long black hair in two plaits, dark against her white angel costume.

Right behind, her arms wrapped around Eliza, was her mother, smiling too. They were almost the same height. To Eliza's left, Maxie; to her right, Olivia. They were like two guardian angels.

Her godmothers stayed for three nights. Eliza went to bed each evening to the sound of the three of them talking and laughing, of corks regularly being taken out of bottles. It felt different to Eliza, much better, to hear the cork noise when there were others with her mother.

At some stage over that weekend, the godmothers' holiday plan was hatched.

'We made a solemn promise about it,' her mum told her the morning they left. 'I wanted to seal it in blood but we shook hands instead.'

Every year from now on, she explained, Maxie and Olivia would take Eliza away for a week or so each. It would mean she'd have two holidays a year. She'd get to know her godmothers, and they'd get to know her. It would also give her mum a break.

'Not that I need a break from you, sweetpea. But they said I was being selfish keeping you to myself.'

The first year, both holidays were in Australia. Maxie still lived in Sydney. Olivia was based in Scotland but had come back to see her family. But as the years went by, with Maxie moving to the UK for her work too, the destinations became more exotic and interesting. By the time Eliza was seventeen, she'd visited Edinburgh, London, Paris, Singapore, Hong Kong and Hanoi.

Eliza never knew beforehand where she was going. A month before each holiday, she'd receive a letter or, in later years, an email, telling her the departure date and what to pack. On the chosen day, her mum would drive her to the airport or train station. Only then would she learn the destination. Her mum would kiss her goodbye and stay waving for as long as she could see her. When Eliza came home, full of stories, her mum was always waiting for her, eager to hear everything, see photos, exclaim with delight over the gifts Eliza would bring back for her.

The year she was seventeen, she'd been staying with Maxie in New Zealand. It had been a magical, action-packed week, visiting glaciers, lakes and movie sets. She'd rung her mum from their hotel the night before she flew home, as always, to confirm her arrival time.

'Thank God. I'm missing you desperately,' her mum said from their small house in Heathcote, a town one hundred kilometres north of Melbourne. 'Tell the pilot to put his or her foot down. I want all speed records broken.'

'I've got so much to tell you. Today we went to —'

'No, no, don't tell me. I want to hear it face-to-face. Every single juicy detail. Don't forget anything.'

Her mum sent her an email the next morning too, written in their favourite list form.

*Safe*
*and*
*happy*
*travels*
*my*
*dearest*

*darling*
*daughter.*
*I*
*Can't*
*Wait*
*To*
*Hear*
*EVERYTHING.*
*Love*
*You*
*To*
*Pieces.*
*Mum*
*X*
*X*

It was a turbulent flight from Auckland to Melbourne, but knowing her mum would be at the airport made it bearable. Sometimes Jeannie prepared a sign that she'd wave as Eliza appeared through the doors. WELCOME HOME TO THE BEST DAUGHTER IN THE WORLD, the last one had read.

'Too bad if it's embarrassing,' she'd said to a mortified Eliza. 'It's true.'

It was after eight p.m. when Eliza stepped into Arrivals, smiling, gazing out at the crowd, searching for the beautiful familiar face. An hour later she was still waiting. Their home phone went unanswered. So did her neighbours'. She finally remembered they were visiting their son in Sydney.

Eliza had no choice but to go to the taxi rank and negotiate a fare – far more than she could usually afford. Thankfully Maxie had slipped two hundred dollars into her bag as she left. Several times on the journey to Heathcote she thought about asking the driver to stop at a public phone box so she could ring Maxie, or Olivia. Each time she talked herself out of it. Everything was all right. Maybe her mum had been called into work. Or was having trouble with the car.

The lights were on in the house as the taxi dropped her off. Her mother's second-hand Honda was parked in its usual place. Eliza could hear music. Her heart started thumping as she reached for her keys.

She stepped into the kitchen. There was an empty bottle of wine on the table. More empty bottles by the rubbish bin. The music was coming from the bathroom. Cheerful music. A jazz station, an announcer telling his listeners that coming up was a trio of classics. Eliza kept moving, down the hall, towards the bathroom. The door was wide open.

Sarah Vaughan's smoky voice was playing loudly as Eliza ran forward and frantically tried to pull her mother's lifeless body out of the half-filled bath.

# CHAPTER TWO

*Thirteen years later*

Eliza's working week began as it usually did. She woke at six in her tidy rented apartment on the fourteenth floor of a building near Melbourne's Southbank. It was only a one-bedroom, but all she needed. The living room window looked out across the city, giving her a bird's-eye view of the ever-changing weather. Blue skies in the morning that often turned into wild storms by the afternoon.

She'd selected a week's worth of outfits the night before, as always, to make her morning routine more efficient. Corporate suits in neutral colours, low-heeled shoes. At five foot ten, she didn't need any extra height. She pulled her long black hair into the usual low bun. After a breakfast of cereal and fruit, she left the apartment at exactly 7.15 a.m. It was late March, allegedly autumn, but with thirty-six degrees forecast, it still felt like summer.

It took her twenty-five minutes to walk to her office on the third floor of a building on Exhibition Street. From the air-conditioned café downstairs, she ordered two cups of black coffee, one for her, one for her boss, Gillian, and one tea (white, two sugars) and a croissant (ham and cheese) for Hector, the old homeless man who slept in the alley around the corner. As usual, he interrupted his swearing at the world to shout at her. 'What's the weather like up there, Lofty?'

She was first into her office, as always. She'd already answered her work emails at home. After checking the stationery supplies, thermostat and water level in the cooler, she settled at her desk and began to review all her current projects.

She'd worked for Gillian Webster Enterprises for nearly nine years. Almost a third of her life. After finishing her business degree at the University of Melbourne, she'd sent her CV to ten companies advertising for graduates. Gillian was the first to reply.

'High distinctions in all subjects,' she said. 'You're my type of person.'

During their meeting that same day – 'I don't mess around. How soon can you come in?' – Gillian did more talking than Eliza. She described herself as 'an entrepreneur, a can-do dynamic ideas person'. Gillian's original business was a successful recruitment agency. She'd recently expanded into the conference industry.

'What I need is a right-hand woman, someone to keep an eye on all aspects of the conferences. The delegates, the finances, casual staff, travel arrangements. Detail, detail, detail. Twenty-four seven.'

Eliza pictured lengthy to-do lists needing constant management. Long hours. Weekend work. Exactly what she was
looking for. When she got a word in, she asked Gillian plenty of
questions, taking notes. Gillian was impressed. Eliza's part-time
job as an art gallery attendant during her university years also
met with her approval. Eliza's godmother Olivia had helped her
find that position, calling on one of her many contacts in the
art world.

'I'm an art lover myself,' Gillian said. 'I'll get your advice on
the most collectable artists.'

She remarked on the entry in Eliza's CV regarding her volun-
teer work with the uni's drama society. That had been her other
godmother's idea. Maxie had started her successful international
acting career at uni in Sydney.

'Never tempted to tread the boards yourself?' Gillian asked.

'No,' Eliza said, feeling her cheeks redden even at the thought
of it.

'Good. What I want is a backroom person. I'm the face of
the company and that's how I like it. The job's yours if you want
it.' She named a reasonable salary. 'Give me your answer by
nine tomorrow.'

Overnight, Eliza thought about it. There were three people
she could ask for advice – her two godmothers and Rose, her
best friend from university – but she needed to decide for herself.
She said yes the next day. She was at her new desk the following
Monday. In the nine years since, she'd regularly worked more
than fifty hours a week and rarely taken holidays. When she did

have time off, she was often called back in. She'd had only two small pay rises, both given begrudgingly.

Rose couldn't understand why Eliza was still working there. 'Your business card should say slave, not executive assistant.'

Maxie was equally puzzled. 'But you're artistic, not corporate, Eliza!' she'd said once. 'You should be surrounded by paints and canvases, not spreadsheets and contracts.'

Olivia was more astonished that Eliza could actually work with Gillian. 'That woman would drive me nuts,' she said after meeting her in the office during one of her visits to Melbourne. 'I've never met anyone who talked about herself so much.'

That Monday morning, as usual, Eliza heard her boss arrive before she saw her. Gillian spent ninety per cent of her working day on the phone. Eliza handed her the coffee as she appeared, receiving a brisk nod in return. Gillian was perfectly groomed, as ever. Eliza had learned how to dress in corporate style by observation. Rose often teased her about Gillian's influence. 'You were practically a hippy when we met. Now you're so sleek I'm scared of you. Come back, Old Eliza!'

It wasn't a matter of Old or New Eliza. It was Necessary Eliza. If she wanted the safe routine and security of a good job, she had to play by the rules. Look the part. Gillian had insisted.

'Neutral colours, thank you, Eliza. Classic suits. Hair back. Dress smart, think smart, be smart.'

She listened now as Gillian paced around the open-plan office, finishing her call. Her boss had a separate glass-walled cubicle, but was rarely in it. She'd told Eliza she preferred to keep her staff of ten on their toes. Eliza gathered that Gillian was negotiating a fee for a popular speaker, presumably for the conference they were organising for a science firm in Brisbane the following March.

After reaching a deal, Gillian put down the phone.

'Morning, Eliza,' she said. 'Good weekend?' She didn't wait for an answer. Instead, she put her hands on her hips and leaned back, making her heavily pregnant belly appear even rounder. She was expecting twin girls. When the babies arrived in two months' time, Gillian and Kevin, her lawyer husband, would have four children under the age of six.

Eliza never wondered how Gillian 'did it all'. She saw it in action every day. Gillian was constantly on the move, networking with clients and suppliers, firing instructions via email to Eliza at every step. She also knew how Gillian and her husband managed at home: day and night nannies. Eliza had sat in on many of those interviews. Gillian went through a lot of nannies.

Eliza and Gillian always started each day with their coffee and a ten-minute meeting. Eliza had established the routine, as well as streamlining their other office processes. Gillian called Eliza the Queen of Lists. 'All bow to our meticulous majesty,' she'd said once to the staff at a company meeting. They'd laughed obediently. But it was true. Eliza was obsessively organised. She loved lists. They'd been special to her as a child. They kept her life running smoothly now.

That day, however, instead of sticking to Eliza's printed agenda, Gillian pushed it to one side.

'I have news, Eliza.'

Eliza felt a prickle of alarm. 'Is it the babies?'

'The babies are great. It's work news.'

Eliza picked up her notebook.

'You won't need that.'

Eliza put it down. 'Good news, I hope?'

'Wonderful news.' Gillian smiled. 'I've sold the company.'

Eliza blinked.

'It was an offer I couldn't refuse,' Gillian said. 'A takeover. All my clients. All my existing contracts. All my current and future conferences.'

Eliza felt a jolt at the emphatic 'my'. She'd worked on every detail of those conferences. She'd fine-tuned the contracts, liaised with every client, delegate and venue. 'Sold to who?'

Gillian named the buyer. An international operation, based in Singapore. There'd long been speculation in the industry about their possible direct move into Australia.

Still, Eliza was shocked. 'Just like that? Out of the blue?'

'No. We've been negotiating for six months. I've been legally constrained from saying anything to anyone until today.'

'To anyone? Even me?'

Gillian mimed zipping her lips. 'I had to obey.'

Obedient was the last word Eliza would use for Gillian. 'But when? How?'

'I was approached when I was in Sydney last year. Just after I'd found out I was pregnant. Do you remember that huge medical conference I organised in Sydney? The one with a thousand delegates?'

Eliza had organised that huge medical conference. The delegates' flights, the hotel rooms, the speakers' schedules. Gillian was on the ground as the face of the company, but throughout the week Eliza was back in Melbourne working fifteen-hour days, staying one step ahead, double-checking running orders, speakers' needs, even the catering arrangements.

When had Gillian had time for any extra appointments?

It was as if Gillian read her mind. 'It was all done in person. The managing director flew from Singapore especially. I met with him and his lawyer. We've been in touch via my personal email ever since. My husband handled my legal advice, of course. Keep it in the family and all that.' She gave a laugh that sounded fake.

'You couldn't tell me? After working together for nine years?' Eliza couldn't disguise her hurt.

An edge came into Gillian's voice. 'It was my company, Eliza. My decision. I'm going to take six months off, spend quality time with the children. After that, the world's my oyster. I have some brilliant ideas already, of course. But I'm stepping away from company life. It's time to fly solo again.'

Eliza forced herself to ask it. 'Where does that leave me?'

'Sadly, your job is now obsolete.' Gillian didn't look sad. 'They've bought my company in name and intellectual property only. They'll bring in their own team.'

Eliza could hear the *buzz-buzz-buzz* of incoming calls on Gillian's phone. If she wanted more answers, she'd need to be quick.

'How long have I got?'

Gillian laughed. 'It's not a diagnosis, Eliza. Or a death sentence. I'm legally bound to give you a fortnight's notice. I'll be telling the others when they come in this morning.'

'Two weeks? For everyone to find another job?' Eliza named her colleagues. It seemed important to remind Gillian of the personal impact of her decision.

Gillian's voice grew steely. 'They'll be fine. They'll have my company name on their CVs. As will you. There's also a severance package, obviously. You didn't think I'd leave you in the lurch, did you?'

Eliza didn't know what she thought.

Gillian reached over and unexpectedly took Eliza's hands. It didn't feel affectionate.

'I know this must come as a shock, Eliza, but remember, one door closes, another opens. I'm doing you a favour, if you ask me. Let's face facts – you're stuck in a rut. What have you done with your life so far? It's time you stepped outside your comfort zone. I'm a risk-taker by nature, so it's easy for me to say this, but in my opinion it will do you good to try something new, spread your wings. Once you get over that silly fear of flying, of course!' She laughed again.

Eliza was suddenly glad she'd never explained what had triggered her fear of flying, why she hadn't flown since she was seventeen years old.

Gillian handed Eliza a copy of her severance agreement. 'You can get legal advice at your own expense, but I assure you it's watertight.'

'Thank you,' Eliza said, taking it.

'That's it? "Thank you"?' Gillian's expression hardened. 'I have to say your response is, frankly, disappointing. After everything I've done for you. I took a chance on you as a graduate. You have my name on your CV. This deal is also wonderful news for me as a woman. Yet you haven't even said congratulations. I thought we were friends. Now I'm not sure.'

Eliza watched silently as her boss stalked off. Alone at her desk, she read the five-page document. She'd negotiated enough contracts to realise there was no point disputing it.

Her colleagues arrived before nine a.m. They were cheerful, talking about their weekends. All in their twenties, hardworking, enthusiastic. At nine-ten, Gillian called them together.

There was shock, even tears, from the younger ones. Gillian had their severance agreements ready too. It was wonderful news, she insisted. She kept giving the fake laugh Eliza was starting to hate.

At ten a.m., Gillian called her in. She'd drafted an email announcing the takeover. She instructed Eliza to send it to all their contacts: clients, venue managers, speakers' agencies, business media. It was upbeat, announcing a wonderful success story, a small Australian company sought after by an international leader in the field. It glossed over the redundancies. Only Gillian was named and quoted. 'I am very proud of my achievements and so excited for what the future may hold for me.'

The calls flooded in as soon as the email was sent. Mostly from clients who already had conference contracts with them, concerned about their future. Eliza transferred them all to Gillian. Twice, Gillian called her in, crossly saying that surely Eliza could handle 'the minor ones'.

Eliza knew what she wanted to say. 'But it's you they want to speak to. It's your company. Your big news.' She didn't, of course. It wasn't her way. She preferred to stay quiet. Hide her feelings.

She left the office at six, one hour earlier than normal. Gillian had left at five, as usual. Eliza would have followed, but one of her younger colleagues came to her, upset, asking for help to update her CV. Afterwards, she gave Eliza a hug. 'You're the one we'll all miss. We hope she falls apart without you.'

The heat outside was still fierce, but Eliza barely noticed it on the walk to her apartment. In the foyer, she picked up her mail. Three advertising circulars and an envelope with her name typed on the front.

She opened it as she went up the stairs. There was a lift, but the hundreds of steps each day were her regular exercise. She stopped on the third landing, trying to take in the letter's contents.

*Dear Ms Miller,*

*I am writing to advise you that your landlord is returning from overseas and wishes to take occupancy of her apartment. As per your tenancy agreement, I'm henceforth giving you three months' notice to vacate. We would like to take this opportunity to thank you for your excellent tenancy over the past eight years.*

Inside her apartment, she sat down on her sofa, still holding the letter. She could feel the sting of tears, but she did her best to blink them away. She stared out the window at the flurry of dark clouds now buffeting across the sky.

For the hundredth, perhaps the thousandth, time in her life, she thought it.

*I want my mum.*

*I want to talk to my mum.*

It wasn't possible.

She needed to talk to someone. She took out her phone, going to her most frequent contacts.

Top of the list was Rose, but Eliza never liked to ring her at this time of day. After graduating, Rose had married her childhood sweetheart Harry and gone back to live in her home town of Colac, two hours west of Melbourne. She was now busy with their three young kids and their stock supplies business. Eliza had stayed with them often enough to picture the scene: a cacophony of background noise, the kids having baths, the table being set, piano practice, Harry in the kitchen making elaborate meals and lots of mess. Rose always preferred long leisurely phone conversations late at night, enjoyed over a glass of wine.

Eliza scrolled down to the next two names. They were in alphabetical order. Maxie and Olivia. She was calculating the time difference, trying to decide who to call first, when the landline phone rang beside her. The caller's name flashed up on the small screen.

*Olivia.*

It happened so often. One of her godmothers there just when she needed them, in person or on the phone. On the day of Eliza's university graduation, Olivia had stood clapping and cheering when Eliza's name was called and she stepped onto the stage. Maxie sent a big bunch of flowers when Eliza emailed them about getting the job with Gillian. Olivia sent her a department store voucher to buy a 'work wardrobe'. Maxie surprised her with a visit on her twenty-first birthday, flying across the world to spend a long weekend with her. Olivia did the same for her thirtieth birthday.

Maxie had been the first to arrive at the hospital that night thirteen years ago, followed as quickly as possible by Olivia. The night Eliza had flown home after a wonderful holiday and —

No. She couldn't think of that now.

She answered, forcing a smile into her voice. 'Olivia, hi!'

'Drat,' Olivia said. 'I wanted your voicemail. That's why I rang your home phone. Are you sick?'

'No, I finished early.' About to explain, she stopped. 'Why did you want to get my voicemail?'

'Because Maxie's dropped some bombshell news. I was in London with her on the weekend. She's sworn me to secrecy but I'm disobeying her. She and Hazel are getting married! Not just anywhere, either. In Gretna Green. They're practically eloping!'

Eliza had never heard Olivia sound so excited.

'I begged her to let me be one of their witnesses. Of course, she said. Then this morning I had a brilliant idea to surprise Maxie. I'm ringing to make you an offer I hope you can't and won't refuse.'

'Olivia, I —'

'Please, Eliza, at least listen before you say no. My plan was to leave a long message to give you time to think about it. And then I wanted you to ring me tomorrow and say yes.'

'Where are you? Still at Maxie's?'

'No, back in Edinburgh,' Olivia said. 'I got the sleeper train last night. Except I didn't sleep. I was too busy coming up with my ingenious plan. Are you sitting comfortably?'

At first, Eliza listened closely. Out of habit, she even took notes. Then, as her godmother kept talking, she put down her pen and gazed around her apartment, noticing every detail as if for the first time.

She'd lived here for eight years but had barely made her mark on it. She had few belongings. In the bedroom was a tidy rack of clothes. In the living room, her books and a box of painting materials. On a shelf, the tall green vase and three coloured bowls her mother had loved. There was a postcard of her mother's favourite painting on the fridge. On the wall, the framed enlarged photograph of her eleven-year-old self with her mum and godmothers, taken after the school concert. Everything else – the furniture, crockery, even the cutlery – belonged to her landlord.

Her entire home life could be dismantled in less than an hour if she wanted. As quickly as her work life had collapsed today.

*'I'm doing you a favour, if you ask me. Let's face facts – you're stuck in a rut.'*

Olivia was still talking. 'I'm not putting pressure on you, Eliza, though of course that's exactly what I'm doing. Please think about it. I know it's short notice. And yes, of course I know how you feel about flying. But we'll deal with that, even if it takes a wheelbarrow of drugs. I know you'll say you're too busy at work, but you're owed weeks of holidays. I also know Gillian still pays you a pittance, so I'll cover your costs. Let's call it an extra thirtieth birthday present. An early fortieth present. Please say yes. It would make Maxie's day. Mine too. The three of us haven't been in the same place together for —'

'Yes,' Eliza said.

There was a brief silence. 'What did you say?'

'Yes. Thank you.'

'Just like that?'

'Yes.'

'Without any excuses about busy schedules, or Gillian's demands, or needing to be in Melbourne to make sure there's a glass of water for the keynote speaker at a conference in three months' time?'

Once, Eliza might have taken offence. Today, she almost laughed. 'None.'

There was a pause. 'Eliza, have you started drinking?'

'No.'

'Let me get this straight. I've asked you out of the blue to do something completely unexpected, on the spur of the moment, and —'

'I've said yes.'

Eliza held the phone away from her ear as Olivia uncharacteristically whooped down the line.

# CHAPTER THREE

As soon as Eliza hung up, she rang Rose's mobile. Her friend picked up after five rings. Eliza could hear children shouting and laughing in the background.

'Rose, I'm sorry. I know it's hell hour. Can you talk even for a minute?'

'Every hour is hell hour. My children are demons. Hold on, I'll lock myself in the laundry.' After a pause, Rose's voice came on the line again, the background quieter now. 'Is everything okay?'

It only took Eliza a few minutes to explain all that had happened.

'That selfish cow,' Rose said about Gillian. 'I hope she has a fifty-hour labour and those twins don't sleep until they turn ten.'

She sympathised about the eviction notice. 'At least it will only take you five minutes to pack up.'

She also wanted to know every detail of Maxie's surprise wedding. Eliza explained that Hazel had been offered lighting design work on Broadway, for a big production of *The Railway Children*. She'd be away for at least a year. It had made Maxie realise just how much she loved her and she'd proposed. Hazel immediately said yes. Not only were they getting married, Maxie had decided to press pause on her UK acting career and move to New York with her. Perhaps even make time for the playwriting she'd been talking about for years now.

'But they don't want a big fussy wedding,' Eliza told Rose. 'Hazel's so private. So they decided on Gretna Green, the eloping place in Scotland. Olivia said she'd secretly organise for me to be the second witness. She wants it to be a complete surprise for Maxie.'

'What a wedding present! And then what will you do afterwards?'

Eliza shared that news too. After Olivia heard what had happened with Eliza's job and flat, she'd invited her to stay at the Montgomery for as long as she wanted.

Rose repeated the name of Olivia's hotel, sighing. 'It even sounds fancy.'

Olivia had recently sent Eliza a link to the hotel's redesigned website. It was as elegant as the Montgomery itself. The logo was a stylised flower, the line 'Family-run for four generations' beneath it. The main photo showed the hotel's exterior, three adjoining Victorian terrace buildings in Edinburgh's West End. Ivy covered all three storeys of the middle building. A photo gallery displayed an inviting sitting room complete with open fire, a formal dining room with crisp linen and gleaming glassware, luxuriously cosy bedrooms, each designed to reflect a floral theme. Evident in every image was the art collection: portraits and landscapes from all around the world.

'Are Olivia's stepsons still working there?' Rose asked. 'That mean one, more to the point?'

Eliza sometimes wished Rose didn't remember every story she'd ever heard. Thinking back to that time still made Eliza want to cringe. 'Yes, they both are. But that was years ago. I'm sure they've forgotten about it.'

'I haven't,' Rose said. 'He'd better be nicer to you this time.'

Alex and Rory weren't the only family members living in the hotel at present. Olivia had told Eliza that another one had recently moved in. Alex and Rory's grandmother Celine. Edgar's first wife's mother.

'An in-house almost mother-in-law? Poor Olivia!' Rose said when Eliza told her. 'How old is she?'

Somewhere in her eighties, Olivia had said. Scottish-born, but she'd been living in the south of France for years with her third husband. By all accounts, they had a stormy relationship. She'd walked out on him yet again in January and returned home to Scotland. Edgar had promised Celine she'd always be welcome at the Montgomery. 'Olivia assumed he meant for a holiday, but she's been there for more than two months now, with no talk of leaving.'

'How is there room for guests with so many Montgomerys everywhere?' Rose asked.

The family occupied two private floors in one of the three

hotel buildings, Eliza explained. But Olivia was putting Eliza in her own favourite suite in the hotel itself. The Iris.

Rose sighed again. 'I can't believe you said you could only go for three weeks.'

'I can't stay longer. I need to find a new job. A new flat.'

'But you'll be flying all that way just to fly back so soon.' A pause. 'Sorry to mention flying.'

Eliza swallowed. 'I'm trying not to think about it.'

'On the bright side, you'll get to sit still for twenty-two hours. Eat hand-delivered food. Watch back-to-back movies. You'll also be landing into the arms of the two women who love you most in the world, apart from me. It's like an updated version of your childhood holidays, isn't it? Even better.'

Rose was right. Olivia had emailed Eliza straight after her call.

*I'll book all your flights and meet you at the airport, of course. Please don't breathe a word to Maxie. TOP SECRET!! Thank you so much for saying yes. O xxx*

There was a voice in the background. Rose's husband, Harry. Rose spoke briefly to him, then came back on the line. 'Eliza, I'm so sorry. Harry needs help. The kids have washed the dog in golden syrup. Can you hold on? I'll be back as soon as I can.'

Eliza was happy to wait. Phone in hand, she walked across to her window. The heavy clouds had gone now. The sky was clear. Below her, the city lights flickered in different colours.

She imagined the scene in Rose's house. The mess. The noise. The laughter. Rose always showed such love, humour and patience with her three kids. They constantly sought her out, tucking themselves beside her, getting hugs, quick kisses. Harry was hands-on too. On Eliza's most recent visit she'd seen him quietly reading with one, then playing piggyback with another. After lunch there'd been a rowdy game of backyard cricket with them all. Eliza had always felt so welcome there too. Even if sometimes she had to try hard to hide unexpected pangs of sadness. Not that she would ever have told Rose that. Their friendship meant everything to her.

She hadn't had close friends growing up. The constant moving and new schools had made it hard. She was always self-conscious about her height. Overly studious. She stood out while trying to blend in. Rose's friendship had been as sudden as it was unexpected, all sparked by a lost student ID card, six weeks into her studies at university.

Eliza hadn't even realised she'd lost the card. Rose found it on the floor of the library, tracked Eliza down to their residential hall and handed it over, introducing herself with a warm smile.

'We're nearly birthday twins! I'm only a day older than you. Did you have a big eighteenth party? My parents insisted. Mortifying baby photos and all!'

Eliza hadn't marked her birthday in any way. Olivia and Maxie rang, trying hard to be cheerful, but it was too difficult for all of them. All Eliza wanted was for the day to be over.

Caught off guard, she told Rose the truth. No, she hadn't had a party. She didn't say why.

The next morning, she was woken by a knock on her door. She opened it to find a card on the floor. *Happy Belated*

*18th Birthday!* Rose had written. *Part two tonight!* That night, Rose arrived at her door carrying a bottle of cheap sparkling wine, two glasses and a shop-bought cake covered in eighteen candles. She came into Eliza's room, ignoring her protests, opening the wine.

'You don't drink?' she said, mid-pour. 'Good for you and more for me!' She gazed around. 'Can you please teach me to be tidy? I'm just a floor below, but your room looks so much nicer than mine.'

She noticed the small framed photo of Eliza with her mother and two godmothers. 'What a wonderful photo,' she said. 'I don't need to ask which one's your mother. You're the image of her. Isn't she gorgeous? Look at that dimple! She's so young too. Who are the other two women?'

Eliza briefly explained.

'Two godmothers? Brilliant. How did you manage that?' Rose put a cocktail umbrella into a glass of water for Eliza, sat down and said, cheerily, 'Now, why did you ignore your eighteenth? Because you're actually fourteen and used a fake ID to get into uni?

Eliza hadn't intended to tell her anything. It was hard enough carrying the knowledge of it herself, let alone having other people know. No one at the uni knew what had happened. But she hadn't expected anything like this friendly, open girl asking her questions. Looking at the photo from the concert with such interest. Asking about her godmothers. Her mother.

Once she started talking, it was impossible to stop.

Rose was in tears by the time Eliza finished. 'I'm so sorry,' she said. 'Oh, Eliza, how can you even be here, after something like that?'

It was as if those words needed to be released too. She'd felt like she had no choice, she said. Her mother had always wanted her to go to uni. She had to be here, for her.

They talked late into the night. When Rose eventually asked the question, she was gentle.

'Eliza, when Jeannie died. Was it —'

She stopped there. She didn't need to say the words out loud. Was it suicide?

No, Eliza told her. There'd been an autopsy. A coroner's report. Interviews with Olivia, Maxie, Eliza, the ambulance team, the hospital staff. All the facts of that night were analysed. The cause of death was drowning. Excessive alcohol was a factor. Jeannie had also taken a prescription-only sleeping pill. Tests showed she'd been eating very little. But there was no note. No proof of intent. She'd emailed Eliza to say how much she was looking forward to seeing her. She'd rung Olivia five times that night to say how excited she was that Eliza was coming home. She'd said how happy she was that Eliza was going to uni. How she couldn't wait to visit her in Melbourne as often as possible. The coroner's ruling was decisive. It was declared a tragic accident.

By the time Eliza stopped talking, she felt hollowed out. She was now regretting saying anything. It was as if Rose guessed. She promised never to tell anyone else. She said she was so sad but also grateful that Eliza had told her. Then she did something so special and so thoughtful. She asked Eliza to tell her what Jeannie was like.

It was the best eighteenth birthday present Eliza could have hoped for. An evening talking about her funny, naughty, wonderful mother. Rose listened to all of her stories. She laughed often. She studied the photo of Eliza with her mother and godmothers again. It was only towards the end of the night that she asked about Eliza's father. Eliza didn't go into detail. Those stories came later in their friendship. That night she simply said that he wasn't in her life.

It was Rose who encouraged her in the following weeks to get the school concert photo enlarged and framed. She also insisted on a ceremonial unveiling, helping Eliza to hang it, then cover it in a scarf. She produced sparkling water and champagne glasses and insisted they make a toast as Eliza pulled off the scarf.

It was that day that she also realised who one of Eliza's godmothers was. She leaned forward, inspecting the enlarged photo.

'One of your godmothers looks just like that TV soap actress, doesn't she?'

Yes, Eliza said, enjoying the moment. Because one of her godmothers *was* that TV soap actress.

It had been Eliza's pleasure to get Maxie to autograph a dozen photographs for Rose and her family.

In the years that followed, Rose became the friend Eliza had always longed to have. It didn't matter that they didn't often see each other face-to-face now. They spoke on the phone, sent emails and photos, always knew exactly what the other was up to.

Rose had also appointed herself as Eliza's matchmaker. She'd told Eliza that it was her civic duty. That Gillian worked Eliza so hard she had no time to socialise. Outside help was needed. After several excruciating first dates, there'd finally been a spark between Eliza and one of Harry's friends. The tallest one. Eliza dated him for six months. Until he told her, kindly, that he'd been offered a job transfer to Perth. They mutually decided to call it a day. There'd been no one in the four years since, despite Rose's best efforts, fully backed by Olivia and Maxie.

Over the years, Rose had regularly met Eliza's godmothers. They got on very well. In recent years, though, a slight tension had entered Eliza and Rose's relationship in regard to them. Rose still couldn't understand why Eliza wouldn't ask Olivia and Maxie about her father.

Eliza had finally told Rose the little she knew. About the promise her mother had made to tell her the truth on her eighteenth birthday. She'd shared some of the stories Jeannie had made up about him over the years, thinking Rose might enjoy them. Rose hadn't seemed to find them funny.

She kept raising the subject. 'Aren't you even a bit curious about him, Eliza? Wouldn't you like to know who he is?'

Of course she was curious, Eliza said. Of course she wondered about him. But it had never been straightforward. Her father's identity had always felt like a special secret between her and Jeannie. A special bond. A birthday promise, unfulfilled for the saddest of reasons. If she hadn't been able to hear it from her mother, she wasn't sure she wanted to hear it at all.

In any case, she said to Rose, her godmothers might not even know his name. Jeannie had always said she'd tell Eliza first, then Olivia and Maxie.

Rose had persisted. 'But they must know something, Eliza. They were best friends. If I got pregnant again, you'd be the first to know. Your mother might have mentioned his name to them even in passing. Perhaps if the three of you sat down together and swapped all the little things she ever said about him, joking or not, you'd figure it out.'

But that hadn't been possible. For work and family reasons, Olivia and Maxie had only visited Australia separately over the past thirteen years. Eliza told Rose she couldn't ask them to come to see her together. She wasn't the only one avoiding the subject, either. Olivia and Maxie had never raised it with her, had they?

'Maybe they've been waiting for you to ask first,' Rose said. 'Or waiting for the right time. Perhaps he's even out there waiting for you to find him. He might have known your mother was going to tell you on your eighteenth birthday. He might not have heard the news about Jeannie. He might be wanting to meet you himself.'

'Why didn't he ever come looking for me, then?' she asked.

'Maybe your mum asked him to stay away. Or he was with someone else then, or even now, and she's jealous of his past. There could be hundreds of reasons.'

Rose had apologised eventually. 'I'm sorry if it feels like I'm nagging. You know I only ever want what's best for you. So do your godmothers. Because we love you.'

Standing at the window now, Eliza thought back to all those conversations with Rose. She thought about her godmothers too. She pictured Olivia meeting her at Edinburgh Airport in a fortnight. She imagined Maxie's surprise when she appeared at Gretna Green moments before her wedding. She pictured the three of them in one place again.

She'd known them all her life. They had been her mother's best friends. They had to have the answers to so many of her questions. Before she could change her mind, she went to her laptop and wrote an email. She'd just pressed send when Rose came back on the line.

'Eliza, are you still there? Sorry about that. So, will you stay on in Edinburgh long after the wedding? Or go travelling?'

She'd just decided what she was going to do, she told Rose. 'You're right. I've put it off for too long. This could be my best chance. While the three of us are together. Before Maxie goes to New York.'

Rose stayed quiet. Waiting.

'I'm going to find out who my father is,' Eliza said.

# CHAPTER FOUR

In Edinburgh, Olivia was in her office at the Montgomery, phone to her ear, impatiently tapping a pen on the antique desk. Another two minutes passed before Maxie finally came on the line.

'Olivia? Are you there?'

'I've aged ten years, but yes. Where are you? I've been leaving messages all day. And when did your publicist's assistant get an assistant?'

'Sorry. I'm on an all-day photo shoot. And I left my mobile at home, again. Hazel says I —'

'Tell me later what Hazel says. Eliza said yes.'

'She *what*?'

'She said yes. On the spot. She's coming.'

'Oh my *God*, Olivia! That's fantastic! Did you bribe her?'

'I didn't have to. Turns out our timing was perfect. I'll explain why later. I also lied. I told her you know nothing about it.

So make sure you act surprised when she arrives in Gretna Green with me.'

'Act? How do I do that? Liv, I can't believe it! But what about the flight?'

'She's scared witless. But she told me she's determined to try again.'

'The fearless Jeannie in her, coming out at last! Oh, this will make my wedding day! Hazel can't wait to meet her too. What fantastic news!'

'Yes, except for one thing. She also emailed me. To ask if the three of us could have a few hours together before you go to New York. She said she has lots of questions she hopes we can answer. About her father. Jeannie.' She hesitated. 'Jeannie's family.'

There was a long pause before Maxie spoke. 'Oh, fuck.'

'Yes.'

'What did you say?'

'I said yes, of course. I could hardly say no.'

'No. And at least we've had warning. There's time to work out what we can tell her.'

'What do you mean "can"? We tell her the truth. Everything we should have told her years ago.'

'We can't! You know what we promised Jeannie, that —'

'Maxie, how many times can we argue about this? We were practically kids when we made that promise. We've also been waiting for years for Eliza to ask us anything at all.'

'What if she gets upset? We'll ruin her holiday. My wedding. She might never talk to us again.'

'Stop being so dramatic. She's thirty years old, Maxie. A grown woman. While we're on the subject, I also think she needs to hear about that night in Carlton.'

'*What?* Why? That happened long before Jeannie was even pregnant. It didn't even go to court.'

'No, but it will help us explain why Jeannie and her parents —'

A voice was audible in the background calling Maxie's name.

'*Coming,*' Maxie called back. 'Olivia, sorry, I'm needed. Thanks so much again. It's wonderful news. It will make my wedding, it really will.'

'Maxie, wait. Before she gets here, can you please try to find those postcards?'

There was no reply. Maxie had hung up.

Olivia put down the phone with a deep sigh. She sat still for a moment, staring out the sash window opposite her desk. It was raining, turning the rooftops of Edinburgh to a glistening sheen. At least there was a fuzz of soft green appearing on the oak tree outside her window. It had been a long, cold winter. Spring seemed to be taking forever to arrive.

She massaged the back of her neck, trying to ease the sudden tension. *We tell her the truth*, she'd insisted today. If only it was that simple.

She stood up and walked across the room. A large framed photo had pride of place by the window. It had been a farewell gift from Eliza, at the end of Olivia's last trip to Australia. Maxie had received a copy in the post too. An enlarged version of the school concert photo taken all those years ago.

Olivia studied it again now. It always made her smile. Not least because of their terrible hairstyles. Admittedly, it had been the early 2000s, but what had she been thinking with those feathery waves? Thankfully, soon after that photo was taken, she'd decided on what was now her signature style: a sharp dark bob. Maxie was barely recognisable in the photo, her hair a mass of red curls for her Australian TV soap role at the time. Since then, she'd had multiple hairstyles, usually for roles, sometimes for fun. She now had a flattering pixie cut, dyed white-blonde. It was much copied by fans of her current hit TV series.

Eliza had changed the most since that photo had been taken, of course. The pale, red-cheeked eleven-year-old girl with long black plaits had slowly transformed via awkward teenage years into a tall, striking woman. In the photo she was wearing a cherry-red dress and bright-yellow cardigan. Jeannie had always dressed her in bright clothes. As a teenager, and then afterwards, at university, Eliza had kept dressing in colourful op-shop finds, wearing her hair long and loose. The casual near-hippy look had belied what a serious student she'd been.

All that had changed overnight once she started full-time work. Olivia had often wished her goddaughter hadn't adopted Gillian's bland corporate style of dressing so obediently, or started tying that glorious long hair into a too-tight low bun. At least she seemed to have finally grown comfortable with her height. Over the years, she and Maxie had often had to gently tell her off for hunching her shoulders, for trying to appear smaller than she was.

But some things hadn't changed. Eliza still had that lively, alert expression. And those spots of red on her cheeks. Olivia had always loved how easily Eliza blushed. She knew Jeannie had loved it too.

Jeannie. There at the centre of the photo. Petite, with that mop of black curly hair, the wide, cheeky smile, the dimple. Mischievous in looks and in personality. Naughty. Bold. So many words always came to mind when Olivia thought of her friend. Wild. Quick-witted. Loyal. Fun. Defiant. Reckless.

Troubled.

She and Maxie hadn't realised until too late how troubled she was.

More than thirteen years had passed since that awful night, yet Olivia still often felt the punch of grief. The sadness. The guilt, most of all. She'd relived it so many times: Eliza's panicked phone call from Australia, her voice unrecognisable, babbling, talking about the bath, the water, her mother, how she'd tried to ring Maxie, she wasn't answering . . . It had taken a few moments to make sense of what she was saying. Once she had, Olivia had needed to shout at her, to order her to hang up *quickly*, to phone for an ambulance, *quickly*, now, Eliza, *now!*

The hours following had been like a nightmare. Olivia could still recall the flight she'd taken that same day, cursing the distance between Scotland and Australia, wishing she could be there instantly, beside Eliza in that shabby house. Wishing she'd somehow been able to protect her goddaughter from what she'd seen in that bathroom, all she now had to go through.

Thank God Maxie had still been in Auckland, able to get to her within hours, to stay close until Olivia's arrival. In the days that followed, the two of them had so often wanted to fold themselves around Eliza, to shield her from more hurt, even as they grieved for Jeannie themselves.

They'd always taken their role as godmothers seriously. Jeannie had made sure of it.

'I don't want two wishy-washy godmothers,' she had said that afternoon in the country hospital when Eliza was only a day old. 'No dolls. No pink dresses. Just lots of adventures. Lots of spoiling. The pair of you like two mighty warriors protecting her at every step.'

They'd laughed, imagining themselves in suits of armour, clanking bodyguards shadowing a little girl to the playground. But they agreed to everything Jeannie asked. They took turns holding her, amazed at how tiny she was, how lovely, how cross. Olivia smiled now at the memory. Baby Eliza's constant frowns had made them laugh. It was a deceptive start. As she grew older, she turned into the sweetest of children. So clever. So watchful, too, of Jeannie and her moods especially.

Olivia felt a flash of guilt again. Eliza should have had a much happier childhood. Known nothing but security, safety. Not the constant moves Jeannie insisted on, the upheaval of new houses and schools, trying to cope with her mother's mood swings. Her temper. Her drinking.

If only Olivia and Maxie had known how bad things were. But they'd been living in other states, then countries. Caught up with their own careers and lives. They'd always stayed in touch with Jeannie, of course. Sent Eliza birthday and Christmas presents, receiving sweet handwritten thankyou cards in return. Their relationship might have stayed like that, fond but distant, if Jeannie hadn't contacted them out of the blue the year Eliza was eleven, begging them to come to her school concert.

'I wouldn't ask you if it wasn't important, I promise. She's the only one in this town without any family nearby. Please, can you both come? For her? For me?'

Olivia had fortuitously been back in Australia at the time, visiting her family. Maxie had still been living and working in Sydney. That three-night stay with Jeannie and Eliza shocked them both. The house Jeannie and Eliza shared was so run-down. Jeannie's fragility was immediately apparent. So was her heavy drinking. But they'd also seen firsthand Jeannie's intense love for her daughter. Their close bond. Eliza was the best thing that ever happened to her, Jeannie said often, over too much wine each evening.

It had been an important weekend in so many ways. Maxie and Olivia realised they needed to pay more attention to their goddaughter. That Jeannie needed more support, not only financial but practical. On the second night, while Jeannie was helping Eliza get ready for bed, they'd hatched up the holiday idea between them.

It hadn't gone down well. Jeannie was fiercely proud. She didn't want their charity, she'd practically spat. She'd already drunk three times as much wine as them. Eliza was now asleep down the hallway. They'd chosen their words carefully, spoken softly, slowly defusing Jeannie's temper.

It wasn't a question of charity, they insisted. Jeannie would be doing them a favour. Neither of them had children yet. Jeannie was the lucky one, a mother already. That's all they were asking, that Jeannie share her beautiful Eliza with them. And yes, of course they'd cover all the costs. Spoil her rotten. What had she expected, a birthday card and a packet of hankies once a year? No, they continued, hoping their lighthearted tone was hitting the right mark, Jeannie was just going to have to accept it. They'd whisk Eliza away on two godmotherly holidays a year, in Australia or even overseas sometimes, and that was that.

'We'll supply you with all the receipts, of course,' Maxie joked.

'We also expect Eliza to pay us back in the years ahead,' Olivia said.

'We have an ulterior motive, obviously,' Maxie said. 'We spoil her now with all these exotic holidays. When we're old and grey, she visits us in our nursing homes.'

'To fill our drips with gin,' Olivia said.

'Spoon the finest of pureed food into our drooling mouths,' Maxie said.

'Nursing homes plural?' Jeannie said, smiling by then. 'No way. We'll end up in the same one, won't we? In the same room. Three beds in a row.' She'd lifted her glass and made them toast the idea.

'Together till the end!' Jeannie had shouted, before laughing, also too loudly. 'Wouldn't Sister Teresa spin in her grave at the idea! All those years she tried to separate us!'

They spent the rest of the evening reminiscing about their Catholic boarding school days. It still caused them great hilarity, the idea of them being sent to such a strict and religious school. What on earth had their parents been thinking? That they might consider becoming nuns themselves?

At least they'd all got neat handwriting out of it, they agreed. And Olivia might never have developed an interest in art history if it hadn't been for cranky old Sister Bernadine. Would Maxie have become an actress if Sister Frances hadn't insisted she take the lead role in their all-female version of *The Crucible*? And while none of them went to Mass any more, they could hold their own in religious discussions, after being taught politics and theology by the fierce Sister Roberta.

'As for me,' Jeannie said as she refilled their glasses, 'I'd definitely have been locked up if it wasn't for the Catholic network. I might not have a good career like you two, but at least I'm not a jailbird!'

For the rest of the weekend, Jeannie had been in great form, making them laugh, exaggerating as always. She'd been full of fanciful yarns at school too. They'd all heard of Jeannie's adventures when she was left alone in the family car as a nine-year-old. A thief had leapt into the driver's seat and taken off, with her in the back. It involved a police chase, blaring sirens, until the car was cornered and Jeannie rescued. Ironic, really, considering what happened all those years later in Carlton.

Mind you, Olivia had to concede, Jeannie's quick wit had been handy whenever one of the nuns or teachers caught them out of bounds or up past curfew. In the blink of an eye, she was always able to come up with an elaborate and convincing story about a bad nightmare causing one of them to sleepwalk, or a sudden debilitating cramp requiring an urgent late-night visit to the first-aid room.

It was in the years following that visit to Jeannie and Eliza that they had become more concerned about her gift for storytelling. Or compulsive lying, as Olivia began to think of it. They slowly discovered she'd been telling Eliza increasingly fanciful tales about her own childhood, her school days, her overseas travels. Eliza occasionally shared details of them during her annual holidays.

'Well, I don't think it was *exactly* like that,' Olivia remembered saying once, after twelve-year-old Eliza earnestly told her about Jeannie running away from home as a child. According to Eliza, Jeannie had stowed away in the back of a semitrailer until she reached the outback, where she spent a week living in a tent made from leaves and branches, surviving on ants, berries and dew, until the police arrived in a helicopter and brought her home again. Yes, Olivia had said, carefully choosing her words, Jeannie possibly had once run away from home. Most children did at some stage. But for a week to the outback? Living on insects? Rescued by helicopters? No.

'But Mum told me it happened,' Eliza insisted. 'She said it was the truth, the whole truth and nothing but the truth. She even said, "Cross my heart and hope to die."'

Olivia had challenged Jeannie about that story, ringing her during school hours once Eliza had arrived back home. She'd kept it light, treading gently, joking that she hadn't realised Jeannie had had such an adventurous childhood. 'Huckleberry Finn had nothing on you,' she'd said, before sharing some of the stories Eliza had told her. Halfway through, Jeannie had started laughing.

'I'm a master storyteller, if I do say so myself. Did she tell you I was also winched up into the helicopter, when it wasn't safe to land? And that there was a glitch and I had to travel fifty kilometres swinging from the rescue rope like a trapeze artist, until they pulled me up properly?'

'Jeannie, she believes every word you tell her. I really think you —'

Jeannie interrupted. 'She's a child, Olivia. My story-loving child. She also believes in giant peaches, chocolate factories, lands at the tops of trees and chairs that grow wings. Should I stop reading those books to her too? Only read her bedtime tales from *Encyclopaedia Britannica*?'

Olivia backed down. Jeannie had been surprisingly fierce. She knew what she was doing, she insisted. She was nurturing Eliza's imagination. Giving her a childhood filled with fun, stories and adventures. All that Olivia knew Jeannie hadn't experienced in her own childhood. She'd only met Jeannie's parents twice during their school days. She'd been struck by how cold they were. How formal.

Jeannie's stories continued, many colourful ones about Eliza's father among them. Olivia and Maxie often discussed it.

They felt it wasn't fair to fill Eliza's head with elaborate stories of a father who was an astronaut, or a circus performer, or whatever occupation took Jeannie's fancy at the time. They'd carefully raised that with her too. Jeannie laughed it off.

'It's just a bit of fun. I told you, I've promised to tell her everything when she's eighteen. Not just about her father. All my dark secrets. You have to promise not to say a word to her until then, too.'

They'd promised. They'd kept their promise. It was Jeannie who had been unable to keep hers, through the cruellest of circumstances.

They had been such terrible, dark days. Eliza was inconsolable. There was the added distress of an autopsy and coroner's report being ordered, due to the tragic circumstances. Jeannie's funeral finally took place, the weather as bleak as their hearts, the gathering in the country church surprisingly large for a small town. Jeannie's colleagues from the supermarket. Teachers and classmates from Eliza's school. Throughout it all, the two of them tried to keep Eliza afloat, while dazed with shock themselves. Every night, the sound of her weeping filling the house. Every day, her initial shock turning into the deepest of grief. The plaintive questions that broke their hearts. 'Was it my fault?' 'Did I do something wrong?' And even more heartbreakingly: 'What if I forget her?'

'You never will, darling, I promise. Never. We'll always help you remember her.' Olivia clearly recalled saying it, holding the seventeen-year-old Eliza tightly.

'We'll always be here for you, Eliza,' Maxie had said. 'We promise.'

Each day, Eliza asked them to keep telling her the stories about Jeannie. It had been so urgent, almost panicked. 'Which ones?' Olivia remembered Maxie asking. The one when the three of you shoplifted the chocolate and the nuns made you crawl on your hands and knees to return it to the shop. The one when she went backpacking around Europe and she slept on a beach and woke up to find a snake in her sleeping bag.

They'd never heard those stories. As far as they knew, none of them was true. But how could they say that to Eliza? She was so frightened, so devastated. She was gathering memories of her mother around her like a comfort blanket.

Maxie took as much leave from her TV series as possible, but after two weeks she'd needed to fly back. Edgar had been so understanding, assuring Olivia that he and the boys were fine in Edinburgh, that she must stay in Australia with Eliza as long as she was needed.

Olivia helped her pack up the house, reducing what had been Jeannie and Eliza's home into two suitcases for Eliza to take to the university residential hall. She'd surprised them by switching from an arts degree to a business one. They begged her to consider deferring for a year. She'd been adamant: she had to go to uni. It was what her mother had wanted.

Two months later, the coroner's verdict was announced. Jeannie's death was declared to be a tragic accident, not an intentional act. The coroner stated his belief that her calls to Olivia and her final email to Eliza showed she was not suicidal. She was making plans for the future.

Olivia had given a long statement. The phone records had shown she was the last person to speak to Jeannie that night. She'd put in writing how happy Jeannie had sounded. How excited she was to be seeing Eliza again. How much she adored her daughter. Eliza had read the coroner's report. It gave Olivia great comfort to know Eliza had been able to see in black and white how much she was loved.

Olivia gazed at the photograph of the four of them again. Perhaps she'd made a mistake hanging it in her office. She'd thought it would be good to see it every day. Instead, today especially, it made her heart ache. But she'd leave it for now. She knew Eliza would like to see it hanging so prominently.

# CHAPTER FIVE

Olivia returned to her desk, forcing her attention back to her working life. Who'd have thought her art history degree would bring her to this point, working full-time as the Montgomery's guest relations manager? She checked her watch. Ten-thirty. The hotel's general manager, Lawrence, had phoned earlier, asking for an urgent meeting. They'd agreed on eleven a.m. He was only in his late thirties, but the calmest, most efficient manager they'd ever had. Hired by Edgar in one of his last – and best – business decisions. Barely a day passed without Olivia being thankful for Edgar's wisdom. Lawrence had been with them for more than three years and nothing seemed to trouble him, be it difficulties with staff, suppliers or guests. So his use of the word 'urgent' was important. When she'd asked what it was about, he'd hesitated, then said a name.

Alex.

Of course, Olivia thought.

Alex had always been the trickiest, most headstrong, most difficult of Edgar's two sons. She'd clashed with him from the first day they met, nearly twenty years ago. 'You'll never be my mother,' he'd shouted at her, aged thirteen. They still clashed. If it hadn't been for his younger brother Rory – sweet, dreamy, welcoming Rory – she often wondered if she'd have stayed the course as Edgar's second wife at all.

She'd known it would be a delicate situation, arriving into their young lives as their father's new wife, not only Australian but, at thirty-three, ten years his junior too. Their mother had died five years earlier. It wasn't a swift remarriage, but even so, Alex resented her. He'd been an angry child. Angry at her. Angry at his father. Angry at his mother for getting cancer and leaving him. His anger had evolved into sharp wit and charm, but there was often still tension between him and Olivia.

In recent years they'd at least established a working relationship. All assisted by Edgar's foresight. Dementia was a cruel disease, but they'd had some warning. Edgar put in place as much as possible before his decision-making ability was taken away completely. Olivia had been surprised to come into her office one day to find the Montgomery family lawyer there, a stern woman in her sixties called Deirdre. She'd informed Olivia that Edgar had appointed her, Deirdre, his power of attorney. Edgar had later explained it to her, so lovingly. He didn't want Olivia to have the worry of running the business side of the hotel. He wanted her to enjoy the guest relations role, manage their art collection. Deirdre and their general manager would always keep Olivia informed, but they would make any major decisions. It had been such a relief.

He'd also told Olivia his great wish was that the Montgomery hotel would continue under the next generation. That one of his two sons would eventually take over as general manager.

A family meeting was called – Edgar, Olivia, Alex and Rory. It was a very sad day. First, Edgar had shared the news of his diagnosis with his sons. Olivia fought tears as she saw their shock, as they asked the questions she'd asked Edgar too. How fast would it progress? What would happen to him? Edgar was matter-of-fact. It could be months or it could be years. But he was grateful for this chance to prepare. He told them he loved them. He asked them to honour him and the Montgomery name by continuing to work at the hotel. To gain experience in all aspects of the business. He shared his hope that one of them would take over as manager one day. Rory was in tears by the end of the meeting. Alex was subdued. They both promised to do as their father asked. For the past three years, they'd worked in the hotel in a variety of roles, both paid well. They were shackled to the hotel, yes, but the handcuffs were golden and mostly comfortable.

The arrangement had suited Alex most of all, surprisingly. Edgar had recognised his oldest son's strengths and weaknesses. Alex was over-confident, Edgar had said once to Olivia, but that could also lead to innovative risk-taking. He'd been proved right.

Two years earlier, Alex had called a meeting with Deirdre to propose turning the mews at the end of the hotel's long garden into upmarket hostel accommodation. He'd got the idea while spending a month travelling Europe after finishing his hospitality management degree. Deirdre had seconded Lawrence, as general manager, to assess its potential.

They'd asked Alex for a business plan and sought more clarification about his investors, funding model, architectural plans, budgeting. Six months passed before they agreed to go ahead with the project, after seeking further assurances that there would be no impact on the Montgomery's core business. No noise issues, specifically. Young travellers in hostels were notoriously more spirited than the hotel's usual well-heeled guests.

The Monty Hostel had now been operational for five months. It was still early days, but so far, it was successful. Its occupancy rate regularly hit seventy per cent. A living wall of plants shielded the hostel from the hotel. That, and the separate entrance, minimised any impact on the Montgomery. The hostel was already showing a small profit. It was still considered to be Alex's solo project, under Deirdre's supervision, but Lawrence and Olivia both received weekly updates.

As for Rory – Edgar had never quite 'got' his second son. Rory was very different to Alex, Olivia often told him. More artistic. Dreamier. But still intelligent. He just needed to find his own way.

While Alex had studied hotel management, Rory chose art and design. Olivia had hoped it might be useful at the Montgomery – with a refurbishment, perhaps. But Rory simply returned to working full-time in different roles: as concierge, in reception, even occasionally as a waiter. He was good with people.

Sweet-natured. Guests enjoyed meeting a 'real' Montgomery too, Olivia knew.

In the following months, Olivia had often diplomatically enquired about him putting his design degree to use. Each time, he'd given her the same gentle smile she remembered from his boyhood.

'I do have something in mind, Olivia. But I need to give it more thought. Talk it over with Milly.'

Milly was his long-term, now long-distance girlfriend. They'd met at university. In the bar, not in class. She was a gifted IT specialist. Her parents had come to Britain from India when she was only a baby. Olivia had met them at her and Rory's graduation day. They'd been so proud of her. 'I taught her everything she knows,' her mother had said with a laugh.

Within a year of graduating, Milly had moved to Berlin after being approached by an American tech company based there, developing new apps and digital solutions for the insurance industry. Berlin was where it was all happening tech-wise these days, Olivia learned.

She'd half-expected Rory to follow Milly, turn his back on the hotel. But instead, they kept their relationship alive with regular trips between Edinburgh and Berlin. When Rory turned thirty, and told Olivia he had some big news, she'd felt sure it would involve an engagement. He surprised her. Six years after graduating, he told her he'd finally decided to put his design degree to practical use by opening a side business. Designing and handcrafting children's jigsaw puzzles, of all things.

It was well underway by the time he told her about it. He'd rented workshop space in an industrial estate half an hour from the Montgomery. Everything was done by hand, to Rory's designs, using high-quality wood and paint. He sold some via the Internet, he told her, but mostly at craft fairs and markets. Olivia had studied the website, designed and coded by Milly. The puzzles were beautifully made. When she asked if he was making any money or even covering his costs, he just smiled.

'It's not always about profit, Olivia. Sometimes art should exist for art's sake, don't you think?'

Olivia had decided not to share that particular conversation with Edgar, in case he was able to take any of it in. She could too easily imagine his reaction to Rory describing jigsaw puzzles as 'art'. But she told Edgar everything else that was happening with his sons.

She visited him most days, for two hours at a time. His nursing home was the most expensive in Edinburgh, but it meant he received first-class care. She couldn't have settled for less. Fortunately, Deirdre – in charge of paying the bills – seemed to agree.

At each visit, Olivia would sit in the comfortable chair beside his bed and smooth down the quilt she had chosen herself for the room she had helped decorate, knowing he would never notice it. She would hold his hand and try to convince herself she was feeling an answering squeeze. Sometimes he was conscious and she would pretend he was looking at her. That his now faraway, faded-blue eyes could still actually see her.

Even though he couldn't respond, she read out all their

business reports and occupancy updates. As she rubbed cream into Edgar's hands – he sometimes seemed to like it, sometimes pushed her hands away – she would share any funny stories with him, especially tales of difficult or unusual guests. There were always plenty of those. Part of her role was to respond to any online praise or criticism of the Montgomery. There was no way of knowing if he understood even a word she said or read to him, but she found it calming. Saying everything out loud had helped her many times to make decisions or reach some clarity on issues, be they business problems or tensions with his sons.

She recalled something now that he'd said about Alex, years earlier. 'He's a maverick and we need to keep our eyes on him. But I believe there's more good than bad in him.' Olivia hoped he was right. Perhaps she was jumping to conclusions about Lawrence's urgent meeting today.

She heard footsteps in the hall outside. It was five minutes to eleven. Lawrence was always punctual. There was a loud knock at the door. It flung open before she had a chance to respond. A woman in her mid-forties walked in, stopped in front of her desk and crossed her arms.

'I quit, Olivia.'

'Susan, please —'

'I mean it. Don't try to talk me out of it again. Life's too short to spend time with that monster.'

'Susan, I know —'

'No, you don't. Yes, you told me it might be difficult at times. Yes, you told me she might be a hard taskmaster. What you

57

omitted to tell me is that she'd be the most bad-tempered, vicious, selfish woman I'd ever have the misfortune to work for, be it temporarily or not.'

'Please don't make a rash decision. I know she's been having a few bad days.'

'A few? A lifetime's worth. And don't tell me I'm overreacting. Hear that noise? *That's* overreacting.'

Olivia faintly heard something smashing in the room above them.

'You're going to need a dustpan and broom,' Susan said. 'Maybe even a skip. I dodged three cups as I left her suite and she was heading for a vase. I'd sue her for assault if I didn't like you so much. You'll also need a new temp agency. I'm telling my supervisor not to send anyone else here.'

'Susan, please, she's an old woman. The project means a lot to her. I know she's contrary —'

'Contrary? Olivia, she's a bloody witch. She should be tied to a stake. If I stayed an hour longer, I'd light the match myself. I'm going straight to the agency now to get another job. Enough's enough.'

Susan had barely left when Olivia's phone rang. She considered letting it ring out, then answered.

'Olivia speaking.'

'Get up here. Now. It's an emergency.'

Olivia thought of all she'd like to say to the caller. She forced herself to remember the promise she'd made to Edgar, before that awful disease laid waste to his mind. He'd been so persuasive.

'She mightn't ever come back to Scotland, Olivia. But if she does, please always make her welcome.'

Olivia had followed his wishes. Celine was family, after all. Edgar's first wife's mother. His sons' grandmother. And truly one of the most difficult, selfish, self-centred women Olivia had ever met. Susan was right. Celine was a witch. A foul-mouthed witch.

'Olivia? Are you fucking deaf? Did you hear what I said? Get up here. Right now.'

Olivia counted to five before replying. 'I'll be up as soon as I can.'

'Run,' Celine said.

# CHAPTER SIX

It was late evening in Melbourne, after another unexpectedly hot April day. Eliza was in the middle seat of a row of three on a plane sitting on the tarmac of Tullamarine Airport.

Fifteen days had passed since Gillian's shock announcement. Now here she was, in her seat, about to take off on her first flight in years.

She wanted to be sick.

She'd imagined this entire scene so many times since Olivia's surprise invitation. Pictured herself walking down the aisle, stowing her bag, taking her seat, willing herself to stay calm, to keep breathing, to somehow endure the two flight legs. The long one to Dubai first, broken by the shortest of connection times, less than two hours, then an eight-hour flight to Edinburgh. Each time, she'd had to fight an overwhelming feeling of nausea. Of panic. Of building terror.

Olivia had sent links to conquer-your-flying-phobia podcasts.

Rose gave practical advice: 'Distract yourself as soon as you board. Watch back-to-back movies. Binge on TV shows.'

Unfortunately, Eliza hadn't had a chance to switch on her TV screen, let alone watch anything. When she reached her row, a dark-haired, bright-eyed boy of about eleven looked up from the window seat and beamed at her.

'You look nice,' he said. 'I'm Sullivan. I'm an unaccompanied minor on my way to Edinburgh. But don't worry, I don't need looking after. I've done this flight six times. My parents are separated. Mum lives here in Melbourne. Dad lives in Scotland. The court ordered that he gets me for a month every year. I'm not sure he wanted to win the case, but he did, and here I am.'

Eliza had barely taken all that in, sat down and introduced herself in return, before she heard what sounded like a sob from down the aisle. It was an older woman, her dark hair flecked with grey, wearing a blue tracksuit. She looked like she'd been doing a lot of crying.

The flight attendant helped the woman stow her bag, then settled her in the aisle seat beside Eliza.

'Now, we'll be close by if you need us, Judith. You've nothing to be frightened of. We take these flights several times a week. We wouldn't do it if it wasn't safe, I promise. It's statistically safer —'

'Than driving a car,' Judith said, stifling another sob. 'I know. But I hate driving too.'

The flight attendant patted her on the shoulder, promised to be back soon, then moved down the aisle. Before Eliza had a chance to speak, Sullivan leaned across.

'Hello, Judith, I'm Sullivan. Are you a nervous flyer? What a shame. This is Eliza, by the way.'

Judith gave them both a watery smile, then took a tissue from her sleeve. She began to pull it to pieces. 'I'm not nervous. I'm completely terrified. I've never flown before. I have never wanted to fly. I want to get off this plane and never set foot in an airport again but I can't, because in Manchester,' she faltered then, 'in Manchester my darling only daughter is waiting with her two little babies, twin boys, born a month ago. I want to see them so badly but they were born premature and it could be a long time before they can take a big flight. I can't even take tablets to knock myself out. What if something happened and I slept through it? If we crashed into the sea? At least if I was conscious, I'd have a chance at swimming, like that Kate Winslet, hanging on to that piece of ship for hours.' She finally stopped and drew a breath.

Sullivan had been listening intently. 'I don't think you'd survive if we did crash into the sea,' he said. 'The impact would be catastrophic. So in that instance it probably would be better to be asleep.'

Judith shuddered. 'That's what my husband said. He hasn't been at all sympathetic. He said this trip has cost so much he hopes I don't sleep a wink. That I have to get my money's worth of movies and meals and drink. But I don't hold my drink well. At Christmas I had a gin and tonic and I was crying by the time we had the pudding, thinking of Cathy on the other side of the world, about to have her babies. And I like her husband – he's a nice Welsh boy – but why did she have to fall in love with a foreigner, rather than an Aussie? But the babies are so gorgeous. It will be worth it, won't it, to hold them?'

For the next five minutes all Eliza had to do was nod and listen. Whenever there was a lull in Judith's monologue, Sullivan jumped in with a question. Around them, other passengers filed in. Flight attendants began closing overhead compartments. Ground staff were asked to leave the aircraft.

'— and so they all came to Australia for the wedding, a huge gang of them. It's true what people say about the Welsh, they really do love to sing — Bloody hell! What was *THAT*?'

The plane had given a jolt as it moved back from the docking area. Eliza's heart leapt at the movement too. She felt her pulse start to race. Beside her, Judith started to cry.

Sullivan leaned across again. 'Don't worry, Judith. That's perfectly normal. We have to get out on to the runway. There'll be plenty more little noises and bumps. I can explain them if you want.'

'Do you want to swap seats?' Eliza asked him. She could take the window seat, and concentrate on her own terror. It was now slowly threatening to overwhelm her.

'Thank you but no, Eliza,' Sullivan said. 'Unaccompanied minors are always given the window seat. We're usually placed beside women too, to guard against creeps, basically. Of course there are creepy women too, but I've been taking this flight for four years and, hand on my heart, I haven't had a bad experience yet. I also prefer the window seat. Did you ask for an aisle seat specifically, Judith?'

She nodded. She was now shredding a new tissue, the pieces fluttering around her like snowflakes. 'My neighbour told me to. She also said I should take lots of walks so I don't die of a blood clot. Also, when I get scared I go to the loo a lot. I didn't want to disturb anyone. I have to go to the loo now.'

'You can't,' Sullivan said cheerfully. 'We're taxiing. That means making our way to the runway.'

'But the flight attendants aren't sitting down. What's wrong? Do they know something we don't?'

'No, they get dispensation to make last-minute checks. Excuse me,' he called as a well-groomed young woman passed by. She stopped. 'I'm Sullivan, the unaccompanied minor. This is Eliza and Judith. Judith's a terrified flyer. But she'll be fine, won't she?'

The attendant smiled a white-toothed, red-lipsticked smile. 'We'll all be fine. I've done this flight a dozen times. It's safer than —'

'Driving,' Judith said. More tissue floated around her. 'I hear it but I don't believe it.'

The flight attendant lowered her voice. 'Would you like a drink to steady your nerves? I could get you a brandy if you think it would help?'

'Brandy would be great,' Sullivan answered for her. 'Anything but gin. That makes her maudlin.'

The plane made another slow movement, getting closer to the runway. Judith gasped. Beside her, Eliza was clenching her fists, forcing her nails into her skin, trying to stay calm.

The flight attendant returned with a small bottle. 'You can't use the tray table but a little sip might help.' She lowered her voice. 'My mum's a bit frightened of flying and this works wonders on her.'

Eliza wished she could have a brandy too. Instead, she clenched her fists even tighter.

Sullivan noticed and frowned. 'Are you nervous as well, Eliza? Do the airlines ask people when they book if they're nervous? I don't book my flights. My father's secretary in Edinburgh, Ann-Marie, takes care of my arrangements. Would a flying phobia be considered private information?'

'I don't know, Sullivan, sorry.' She was swallowing hard. Her heart was racing. All the flight attendants were now sitting down. The plane was moving faster. She really did want to be sick. Beside her, Judith had drunk all the brandy. The tissue was a crumpled ball in her lap.

'Would it help if we all held hands?' Sullivan asked.

Eliza and Judith turned to him. 'What?' they said.

He shrugged. 'Sometimes it helps to feel human touch when you're scared.'

'You are a very odd little boy,' Judith said.

'You're not the first person to say that,' Sullivan said. He held out his right hand.

Eliza hesitated, then took it in her left. She held out her own right hand for Judith. She winced as the older woman squeezed it tightly. As the plane gathered even more speed, she shut her eyes.

'It's best to open your eyes, Eliza,' Sullivan said. 'Your imagination will make it worse. You'll picture us crashing into another plane, for example. Look outside. We've got the runway all to ourselves.'

Judith moaned softly and crunched Eliza's hand more tightly.

Eliza kept her eyes shut, ignoring Sullivan's advice. She was now extremely queasy. Her breathing was too fast. She felt beads of sweat on her forehead. She wanted to be in her flat, getting ready for work or ironing her clothes, or talking to Rose on the phone or doing anything but being on this plane —

'We're aloft!' Sullivan said. 'Well done, Eliza,' he whispered as she opened her eyes. 'That was kind of you not to show Judith how bad you were feeling.'

Judith looked over at them both, eyes wide. 'What are you whispering about? Is something wrong?'

'Nothing at all,' Sullivan said. 'It was a textbook take-off, as far as I can tell. We'll feel a bit odd for a little while, until the plane levels off. And don't worry about odd noises either, like the wheels retracting. That's normal too. So, have either of you had a chance to look at the films on offer?'

Eliza shook her head. She was slowly starting to breathe more normally. She'd been so terrified of the take-off, worried it would spark an embarrassing panic attack. But there hadn't been time to think about a panic attack, let alone have one, between Sullivan's chatter and Judith's nerves.

'We can let each other's hands go now,' Sullivan said. 'If you're both feeling less anxious.'

'Both?' Judith turned to Eliza. 'Is this your first flight too?'

Eliza shook her head. 'But I haven't flown for a few years.'

'Why? Did something put you off? Did you once nearly have a crash?'

'I've been too busy at work to go travelling,' she lied.

'Really?' Sullivan said. 'What do you do that keeps you so busy, Eliza? Let me guess. Guessing games are good on flights. Shall we play a game? We can watch films later.'

Eliza didn't have a choice. Judith and Sullivan took turns trying to guess her occupation. Nurse. Doctor. Lecturer. Teacher. Lawyer. Astronomer. They finally gave up.

'I'm actually unemployed,' Eliza said. 'I was made redundant two weeks ago. I was a conference organiser for nine years. But the company was sold and we were all let go.'

'I'm sorry to hear that,' Sullivan said. 'Best of luck job hunting.'

'So you're having a holiday in the meantime?' Judith asked.

'That's right,' Eliza said.

'Have you been to Edinburgh before?' Sullivan asked.

'Once, when I was sixteen. Fourteen years ago.'

'It's a charming city,' Sullivan said. 'Beautiful architecture and gardens. If you need any sightseeing tips, please do ask. I haven't been to Manchester unfortunately, Judith, but I presume your daughter and son-in-law will have places to show you, if the twins allow them out of the house at all.'

'I don't want to see the city. I want to see the babies.'

'And so you will, in less than twenty-two hours. Look, nearly half an hour has gone by already. Would you both play I-Spy with me? I know it's a child's game but it does pass the time.'

He was so earnest, so eager, it was impossible to say no.

During their fifth round of I-Spy the flight attendant came back, pushing the drinks trolley.

'Don't risk it,' Sullivan advised Judith. 'I know the first one steadied your nerves, but the second will begin to distort reality. You don't need it.'

'How do you know that? How old are you?'

'Seven weeks from being twelve. My mother's a psychologist, specialising in addiction therapy. She sees her patients at home. I like to eavesdrop.'

'Does she know?'

'No. She'd soundproof her office if she did. I don't do anything with the information. I just store it up. I might be a psychologist when I'm older. Or a surgeon like my father. I haven't decided yet.'

He enthusiastically shared details of his father's recent operations. He was a world leader in reconstructive surgery, he explained. Two of his operations were available on YouTube. He offered to use the onboard wi-fi to show them. They declined.

It wasn't until after their first meal was served that Eliza's companions left her in peace. To her left, Sullivan began watching what appeared to be a program about ring-tailed lemurs on the wildlife channel. To her right, Judith began what she announced would be a 'bungee-watch' of *Downton Abbey*.

Eliza put on her headphones, selected a film at random and stared at the screen as though she was watching it. She wasn't.

# CHAPTER SEVEN

Until now, Eliza hadn't had a chance to think about anything beyond the imminent flight. Her final days at the office had been so busy there'd been no time for anything but work matters. The new company's representatives had arrived the day after Gillian's announcement, professional and relentless in their questions. She'd shown them every process, file and conference plan, all the while fighting the realisation that she was leaving her safe, organised, constant routine behind her.

Packing up her house had been straightforward, at least. Rose offered to store her books and other belongings and take good care of the plants, bowls and vase. She'd also asked if she could hang the framed photo of Eliza with her mother and godmothers in her house, rather than store it away.

'To show you off, of course. And maybe to do a tiny bit of boasting that I've met Maxie, too.'

As the day of her flight approached, Eliza's anxiety levels rose.

It wasn't just the thought of the flight. The packing kept prompting bad memories of packing up the house after her mother died. After four sleepless nights and too many daytime hours spent with a racing heart, she knew she had to do something. She took out her address book, found the clinic's number and made an appointment.

Three days before her flight, Eliza caught the tram and got off at the familiar stop in Camberwell. She'd come here once a fortnight for nearly three years. From the outside, it looked like a normal house in the leafy inner-eastern suburb. She was early, as always. She sat in the waiting room. Her hands were clenched. Her breathing was tight. She was overwhelmed with memories of the many hours she'd spent here, as she'd tried to get answers to impossible questions. *Was it my fault Mum died? Was there something I should have done? Should I have helped her to stop drinking? Was it my fault for going away with Maxie? Could I have stopped it from happening?* And the most unanswerable question of all. *How do I live without her?*

Her counsellor, Caroline, greeted her with her usual warm professionalism. 'It's good to see you again, Eliza. Tell me, why are you here today?' The same question had opened all her appointments.

Eliza told her the truth. The stone was back. She could feel it deep inside her. It had never really gone away, she knew. Sometimes it grew lighter, or shifted, but it was always part of her. A stone made of pain, grief and guilt. Caroline talked it through with her again, as she had so many times before. Told her, again, that she wasn't responsible for her mother's death. It was an accident. The coroner had said so, the police had said so. A tragic accident. She had to look at the facts, as the inquest had done. Re-read the last email her mother had sent. Remind herself how much she'd been loved.

Eliza explained all that had happened in the past days. Her job, her flat, the imminent flight. How it had all triggered her anxiety again. How it was affecting her sleep. How she was reliving scenes she never wanted to see again, but never wanted to forget, either.

Caroline took her through helpful breathing exercises again. Reminded her to keep updating what they'd previously named Eliza's 'jukebox of memories'. Happy images and stories about her mother that Eliza could choose from whenever she was feeling troubled, overwhelmed or panicked.

Caroline helped her work through another recurring question too: about her own mental health. Was she destined to follow in her mother's footsteps? Find life as difficult as Jeannie had? Yet again, Caroline was reassuring. She gently praised her for already having sought professional help with her anxiety. For taking the good step of avoiding alcohol. Small steps with helpful outcomes, she said.

'And tell me, Eliza, are you still painting?' Caroline asked. 'That used to give you great solace.'

Eliza shook her head. She'd stopped in the past year or so, after her work with Gillian became more intense, the hours even longer. Her painting items – the small canvases, the paints, the brushes – had sat on the table in her flat unused for weeks. Eventually, she had packed them away rather than constantly feel guilty seeing them there.

She had always loved painting, even as a child. Her mother had encouraged her, always making sure she had paper and paints, no matter how cheaply made they were. After that terrible night, after she'd moved to Melbourne and started uni, it was painting that helped keep her afloat. Night after night, rather than meet the other students down at the campus bars, she sat at the desk in her room. Her subjects were always the same four items. The tall green vase and the three coloured bowls that had belonged to her mother. She rearranged them into different configurations or with different light falling on them. She painted them so she could imagine her mother's praise.

*'Eliza, they're gorgeous! You've got the colours exactly right. Can you please do me another one?'*

She re-used each canvas, many times. She discovered that for the hour or so it took her to do each painting she would become so absorbed, be concentrating so intensely on getting just the right shade of green, red, blue or yellow, that her mind would become still. For a short time, she could forget Jeannie was gone. Forget that she'd never hear her voice again.

At uni, she'd kept her painting secret. It was only several years after they graduated that Rose saw any of her artwork. On a rare trip to Melbourne, she'd surprised Eliza with a visit to her apartment.

A half-finished still life of the vase and one of the bowls had been drying on the table. She hadn't had time to hide it.

'Eliza, that's beautiful!' Rose said. 'I can't even draw stick figures. I didn't know you were so artistic.'

Eliza batted away the compliment. Rose was undeterred. Ever since, she'd constantly encouraged Eliza, often giving her unexpected parcels of paints, or small canvases. 'Just in case you get the urge,' she'd say.

Her counsellor didn't tell her to start painting again. She never issued instructions. She let Eliza talk. Listened as she came to the realisation herself that it might be good for her to start painting again, when she got back from Scotland.

Eliza noticed Caroline's subtle glance at the clock. Their session was coming to a close. She needed to discuss one more thing. About her decision to finally ask her godmothers about her father. About her mother's family. Was there something wrong with her, that it had taken her this long to want to talk to them about it all?

There was nothing wrong with her, Caroline reassured her. There wasn't one right way of coming to terms with all that had happened to her.

'What's important is you now know you're ready to ask those questions.'

Talking to Caroline helped, as it always had. That night, Eliza continued packing. At the bottom of her wardrobe, she found something she hadn't looked at in some years. A folder of paperwork. Everything that had been in her mother's bedside table. She'd looked through it so many times in the early months, desperate to find something new: a note to her, a new detail about her mother's life. It was only a collection of bank statements, a letter from the council about an overdue parking fine, a note from the library to say the books she'd ordered had arrived. But among them were two special items. Her mother's passport, filled with stamps from her travels around Europe. And, at the back of the folder, something that even all these years later gave her a dart of joy to see.

It was a stapled set of A4 pages. A school project Eliza had done the year she turned twelve, an assignment entitled 'The Person I Admire Most in the World'. Most of her classmates had chosen footballers or cricketers. Two chose Mother Teresa. Eliza wasn't the only student who chose her mother. But she was the only one who handed up a ten-page document, complete with handwritten notes, drawings, long captions and plenty of spelling mistakes.

It had taken three nights of questioning her mum to get the facts.

'Stop joking, Mum,' Eliza remembered saying. 'This is serious.'

'I couldn't get more serious if I tried,' Jeannie said with a studious expression. 'So, where shall I begin? I was born in the Amazonian jungle, in a straw hut dangled over a precipice, to a soundtrack of monkey howls and toucan cries. Do toucans cry?'

'Mum, stop it.'

Eventually, they got through the long list of questions suggested by the teacher.

*Date and place of birth.* 'Darling, you already know my birthday. It happened in a hospital. I can't recall the name. But it smelt of bleach, I do remember that.'

*Names of parents.* 'Mum and Dad,' Jeannie said.

'But what were their names?'

'I don't know. That's all I ever called them.'

Eliza sighed and wrote that down. 'Any brothers or sisters?'

'Alas, no. But we did have three cats. I thought of them as my sisters. Sisters with severe facial hair problems, but sisters nevertheless.'

'Mum, this is serious.'

'So was their facial hair. Go on, next question.'

*Schooling.* Her mum always made her boarding school sound like a cross between Hogwarts, Malory Towers and a haunted house. That night, Eliza wrote down Jeannie's descriptions of evil teachers and midnight feasts. She also added a final line. *My mum met her two best friends in the world at boarding school, which she said made up for the terrible food and inadequit teaching. Their names are Olivia and Maxine, but we call her Maxie.*

*Achievements.* That one was easy. Eliza had always thought it was amazing that her Mum had gone travelling overseas at the age of nineteen, only seven years older than she was right now. With just a backpack. She'd written a full page about it.

*Mum flew to London first. It was cold but it looked like it should and there was snow one day. She got a job in a bar and lived in a big house called a squat and made a good friend who lived there too. The friend's name was Emma. Emma was funny and kind and Irish. On Mum's days off she would go to art galeries and look at her favrite paintings. We have a postcard of her favrite on our fridge. When her job ended she went travelling to France and Italy and Spain and to the place in Ireland where Emma was from. She saw the Eiffel Tower and also the Collaseeum and she went to an incredible church which looks like a forest of bare tree trunks and a cave inside. She said there were fifty shades of green in Ireland because she counted them one day. She had lots of adventures and once someone tried to steal her backpack and if Mum hadn't fought back all her wordly goods would have disappeared forever.*

The other answers were shorter.

*My Mum's favourite colour is: red.*

*Her favourite food is: chips.*

*Her favourite flower is: a daisy.*

*I admire her because: she makes everything fun and she loves me so much that she says sometimes her heart feels like it might burst with all the love for me it holds.*

Her teacher had given her an A. At some stage, Jeannie had added her own comment to the final page. *I give it an A++++++++++++++++++++. Best school report EVER!!!! Best daughter EVER!!!!!!!!*

Eliza had planned to leave the folder with Rose. At the last minute, she put it in her suitcase. It still meant so much that her mother had touched those pieces of paper. She thought Olivia and Maxie might like to see the school report too. She couldn't remember if she'd showed it to them before.

The detail about her mother's Irish friend Emma had also planted the seed of an idea. Perhaps Olivia and Maxie knew more about her. Her surname, where she was from. She'd only been a name in a school report for years. But what if Eliza was able to find her? Perhaps Emma might even have met her father too? She might be able to hear a new story about her mother. Something else to treasure.

Eliza gave up pretending she was watching a film on the screen in front of her. She leaned back and shut her eyes. As the plane brought her closer every minute to her godmothers, to the possibility of answers to so many of her questions, she gave in to her favourite pastime. One her counsellor Caroline always encouraged. Remembering moments with her mother.

# CHAPTER EIGHT

Jeannie had long planned a big eighteenth birthday celebration for her. She'd even promised to bake a huge cake. 'I might jump out of it. Naked. Give you a real birthday to remember.'

'Of course I'll remember it,' sixteen-year-old Eliza had said. 'I've been counting down the days. I still think it's unfair you haven't told me anything about my father. I'm not a child any more.'

'Legally, yes, you are.'

'Why not tell me now? It's something terrible, isn't it?' She made herself ask the question. 'Were you attacked by some man? Is that why you won't tell me? I'm the result of a rape?'

Her mother hadn't joked then. 'I promise that wasn't the case. I swear that it wasn't.'

'Then why wait until I'm eighteen?'

'Because it's complicated, sweetheart.'

'I'm almost an adult. I can cope with complication. Can't you tell me even one thing about him?'

'One?' Jeannie considered it. 'All right. What do you want to know?'

Her mother's answer shocked her. Where did she start? She wanted to know everything. His name. Where he was from. What he looked like. She finally settled on one. 'Where did you meet him?'

Jeannie smiled. 'Overseas, when I was travelling. And I described Australia in such a beguiling and magical way that he had to come and see it for himself.'

'Where overseas?'

'One question, not two.'

'That's not fair! You didn't give me any detail at all. You didn't say what country, or what city.'

'I'm naughty, aren't I? Incorrigible, really. That's what Sister Teresa used to say. I asked her to spell it once. She threw a piece of chalk at me.'

Eliza sighed in exasperation. At sixteen, sighing was one of her favourite things to do. Her mother laughed, reached over and tweaked her cheeks.

'You know the real reason why I haven't told you the whole story before now, don't you?'

'Because you don't know who my father is?'

'Eliza!' Her mother put her hand on her heart in mock outrage. 'How dare you cast aspersions on my character? Don't forget I was locked up in a Catholic boarding school for years. You're lucky I didn't run away the first time I saw a man, or you wouldn't be here to bring me such joy and delight.'

'So what is the real reason?' She knew what her mother would say. She just wanted to hear it again.

'Because I don't want you to go looking for him. Because then I'd have to share you with him. And I've wanted you all to myself from the first moment I saw you.'

'You share me with Maxie and Olivia.'

'That's different. That's so they can spoil you senseless. Without singing my own praises too much, because, as you know, I place modesty as one of the highest human attributes, I played a blinder when it came to your godmothers. I might not have been able to deliver much to you in the way of loving grandparents, aunties and uncles, my darling, but I did my best in other ways.'

The year Eliza turned ten, her mother had told her sad news about her grandparents. They'd died two months before Eliza was born, in a car crash on the Hume Highway. It had been so tragic – three other people died in the four-vehicle pile-up caused by a truck driver falling asleep. Eliza clearly remembered the tears in her mother's eyes.

'I wish it had been different, sweetheart. That they could have met you. Maybe if I'd had brothers or sisters it might have been easier too. We could have grieved together.' Then she sat up straighter. 'But we did our best, Eliza, didn't we? We made our own little family, in our own way. You and me, with Maxie and Olivia like our sun and our moon, shining down on us. That's poetic of me, isn't it?'

Then, three years later, Eliza had been told a different story. That her grandparents had been part of a right-wing religious cult in which women were only there to serve. That Jeannie had run away from them.

And gone to a Catholic boarding school? Eliza had asked, truly bewildered.

'It seemed like a good hiding place,' her mother said. 'Who would think to look for me there?'

During one of her holidays with Olivia, a sunny beachside stay in Queensland, Eliza summoned up the courage to ask about her mother's family. Which of the stories was true? She'd tried to be lighthearted about it. Make it sound as if her mother's ever-changing tales were all just great fun.

Olivia hadn't found it funny. She had quietly asked Eliza questions. That night, when Eliza knew Olivia thought she was asleep, she'd heard her phone Maxie. She crept to the door to eavesdrop.

'I can't believe it, Maxie. Jeannie clearly thinks it's funny, but it's almost child abuse. One minute her grandparents are dead in a terrible car crash, the next they're leaders of some kind of religious cult.' Eliza wished she could also hear what Maxie was saying. 'No, don't you remember? That time they visited? I know, cold as ice but —' It was all she'd heard before Olivia shut the door.

Eliza and her mother didn't have a phone at that time. It had been cut off. Olivia handed Eliza a sealed envelope to give to Jeannie as soon as she arrived home. 'It's me telling her how wonderful you have been and what a great traveller you are,' she said. 'But even so, please don't read it.'

Jeannie was at the airport to collect her. She'd swept Eliza up into a hug, showered her with kisses. It was only when they got home that Eliza remembered Olivia's envelope. She gave it to her mother and went to unpack, imagining her mum reading all the nice things Olivia had said about her, smiling as she refolded her T-shirts and dresses, then neatly arranged her shoes inside her wardrobe.

The smashing of a glass in the kitchen made her leap. Her mother was shouting.

'Fuck you, Olivia, Mrs Fucking Know-It-All without any fucking kids of her own telling me how I can or can't raise my daughter. Well, fuck you. That's the last time you see Eliza again, you interfering —'

Eliza ran out, heart pounding. 'What's wrong? Was it me? Doesn't Olivia want to see me again?'

Her mother stopped tearing the pages into tiny scraps. 'What, Eliza?'

'Olivia said she was writing to you about how good I'd been. Did she say something else? Was I bad?'

Her mother's mood changed instantly, as it often did; sunshine after a storm. She opened her arms. 'Sweetheart, of course she didn't say that. She thinks the world of you. Maxie thinks the sun shines out of you. They're both right, of course. You are the most wonderful girl in the world.'

'Then why are you so cross?'

'Olivia and I have, over the years, had cause to disagree on occasional matters. This, sadly, is one of those times.' Her mother was speaking now in a posh accent, sounding like a TV news-reader. 'Olivia is an art historian, darling. She loves details and facts. I must remind her that it's humour and imagination that will keep the human race afloat, not rigid adherence to some dry fucking truth.'

Eliza winced at the swearword. Her mother noticed.

'Oops, I better not swear in front of you either, should I, or Police Commissioner Olivia or Nazi Nanny of the World Maxine will have something to say about that too, won't they? You think I'm a good mother, Eliza, don't you? You love me? Love the games we play, the stories I tell, the fun we have?'

There was a strange, urgent tone to her voice. Eliza almost preferred the newsreader one. 'Of course, Mummy.' She hadn't called her that in years. 'I love you. You're the best mother in the world.'

'Write that down for me, darling, would you? Here, on this piece of paper. Use this black pen.' Eliza found herself almost dragged to the table, the pen put in her hand, the paper in front of her. 'I'm going to write to Olivia tonight and I think it would be marvellous to include that as well.'

She never knew if her mother posted that letter. She didn't know if Jeannie and Olivia had a fight about it. She spent the next months wondering if that was the last godmother trip she'd ever have.

But, six months later, Maxie's holiday plan arrived. After that, Olivia's. If there had been a rupture between her mother and godmothers, it was healed, as if nothing had happened.

Except something did change. Eliza made sure never to tell Olivia or Maxie any more of the stories her mother told her.

As Eliza became a teenager, she and her mother began to argue more often. Sometimes it was about Eliza's plans after she left school. Jeannie was insistent that she go to university.

'It's one of my biggest regrets that I didn't go, Eliza. Oh, I thought I was so rebellious, thumbing my nose at studying, heading off overseas to go travelling.' She'd told Eliza she'd received an unexpected inheritance from her grandmother and used every cent to go backpacking. 'I was horrible to Maxie and Olivia too, I'm sure. Sending them gloating postcards from all sorts of places. I might have gone to uni when I got back, but then when you came along – well, of course I'd much rather spend hours staring at your beautiful face than any study papers or history books.'

'Do you wish you had had a proper career? Instead of having to look after me?'

Her mother got cross then. 'I've had lots of proper careers, Eliza. Don't be snobby about the different jobs in the world. No, I'm not a glamorous actor or an art expert, but how long would the world keep going without someone like me stacking supermarket shelves? What would people eat if there weren't hard workers like me in food-processing factories, or waitressing in cafés, or serving drinks in bars? I choose to do the kind of work I do and I don't regret it for one minute.'

The teenage Eliza pushed it. 'So you won't mind if I do waitressing or factory work instead of uni?'

'If you don't go to uni, I will kill you. And that's a promise.'

'That's hypocritical, isn't it?'

'I'm your mother. I want the best for you. That allows me to be as hypocritical as I want.'

There was one subject they fought about more than anything. Her mother's drinking.

It had been part of their lives for as long as Eliza could remember. Her mother called it a way to relax at the end of a long day. To Eliza, it seemed more like desperation than relaxation. It worried her how quickly her mother drank. Sometimes, after work, she'd drink two glasses of wine as if they were water.

'I'm dying of thirst today,' she'd say if Eliza was there doing her homework. Eliza would stare down at her book, wishing her mother would quench her thirst with water like most people.

It took years for her to summon the courage to say anything. She knew how hard her mother worked. Who was she to tell her how to relax? But one month in particular, the year Eliza was fifteen, her mother drank a bottle of wine a night. One night it was two bottles. The following morning, as Eliza was leaving for school, she emerged hungover, eyes panda-like with mascara.

'I think I have a touch of that flu going around,' she said. 'Call in sick for me, sweetheart, would you?'

Eliza had made that call before. She had the phone in her hand and was about to dial when something made her put the receiver down and turn back to her mother.

'It's not the flu, Mum. It's a hangover.'

'I think I can tell the difference, Eliza. Fine, if you won't phone them, I will.'

It was hard, but she stood in front of the phone. 'I think you have a problem.'

'Oh, you do, do you? And what kind of problem is that?'

'Mum, please don't use that tone with me. You know what I mean. I think you're drinking too much.'

'How much am I allowed to drink?' She laughed and then abruptly stopped. 'I don't tell you how to live your life. So please don't start on me, missy.'

'But you do tell me how to live my life. And I don't want you to kill yourself.'

'I'm not killing myself. For God's sake, Eliza. One night of one-too-many wines and you've got me in an early grave. Okay, forget about it. I'll ring them myself. Off you go to school, like the good holy girl you are.'

All day Eliza felt sick with guilt and shame. That night, she came home to a spotless house, a home-cooked dinner in the fridge and a note on the table. *My flu was gone by lunchtime so I've gone in for the afternoon shift. Home by 8. See you then, darling. Xxxxx*

When her mother came home, it was as if nothing had happened. There was no wine for the next four nights. Only a glass on the fifth. Until it went back to a bottle or more a night again. It became a cycle. They would argue, it would stop, then start again. All through her final years of school.

She never spoke to Maxie or Olivia about it. It felt too shameful, too private. Afterwards, she cried herself to sleep many nights, wishing she had told them. Perhaps they might have done something to stop it from happening. Stop Jeannie deciding to have a drink that night, after filling her bath —

Eliza opened her eyes. No. She couldn't revisit memories of that night again. Not here, on a plane, far from all she knew, with so much uncertainty about her future, no job to distract her, no —

*Ding.*

Her thoughts were interrupted by the plane's announcement bell.

Beside Eliza, Judith's eyes were wide. The 'Fasten seatbelts' sign had come on. The pilot advised that they were approaching an area of turbulence.

'I knew it would get bad,' Judith said, her voice rising. 'We're going to crash, aren't we?'

Sullivan consoled her. 'It'll be fine, Judith. They're just being cautious. Let's hold hands again.'

Eliza had no choice but to join in. It was surprisingly comforting.

# CHAPTER NINE

Two hours later, they landed in Dubai on schedule. They held hands once more. Eliza shut her eyes as the plane descended. Judith was praying. There was a squeal when the tyres hit the tarmac. She wasn't sure if it was her or Judith.

Sullivan beamed proudly at them both. 'You did it. More than halfway there.'

'But now what do I do?' Judith said. 'How will I find the next plane? My husband and friends said to ask someone but I don't speak the language here. I don't even know what the language is.'

'You'll find most people in Dubai speak English, Judith,' Sullivan said.

'But I can help you find your gate, if you like?' Eliza said.

'Good idea, Eliza,' Sullivan said. 'I'll come too.'

The ground staff member charged with looking after Sullivan wouldn't pass him over to a stranger. There were rules and regulations, she said.

'Never mind. At least I tried,' Sullivan said. 'Eliza, I'll see you on the next leg. Judith, it's been a pleasure. Have a great time with your grandchildren.'

Judith was calmer now. 'If you're ever in Bendigo, come and visit,' she said.

'I doubt I ever will be, but thanks all the same,' Sullivan said.

He went off, already chatting to the airline representative. 'And what part of the world do you hail from?' they heard him ask as they walked away.

'Imagine living with that all day,' Judith said to Eliza. 'Do you think he's got that ABCD brain thing?'

Eliza suspected there wasn't a label for Sullivan.

After leaving Judith at the right gate and making sure she knew what to do, Eliza walked around the terminal. It was like being in a 24-hour department store, lights flashing everywhere, the air heavy with too much perfume. It was a relief when it was time to board her flight to Edinburgh.

Even before she reached her gate, she heard Sullivan calling her name. He was in the front row of the waiting area, his neat backpack beside him.

'Great news, Eliza! The flight isn't full. I've asked the ground staff if it's possible for you and I to sit together. I explained you're an extremely fearful flyer and you need my support.'

Shortly after, Eliza found herself in the same row as Sullivan again. He was in the window seat, she was on the aisle. Sullivan held out his hand, measuring the space between them.

'Yes, we'll be able to reach. Excellent. Thank you, Mosal,' he said, reading the flight attendant's badge. 'I'll be sure to mention you by name when I send my follow-up email to the airline.'

'I'd appreciate that, Mr Farrington, thank you.'

Eliza bit back a smile. She'd spent hours with Rose's children, but they'd certainly never had these kinds of grown-up conversations.

'Are you an only child, Sullivan?' she asked.

'I was, Eliza, yes. But now I have a half-sister. She's only three months old. I'm actually meeting her for the first time this trip. My father got remarried to a much younger English woman. Mum hates her, of course. She's repartnered herself, though. He's a fellow psychologist. They're undertaking a lecture tour of America together as we speak. You'd think that would mean a harmonious home life, all that knowledge and insight under one roof, but they squabble a lot, actually.'

'And you go to school in Melbourne?'

'Yes, an expensive private school. Dad pays for it. Mum had an excellent lawyer.'

'Do you play any sport?'

He shook his head. 'I'm more cerebral than physical. I have an aversion to running around muddy paddocks or standing in steamy changing rooms. Fortunately, I get asthma occasionally so that gets me out of most sporting requirements.' He gave an impish smile.

'And do you have many friends at school?'

'Not many. Actually, none. I don't mind. I read, listen to podcasts, do my study. I top my class in most subjects. I always have done. It doesn't help my popularity.'

'And what do you think you'll do when you finish school?'

'Go on a bender? That was a joke, Eliza. University, I expect. But it's early days yet. I might end up doing something unexpected, like pottery. Or DJ-ing. Look, we're beginning to taxi already.'

Eliza hadn't noticed the plane moving. She felt her heart start to race. She tried breathing deeply, closing her eyes, counting to ten. It didn't seem to be working.

'You do have it bad, don't you?' Sullivan said. 'What caused it, if you don't mind me asking?'

She opened her eyes and told a portion of the truth. 'I had very bad news after a flight when I was seventeen. It set up an association between flying and trauma.'

'What sort of bad news?'

'I'd rather not say.'

'I respect your privacy. But my mother would love to get her mitts on you. I can give you her card?'

'Thank you but no.'

'If you change your mind, just ask. Will we start holding hands now?'

Eliza held out her hand. He took it in a firm grasp.

'Thanks, Sullivan,' she said. 'If the pottery or DJ-ing doesn't work out, you could have a career helping people face their fear of flying.'

He gave his funny little bark of a laugh. 'I'll keep that in mind, Eliza, thank you. Further to our earlier conversation, do you have any brothers or sisters?'

She shook her head. 'I'm an only child too. I'd have loved a brother or sister.'

'Younger or older?'

'One of each.'

'If you had to choose?'

'A younger brother. Like you.'

'You flatter me,' he said. 'If I ever decide to hire out my sibling services, you'll be the person I call. Look, we're up in the air. Well done, Eliza. You've got through it again. Now, it's time to relax.' He let go of her hand, put on his headphones and began scrolling through the wildlife documentaries.

To her surprise, she did relax. Mostly. Two bouts of turbulence set her heart racing. But the hours passed with the help of three movies, two meals, even a nap. Sullivan only interrupted her twice.

'You don't play online Scrabble by any chance, Eliza, do you?' he asked. 'It would be fun to keep in touch that way. I don't use social media. I prefer to leave as little trace of myself online as possible. But I do enjoy Scrabble and its messaging feature. If you don't mind me using your phone to access the onboard wi-fi, I can set us up online as opponents. I'm good, though, I must warn you.'

She found her phone in her bag. He switched it on and pressed the keys.

'There you are. I've started a game with you. I called you Fearless Flyer. I hope that's okay?'

'I like it very much,' she said.

'I'm Navillus. Sullivan backwards. Catchy, isn't it?' He took out his own phone from the backpack at his feet. 'Will we have a quick game now?'

They played two games – Sullivan won both – before the announcement that they were soon landing.

'Who'll be meeting you, Sullivan?' Eliza asked, as she put her phone away.

He shrugged. 'I never know. Sometimes Dad. Usually his secretary, Ann-Marie. She's very likeable.'

'Will you be okay? You'll get to do some fun things?'

'I imagine so. If not, I'll get plenty of schoolwork done. I've been given projects to complete. Usually I come in the holidays, but they got special dispensation this time, due to my mother's American trip.'

'When you're not doing school projects, I look forward to thrashing you at Scrabble.'

'Not a chance. Prepare to die, Eliza.' He pulled a face. 'Sorry. That was an unfortunate choice of words in light of your flying phobia. Prepare to be slaughtered by my word prowess, I meant.'

'The game is on, Navillus.'

She was rewarded with another smile before she shut her eyes, trying not to think of the landing. She searched for a good mental picture to replace her anxious thoughts. It was easy this time.

She pictured her two godmothers.

# CHAPTER TEN

Maxie was at the kitchen table in the apartment she and Hazel rented in central London. She'd just written a note to accompany the newspaper article she was posting to her mother in Australia. Her mum loved reading any of Maxie's publicity, as long as it wasn't online. She'd told Maxie she got too angry reading the mean things trolls said about her in the comments. Maxie secretly loved that her mother even knew what an online troll was.

She hoped she'd enjoy this latest article. It was a two-page spread, with one big photo that had required an all-day shoot. Most of the content had been recycled from earlier interviews Maxie had done in the UK and Australia. The old anecdote about her nearly becoming a nun had been trotted out too. Not true, of course, but the media always managed to twist that out of the fact she'd gone to a strict Catholic boarding school that had once been for novitiates. Today's article even re-used an old quote from her first drama teacher Sister Frances, now in a retirement home for nuns, about Maxie's early acting talent. 'She was always a great mimic, and a scallywag. There were three of them – the Terrible Trio, we used to call them.' Somehow, the newspaper had tracked down the photo of the three of them with Eliza, taken at the school concert nineteen years ago. An enlargement of that same photo now hung in Maxie and Hazel's study. It would be coming to New York when they moved in a fortnight's time.

Still, all publicity was good publicity, apparently. Not that the final episode of the current series needed much official promotion. The fans were making enough noise about it online themselves.

Her final episode. It seemed impossible. How many had there been? Two hundred? More? She'd played a baddie on TV for so long now she had almost become accustomed to the reaction from people in the street, if and when she was recognised. It didn't happen often. Her own usual expression was so cheerful, her smile so broad, that she was the opposite of the angry, bitter woman she played. She knew she had her voice to thank for her acting career, her gravelly, husky voice, which always seemed such a surprise coming from someone as petite as she was.

After starting her career on Australian soaps, a trip to the UK sixteen years earlier had been a gamble, but one that paid off. Olivia and Jeannie had urged her to go. Her agent in Australia had recommended an agent in London. She'd shown her a highlights reel. She also had a British passport, courtesy of her English grandfather.

Her timing was perfect. A gritty crime drama was in development. The producers were seeking an actress for the lead role. She auditioned three times before she got it. In the years since, her character had been through three husbands, had gone to jail twice, had embezzled, burgled, stolen, deceived. The season was finishing with a bang, literally. Her character's rival had arranged for a Molotov cocktail to be thrown through the window of Maxie's character's house.

The publicity department had kept under wraps whether she survived or not. That evening, when the episode aired, a nation of viewers would learn that she'd survived, angrier than ever. She was seriously injured in hospital, however. She'd need extensive plastic surgery and a long rehabilitation. The producers hoped that would cover the fact that when the TV series returned for its next season, her character would only be heard in voiceover, phoning from abroad, where she was recovering.

Maxie had loved her time on the show, but she'd known it was time for a change. Hazel coming into her life had given her all the impetus she needed. She was not only happier than she'd ever been in her personal life, she was ready to take a step back from her acting career, even temporarily. Explore other creative possibilities. The playwriting. Perhaps even a TV script too.

A week after their wedding, Hazel would be moving to New York to work on *The Railway Children*. Maxie would follow her as soon as she'd packed up their flat. The TV network hadn't been happy about her decision to leave, of course. Nor had her agent. The regular fee from her starring role benefited him too. Recording the voiceovers wouldn't pay as well as day after day on set. But she knew it was the right decision for her for now.

She sealed the envelope. She'd take it down to the post office later. It was a surprisingly good interview. They weren't always. She knew from her publicist that the newpaper had asked for a photo of Maxie and Hazel together to use in the feature, too. There had been no chance of that.

It was common knowledge that Maxie was gay. She'd never hidden it, either at work, with friends or in interviews. 'If I could come out to the head nun in my final year of school, I can handle the British media,' she'd told her agent when the subject first came up years earlier. She'd told her parents while she was at uni. She'd been lucky. They were liberal-minded, progressive Catholics, non-judgemental. Her two older brothers had taken it in their stride too.

Hazel had also been fortunate. She had brought Maxie home to meet her family two months after they started dating. They'd welcomed her warmly. Hazel's grandfather even asked for her autograph. Hazel had smiled at that. It was a running joke between them that Hazel had had no idea who Maxie was when they first met at a theatre fundraiser for a refugee charity. She rarely watched TV.

Maxie had thought she was joking that first time they talked backstage. There had been a break in rehearsals while a sound problem was being fixed. Hazel had taken the opportunity to tweak the lighting design and come down to the stage.

They'd fallen into conversation. Hazel hadn't realised Maxie was one of the stars. With that pixie cut she looked like a chorus member.

Hazel had asked her what other work she'd done, presumably imagining Maxie would list off other West End shows. Instead, she mentioned her Australian soap and her long-running starring role in the gritty English drama. Hazel apologised that she'd never seen either. She'd given a soft laugh – Maxie still loved the way Hazel laughed – and confessed that she didn't own a TV.

'You watch everything online?' Maxie asked.

'No,' Hazel said. 'I barely watch TV at all. I read.'

That started a conversation about favourite books. Fortunately Maxie read as well as watched TV. They went for a drink that night. To talk more about books, they said. The next night too, to talk about more than books. They spent the weekend together. They'd been together ever since.

From the start, Maxie had wanted to shout from the rooftops about Hazel. She still did. But that was the one sticking point between them. Hazel hated the spotlight. Ironic, considering what she did for a living. But she'd been insistent.

'You know I love you, Maxie,' Hazel said one night. 'But I never want to be seen publicly with you.'

'You're ashamed of me?'

'No, I'm mad about you. When you're yourself, when you're my Maxie. But I don't want to be part of your world when you're being Maxine Hill.'

She'd tried to change Hazel's mind over the years, of course. Invited her to gala award ceremonies. Weekends away for photo shoots in glossy magazines.

'No, thank you,' Hazel said each time. 'I'd rather eat my own arm.'

'But you're in show business too,' Maxie argued. 'You know how it works. Publicity equals viewers and ticket sales.'

'You do any publicity you like,' Hazel said. 'Run naked through Soho if you want. But leave me out of it.'

Hazel loved the theatre world, but only the backstage world. She'd started as an assistant stage manager in regional theatres, before discovering her interest lay in the magic and illusion that proper lighting design could create. She'd graduated from smaller to bigger theatres, her reputation for originality, dedication and calm humour growing. All leading to this wonderful job on Broadway.

Maxie was so proud of her. Hazel made her so happy. Made her feel so loved. So safe, secure, supported. Energised, encouraged, entertained. She loved talking to her, cooking together, sleeping with her, planning their lives together. The thought of being away from her for even a few months was what prompted their forthcoming marriage.

Maxie had done the proposing. Hazel immediately said yes. Maxie burst into tears, in happiness and relief. They'd opened the champagne Maxie had secretly hidden in the fridge, and toasted each other. Then Hazel had got to work, taking out her laptop and beginning to research venues. It was only six weeks until she was leaving for New York. Was there time before she left?

It was Maxie who jokingly suggested running away to Gretna Green. A colleague had done it the previous year. It had sounded like great fun. Simple, quick, no fuss. Like an old-fashioned elopement. She and Hazel had sat in front of the laptop sipping champagne, scrolling through the various Gretna Green wedding websites, getting more amused as they read about ceremonies held in an old blacksmith's cottage, the striking of an anvil marking the marriage. They wouldn't even need to tell anyone. The staff at the cottage could apparently step in as the two witnesses required.

They decided that night. Sent off an email to an agency there to organise it, under Hazel's name to keep it as private as possible. Maxie assured Hazel that of course she was happy for their wedding to be secret, that she was happy to have two strangers as witnesses. Even if secretly she'd love to throw an enormous party, inviting her family from Australia and all of Hazel's family from Wales.

Then Olivia had visited her in London. They'd gone to dinner. After too many cocktails, Maxie blurted out the whole story. Had she actually asked Olivia to join them at Gretna Green or had Olivia invited herself? Maxie couldn't remember. All she knew for sure was that by the end of the night, Olivia was coming to their wedding and had declared she was going to convince Eliza to come too.

She'd done it, of course. Olivia was a great convincer.

Miraculously, incredibly, Eliza was in the air right now, en route to Edinburgh. She'd have just a day or so to get over her jetlag before she and Olivia would drive down to Gretna Green to 'surprise' her.

Maxie already knew she'd burst into tears as soon as she saw Eliza. Since she'd turned fifty, three years earlier, she'd found herself crying easily and regularly. Perhaps it was just as well she was stepping back from her role as the tough crime gang leader. God knows how she would react the moment the celebrant declared her and Hazel married.

She really should start packing for Gretna Green, she knew. All she'd done so far was carefully put their two wedding dresses into protective covers. They were hanging on the back of their bedroom door. She also needed to pack for their honeymoon. A TV producer friend had loaned them his cottage in the Highlands for a week. It was in the wildest of locations, perfect for the hill-walking and relaxing they had planned. She also needed to pack up this flat.

They would miss living here. It was small but in such a wonderful location, in exclusive Mayfair, a street back from Park Lane, across from Hyde Park. It had been left to a theatrical trust fifty years earlier by a wealthy producer, who'd decreed that it always be rented cheaply for two-year periods to up-and-coming technicians. Hazel's turn had come eighteen months ago, after years on the waiting list. Maxie had joined her. A rising star in costume design was moving in the day after they moved out.

It had been a very happy home. Unfortunately, it was also a cluttered home. Her fault. She was a terrible hoarder. The plan was that once she'd spent a few days with Olivia and Eliza in Edinburgh – after the honeymoon and Hazel's departure, of course – she'd come back to London, spend two full days packing, then join her new wife in New York.

Perhaps she should do a bit of sorting now. A bit of looking-for-something too. The postcards. Olivia had rung her again that morning to remind her.

'Maxie, please stop putting it off. It's important. You need to bring them to Scotland with you.'

'I know. I will, I promise. I think I know exactly where they are.' She hadn't even started looking yet.

She tried to put off her search again. She started watching the latest hit series on Netflix, but the lead actor's bad performance annoyed her and she turned it off. She opened her laptop, glanced over her most recent writing project, then closed it again. She made herself a herbal tea. Usually that calmed her down. Not this time. She knew what she should be doing.

She went into their tiny spare room. Hazel called it The Valley of Lost and Found. It was apt. It was such a mess, a gathering place for their joint belongings when they first moved in together, and now two cupboards of combined chaos they'd never got around to sorting.

What she was looking for was at the very back of a cupboard. A box of material for the scrapbook she'd started putting together fifteen years ago, depicting her, Olivia and Jeannie's friendship.

Her plan had been to present it to Eliza on her eighteenth birthday. A surprise, for her and Jeannie. A surprise that never happened for the most terrible of reasons. She'd kept telling herself that one day she'd finish it and give it to Eliza. She never had. Instead, she'd kept moving it from house to house.

She began to leaf through the box of material now. She'd been arranging the contents chronologically, starting with photos from their first school days, aged thirteen. Their uniform truly was the ugliest garment known to woman or nun. She'd also included photos they'd taken in kiosks as teenagers, crammed into the booth, smiling faces pressed together. A photo taken at their formal school dance, when they'd deliberately worn the same colour and style of dress, the rich red standing out against the prim, pastel outfits of their classmates. Jeannie in the middle, Olivia on the left, Maxie on the right. They looked so young. Who could ever have known what lay ahead for the three of them?

She forced herself to put the photos to one side. She was here to find the postcards. Jeannie had sent dozens during her European backpacking days. Maxie had planned to include a selection in the scrapbook. She'd known she'd have to read them all first. Censor them, more accurately.

There they were, the large bundle still held together by an old shoelace. All addressed to Madam Olivia and Madam Maxine, c/o Maxie's fortunately unshockable parents.

Jeannie had always written on the postcards in vertical fashion, never landscape. She insisted she could fit more in that way. She'd been prolific, sending two or three a week. Even before the ink faded, they'd been hard to decipher. Jeannie's handwriting had got tinier the more she had to say.

Maxie picked one out of the bundle. The photo showed an exhibit at the British Museum, an Egyptian cat. On the back was a dramatic account of a hitchhiking drama Jeannie had in France, when she'd been picked up by an elderly man she'd quickly realised had an ulterior motive. When he slowed the car, she'd leapt out while it was moving. *A narrow escape!* she'd written. *Those gymnastic lessons finally paid off! I executed a perfect tumble and roll!*

Another went into detail about an American girl she'd met on her travels, an accomplished shoplifter. *No Catholic guilt for her!* The American specialised in stealing bottles of wine. *I'm writing this with a glass of fine Burgundy in my hand. Only the best for your travelling friend!*

There were at least sixty more, from London, Paris, Rome, Barcelona, Dublin. Some featured just a few scrawled lines. *Have been offered work as a chambermaid in Paris. Ooh la la!* Several from Ireland. *Learning how to pour the perfect pint of Guinness, to be sure! In an Irish pub in Ireland that's in sight of an ACTUAL IRISH CASTLE!!!!* One from Rome, describing a wonderful meal she'd had, with a P.S. that she'd run away without paying. *The prices were a rip-off, anyway!!* And on most of them, mentions of the different men she'd met, implying that she'd done more than meet them. *I'm working my way through the United Nations!!* she'd written on one.

As Maxie leafed through them, her heart felt heavy. It was as if Jeannie was suddenly in the room with her. All that vitality, all those adventures, her spirit leaping off the postcards. All of it now gone.

Thirteen years had passed, yet Maxie still could barely believe Jeannie was no longer with them. Wild, unpredictable Jeannie. Troubled, lost Jeannie. Their oldest friend. Their most difficult friend.

'We have to tell Eliza everything we know,' Olivia had once insisted. 'She needs to hear the truth.'

But did she? What good would it do now?

Maxie couldn't look at any more of these tonight. They were making her too sad. Bringing back too many bad memories. As she pushed the box and the postcards to the back of the cupboard again, she found herself in tears.

# CHAPTER ELEVEN

Olivia was tracking Eliza's flight. In less than two hours her goddaughter would arrive at Edinburgh Airport. Which was why she was only half paying attention to this meeting with Lawrence.

Their general manager had updated her on their latest, excellent, occupancy rates. Outlined a new staffing overtime arrangement. Shown her quotes for the maintenance work needed for the refurbishment of two rooms after a recent water leak. It was all a courtesy to her. She knew he had it under control. He was always so reliable. Olivia had been concerned when the three-year contract he'd negotiated with Edgar came to an end four months earlier, but Deirdre had informed her that Lawrence had agreed to a month-by-month extension.

She had worked side by side with Lawrence all that time, but she still couldn't say she knew him well. She'd seen his CV, of course. He was in his late thirties. He'd been educated in a small but prestigious boarding school north of London. Done a business degree at the London School of Economics, and then moved into hotel management. He'd come to them from a luxury hotel in New York, after stints at a five-star boutique hotel in Paris, a discreet and expensive London hotel and two others in mainland Europe. Madrid and Geneva, if Olivia remembered rightly. Or perhaps it was Vienna. He spoke French, German and some Italian, she knew. He had Spanish blood in his family tree, she'd learned. Only in passing. Lawrence rarely spoke about himself. Was it his grandmother or grandfather? He'd inherited his olive complexion from one of them, at least.

She did know one detail of his life that no one else at the Montgomery knew. Lawrence had asked Edgar to keep it private. He'd come to Edinburgh from New York after suffering a great loss. Four years earlier, his wife of two years had been diagnosed with heart disease, dying only eight months later. Lawrence and Edgar had met previously at an industry event and exchanged contact details. When Lawrence contacted him out of the blue, asking if there were vacancies at the Montgomery, Edgar had been sympathetic to Lawrence's need to be far from New York. He was Edgar's last appointment. One of his best, Olivia knew.

Lawrence had been offered a flat in the hotel, but he'd chosen to live 'off campus'. He still did. The staff liked him, Olivia knew, but he kept his distance. Edgar had been the same. In many ways, Edgar had chosen a manager in his own style. Professional but private.

She checked her watch. Twenty minutes before she'd need to leave for the airport. 'I'll look through the other figures later, Lawrence. I don't want to be late for Eliza. Any further issues for now?'

'Two more. Alex again. And Celine.'

'Which is worse?'

'I'd say equal footing.'

'Let's go alphabetical. Alex?'

In their last weekly meeting, the one Lawrence had deemed 'urgent', they'd spoken candidly about the situation with Alex. They'd adopted a 'wait and see' position, on Lawrence's advice. He felt it could become too awkward otherwise. It seemed the waiting was over.

'It's happened again,' Lawrence said. 'Five crates last night. All caught on CCTV.'

'That bloody idiot.' Olivia said it before she could stop herself. But she meant it. What a bloody idiot indeed. Alex had already had everything handed to him on a plate. A good education in a fine, if tough, boarding school. Support throughout his university years. A hotel management job waiting for him, if he was the successful son. Backing for his possibly risky idea for an upmarket hostel, which had, frankly, confounded all their expectations. Yet that still wasn't enough for Alex.

He was stealing from the Montgomery. Crates of wine. Gin. Champagne.

Lawrence had brought her after-hours to the hotel's small security office. He'd shown her the footage. It was definitely Alex.

The time stamp was two a.m. Six cases, from the storeroom, through the hallway across to the mews hostel. Not once. On three separate dates.

It wasn't the first time. Four months earlier, Olivia had been approached by the bar manager. Several bottles of their most expensive whisky had gone missing. It was literally top shelf, and locked away too, in a glass cabinet made especially to display their range.

'It wasn't broken into,' her manager said. 'There are only two keys. I have one. Alex has the other.'

She'd called him into her office. Expected him to deny it. Instead he sat back and smiled. 'My family hotel. My family whisky. Surely I don't have to ask permission to take what is already mine, Olivia?'

'It's a family business, Alex. It's not a family pantry. And you're not taking boxes of cornflakes. Each bottle you took was worth nearly two hundred pounds.'

'I have good taste, don't I? Wouldn't my father be proud of me?'

'You are putting me, and the bar manager, in a difficult position. We'll be keeping an eye on stock levels from now on. Especially of those rare whiskies.'

'I'm sure the ignorant tourists who come here wouldn't know a fine drop from a supermarket brand, Olivia, as you well know. Why waste our good stuff on them?'

'What are you doing with it?'

'I have it for breakfast. Poured over the cornflakes I also steal.

Whoops. Loose lips sink ships. I shouldn't have mentioned them, should I?'

She'd raised it with Deirdre. In her usual cool, official way, Deirdre had outlined their options. Threaten him with prosecution. Report him to the police. Neither was possible, as Alex well knew. A court case? One of the Montgomery heirs prosecuted? Edgar would never know about it, but Olivia still couldn't let it happen. Deirdre had advised caution, a slow gathering of further evidence, but also to let Alex know they knew what he was doing.

For a while it seemed to have worked. Or perhaps he'd been so busy with the hostel that it hadn't occurred to him to steal anything. Until lately.

'How much?' she asked Lawrence now.

Lawrence listed it, reading from a printout. More than £5000 worth. 'It will be hard to prove what he's doing with it. My guess is he's selling it on, either to hostel guests, or others in Edinburgh.'

'He knows about the cameras. What do you think he's doing? Waiting for us to confront him?'

Lawrence stayed silent. Diplomatic as ever. But that would match Alex's personality – to brazen it out until he was cornered, and then fight back against it if he was. Was he doing this for sport?

'I'll try to talk about it with him. And Rory? Please don't tell me he's selling the hotel linen on eBay?'

Lawrence smiled. 'If he is, he's better at covering his tracks. No, Rory is doing well. His time-keeping is still a problem, but our guests love him. He's asked for more days off than usual recently, to go to craft fairs for his puzzle business. I've agreed each time. Did you want me to run that by you first?'

'No, thank you.' She didn't want to micromanage Lawrence.

'The other issue is Celine. I'm sorry, Olivia, but my PA can't spare any more time with her.'

'Are you being polite again, Lawrence?'

'I can tell you exactly what she said?'

'Please do.'

She was taken by surprise when he mimicked his assistant Hilary's Scottish accent perfectly. '"That hag up there has pushed my buttons too many times. Either you stop sending me up to her, Lawrence, or I hand in my resignation now."'

Olivia sighed. 'Please give Hilary my apologies. She was always a stopgap. I did try a couple of other temp agencies but they were mysteriously unable to send anyone.' It seemed her last temp, Susan, had been true to her word. She stood up, signalling the meeting was at an end. 'I'll try to think of a solution about Celine. One that doesn't involve rat poison. For now, I'm off to the airport.'

He stood too. 'The Iris suite is ready. Fresh flowers, fruit basket. You said no to the champagne?'

'Thanks, Lawrence. Eliza's a nervous flyer, so I'm not sure what state she'll be in when I collect her. I'll introduce you as soon as I can.'

'I look forward to meeting her,' he said.

*

Thirty minutes later, Olivia was at the airport. Eliza's flight was now minutes from landing. She could feel emails arriving via her phone, but she ignored them. This was Eliza Time. Even so, thoughts about Alex, Rory and Celine kept darting into her mind. Small annoying thoughts, like mosquitos.

Both boys – men – were now in their early thirties but still keeping her awake at night worrying. If it wasn't Alex's thieving or arrogance, it was Rory's dreaminess and lack of direction. As for Celine – or Bloody Celine, as Maxie dubbed her, when Olivia rang her, needing to unload . . .

'Just kick her out,' Maxie said. 'Tell her you need the room for your beloved Australian goddaughter.'

'I can't. At least this way she's only keeping the family awake. It would take a week to shift her anyway. You should see the state of her suite. The cleaning staff have complained to Lawrence that there's so much paper everywhere they can't clean properly. She still abuses them.'

As she'd said to Maxie, if this was simply business, she would deal with it all quickly, efficiently. If any other staff member had been caught on CCTV stealing valuable hotel property, she'd have reported them to the police. If Celine was any other guest, they'd have politely asked her to leave. If she refused, they'd have firmly asked her. Olivia was having to make so many allowances because they were both family. Even though, as an insistent inner voice kept reminding her, they weren't even *her* family.

Back came that memory of a teenage Alex shouting at her, during her first days in Scotland. *'You're not my mother.*

113

*You'll never be my mother. So don't you ever even think about talking to me as if you are my mother.'*

She had never forgotten it. As she had also never forgotten Rory quietly coming over to her later that same night, after Edgar had sent Alex to his room. She had been sitting on her own in the family's living quarters, blinking back tears, wondering if she was going to be any good at this stepmother business. She'd looked up to see Rory, aged eleven, standing in front of her, his forehead furrowed.

'Please don't cry, Olivia,' he'd said. 'You're not my mother either but I still think we're going to get on very well indeed.'

Such a funny formal speech, possibly copied from a film he'd seen, but it made her heart swell. It felt the most natural thing in the world to open her arms to him. He'd stepped forward and she'd given him a hug. She'd never told Edgar, but she'd always loved Rory that bit more from that moment on.

She glanced up at the screens. Eliza's flight had just landed. She made her way over to the arrivals area, passing a bank of TVs as she walked. They were tuned to a news channel, reporting on record prices paid for a contemporary painting at a New York art auction. It was an extremely ugly painting. 'What a waste of money,' Edgar would have said. 'Where's the beauty in it? Who would possibly want that hanging in their house or gallery?'

It gave her such comfort that she could still imagine conversations with Edgar. He'd always been old-school in his artistic taste. Just as well, or he'd never have had to hire the services of one of Australia's top young experts in modern art during his Sydney buying trip. In their years together, they'd enjoyed many spirited arguments. Many passionate sessions of making up afterwards, too.

Oh, she missed him so much. Not only his wit, his company, his wisdom, his kindness. She missed the spark between them, how playful he was in private, compared to his chilly public persona. The way he'd hold her tightly after they made love. The surprises he'd give her: a piece of antique jewellery, a bouquet of spring flowers. So thoughtful and loving. And now so far away from her, his body alive, but his mind long succumbed to confusion and bewilderment.

Passengers from Eliza's flight started to appear. Olivia took a deep breath, making herself focus on the present, not mourn for the past. Yes, life could be so sad. But it could also be beautiful. Like now. Her darling Eliza was about to arrive. At last.

# CHAPTER TWELVE

They spotted one another immediately.

'You made it, you made it, you're here,' Olivia said, hugging her close.

Eliza hugged her back. 'I'm sorry it took me so long.'

'Was the flight all right?' 'I survived the flight!'

They laughed at the clashing sentences.

'I'm so happy to see you,' Olivia said as they started walking to the exit. 'Can you stay for a year?'

'I might need to. I never want to get back on a plane again.'

'Our evil plan worked. We hoped this would put you off flying home.'

'We?'

Olivia cursed herself. 'Me. But I know Maxie will want you to stay forever too.'

They'd just reached the doors when Eliza stopped and called a name. 'Sullivan!'

A boy, eleven or so, turned. He was with a young woman in a business suit. Eliza walked over, crouched down, laughed at something he said and then came back.

'You made a friend on the flight?' Olivia asked.

'A lifesaver, to be honest.'

'I can't wait to hear all about him,' she said. 'Tonight, over dinner.'

As they drove into the city, Olivia watched with pleasure as Eliza marvelled at everything. The silver light in the sky. The terraced buildings. The glimpses of the Castle. The cobblestones, the spring growth on the trees in the city parks, the hills in the distance.

As they reached the Montgomery, the clouds cleared. The stone of the hotel momentarily glowed. The ivy covering the middle building was a light spring green. The glass of the windows sparkled.

'It's beautiful, Olivia,' Eliza said. 'I'd forgotten just how beautiful.'

Olivia took her in through the staff entrance. Alex was on the front desk today, and she didn't want Eliza meeting him yet. She knew some of what had happened between him and Eliza all those years ago. It hadn't surprised her. Alex had always been too aware of his charms. It was a shame Rory was away at that craft fair today. He'd at least remembered Eliza was arriving, asking Olivia to apologise for his absence and to offer his services as a tour guide.

'You know I'm hoping that Eliza will fall in love with one of your stepsons and live with you forever,' Maxie had said the last time they spoke.

'I'm not sure Rory would make a good husband, even if Milly wasn't on the scene. He'd wander off and forget he was married. And Alex would probably cheat on her before the honeymoon was over.'

The Iris suite was on the third floor of the first terrace. It was Olivia's favourite in the entire hotel. Where she and Edgar had spent their wedding night, in fact. Not that she'd let Eliza in on that piece of the Montgomery's history. She opened the door with the heavy key – no modern key cards yet – and stood back as Eliza walked into the centre of the room.

She was wide-eyed. 'Are you serious? This is for me? Shouldn't it be kept for your VIP guests?'

'You are our VIP guest. I actually had a suite in mind for you in our private wing, with an even better garden view. But it's still unfortunately occupied by a certain Celine.'

'Your guest from hell? When do I get to meet her?'

'As soon as your jetlag passes. My advice is to make it last.'

Eliza moved from the four-poster bed to the antique dresser, taking in the mahogany wardrobe, the floor-to-ceiling window framed by thick curtains of blue fabric. Everything was in shades of blue and purple, subtly evoking an iris. The artwork – three framed paintings – featured the flower in some way, in a bouquet, in a vase in a portrait of a young woman, and then in a modern sketch.

She turned back, her cheeks bright red. 'It's the best room I've ever seen. Thank you, Olivia. I'm so glad I'm here.'

Olivia smiled. 'So am I, darling.'

*

Fifteen minutes later, Eliza was under a hot shower. Olivia had left her to unpack, arranging to meet her in the bar whenever she was ready. She breathed in the citrus-scented bodywash, rinsing the last of the long flight away. She'd made it. She was here, with Olivia, in Edinburgh.

As she stepped out into the beautiful bedroom again, it hit her. Out of the blue, as always. The strongest of urges to talk to her mother.

When would it ever stop, that missing feeling, that longing? Not just to tell her mother where she was, what she was doing, but to ask her all the questions she hadn't had time to ask, too.

What had her mum done on her first day in Europe, on her big backpacking adventure? Where had she stayed? A cheap hotel, a hostel, a B&B? Nowhere as fancy as the Montgomery, Eliza felt sure of that. Money would have been tight. What did she think when she first saw those low grey skies, the terrace houses, the sheer size of the cities. What did she eat and wear? Where did she socialise? What did she do every day? Was she ever nervous? Worried?

'She was fearless,' Maxie always said. 'If we were ever in trouble, it was because of her.'

It came over Eliza again, a wave of something that felt like homesickness. She took herself through the familiar steps, the ones she'd forced herself to learn over the years. Slow deep breaths. Don't dwell on sad times. Focus on a happy thought.

Remember one of the good stories. Choose from her playlist of happy memories.

It worked. Slowly but surely, the sad feeling ebbed away.

As she was drying her hair with a thick white towel, her phone beeped. Rose. She'd sent several messages since she'd waved her off at the departure gates, all checking she was okay. There'd been a message when Eliza landed in Dubai: *One down, one to go!* Another on her arrival in Edinburgh: *YOU DID IT!! I AM SO PROUD! xxx.*

She read the new one. *Is everything okay? Was Olivia there to meet you? Xx*

She quickly replied that everything was great. She sent several photos of her room.

*How will you ever leave?? Any sign of Alex the Cad yet?*

*Not yet.*

*Please send constant details. So proud of you. Xxxx*

Eliza sent back her love and a row of kisses too. Her phone beeped again. A Scrabble notification from Navillus, saying it was her turn to play. She hadn't expected to hear from him so quickly. She chose her letters and pressed send. Moments later, it pinged again with a message.

*Hello Fearless Flyer! I hope you're settling in well? All good with me and the Scottish wing of my family. I hope you'll keep in touch. Navillus* ☺

She typed back. *All good here too, Navillus. Hope your jetlag isn't too bad. FF*

*I'm eating a banana. The potassium helps reset my internal body clock. Your turn to play a word!*

After playing her letters, she fixed her hair into a long plait again. She hadn't worn it in a bun since she'd left Gillian's office. As she got dressed, the jetlag made her movements clumsy. The idea of running into Alex again soon had also become real.

Rose had coaxed the entire story out of her again before she left. 'Please. It will be therapeutic for you.'

'It won't be. It will only be mortifying,' she said, before giving in.

She'd met Alex on her first day in Edinburgh. She was sixteen. He was nineteen. It was like being struck by hormonal lightning, she told Rose.

She'd had crushes before, kisses at school dances too, but nothing serious. She'd been shy about such things. Her mother had sat her down some weeks earlier and asked if she wanted to go on the Pill. Eliza was so embarrassed she'd pulled her jumper over her head. Jeannie laughed and hugged her. 'Not yet, then. But let me know when and if you do.'

Eliza peeked over the jumper. 'Aren't you supposed to be warning me against premarital sex?'

'I'm being responsible. I also don't want you to miss out on any fun. Sex can be a glorious thing. Don't be frightened of it. Choose your partners wisely and well. Always use contraception. Mind you, I'd love you to have an unplanned pregnancy. I'd make a wonderfully groovy granny, don't you think?'

'Mum!'

'I'm serious. You mightn't realise it yet, but you're officially a seething storm of hormones. A sudden urge to lose your virginity might leap out unexpectedly. Let me know if you start to feel any lustful stirrings and I'll whisk you off to get the Pill quicker than you can say, "Wear a condom, please, sir."'

'Stop it!'

Her mother just laughed, of course. She loved shocking Eliza.

Alex had been lying stretched out on the sofa in the Montgomery's family apartment. When Olivia introduced her, he leapt up, tall, graceful, his hand held out. 'So she is real, this mysterious goddaughter! I'm Alexander. And I'm so pleased to meet you.'

She'd never seen anyone as good-looking. Never heard such a voice, his Scottish accent smoothed to a musical polish courtesy of his boarding school education. His eyes were blue, sparkling.

Rory joined them soon after. Aged seventeen, he was the opposite to his brother in every way. Shy. Awkward. A bit goofy, even. It was as if Alex had received the quality ingredients and Rory was left with the offcuts.

'Don't get too interested, Eliza,' Olivia warned her later. 'Yes, Alex is charming, and popular too. Especially with the girls. It's because he's had lots of practice.'

His attention felt so genuine, though. She felt her heart beat faster whenever he appeared. He even joined her and Olivia one afternoon for a trip to the art gallery. She barely noticed the paintings.

Her feelings towards him became more fervent as her departure approached. She wanted to kiss him. Do more than kiss him. She kept recalling her mother's advice. She was definitely ready. She wanted to make her first time something special, and yes, also be prepared. But how to make it happen?

She tried to get time alone with him, but it was impossible in a busy hotel. She wrote to him instead. She borrowed phrases she remembered from romantic fiction, about feeling dizzy and full of longing for him. She told him she was leaving soon, but it would make her so happy if he'd spend an afternoon or even longer with her? She fantasised constantly about it.

She knew he was having friends over. She slipped up to his room while they were downstairs and left the letter on his pillow, thrilled to be in his private space. She was relieved that she and Olivia were going to a play that night. She needed the distraction while she waited for his reply.

She was going downstairs to meet Olivia when an urge like a drug craving made her want to see him. He and his friends were in the back bar. She could hear laughter. Alex's voice. She stood at the door, summoning the courage to say hello, meet his friends. She'd already pictured them all out together, Alex's arm proudly and possessively around her. Then she stopped, and listened.

He was reading her letter out to his brother and his friends, in an exaggerated coarse Australian accent, overlaying it with swoons and gasps. They were all roaring with laughter, wolf-whistling too.

The door she was hiding behind squeaked. They all turned to see her standing there, bright red with shame. She was frozen for a moment, before she ran back up the stairs.

It wasn't Alex who followed her. It was Rory. She started talking as soon as he caught up with her.

'Don't feel sorry for me. Please, don't talk to me.'

'Eliza, I'm sorry. He didn't mean any harm. It was just —'

She didn't wait to hear the rest. Nor did she go to the theatre that night. When Olivia came looking for her, she pretended she was getting the flu. She hid in her room for the next two days, curled up, feigning symptoms. She was never so glad to get to the airport at the end of a godmother holiday.

She eventually told her mother. Jeannie had guessed something had happened and hounded her until she confessed. Afterwards, she insisted Eliza do a sketch of 'This Alex'. The two of them took it outside and set it on fire, under the stars. She still remembered her mother's gleeful face as she lit the match. 'We've cursed him now, darling. Two Australian witches. He'll never be happy in his life.'

Afterwards, back inside, they'd talked more. Eliza had felt so loved.

Her mother had been as straight-talking as ever. 'Thank God you didn't have sex with him. What a waste that would have been. He didn't deserve someone as special as you.'

She'd eventually felt glad too. When she finally did have sex for the first time, four months later, it had been with a kind, gentle boy from her high school. They'd been dating for six weeks.

Jeannie guessed immediately, somehow, when Eliza came home from a sleepover at his house.

'Did you use protection?'

'*Mum!*' she'd said. Yes, she admitted.

'And did you enjoy it?'

'*Mum!*' Yes, she admitted.

'My little girl is a woman,' Jeannie said.

'*Mum!*'

'Sorry. My tall beautiful girl is a woman.'

You were so lucky, Rose had said, when they swapped stories early in their friendship. She'd come from a large Catholic family. Sex had been taboo. Her brothers had all been told to 'keep it in their pockets' and there had been the assumption that the girls simply weren't interested in sex.

In her hotel room, Eliza made a decision. She wouldn't wait for Olivia to introduce them again. She'd go and find Alex now. Get it over and done with. She imagined what her mother would say. She could almost hear her voice.

*That's my girl.*

Two floors down, at the desk in her office, Olivia was on the phone to Maxie.

'She's as gorgeous as ever. A bit frazzled from the flight, and she still seems to be dressed in Gillian's cast-offs, but she's here and that's all that counts.'

'Has she asked you any questions about Jeannie yet? About her father? Any of it?'

'Maxie, she's hardly off the plane. She also wants to wait until it's the three of us, remember?'

'I'm feeling sick every time I think about it.'

'Can you please stop being so dramatic?'

'You know I can't. I always ring her on a Monday, around now. Will she be suspicious if I don't?'

'Maybe. Ring her now, before we go to dinner. And remember —'

'Do some acting? Seriously, Liv, what do you think I've been doing for the past twenty years?'

'Sorry. Break a leg.'

'Now you're being mean.'

Eliza was leaving her room when her mobile rang. *Maxie calling.* She answered, remembering in time that Maxie thought she was still in Melbourne.

'Good morning!' she said, looking through her bedroom window at the darkening Edinburgh sky. 'I could set my watch by you, couldn't I?'

'I've always been your favourite godmother, haven't I? Olivia is more the bossy but boring type. I'm the exciting yet still reliable one.'

'Exactly,' she said, sitting down on the bed. 'How are you, how is Hazel, how is work?'

Maxie told her a story or two from the set, spoke about a good film she and Hazel had seen, passed on some salacious gossip about an American actor who was appearing in a West End show a friend of Hazel's was working on. 'And how are you, darling? All good at work? How is the demure Gillian?'

'Same as usual,' Eliza said.

'And the Melbourne weather?'

'As contrary as ever,' she said.

After a few more minutes, they ended their conversation as they always did.

'Love you,' Eliza said.

'Love you even more,' Maxie answered.

Moments later, Olivia knocked on the door. Eliza told her about the call from Maxie as they began walking down the corridor. The walls were lined with artwork. Olivia stopped in front of a small, gold-framed painting.

'This is by an Australian artist. It was the first painting Edgar bought via my gallery.'

Eliza gazed at it. The colours were muted, yet still so layered and rich. A landscape, Australian gum trees and a dirt road, the light and shadow playing against each other.

'Can I go and see Edgar with you one day, Olivia?' she asked as they continued walking.

'Thank you for asking, Eliza, but no, it's best you don't. It's too confusing for him to meet anyone new. Some days I'm not even sure if he remembers me, or Alex and Rory.'

'I'm so sorry.'

Olivia gave her hand a quick squeeze. 'I know you are. Thank you.'

They reached the foyer. Olivia watched Eliza take it in. It was lit by standard lamps and a chandelier. Well-groomed staff were moving from one area to another. Guests filled the bar and dining area. Behind the front desk, a man in his thirties with a big smile and glossy dark hair was giving a well-dressed elderly woman his full attention. It was Alex.

'Head up,' Olivia whispered. 'Shoulders back. Smile. And get it over with.'

Eliza spun around. 'You know? Who? How?'

'Rory, at the time. And don't worry, I told Alex off.'

'That makes it worse.'

'No. Hopefully it stopped him from being so cruel to someone else.'

The elderly guest moved to the lift. Olivia put a reassuring arm around Eliza as they stepped forward.

'Alex, not that you need an introduction, but let me reintroduce you. My goddaughter, Eliza. Eliza, you remember Alex, my stepson?'

'Of course.' She held out her hand, feeling as though she was channelling Audrey Hepburn in *My Fair Lady*, pretending to be polished. 'It's good to see you again.'

'Is it?' Alex said. 'I bet you're thinking, I wish he'd moved away. I wish I didn't have to see him again, the mean self-obsessed spoilt brat, who humiliated me so badly the last time I was here.'

Eliza was too jetlagged to pretend otherwise. 'Yes, I am.'

Alex stepped out from behind the desk. 'That was juvenile of me. I was trying to show off to my friends. I'm sorry. It was a very sweet letter. If you write to me again, I promise I'll take it much more seriously.'

Eliza glanced at Olivia. She was watching with one eyebrow raised.

Alex noticed. 'Olivia, do you doubt my sincerity?'

'Never, Alex.'

He grinned, as charmingly confident as he'd been all those years ago. 'Shall we start afresh, Eliza? We're practically cousins, after all. No, let's forget being related and start afresh as friends, yes?'

Disarmed, she took his outstretched hand as he gave a bow.

'Thank you,' he said. 'I can start sleeping at night again. Olivia gave me such a telling off. I've been riddled with guilt for the last, what is it, ten years?'

'Nearly fourteen,' Eliza said.

'That long? What kept you?'

A guest came up to the desk.

'Excuse me,' Alex said, 'but duty calls. So good to have you here, Eliza. Settle in, and then we'll plan some outings together. If you can bear to be in my company unchaperoned?'

Olivia was openly rolling her eyes. 'Thank you, Alex.' She waited until they'd walked away before she spoke. 'He should come with a health warning.'

'He was so nice.'

'Like a charming crocodile, yes. Don't fall for it again. He is Edgar's son, and I'll always love him for that, but proceed with caution.'

After their pre-dinner drink in the small bar, they were escorted by a smiling waitress to the opulent dining room, with its low lights, linen tablecloths and gleaming silverware. Midway through her main course of grilled trout and crisp vegetables, Eliza's eyelids began to grow heavy.

'If you can last one more hour, I'll let you go,' Olivia said. 'The closer you get to local time —'

'Excuse me, Olivia.'

A serious-faced man with grey-flecked dark hair was standing by their table.

'Lawrence,' Olivia said. 'Let me introduce my goddaughter, Eliza Miller. Eliza, this is our general manager, Lawrence Greene.'

They exchanged greetings, then Lawrence turned to Olivia. 'I'm sorry to interrupt but —'

'Celine?'

He nodded.

Olivia stood up. 'Excuse me, Eliza. I'll be right back.'

Eliza watched as her godmother and Lawrence walked out of the dining room. Through her jetlag, she suddenly recalled Olivia mentioning a sadness in his past. After a moment, it came to her. His wife had died tragically young some years earlier, not long before he'd come to the Montgomery. It must have been so hard for him. Edgar had thought highly of him, Olivia had told her. Eliza knew Olivia did too.

Five minutes passed, then ten. Eliza was content. She often dined alone. She was also so cushioned by tiredness that everything had a soft glow. It hardly seemed possible she was in Scotland. That she'd managed the flight. That she no longer lived in a flat overlooking Melbourne. That she no longer had a job. Gillian's words jabbed her memory again. *What have you done with your life so far?*

'Are you deep in philosophical thought or drowning in jetlag and trying to stay awake?'

It was Alex. He took the seat Olivia had vacated fifteen minutes earlier.

'Olivia phoned me at the front desk,' he said. 'She's asked me to apologise profusely. She's unexpectedly detained upstairs. She said she'll understand if you go to your room but she hopes to be back soon.'

Eliza thanked him and glanced at her watch. Still not nine p.m. 'I'm happy to wait.'

'Good,' he said. 'I'm on a break. What can I get you? Brandy? One of our fine whiskies?'

She shook her head. 'Chamomile tea, please.'

'So sensible, but yes, of course. We have more than thirty tea varieties. Handpicked by elves in the mist, I believe.' As a waitress appeared, he ordered brandy for himself, tea for her.

He sat back and smiled. 'Olivia and our general manager are up there trying to tame my wild grandmother, you know. Good luck with that, I said to Olivia. Celine's quite something when she gets going. She's writing her biography at the moment.

I asked her if Rory and I will be in it. Yes, if we ever do anything interesting, she said. You have to laugh. It's either that or want to kill her.'

The waitress reappeared, putting the tea in front of Eliza, the brandy in front of Alex.

'No drinking in work hours, please, Alex,' Olivia said. They hadn't noticed her return.

'Officially speaking, Olivia, I'm not at work,' he said. 'I'm on my break.'

'But you'll be back behind the front desk in ten minutes. Without alcohol on your breath. Please.'

It was a subtle stand-off. Olivia won.

Alex stood up. 'Apologies that our reunion was so brief, Eliza, but we'll see each other again. Only on my days off, Olivia, promise.'

After he'd left, Eliza looked more closely at her godmother. Something was different.

'Let me guess, you're wondering if it's jetlag?' Olivia said. 'No, I am wearing different clothes. I'll explain why shortly. Do you really want that tea or will I finally let you go to your bed?'

She escorted Eliza to her room. 'I won't stay long. Just to apologise for the interruption. Our special guest threw what I can only call the mother of all tantrums. She's very unhappy with our secretarial services. Or lack thereof. She showed it by throwing a cup of tea at me. Fortunately cold tea.'

'Olivia!'

'It could have been worse. She nearly hit Lawrence with the actual cup.'

'Can't you ask her to leave?'

'I wish I could. Unfortunately Edgar was so honourable, he put it in writing that she always has a place here with us. She threw that at me today, too. Literally. A balled-up piece of paper. Not the original, of course. A certified copy. She's had it all confirmed by lawyers.'

'I don't know now if I'm dying to meet her or if I never want to.'

'Go with option two,' Olivia said as she gave Eliza's plait a gentle tug. 'Forget her. I want you to wash your face, clean your teeth and get into bed. There's a room-service menu for breakfast beside your bed. If I see you before eleven, I'm sending you straight back to Melbourne. Yes, on a plane.'

Eliza did as she was told, luxuriating in the touch of the soft cotton sheets, the weight of the down quilt, the feeling of being completely and utterly looked after. She was fast asleep in minutes.

# CHAPTER THIRTEEN

It was after ten by the time Eliza woke. Her first thought was disturbing. She had nothing to do.

It had been years since she could say that. Even at uni, her life had been ruled by lengthy to-do lists. Preparing for this trip to Edinburgh had fulfilled that need too. Packing. Finishing up with Gillian. There had been no long lunch or farewell ceremony. On her last day, at four p.m., Gillian declared she had an urgent appointment with her obstetrician. Eliza had literally turned out the lights.

She would need another job soon, but her redundancy and savings would cover the next few months. She reached for her phone. The diary had always been crammed. Now there was only one entry. Her return flight in just under three weeks.

Olivia rang just as she'd finished a delicious room-service breakfast.

'Please tell me you're not out in the city applying for jobs?' her godmother said.

'I'm down in the kitchen. They've taken me on as a dishwasher.'

'Don't even joke about it.'

Olivia told her she had one more appointment and then had taken the afternoon off. They agreed to meet in the foyer at midday.

Eliza used the time to explore the Montgomery again. She walked down each hallway and into every public room, noticing the antique furniture, patterned wallpaper and sumptuous drapes. She admired the artwork, particularly. She appreciated it more now than she had as a teenager. The collection was so varied, delicate watercolours alongside darker oil paintings, portraits alongside landscapes. The artists were from all over the world, Scotland, Italy, France, Australia. Underneath each painting was a brief description of the artist, and then his or her technique and intent. All written by Olivia. Her godmother was so knowledgeable about art.

Eliza was making her way down the wide stairs to the foyer, stopping every few steps to look at the paintings hanging there too, when she heard her name being called. It was a man in his early thirties, wearing a suit. He had pale skin and strawberry-blond hair. He was smiling.

'Eliza? You probably don't remember me. I'm Rory. Welcome back to our humble abode.'

She instantly warmed to him as he asked about her flight, her jetlag. There was none of Alex's practised charm. He still had the sweet shyness she remembered.

'You're taking the self-guided art tour? Any favourites yet?'

All of them, she said truthfully. He was so lucky to have grown up surrounded by such special art.

'I know. Alas, none of it rubbed off. Neither Alex nor I have our father or Olivia's knack for spotting good art. It must be true, talent skips a generation.'

At dinner, Olivia had told her about his jigsaw puzzles. She mentioned them. He smiled shyly again.

'It's not working for the Tate, but I love it. I spend half my time dressed like this' – he gestured at his suit – 'the rest covered in paint and sawdust. I can show you my workshop one day if you like?'

She'd love to see it, she told him.

They walked downstairs into the sitting room. The thick curtains were pulled back. An ornate church was visible in the distance. Rory was sharing its history when he was interrupted.

'Don't believe a word he says, Eliza. If Rory doesn't know something, he makes it up.'

It was Alex, also in a suit, loosening his tie. 'Early shift done. All yours, Rory. A party of twenty Americans checking in shortly. Good luck satisfying their every fuc—'

'Language, Alex, please,' Rory said. 'We have company.'

'Oh, I'm nothing but charm personified with them, Eliza, I promise. But we Montgomerys have to let off steam sometimes, don't we, Rory? We're human beings under these incredibly sophisticated and sleek exteriors. Speaking for myself, of course.'

'He's only trying to shock you, Eliza,' Rory said. 'It's always been his modus operandi.'

'I've already said sorry to Eliza for my lapse of manners years ago, Rory. No need to stir up unease.'

The mood wasn't entirely lighthearted between them, Eliza noticed. Their exchange was halted by Lawrence's arrival.

'Olivia's unfortunately been delayed,' he said to Eliza. 'She's asked me to bring you up to her office.'

'We'll organise that visit to my workshop whenever you're ready, Eliza,' Rory said to her.

'Wow, fast work, Rory,' Alex said. 'Forget Puzzle World, Eliza. I'll take you to my favourite nightclubs. Much more fun.'

She walked up the stairs beside Lawrence. The previous night she'd thought he was much older than her. Now, she saw he was in his late thirties, perhaps. The grey hair was deceptive.

'It's such a beautiful hotel,' she said, needing to break the silence. 'Have you been here long?'

'Three years and four months,' he said. 'Nearly five.'

'You're counting down the days? Like a prison sentence?'

There was a flash of humour in his eyes. 'Not quite that bad, I promise. Here's Olivia's office now.'

Her godmother finished a phone call and opened her arms. 'There she is! I wasn't imagining it! My darling goddaughter in our hotel. Thank you, Lawrence.'

Once they were alone, Olivia fired questions at Eliza. Was the bed comfortable? Had she slept long enough? Did the curtains block out enough light? Did she enjoy breakfast?

'I feel like I've done a customer service questionnaire,' Eliza said, smiling. 'Everything is perfect.'

'As it should be for you.' Olivia came from behind her desk and reached for her coat. 'And now, you and I are going shopping. For Maxie and Hazel's wedding gift first, and then for you. I'm sure I still owe you a thirtieth birthday present.'

'This trip is my birthday present.'

'No, this is a long overdue visit.'

'Olivia, before we go, I need to say something. About the email I sent you after we spoke.'

Olivia waited.

'I know I should have asked you and Maxie so many questions long before now. It's not that I haven't wanted to know. It's just . . .' She faltered.

'There's no need to apologise, Eliza. We knew you'd ask when you felt the time was right.'

'Will Maxie have time before she goes to New York?'

'I know she will.'

'You've asked her already?'

'No, I haven't breathed a word about you coming. But I know she'll make time for you, of course.'


Olivia drove them into the city centre. The last time Eliza had been in Edinburgh, nearly fourteen years ago, it had been summer, the final days of the Fringe festival, the streets still crowded with performers, people giving out flyers. It was a different city now. Quieter, but still beautiful. She loved the distinctive sandstone of the buildings. The green hills unexpectedly visible in the distance. Modern architecture alongside centuries-old buildings. The Castle rising high above it all.

Olivia pointed out other landmarks. The steeple of St Giles' Cathedral visible high above the Royal Mile. The Gothic tower of the Scott Monument, commemorating author Sir Walter Scott. She offered Eliza the loan of her car whenever she wanted to go sightseeing herself. Eliza had to remind her that she still hadn't learned to drive. Her mother had started teaching her the year she died. Afterwards, Eliza had never tried again.

'I'll teach you,' Olivia said. 'Another reason for you to stay as long as possible.'

Olivia knew exactly what she wanted to get Maxie and Hazel and where to get it. Fine Scottish linen from a small store off the Royal Mile. Eliza described the gift she'd brought from Australia, safely packed in her bag. A handblown glass vase. Olivia was sure Maxie and Hazel would love it.

'And now, we're going shopping for you,' Olivia said. 'No objections. You've escaped from Gillian's clutches. You can escape from her wardrobe now too.'

Olivia took her to her favourite department store. Eliza felt as if she was in a film, as her godmother asked the personal shopper to bring a range of items to the dressing room.

'I can't afford this, Olivia. I don't have a job.'

'I can afford it. These are all the gifts I'd have given you if you'd visited me before now. I've saved them up. It only feels excessive because it's arriving in one fell swoop.'

They left the counter with three bags of new clothing and footwear. Shift dresses. Tailored trousers. Wool and cashmere jumpers. None in neutral colours.

Afterwards, Olivia took her to a bistro. Over late lunch, they spoke about Maxie and Hazel's wedding. They'd drive to Gretna Green the next afternoon. The plan was to arrive just before the six p.m. ceremony, to give Maxie the biggest surprise.

As they had coffee, Olivia told stories about Celine. Eliza knew her godmother was trying to make the tales amusing, but her tension and exhaustion were obvious.

'Olivia, is there anything I can do to help? I'm a fast typist. I'm organised. I love sorting out messes. What if I stepped in even for a few hours or —'

'Yes, Eliza, of course. After finally prising you out of Gillian's bossy jaws, I'm going to throw you into a brand new wolf's lair, if you'll excuse all my metaphors. The answer is no. Thank you, but no.'

It was nearly four by the time they walked back to the car together, bags in hand, still talking. Eliza was in a gentle jet-lagged glow. She felt safe, cushioned. Looked after. Many times in Melbourne, the sight of mother–daughter duos out shopping and lunching together sent an ache into her heart. Seeing them talking, laughing. As she walked alongside her godmother, she felt a sudden rush of gratitude. No, she wasn't here with Jeannie. But this felt like the next best thing.

\*

That night, back in her room while Olivia finished some work in her office, Eliza had another message exchange with Rose. Rose had asked Eliza about Olivia, Edgar, the hotel and the two Montgomery Men, as she'd dubbed them. She wanted to know all about Maxie and Hazel's wedding plans. Eliza told her they were arriving just before the ceremony to give Maxie the best possible surprise.

*That's when she'll first see you??* Rose wrote. *I hope she's wearing waterproof mascara.*

Afterwards, Eliza thought about it. Perhaps they could arrive earlier. She couldn't wait to see Maxie herself. She decided to go and talk to Olivia about it.

On the way, she got lost, finding herself on what looked like new staircases, in different hallways, all lined with artwork. She doubled back twice, sure she was now in the family's wing. She heard the shouting before she was halfway down the hall. It was punctuated by occasional thumps.

Unsure what to do, she paused. A door opened. Lawrence stepped out, a red stain on his white shirt.

'Eliza, hello,' he said, calmly. 'You look lost. Can I help?'

'I was looking for Olivia.' She glanced at his shirt. 'Can I help you?'

'Thank you but no. Everything is —' Another thump sounded. 'Fine, thank you.'

'You look like you've been shot,' she said.

'Fortunately only by an expensive pinot noir. I'm going to see Olivia myself. Let me take you.'

Olivia's office was one floor down. She sighed as they came in.

'Another shirt ruined, Lawrence? You are claiming them back on expenses, I hope? You can talk in front of Eliza. She's family. Do you know she offered her services with Celine today? I blame jetlag.'

Lawrence turned to her. 'Do you have experience working for a tyrant? Someone who makes unreasonable demands for no praise?'

'You've just summed up the past nine years of my working life.'

'Stop it, both of you,' Olivia said. 'It's not going to happen. Lawrence, please, give me the latest. And please excuse me silently screaming while you do.'

Nothing out of the ordinary, he told her. Another tantrum. Some wine throwing. He'd cleaned it up.

Olivia thanked him, then glanced at her watch. 'Isn't it supposed to be your night off? Any plans?'

'Gambling or my laundry, I can't decide. Thanks, Olivia. Goodnight.' He nodded at Eliza too.

Olivia waited until he'd shut the door. 'He is so hardworking, has a sense of humour and never tells me anything about his private life. I can't tell you what a relief that is. Now, to what do I owe this pleasure? I thought I'd banished you to your room for the night.'

Eliza explained her idea about an earlier arrival at Gretna Green. Olivia agreed it was a better plan. They'd leave first thing in the morning.

'Now, back to your room, young lady,' Olivia said. 'Order room service again. Hang the expense.'

Eliza stopped at the door. 'Mum used to like saying that.'

Olivia smiled. 'Yes, I know,' she said.

# CHAPTER FOURTEEN

They were on the road to Gretna Green by nine a.m. It was only a two-hour drive from Edinburgh.

Olivia had secretly rung Maxie at her hotel in Gretna Green the previous night to let her know the change of plan. Maxie had been happy to hear it.

'But you don't think Eliza will want to ask us any questions before the ceremony, do you? I'm going to be emotional enough as it is.'

'No. I've said to her that I'll ask you to come to Edinburgh for a few days after Hazel's left for New York. The three of us can sit down and talk about everything together then.'

Maxie swore loudly. 'The postcards! I'm so sorry, Liv. I forgot them. I got upset looking through them and put them back in the cupboard. They're still there. I was in such a rush leaving, I left my walking boots behind too. I can't even ask Hazel to get them. She's already on her way, staying with a friend of ours in

Manchester tonight. I'll have to post them to you as soon as I'm back in London, when I'm packing up the flat.'

Olivia kept her temper with some difficulty. 'Maxie, for God's sake. You knew how important those postcards were.'

'Please don't be mad,' Maxie said. 'I've got a bad case of bride brain. If it's any consolation, I did remember to bring the champagne. And my wedding dress.'

In the car beside her, Eliza was noticing every aspect of the landscape around them. It was so green compared to what she'd left behind in Australia, she told Olivia. So restful on the eyes. Olivia had grown to love the Scottish landscape, she said. Not just the dramatic Highlands further north, but these gentle rolling hills too, green fields on either side of the road, streams visible in the distance bordered by trees springing into leaf.

She was on edge, though, she realised. Waiting for Eliza to start asking her questions, even before Maxie was there. She deliberately kept the conversation to lighter subjects.

After passing through several villages, they began to see signs for Gretna Green. Olivia had booked them into Maxie and Hazel's hotel, opposite the blacksmith's cottage where the ceremony was taking place. They'd look around the village later. There was something important to do first.

Outside Maxie's room, Olivia waited to one side as Eliza knocked.

It was a prize-winning performance. Maxie stepped back, astonished. She laughed. She put her hands to her face, then pulled Eliza into a hug. She asked if she was dreaming, if she was seeing things. Then she burst into tears. For real, Olivia felt sure.

They spent the next hour in the sleek living area of Maxie's suite, talking, laughing. Maxie kept spontaneously hugging Eliza. 'This was already one of the best times of my life. Now it is the best. Oh, I can't wait for Hazel to meet you. I can't believe Olivia kept it secret from me.'

Hazel wasn't arriving until early afternoon. At Maxie's suggestion, they went across to the blacksmith's cottage complex to watch other weddings unfolding. It was like a marriage theme park, so many wedding parties strolling around, some brides in full white regalia, others more casually dressed. There were photographers everywhere. Olivia noticed Maxie put on her sunglasses, even though the sky was cloudy.

Still, she was recognised once, as they stood in front of the information panels lining the walkway to a café and gift shop. She'd taken off her glasses to read it. An English couple in their forties approached. The woman spoke first. 'Excuse me, are you that actress?'

'On that crime show?' the man added. 'Maxine Hill, her name is.'

Maxie answered in a strong American accent. 'I keep being told I'm her double. I must watch that show myself. Is she any good?'

'She's brilliant. Terrifying.'

'You should register with one of those look-alike agencies. You're the spit of her.'

'Awesome idea, thanks!' she said.

After they left, Olivia turned to Eliza, rolling her eyes. 'Last time this happened, she started speaking Spanish. And Maxie doesn't speak a word of Spanish.'

'I thought celebrities all hide under baseball caps,' Eliza said.

'I'm a bride-to-be,' Maxie said. 'I don't want to spoil my hair.'

Hazel arrived in time for a late lunch. Within minutes of the four of them sitting down in a corner of the hotel restaurant, Eliza could see how happy Maxie and Hazel were. They were so interested in one another. Affectionate, loving. She instantly liked Hazel too. She had an open, smiling face, long blonde hair. There was something calm about her. Amused.

She was very welcoming to Eliza. 'Maxie talks about you all the time. You've made her wedding day, I know.'

'Nearly as much as you, Hazel,' Maxie said, overhearing.

The ceremony was due to start at six. They went to their rooms to get ready. Eliza had changed into a long blue gown and was finishing her make-up when her phone pinged. It was Sullivan. He seemed to have stopped playing any words. It was all messages.

*Hello Fearless Flyer! How is your jetlag?*

*Nearly gone*, Eliza replied. *How is your little sister?*

*Very babyish. What are you doing today?*

*I'm in a place called Gretna Green, getting ready for a wedding.*

*Really?!!! Are you eloping???*

She shouldn't have been surprised he'd heard of Gretna Green. *No, it's my godmother's wedding.*

*How exciting! Perhaps we could meet up when you're back in Edinburgh? You could tell me all about it.*

He sounded strangely forlorn, she thought. *Of course, Navillus.*

*Thanks FF! Have a great time!*

At ten minutes to six, they all met downstairs. Maxie and Hazel looked beautiful in their wedding gowns, both in antique cream lace. Olivia was in a flowing green dress. There was no official photographer. Instead, Maxie asked Eliza and Olivia to take photos on their phones.

They walked over to the blacksmith's cottage. Their celebrant and the wedding organiser were waiting, smiling. They made their way through the front rooms of the cottage, past exhibits telling the story of Gretna Green weddings, with examples of wedding dresses over the decades glowing in their glass cases. Then, into the marriage room, the anvil standing in the centre. Maxie became teary as soon as she saw it. Eliza saw her reach for Hazel's hand.

The service was brief, the celebrant sincere. Hazel and Maxie read the vows they'd written themselves, promising to honour, cherish, love and look after one another. They'd asked Eliza and Olivia not to take photographs during the ceremony. Afterwards, they posed arm-in-arm, holding their bouquets, faces alight with love. The celebrant hit the anvil, in keeping with tradition. They all cheered as the sound echoed around the room.

The wedding dinner took place in a private room of the hotel, decorated with flowers, fairy lights and lanterns. It looked like an enchanted garden. Maxie grew tearful as she thanked Olivia and Eliza.

'I knew having you both here would make today perfect. I didn't realise just how perfect.'

'You knew I'd be here?' Eliza said. 'It wasn't a surprise?'

'Oops,' Maxie said.

'Oops,' Olivia said.

'But this morning, when you saw me —'

'The Academy Award goes to Maxie Hill,' Hazel said, smiling at her wife.

'You're both such good liars,' Eliza said to her godmothers after they explained how it had all happened. 'I don't know whether to admire you or be nervous of you.'

'Admire me, darling,' Maxie said, leaning over to touch her cheek. 'It's my wedding day.'

There was one more surprise after dinner. Maxie and Hazel had decided to leave for their honeymoon that night. It wasn't a long drive. Hazel had barely touched her champagne. They wanted to wake up in the cottage, they said. Start their married life in the wild beauty of the Highlands.

*

Downstairs, Olivia hugged them. 'If it wasn't nearly midnight, I'd tie cans to the back of your car.'

'See you in New York soon, I hope,' Hazel said as she hugged Eliza.

'See you in Edinburgh next week,' Eliza said, hugging Maxie.

'I can't wait,' Maxie said.

She did her best to avoid Olivia's gaze as she said it.

Olivia and Eliza had just driven out of Gretna Green on their way back to Edinburgh the next morning when Olivia's phone rang. She pulled over to answer.

Maxie, Eliza guessed. She'd already sent two messages that morning, both with photos. The view from their cottage, heather-covered hills, spectacular mountains in the distance, a weak sun breaking through clouds. The second showed two slices of wedding cake beside a morning pot of coffee. *It was the most perfect wedding,* she'd written. *It felt like a magical dream. We never want to wake up. Thank you both so so much. M & H xxx.*

It wasn't Maxie calling. It was Lawrence.

A woman had arrived at the front desk of the Montgomery saying she was there to provide secretarial services to a guest. She was from a prestigious executive assistant agency in London. She'd been offered a month's employment, with accommodation and all expenses paid by the Montgomery hotel. Celine had placed the ad. Rory had driven the woman back to the train station. Lawrence had covered her travel costs.

Olivia was furious. She told Lawrence they'd meet to discuss it as soon as she and Eliza returned.

Eliza and Olivia began arguing about it even before they got back on the road.

Eliza pleaded her case. 'Please, Olivia. Ask me. I need something to do.'

'You're supposed to be here on holiday, Eliza. Not to tidy up my family messes.'

'Then pretend I'm a temp. Let me step in until you do find someone else.'

Olivia turned in the driver's seat. 'Eliza, Celine's not an eccentric old lady. She's vicious. I've tried to be sympathetic to her over the years – she lost her only daughter to cancer, after all – but it's impossible. All she does is insult people. She told Susan she was fat, had chin hairs, that it's no wonder she's single. She told me that Edgar only married me to get a free nanny. She blames everyone for the fact she's behind with her deadline.'

'Deadline?' Eliza asked. 'So she actually has a contract for her biography?'

'With a vanity publisher,' Olivia said. 'And this is only volume one. Her Scottish years. She said that once it's done she's going back to France to research volume two. She's lived there for years with her French husband, the pair of them constantly fighting and making up again, apparently. He's either a saint or a madman.'

'So let's help her finish volume one. Let me help her. Let me help you, Olivia. I survived Gillian, remember.'

'Celine makes Gillian look like a pussycat.'

'Please, Olivia.'

Olivia started the car, then turned the engine off again. 'One afternoon. No more. And thank you.'

Eliza couldn't stop a smile. 'Will you tell her I'm your goddaughter?'

'She'll be horrible to you either way. We may as well tell her the truth.'

Olivia rang Lawrence. 'Tell her we've found her a temporary assistant. One with nine years' experience at the highest level. Her name is Eliza Miller. She'll be there by lunchtime.'

Lawrence was in the hotel foyer when they arrived. He smiled at Eliza. 'That Anzac spirit coming to the fore, Eliza? Thank you, on behalf of the hotel and every temp agency in a thousand-mile radius.'

'It's just for this afternoon, Lawrence,' Olivia said. 'Can you please take Eliza up? I'm not in the mood to have Celine shouting at me today.'

'Of course,' Lawrence said. 'Ready, Eliza?'

'Ready,' she replied.

# CHAPTER FIFTEEN

Lawrence knocked on the half-open door. A cross Scottish voice summoned them in.

Eliza's initial thought was that there couldn't be room for anyone in the suite. She had never seen such chaos. It was as if fifty boxes of stationery had been upended onto every surface. Teetering towers of books leaned against bundles of newspapers that touched piles of photographs. There wasn't a bare surface in the bedroom or living area.

'This is the whiz-bang new temp?' a voice said from the corner. 'You didn't tell me it was a giraffe.'

Eliza spun around. Her first impression was that she'd stumbled into a wildlife documentary. One starring a furious little animal, like an otter or Tasmanian devil. Celine was tiny. She had short, dyed dark hair teased into tufts around her head. She was wearing pink silk pyjamas. There was a too-taut look to her face, as if she'd had not entirely successful plastic surgery.

Her blazing, heavily made-up eyes were directed at Eliza.

'Do you speak as well as stare?' she asked. 'Your typing had better be an improvement on your manners.'

As Lawrence introduced them, Eliza stepped forward and held out her hand.

'Hello, Celine. I'm pleased to meet you.'

'I don't shake strangers' hands. You'll wear gloves while you work for me. Not only for hygiene reasons. You'll be dealing with a lot of precious items. If you damage even one of them, I'll sue your fucking arse off.'

Eliza didn't react. Gillian had liked swearing too. 'I hope that won't be necessary.'

Celine glared at her. 'I'll issue your instructions shortly. Get lost, Lawrence. You're only in the way.'

'Eliza?' Lawrence asked.

'I'm fine, Lawrence, thank you.'

He gave her the quickest of smiles, mouthed a thanks, then closed the door behind him.

'Thank God he's gone,' Celine said once they were alone. 'I can't decide who I hate the most, him or Olivia. Who the hell are you again?'

Eliza repeated her name. 'I can get started as soon as you tell me what you're doing.'

'What does it look like?' Celine threw out her arms. 'Telling my life story, of course! Readers will lap it up. Filmmakers will snap it up. It will break hearts and open minds. Make a note of that. It's perfect for the movie poster.'

Eliza reached into her bag, took out a notebook and duly made a note.

Celine's eyes narrowed. 'Well, well, a moment of efficiency. It won't last, of course. What qualifications do you have? None, I suppose.'

'I have a business degree. Nine years' experience working in conference organisation. I have an eye for detail, a logical mind and I work very quickly.'

'Big head. They told me I only had you for this afternoon. What the hell use is that?'

'I can get a lot done if you'll let me get started. I just need some direction.'

'Who doesn't? Where do I start? Do I write chronologically? Or do I cherrypick the most dramatic events of my life? It's not as if I've had any help from the fools in this hotel. I've heard them all moaning about me, Olivia and that Easter Island statue —'

'Who?'

'Lawrence. Mr Cool, Calm and Collected.'

'It's his job to be calm.'

'I've tried, you know. Jab jab jab, to see if I can get some sort of reaction from him. No luck. Olivia's the same. She must hate my guts, but no, she's all, "Of course, Celine. Yes, Celine." I suppose you'll be the same. A sneaky backstabber.'

'I think they're being professional. And mindful of your position in the Montgomery family.'

Celine repeated her words in a mocking tone. 'Are you trying to be cheeky, you big lanky brat?'

Eliza had to bite back a smile. She'd suddenly thought of Hector, the homeless man in Melbourne who used to shout insults at her too. 'I'm not, I promise. I'm only here to help.'

'Where are you from? New Zealand, by the sounds of that awful accent.'

'Australia. Melbourne. I'm Olivia's goddaughter.'

'That's all I need. Some religious freak, sponging off her god-mother while her godmother's husband is drooling in an asylum somewhere.'

Eliza's back straightened. 'I'm not religious. And that's a horrible way to talk about Edgar.'

'My daughter never loved him, you know. Oh, she said she did, but I know she was lying. She could have done so much better. She was extremely pretty. Took after me. I've photos of her somewhere. She had a minor aristocrat sniffing around her for a while. I've written about him in one of my diaries. That's where I want you to start. Sort all my papers and photos and put them in chronological order.'

'That's fine. I'll get started —'

'Not yet. Answer my questions first. Why are you here?'

'As I said, I'm an experienced executive assistant.'

'No, in Edinburgh. Did you get your heart broken in Auckland? Come running to your godmother?'

'I'm from Melbourne and no, I didn't. Olivia invited me.'

'Who are your parents?'

'My mother's name was Jeannie.'

'Was? She's dead?'

Eliza nodded.

'Your father?'

A brief hesitation. 'I don't know.'

'What do you mean you don't know? Your mother was a tramp? Couldn't remember which of her many lovers might have been your father?' Celine laughed. 'Look at the blush. Got it in one, did I?'

Eliza kept her voice steady. 'Of course not.'

'What are they paying you?'

'Nothing,' Eliza said, as she got down on the floor and began to empty the first overflowing box.

'Nothing? Are you nuts?'

'I'm doing it as a favour to Olivia.'

'Her? I call her The Nanny. You know that's the only reason Edgar married her, don't you? To get a free childminder. So what happened to your mother? Cancer, like my daughter?'

'No.' She hesitated, then decided to say something. 'I'm sorry about your daughter. Olivia told me about her.'

Celine lifted her chin. 'Mind your own business. I don't want your sympathy or curiosity. You're here to work, remember.'

Eliza was stung. 'There's no need to be so rude.'

'There's every need. What's the point in trying to be good and kind and sweet? Bad things will still happen. They always do. Enough chitchat. Get on with it if you're so efficient. If I can believe a word The Nanny says.'

'Please don't call Olivia that.'

'I'll call her what I want. You've got those two red spots on your cheeks again. I know you're pretending to be Ms Professional but that's a giveaway.'

'I'll wear concealer next time I work for you.'

'If there's a next time.'

'I think I'll be the one deciding that, not you.' Eliza couldn't believe she was talking to her like this. It felt like she was channelling someone else. Someone fearless. Like her mother.

Celine narrowed her eyes. 'So get started, then. But I'm watching you, missy. Like a hawk.'

Or a deranged otter, Eliza thought. Fighting a smile, she turned back to the paper-crammed boxes.

Four hours later, she'd sorted through six full boxes. She'd found photos, letters, theatre programmes and newspapers dating back years. Olivia had told her Celine had shipped them all from France. Billed to the Montgomery, of course.

She'd have done even more if she hadn't been regularly interrupted by messages from Sullivan. His father was at the hospital. His stepmother had gone to visit her parents, taking The Baby – Sullivan always used capital letters – with her, he told her.

*Are you home on your own?* she typed, concerned.

*No, Dad's PA is here. But she's busy working. What are you doing, FF?*

*I'm working too, actually.*

*I thought you were unemployed?*

*I'm doing a temp job. To help my godmother.*

*The one that just got married?*

*Another one.*

*Two godmothers AND a new job. Sounds great! I look forward to hearing all about it!*

'Stop that bloody messaging, would you?' Celine said loudly. 'That pinging is driving me insane.'

There was a knock at the door.

'Get it,' Celine said.

Eliza stood up, found a path through the boxes and opened the door. It was Olivia.

'Is everything okay?' her godmother whispered. 'Do you need anything? Tea? Something to eat?'

'Who is it?' Celine shouted.

'Olivia,' Eliza called. 'She's asking if we're hungry.'

'I'm starving. I want a club sandwich and a glass of red. Same for you.'

'I'm not hungry yet and I don't drink.'

'You don't drink? Jesus, religious *and* a teetotaller.'

Eliza turned back to Olivia and winked. 'Just tea for me, thanks Olivia.'

Olivia brought her hands together in an expression of gratitude, then left.

'Why don't you drink?' Celine asked as Eliza started sorting again. 'Are you an alcoholic?'

'I don't like the taste.'

'What about drugs?'

'No,' Eliza said, moving over to a new box filled with what appeared to be theatre tickets.

'How tall are you?'

'Five foot ten.'

'Too tall. Bet you've had trouble getting a boyfriend. Are you single?'

'Yes.'

'You're not completely hideous-looking. You could make more of yourself if you tried.'

'Thank you.'

'It wasn't a compliment. So are you a virgin as well as a religious teetotaller?'

'No,' Eliza said. 'Not that it's any of your business.'

'I've had more lovers than I can remember. I'm trying to decide whether to weave my love affairs through the book, or have a separate chapter.'

Eliza kept sorting.

'Elspeth?'

'It's Eliza.'

'What do you think I should do? Scatter my sexy tales throughout or in one whole chapter?'

'I don't know, I'm sorry.'

She sorted in silence for another fifteen minutes, before Celine spoke again.

'Was your mother an alcoholic? Is that why you don't drink?'

'I'm not going to answer that.'

'Why not?'

'It's private.'

Celine raised her voice. 'Don't be ridiculous. What's private in this world?'

'Celine, please. It's hard to concentrate when you're shouting at me.'

'I'm not shouting. But if I am, it's because you're so boring.'

Ten minutes later, Eliza stood up, hands on hips, and looked around. She was running out of space.

'What are you plotting now, Ellen?'

'Eliza,' she said. Before she could say any more, there was a knock at the door. Rory, holding a tray. She invited him in.

'Rory, how nice to see you,' Celine said. 'Yes, I'm being sarcastic. What is this, the third time you've visited me since I arrived?' She snatched the tray. 'I want another glass of wine in thirty minutes.'

'Please,' Eliza said without thinking.

Celine just swore at her.

Thirty minutes and two boxes later, another knock. Alex this time, with a single glass of wine on a silver tray.

'Eliza, a pleasure to see you again. Working already, what a scandal. Grandmother, your wine as requested. Our finest shiraz. Not that you specified. I made an informed guess.'

'Don't be such a suck, Alexander. That smooth patter might work with all the waitresses you seduce but it won't cut any ice with me.'

'It really is always such a pleasure to be in your company. You radiate goodwill.' Alex turned to Eliza. 'We're just so grateful our grandmother decided to grace us again with her presence.

She once described Edinburgh as a "mouldering city dipped in grey sludge".'

'Yet here I am,' Celine said. 'The prodigal grandmother. Not that any of you seem to care about me. If my heartbroken husband didn't keep ringing from France, begging me to come home again, I'd never get to speak to another human being.'

'He's begging you? There's a man in need of urgent psychological help.'

Eliza stood up. The tension between them was becoming uncomfortable. 'Excuse me,' she said.

As she walked outside and shut the door, her phone beeped. Sullivan again. She played a word. He played one back, then sent a message.

*Are you having fun at work?*

*Sure am!* she lied.

# CHAPTER SIXTEEN

Next morning, Olivia delivered Eliza's room-service breakfast. They hadn't seen each other since the previous afternoon. Olivia had spent the evening visiting Edgar. Eliza had had a welcome early night.

Olivia pushed the trolley into the room. 'We're not short-staffed. I'm dining here so I can talk sense into you. Lawrence told me you've volunteered again. One afternoon with Celine was kind. A second day is madness. You should be out exploring Edinburgh, not trapped in that room with her.'

'I'll go exploring on the weekend. When you can come. At least this way I feel useful. I'm also salving my guilt about taking up space in this beautiful suite.'

'You've already earned yourself a year in this suite by doing yesterday. That's enough.'

Eliza helped Olivia set out their trays on the table by the window. Golden-yellow scrambled eggs, slivers of smoked salmon sprinkled with chives, hot buttered toast. She poured their coffee.

'I'm enjoying it. Truly.'

'That's because Celine hasn't started insulting you yet.'

'Yes she has.' Eliza repeated some of the insults.

Olivia looked appalled. Before she had a chance to speak, Eliza's phone pinged.

'I hope that's Rose trying to talk sense into you,' Olivia said.

'It's Sullivan. The boy from the plane. I think he's lonely.'

'Why don't you go explore Edinburgh with him? At least until I'm free. That would be much better for you than being Voldemort's PA.'

Eliza told her godmother she was running out of space in Celine's suite. Olivia remembered that the room adjoining Celine's was being redecorated after a leaking pipe. She could use that too.

'You're sure I can't talk you out of this?'

Completely sure, Eliza told her.

'Then I'll ask Lawrence to meet you there with the key.'


Lawrence was waiting outside Celine's suite. 'You've already saved two of our reception staff from nervous breakdowns, thank you. She used to ring them every ten minutes.'

Eliza knocked. No answer.

'Celine?' she called. 'It's Eliza. It's nine-thirty. The time we arranged.'

Another knock. Still nothing. She turned to Lawrence. 'Perhaps she's gone downstairs for breakfast?'

'No,' Lawrence said. 'She said the carpet pattern gives her a headache and the dining room stinks.'

She knocked again. Nothing. 'Could she be —'

'I'll get the master key,' Lawrence said.

While he was gone, Eliza pressed her ear to the door. It swung open. She nearly fell in.

It was Celine, in yellow silk pyjamas. 'Serves you right for eavesdropping. You're late.'

'I'm not late. We were getting worried.'

'We? You're alone. I was meditating.' She gestured to earplugs. 'It keeps me calm.'

Eliza couldn't hide a smile.

'Funny, is it?' Celine raised her voice. 'You have an attitude problem, missy. You're sacked, you —'

'Can't sack her, Celine, because you haven't hired her.' It was Olivia, holding a master key and the key to the adjoining room. She gave them both to Eliza, then made a swift exit.

Eliza opened the adjoining room. There was ample space for all of Celine's boxes and paperwork. Celine had followed her. She looked around.

'This room has been empty all along? Why didn't anyone else suggest I use it? Fools.'

Eliza ignored her and got to work. After a while, Celine turned on the TV, watching at high volume.

Throughout the morning, Sullivan was very active online.

*What's the name of your workplace, Fearless Flyer?*

*It's my godmother's hotel. The Montgomery.*

*I've just googled it. I'm only a 21-minute walk away, according to Google Maps.*

*Where are you?*

*At home with Dad's PA. She's very busy. I wish I had something to do, or someone nearby to visit.*

She couldn't invite him over. He was a child. A near-stranger.

*FF, is your godmother married to Edgar Montgomery? It's very sad about his dementia.*

*How do you know that??*

*I asked my dad's PA. Her dad used to play golf with Edgar. She had her 21st party at the Montgomery. She's met your godmother Olivia too. What a small world Edinburgh is! Would you like to talk to her?*

*About what?*

*The possibility of me coming to visit you.*

*Sullivan, I'm sorry, but I don't think you can. I'm supposed to be working.*

*I'll be good as gold, I promise. I could read quietly while you work?*

*I'd have to speak to your dad, not his PA.*

*I have his contact details right here. Shall I send them over?*

It was becoming clear just how lonely Sullivan was. Eliza too easily remembered what loneliness felt like.

She messaged Sullivan again. His father's contact details arrived seconds later.

Soon after, she took a break, ignoring Celine's taunts that she was lazy as well as inefficient.

Olivia was in her office. Eliza filled her in. Olivia not only remembered Ann-Marie's twenty-first birthday party, she'd also heard of Sullivan's father. 'He made the papers when he took up his position at the hospital. A world leader in reconstructive surgery. It was a coup to get him. He's left his son at home alone?'

Eliza explained the situation.

'The poor kid,' Olivia said. 'How about we invite him here for lunch? As a thankyou for being so good to you on the plane. I'll email his father myself.'

They didn't hear anything back from Sullivan's father until the next morning. He was businesslike but grateful. He'd copied in his PA. Sullivan could come for lunch that day, if it suited.

Moments after Olivia emailed back to say that yes, it would, Eliza's phone pinged.

*Hurrah!! See you soon!!!!!!!!!!!!!!!!!!*

Celine wasn't happy when Eliza told her she'd only be working until Sullivan arrived.

'Bring him up here. I'll order room service for three.'

'No, thank you.' She started sorting a new box.

'You're no fun.'

'I don't have to be fun. I'm here to work.'

A few minutes passed before Celine spoke again.

'Why don't you and Lawrence get together? He's almost tall enough for you. He doesn't have a girlfriend. I asked him. He's probably never had a girlfriend in his life.'

'Celine, please, I'm trying to concentrate.'

'Or one of my grandsons instead. Though they're as useless as each other. This place will go to the dogs if either of them ever takes over.'

When Eliza ignored that too, Celine turned the TV up loud. Her shouted insults at a daytime soap opera provided a surprisingly entertaining soundtrack.

At one p.m., Eliza told Celine she was going for lunch. The older woman turned her head, continuing to watch TV at full volume. Eliza had reached the door before she spoke.

'Club sandwich. Wine. Tell them to send it up.'

'No, Celine. Ring and order it yourself. And say please.'

'Bossy cow!' was ringing in Eliza's ears as she went down the corridor.

*

'Eliza!'

Sullivan stood up from the sofa in the foyer and gave her one of his great smiles. He was wearing a well-ironed white shirt and what looked like new jeans. He took her hand and pumped it like a little enthusiastic businessman. 'It's so good to see you again.'

'You too, Sullivan,' she said. She meant it.

'That's Ann-Marie there,' he said, pointing over at a young woman on the phone nearby. Eliza recognised her from the airport. She finished her call, came over and was introduced.

'Let's go through to the dining room,' Eliza said to them both.

'Oh, I'm not joining you,' Ann-Marie said. 'I'll collect Sullivan again at three.'

'Three?' Two hours away.

'Sullivan said that's what you'd agreed.'

'I'll be so well-behaved, Eliza,' Sullivan said quickly. 'If you're busy, I really can sit quietly and read.'

Eliza gave in. 'Three p.m. is great, Ann-Marie, thanks.'

'Shall we make it four?' Sullivan said. 'That will give Ann-Marie plenty of time to do her work.'

Eliza gave in again.


An hour later, they both put down their linen napkins. She'd expected to find it difficult keeping a boy Sullivan's age entertained over lunch. Instead, they'd had an interesting conversation about Edinburgh. He knew lots of facts. He also had excellent table manners.

'My expensive schooling,' he said, when she remarked on them.

Olivia came to say hello. 'You were so kind to Eliza on the flight, Sullivan. Thank you.'

'Anyone in my position would have done the same,' he said. 'Do you need to speak to Eliza? I'll visit the bathroom and give you some privacy.' He hopped down off the chair and left them alone.

'Did I imagine that exchange?' Olivia asked.

'That was mild, believe me.'

'Celine wants to meet him too. She's been calling me nonstop. Telling me she's dying of loneliness.'

'Olivia, I'm sorr—'

'You've nothing to apologise for. I'd distract her myself, but I have a meeting with our lawyer.' She lowered her voice. 'We're hoping to find a loophole in Celine's agreement with Edgar.' She also read Eliza a message she'd received from Maxie, saying that she was still having a blissful honeymoon, but confirming she'd be with them in Edinburgh by the end of the week. Three days away.

'My list of questions is getting longer every day,' Eliza said. 'I can't wait.'

'Nor can we,' Olivia said.

*

Sullivan was thrilled when Eliza invited him to come upstairs to help her sort Celine's paperwork.

'If I get bored, can I use the empty boxes to build myself a fort?' He sounded like a proper eleven-year-old for once.

'Of course you can,' she said.

—

Sullivan stepped into Celine's suite and held out his hand. 'I've heard so much about you, Mrs Montgomery. I hear you're writing your life story. How fascinating.'

'I'm not a Montgomery,' Celine said. She turned to Eliza. 'You're right. He's a weirdo.'

'I never said you were a weirdo,' Eliza told Sullivan.

'I don't mind if you did,' he said.

'Get to work, both of you,' Celine said, turning back to the TV. 'And don't read anything, kid. Some of the things I've done would make your hair curl.'

Sullivan tugged at his straight dark hair. 'I'd quite like curly hair, as it happens,' he said.

He was quick to learn, carefully taking out photos, theatre programmes and letters, placing them on the right piles. As he sorted, he chatted to Eliza.

'Have you seen much of Edinburgh yet, Eliza?' he asked as

they started on a new box.

'Stop talking and keep working,' Celine called from the adjoining room.

'Not yet,' Eliza said. 'I've been busy in here.'

'Perhaps I could show you around one day. I know where all the sights are. We'd have to get security clearance from my father again but if I return unharmed today, I can't imagine any objection.'

'That would be great, Sullivan, thank you.'

'I'm coming too,' Celine shouted from the other room.

# CHAPTER SEVENTEEN

In her office one floor down, Olivia was finding it hard to concentrate on work. As well as guest relations and online review responses, she looked after the design and printing of the hotel's menus and promotional material. She was supposed to be proofreading table settings and place cards for a forthcoming wedding. She knew she wasn't doing it properly.

She put them to one side and massaged her temples instead. She was feeling unnerved. Not only by the sudden lack of hectoring phone calls from Celine. Eliza was working miracles with her.

Olivia was feeling anxious about Eliza's imminent questions. She wished it was possible to ask her to submit them beforehand, to give her and Maxie some insight into what she wanted to know. She had to be honest with herself: it was also so she and Maxie could get their stories straight. Decide which questions they really could answer truthfully. Work out in advance which ones they couldn't.

Eliza wanted to ask them about her father, of course. They'd been waiting for her to ask for years. Not that she and Maxie would be any help. Jeannie had never told them the whole story, either. She'd insisted she would tell Eliza first on her eighteenth birthday, and then the two of them the next day. But what else would she ask about? Jeannie's childhood? Her family? Her overseas travels?

She and Maxie had never known for sure where Jeannie got the money to go travelling. She'd once mentioned something about a necklace her grandmother had owned and bequeathed. Another time she'd spoken about an inheritance from an old uncle.

She was away for nearly a year. She'd returned full of stories, of this scrape with the law, that late-night adventure. But she hadn't been pregnant. She had even talked about going back to study again, appearing interested in how their courses in Sydney were going. Olivia had been in the second year of her art history degree, while Maxie was studying drama and also getting the occasional bit part on low-budget TV soaps. They were living in a student house in Newtown, run-down but cheap.

But then Jeannie decided she wasn't ready to 'settle down and study' yet. She got a job in a pub in Melbourne, a music venue. She'd spent time working in pubs in London and Ireland, and had more than enough experience to talk her way into a job, in any case. They'd been jealous of her, Olivia remembered. Jeannie was earning money. She got to hear live music seven nights a week if she wanted.

Living in different cities meant they didn't catch up as often as they'd have liked to. She and Maxie were also serious about their studies. They had exams. They'd made other friends from their courses. Still, one cold April during their uni holidays, they bought bus tickets and made the twelve-hour journey from Sydney to Melbourne to visit Jeannie.

They arranged to meet at the Collingwood pub she was working in. The reunion was instantly fun. She'd take them to her share house later, she said, apologising in advance that it would be mattresses on the floor. She showed them around the pub, introduced them to her boss and the other staff. She was excited, sparkly eyed, full of stories about the bands, the customers, her regulars.

She settled them at what she called her favourite table, fetched bags of chips and peanuts, went behind the bar and poured their drinks herself. She peppered them with questions, listening in the intense way she had, wanting to know from Maxie how it felt to be on stage with a whole audience looking at her, how Olivia knew if a painting was good, or was it the market dictating what was valuable. They'd ordered their third round when they heard a voice behind them.

'Jeannie?'

They turned around. A young, lanky, brown-haired man was standing there. He apologised for interrupting. Maxie thought he was Welsh. Olivia later guessed correctly that he was Irish.

Jeannie introduced him with flamboyant enthusiasm. 'This is my darling friend Emmet,' she said. 'Isn't that the most adorable name? And hasn't he got the most adorable accent?'

Emmet shook hands with them both. 'Such good manners,' Jeannie said proudly. He'd come to drop off a new key to their share house, three streets away.

After he left, they interrogated her. 'A charming Irishman? How come we haven't heard about him before now?'

'I was saving him up for you to meet in person. You'll meet him again tonight, when I take you back to your luxurious lodgings on my living-room floor. Tomorrow at breakfast too.'

'You're living with him?'

'Correction. He's living with me. Emmet and his cousin, actually. It was my house first. It's quite the Irish embassy now. But unfortunately in my excitement about your visit I had too much to drink and lost my keys somewhere last night. Or had my keys stolen. So we had to get the lock changed. See how responsible I am these days?'

Maxie ignored the talk of keys. 'Living with as in *living* with? Are you and Emmet a couple?'

Jeannie laughed. 'You're so coy, Maxie. Are we sleeping together, do you mean? Go on, ask me outright, one of you. I bet you can.'

'Are you and Emmet sleeping together, Jeannie?' Olivia asked.

Jeannie put her hands together in a prayer gesture and pulled a sad face. 'For my sins, Father Olivia, yes, we are. Will I burn in hell?'

'Why would you burn in hell? What do you take us for? You're both adults, young, single —'

Jeannie laughed. 'Fooled you. No, he's just a friend. A dear friend. His heart is taken elsewhere. In real life, back in Ireland, Emmet is engaged. Well, to be exact, he was engaged but the engagement is currently on hold. I met him in London first, as it happens. Then he went back home and brought me with him as a souvenir. I worked in his family's pub for a month. That's why I am able to pour such a mean pint of Guinness. I'll show you later. I can even trace a shamrock pattern on top. His girlfriend – sorry, fiancée – announced she thought they needed some breathing space before they got married. So they agreed to "take a break".' Jeannie made quote marks with her fingers.

'I'd told him about the paradise that is Australia, of course, a land of sweeping plains, et cetera. We kept in touch, he rang me one night, a bit drunk, truth be told, said he and his father hadn't been getting on, he'd had enough of being back in Ireland, he and his cousin had decided to come to Australia for a few months. I told him they could stay with me. I got him a part-time job here too. See what a good friend I am? Loyal. Helpful. Supportive. Lascivious.'

Jeannie burst out laughing again, too loudly. She fetched more drinks, then insisted on hearing all about their love lives, their careers. She wanted Maxie to perform a monologue there and then, in the pub. She told a long rambling joke that didn't have a punchline. When the band appeared, she insisted they get up and dance with her. They stayed far longer than either of them wanted to. It was nearly three a.m. by the time they got home. Jeannie was giggly, affectionate and very drunk as she made up their beds on the floor, a combination of sofa cushions and grubby pillows she pulled out of a cupboard. Neither of them slept much that night. The next morning they were up and out early, before any of her flatmates were awake. They treated her to breakfast – 'I love having rich friends!' she kept saying – before making their way to the bus station for the long journey home.

Things changed between them after that visit. Olivia's study program increased. She also began a weekend job at a prestigious gallery, with the possibility of it becoming full-time after she graduated. Maxie's bit part on the TV series turned into a more regular role, involving long hours and a rising public profile. Maxie's elderly aunt died, leaving her flat in Petersham vacant until it was sold. She was offered the chance to house-sit. Olivia moved in with her.

A week went by without them calling Jeannie, or hearing from her. Another week. A month. Two months. A postcard arrived, in her familiar scrawl. A photo of a tram on the front. *Everything is on track down here HAHAHAHAHA*. They laughed when they received it. They both meant to ring her or write back, of course. But again, the days flew by and turned into weeks. Months. Until one day, they came back home after long work and study days to a voice message on their phone.

'*Darlings, it is me. Your long-lost pal in Melbourne. Remember Melbourne, that shabby grey town all those miles away from your glamorous shiny Sydney? Remember me? Your old school friend? The one you used to share a dormitory with? I have some big news. Well, in fact, right now it is tiny news but the doctor tells me it's going to get bigger and bigger. I'd prefer it stayed this size – it'd be easier to have it, if you know what I mean. Anyway, call me when you get the chance in your busy, busy lives, won't you? I'll be home after eight. Do you have my number? I was thinking you might have lost it, seeing as you never seem to ring me any more.'* She recited the number, then hung up.

They guessed immediately what she meant. They rang her that evening, put her on speakerphone.

Olivia spoke first. 'Oh my God, Jeannie, you're pregnant?'

She laughed. 'I knew I hadn't been cryptic enough. But that's it? "Oh my God"? Not, "Oh congratulations, Jeannie, what wonderful news, a new human being is on the way!"'

Olivia and Maxie spoke over each other. 'But how? Who's the father? What are you going to do?'

Jeannie interrupted. 'So many questions! How? Darlings, weren't you paying attention at school? Remember those lessons, how babies are made?' She began to speak in a low, ponderous tone. '"First the lady and man must get close to one another and remove their clothing. Then the man —"'

'That's not what we meant, Jeannie,' Olivia said. 'I mean, whose is it? Is it the Irish guy?'

'The Irish guy? Which one? I've been so busy studying international relations since we saw each other. Let me think, there was also one from Spain, then Venezuela, then Thailand —'

'Jeannie, stop joking,' Maxie said. 'This is serious. Is it Emmet, the Irish guy we met?'

'No, it is not Emmet-the-Irish-Guy-You-Met. Actually, something bad happened with him.'

'His fiancée found out about you and ordered him home?'

'My, Maxie, you do have a good memory. That must help when you're learning your lines. Anyway, I told you they were on a break when he was in Australia.' Her tone changed, grew serious. 'He had an accident. A bad one. And it wasn't completely my fault but some of it was.' Before they had a chance to ask, she went into detail about what had happened. It was impossible to interrupt her.

It had happened near the pub one night, she said, a month after they visited. She, Emmet and the other bar staff had been drinking after-hours.

'Just relaxing, you know, kicking back after a busy night. I hadn't eaten since breakfast. I was starving. I knew a place that did the best chips, and said I'd shout everyone, but no one would come. Then Emmet said he would. We got there, and it was packed, a queue stretching out the door . . .'

Olivia could remember the feeling of frustration, wanting to hear all about Jeannie's pregnancy, instead having to listen to her tell this rambling story about her friend.

'There was a gang of about four fellas behind us in the queue. Aussie guys. Footballer types. One of them said something about me. As in, me physically. Gross. And I said something back. And he said something worse back. And then Emmet stepped in, and there was a bit of shoving and pushing. And one of them, this big drunk guy, started making fun of Emmet's accent, "tirty-tree" this, "tirty-tree" that, doing Irish dancing, and Emmet told him to fuck off. And so they started mimicking the way he said that too, saying "You feck off, Paddy," and I was trying to get them all to calm down, and I shoved one of them – not even hard, a push – but he thought Emmet had done it, and he lost it.

'They all started punching each other. I tried to stop them. I even thought it was a bit of a joke at first. But then one of the other guys, not Emmet, picked up a bottle from the ground and he smashed it against the wall. And he hit Emmet with it, and Emmet went down.'

'Oh, Jesus,' Olivia said. 'Oh, God. Oh, Jeannie.'

'The other guys ran off. They were never caught. I was screaming, asking for someone to call an ambulance. There was blood everywhere, I thought they'd taken his eye out. It was horrible.' An ambulance came, followed by the police. She was taken away in the police car to be checked out in the emergency department too, even though she insisted she hadn't been touched, that Emmet had been protecting her, that he'd been hurt because of her.

'They gave me something, I think, to calm me down. I was hysterical by then.'

Olivia and Maxie now wanted all the details. Jeannie told them Emmet was put into a medically induced coma. His cousin let all the family know. His father came out from Ireland, his mother staying back in Ireland praying and fearing the worst, looking after his three younger brothers. His girlfriend was away travelling in South America, unreachable. They'd left messages for her everywhere they could. It was a terrible, terrible time, Jeannie said.

Olivia was shocked. 'Why didn't you tell us when it was happening?'

'Jeannie, we should have known,' Maxie said.

'I didn't know how it was going to end. I felt so guilty. The fight started because of me. And I was so worried he might die. And that they might press charges against me – Emmet's family – and it would be like last time, with the police involved, but this time I wouldn't be able to get off . . .'

Jeannie began to sob. In Sydney, Olivia and Maxie looked at each other with concern.

'But what happened to him, Jeannie?' Maxie asked. 'Is he okay now? Where is he?'

'He was in a coma for three weeks. I was in there every day. His father and cousin and I started taking turns. We didn't know if he'd ever wake up again or not, if he would be brain-damaged. But then it was like a miracle. His father was in with him one day, reading an Irish newspaper to him, and Emmet woke up. *Bing*, eyes opened, as if he'd been having a nap. They kept him there for two more weeks, and then he flew home, with his father and cousin. Everyone kept telling him how lucky he was. The vision in one of his eyes was damaged, but it could have been so much worse. I felt so guilty, for weeks afterwards. I was the one who wanted the chips, I was the one they'd insulted, and yet he was the one who paid for it.' She was sobbing again.

'But he's okay?' Olivia asked. 'Back home, with his girlfriend?'

'Yes. The engagement's back on, everything. I've only spoken to him once since he got back, but he sounded like himself again. He's so lucky. It could have —'

Olivia lost patience. 'Jeannie, I'm sorry about Emmet and I'm glad he's okay, but can we please talk about you now? How pregnant are you? When did you find out?'

'Just this week. The doctor said he couldn't be completely sure, because my periods are always all over the place, but he thinks I'm about five months.'

'Five *months*!' Olivia said. 'And you're only telling us now?'

'You didn't *realise* until now?' Maxie said.

'God, it's so great to talk to you both again, you know that?' Her voice grew cold. 'Thanks for nothing. You're the first two people I tell, and what do I get? Only judgement and the third degree. It's like being back in bloody boarding school.'

Maxie stepped in. 'Jeannie, don't get mad. We're shocked, you have to understand that. We're worried about you. How you're going to cope.'

Jeannie's tone turned cheery again. 'Oh, women of little faith. I'm young, fit, healthy. We're supposed to have babies young, aren't we? Didn't you listen to anything during those sex education classes? Come to think of it, did we even have sex education classes? Maybe I was sick that day. I thought I could only get pregnant if I went to the cinema with a boy and let him have his way with me in the back row. No cinema involved in this case. Turns out the nuns were wrong about that as well.'

She laughed loudly. 'Hold on, I need to fill my glass. And yes, it is wine. Aren't I naughty?'

Maxie and Olivia exchanged glances again. Before they could say anything, Jeannie kept talking.

'No, I probably shouldn't be drinking. I'm stopping tomorrow. I know I should be thinking of the baby. I am thinking of the baby. Every day, every minute, every hour. And I will love this baby, and I will look after this baby. And I want this baby, otherwise there are ways I could have avoided having this baby, as I'm sure you also recall from our boarding school days.'

They knew what she was referring to. It had never been discussed openly, but their head prefect had gone missing for a month. On her return a rumour spread that she'd gone away to have an abortion. Whether it was true or not, they'd never known.

Jeannie's voice was falsely cheery again. 'So anyway, I wanted you both to know. I hoped you might be happy for me. Not react like two sour old biddies. I can picture you there, with faces like a slapped arse. Do you like that saying? It's one of Emmet's. The Irish have some excellent sayings.'

Olivia ignored the insult. 'Jeannie, are you okay? I'm not talking about you being pregnant. I'm talking about generally.'

'You seem a bit, I don't know —' Maxie didn't want to use the word manic. 'Up and down.'

Jeannie laughed. It was an unpleasant sound. 'Up and down? As in manic one day, depression the next? Alas, Maxie, I can't be labelled so easily. Would that be better for you both, if you could pop me under that description, give me a handful of pills, file me under Old Mad Friend? Send me and my baby to some crackpot institution, so you don't have to think about me again?'

They both stepped in, talking over each other. Of course not. They'd never abandon her. They loved her. She was their closest friend. They were worried about her. They wanted to help.

As quickly as her temper had risen, it went again. They heard the change in her voice. It became calm. Vulnerable. The gentlest version of the Jeannie they knew.

'I'm sorry, Liv. I'm sorry, Maxie. I'm so scared. I don't know if I can do this. But I don't want to not do it. I mean, maybe it's the best thing that could have happened to me. I love kittens and puppies. A baby is just a human version, isn't it?' She laughed softly. Genuinely. 'I know it will be difficult, but I'll try so hard to make it work. I'm not a career woman, not like you both. But I wanted you to know. I wanted to ask for help, if you want to give it to me. Not money, not that kind of help. Your support. Not out of loyalty, or guilt. I hoped you might think it'd be fun to be part of this little baby's life.'

Olivia burst into tears. Self-possessed Olivia, crying so hard her nose started to run. Beside her, Maxie unexpectedly found herself blinking back tears too.

'Are you both crying?' Jeannie asked. 'Oh, thank you so much. Thank you. I've done all my crying already. I've done nothing but cry about it for the past few weeks.'

'Few weeks? So you haven't just found out?'

'No. It's taken me this long to summon up the courage to tell you. To try to decide what to do. Who else to tell.'

'Jeannie, you have to tell the father. He has to know.'

'I have told him.'

'And what did he say?'

'Well, put it this way, congratulations wasn't at the top of his list.'

'Does he want to be involved?' Olivia asked.

'It's his child too,' Maxie added. 'He chose to be in a relationship with you. He has to support you.'

'He doesn't quite see it that way. And I think calling it a "relationship" might be pushing things.'

'What do you mean? Was it a one-night stand?'

'What do you take me for? Not that there's anything wrong with one-night stands. But yes, it was brief. Short but sweet. Which is another reason why it might be a teensy-weensy bit tricky for me to turn up on his doorstep with a little bundle of joy in my arms.'

'But he has to help you out,' Olivia said. 'Financially or practically. Both.'

'Do you want us to talk to him for you?' Maxie said. 'I can fly down, come with you to see him.'

'Oh, I'm pretty sure he wouldn't appreciate a delegation. But thanks for the offer.'

'But what will you do? You can't bring up a child on your own.'

'Yes, I can. I've even been to social security and investigated my rights. See how organised I am?'

'Jeannie, I've got savings. Of course I'll help you too, but I'm sorry, I don't have a lot.'

'You can have mine too,' Olivia said, 'but long-term, your work, where will you live, all of that?'

'I've decided to move out of Melbourne. It's too expensive. I'm going to go to a country town, somewhere with a good hospital, nice schools, cheap rent. See, I'm responsible *and* organised.'

'Have you told your parents?' Olivia asked.

'Of course!' Jeannie's voice was bright. 'They were so supportive. They think it's wonderful news. They can't wait to meet the baby.'

'Really?' Maxie said. 'But that's fantastic. I thought —'

'Don't be so stupid, Maxie. Of course I haven't told them. I'm not going to.'

'But they need to know too. It will be their grandchild.'

'Olivia, when will you realise my family is not your family? We don't like each other. Or to be more accurate, my father hates me and my mother is ashamed of me. You think they'd leap joyously at this news? That my mother would call her fancy friends and say, "Wonderful news. Not only was Jean nearly a jailbird, but now she's having an illegitimate child! I'm so proud of her!"'

For the rest of the call, Olivia and Maxie did all they could to assure Jeannie they'd help as much as they could. Visit as soon as they could. Did she need anything now? Did she have enough money? She insisted she was fine.

They kept in touch constantly from then on, with phone calls several times a week. Jeannie moved to a country town, as she'd said she would. It was north of Melbourne, in the goldfields. She rented, cheaply, a two-room flat at the back of a bigger house in the town. She struck it lucky. The elderly couple who owned the flat were kind, understanding, non-judgemental.

'I think they're religious. Possibly Quakers,' Jeannie told Maxie and Olivia. 'They're very quiet and un-nosy. That's not normal, is it?'

It was Mrs Quaker, as Jeannie always called her, who rang Olivia to say Jeannie had gone into labour, two weeks earlier than expected. It was Mr Quaker who rang again to say it had been fast, that Jeannie had only been in the small hospital for two hours before the baby arrived. His wife was in there with her now. 'It's a girl. A beautiful little girl.'

Olivia and Maxie flew to Melbourne the next day, drove a hire car for two hours and met the beautiful little girl. Jeannie had already named her. Eliza Maxine Olivia Miller.

Jeannie smiled up at them, her baby daughter asleep in her arms. 'I appointed you joint godmothers in your absence. I hoped you wouldn't mind. I tossed a coin to see whose name went first.'

They were thrilled. They didn't care about the order of their names. They took turns holding the tiny baby. Mrs Quaker – whose first name was Elizabeth – was there too. Maxie and Olivia immediately noticed the bond between her and Jeannie. Elizabeth was so touched to have the baby named after her, she told them, her face glowing.

'I was tempted to name her after your husband too,' Jeannie said, smiling. 'Eliza-Douglas.'

After two days with her, Maxie and Olivia returned to Sydney surprisingly content. It truly felt as though everything would be all right for Jeannie and her baby. They were further buoyed by regular phone calls, by the photos Jeannie sent every couple of weeks: Eliza in different poses, sleeping, crying, always with that funny cross expression. They came back to Victoria for her christening, staying with Elizabeth and Douglas. It turned out Jeannie was right. They were Quakers. They were there for her first birthday party too. It was a happy occasion. Eliza had become a very smiley baby. They'd never seen Jeannie so happy.

'Thank you for being so kind to Jeannie and Eliza,' Olivia said to Elizabeth and Douglas privately that weekend.

'It's the easiest thing we've ever done,' Elizabeth said. 'Life was dull before they came along. They're welcome with us for as long as they want to stay.'

And perhaps everything would have been different if Jeannie and Eliza had stayed there, Olivia thought now. If Mr and Mrs Quaker hadn't decided to take that daytrip to Melbourne two weeks after Eliza's first birthday, heading off after breakfast in their reliable old Toyota. If the driver of the semitrailer on the same highway had slept more the previous week, and not taken caffeine tablets to keep him awake. If he hadn't decided to light his cigarette at the moment that he was coming abreast with the Quakers' car. If he hadn't sideswiped them, killing Mr Quaker outright, giving Mrs Quaker severe brain injuries, putting her into hospital for the next two months until she died of complications caused by a bacterial infection. If their next of kin, a grand-niece in Toronto, hadn't instructed the family solicitors to put their house on the market immediately. If Jeannie, and little Eliza, hadn't been given their notice and had to move not just house but towns, when nothing cheap enough was available where they were. The first of many moves, many new towns, many new houses, over the next sixteen years.

Did Eliza know any of that story? Olivia wondered now. Or had Jeannie told her some of it, embroidered other parts, or made up an entirely different story instead? There was no way of knowing, she realised. Not until the three of them sat down together and talked.

# CHAPTER EIGHTEEN

Maxie was alone in the cottage in the Highlands. Hazel had driven to the nearest town for supplies and to check her work emails. The phone coverage was very patchy, they'd discovered.

It had been a wonderful honeymoon so far. Not that Maxie had another to compare it to, but theirs had felt enchanted. The cottage was in the wildest of locations but was filled with such luxurious contents. They'd enjoyed delicious food and wine every evening. Early nights and sleep-ins. Days of fresh air and walking. They were treasuring every lungful of that fresh Highlands air, talking so often about what their lives would be like soon in New York.

Maxie hadn't only been thinking about New York. She knew Hazel had noticed how preoccupied she sometimes was. How anxious she was about the conversation she'd soon be having with Eliza and Olivia.

'What did you think of Eliza?' Maxie had asked as they drove to the cottage on their wedding night.

'I liked her very much,' Hazel said. 'She's smart. Witty. She loves you both dearly.'

'We love her dearly back,' Maxie had replied.

Over the following days, she'd tried to imagine Eliza's reaction once she'd heard what they had to tell her. Would it be tears? Anger? An icy silence?

Hazel tried to keep her calm. 'You might have it completely wrong. Eliza didn't strike me as the melodramatic type.'

'Are you saying I am?'

Hazel diplomatically didn't answer that.

Perhaps it was due to being on her own in the cottage for the morning, having all this time to think, but Maxie couldn't stop going over every detail of Eliza's life. Should she and Olivia have stepped in earlier? Would it have even been possible? What could they have done?

They could see it all so much more clearly now, now it was far too late. But it hadn't ever been easy. Jeannie had always insisted she was managing, that she was getting enough work, that her part-time earnings alongside her pension were enough.

She and Olivia sent her what they could. Even so, their cheques were often not cashed. They sent parcels as often as possible instead. Books and clothes for Eliza. Treats for Jeannie, too. They were rarely acknowledged, but the two of them persevered, ringing her at least once a week. So much began to happen in their own lives. Maxie landed a key role on her popular soap opera. Olivia graduated top of her year in art history, and was offered a full-time job in the gallery she'd worked weekends in throughout university. Their weekly phone calls became fort-nightly calls, then monthly calls.

But they still tried to visit Jeannie and Eliza, even if only for a night or two. They'd arrive with more gifts, spoil Eliza, gen-uinely delighting in their goddaughter: how tall she was getting, how sweet she was, how clever she was. They'd try not to show how surprised they were by how shabby the rental flat or house was, or to appear shocked when Jeannie told them that she'd decided to move yet again. They liked the change in scenery, she always told them. She and Eliza might not be able to travel the world together yet, but they could travel around Australia, couldn't they?

It was only when they visited the year Eliza was eleven, for her school concert, that Jeannie told them she moved so often to avoid being arrested for shoplifting and burglary. When, fuelled by too much wine, they all spoke more than they had for years, as if they were back in the time of middle-of-the-night conversations and confidences whispered in their boarding school dormitory.

Maxie had admired a tall green vase in the kitchen and asked where Jeannie had got it.

'I stole it,' Jeannie said cheerily. 'From the house beside the school, two towns ago. The owners worked full-time. It was easy.'

They'd laughed, thinking she was joking. Then stopped laugh-ing when they realised she wasn't.

Jeannie started pointing out different objects in the kitchen and living room. Telling them when and from where she'd taken them. Shops sometimes. Usually private homes.

'Where was Eliza when you were doing this?' Olivia asked, trying to hide her alarm.

'With me, obviously. I trained her from an early age how to undo window locks and slither through tiny spaces. The best little accomplice I could hope for.' She laughed. 'You should see your faces.'

'Are you joking?' Maxie said. 'You are joking, aren't you?'

'Of course I am. I'm not that bad a mother. I did all my stealing while she was having her nap. For the first five years, you could set your clock by her. Asleep every day from eleven a.m. until two p.m. A bomb could go off and she'd sleep through it.'

'Jeannie, stop messing around,' Olivia said.

'What if something had happened while she was home on her own?' Maxie said.

She turned on them. Like a tropical storm, blue skies one moment, wild wind and rain the next. 'Don't you both fucking preach to me about what's right or wrong. I did what I had to do, because it was just the two of us, and I never did anything that could bring harm to her. Ever.'

'But what if she woke up and you weren't there?'

'It never happened. She never did.'

'But you don't know that.'

'I do know. It never happened.'

'But stealing, Jeannie. That's wrong.'

'No! Having more than you need when people around you are hungry or unable to sleep at night because they're so worried about food or rent or buying clothes – *that's* wrong. And nothing

I stole was ever too valuable, or too personal. Half the time I don't think they even noticed what was missing, they had so much. I was selective.'

'But what if you were caught?'

'I never was.'

'But what if you *had* been, Jeannie? If you'd been sent to jail? What would have happened to Eliza?'

Jeannie laughed then. Too loudly. 'You should see your faces. It's as if I've told you I'm secretly Wonder Woman.'

'Wonder Woman wasn't a thief.' Maxie said it before she could stop herself. She'd had more wine than usual. She tensed, waiting for Jeannie to flare up at her again.

Jeannie just laughed. 'You're right, Maxie, of course,' she said. 'Imagine that being phoned through to a country cop station. "I think someone robbed my house." "Can you describe them, madam?" "Yes, she was wearing a low-cut red top, a short blue skirt covered in stars, and red, shiny thigh-high boots. Oh, and a gold amulet in her hair."' She took a sip of her wine. 'Look, calm down, would you both? No one was hurt. I only took things that were small or easy to sell on. I kept a few things – that vase, for example. A few books now and then. You wouldn't believe how much some people have. Cupboards full of toys their kids will never play with. Shelves and shelves full of books. Pantries full of food.'

'But how did you break in?' Maxie was trying to appear calm. She wasn't.

'I didn't have to.' Jeannie grinned. 'One of the joys of

country living. Everyone trusts everyone. No one locks their door. I'd save up a pile of leaflets from the post, make sure Eliza was fast asleep, then go off on my rounds. Knock on the front door, then on the back door. No answer, in I'd go. I'd be out again in five minutes. I never did any damage, broke anything. I took what I needed for us, or what I could sell easily. A necklace, or anything gold. Silverware was surprisingly lucrative. That was also a great thing about country towns. Several generations, heirlooms handed down. And let me tell you, girls, those snooty antique dealers aren't as ethical as you might expect.'

Olivia and Maxie were now speechless.

'Anyway, I was a communist back then, so it was okay in terms of my ethics,' Jeannie continued, topping up their glasses. 'Property belongs to all.'

'That's communism?'

'Communism Jeannie Miller–style, yep.' She sat back then, looking from one to the other. 'Oh, if you could only see your faces.'

'What do you mean?'

'You believed me, didn't you? That I would leave my baby daughter, the absolute light of my life, on her own while I went sneaking around a country town, where everybody knows each other, where people notice if a fly from out of town happens to buzz in. Yet I somehow managed to gaily flit in and out, stealing family heirlooms and fluffy toys?' She began to laugh, the laugh Olivia and Maxie now hated hearing. 'I wish I had done it. It's a fucking ingenious idea, actually.'

She picked up the blue bowl. 'Maxie, I bought this in a charity shop. It cost me two dollars. And I bought that in a charity shop' – she pointed to the sofa – 'and those curtains. And my food? I bought that with money I saved from my pension, or money I earned in the part-time job I got while Eliza was in crèche, like thousands of other single mothers before me. Will I run through my CV for you now? Hospital cleaner. Filing clerk. And currently the finest shelf-stacker in all the land. See these hands?' She held them up. 'They can stack twenty cans on a single shelf faster than you can say Beanz Meanz Heinz.' She laughed again. 'More fool me, in hindsight. Being Australia's answer to Robin Hood would have been far more lucrative.'

They tried to laugh it off that night. It wasn't easy. They really had believed her. They still weren't entirely convinced it was made up. But in an unspoken agreement they decided to let it go.

It was the next night, their final night, that they proposed the godmother holiday plan. After years of asking, they also persuaded Jeannie to share her bank account details. The excuse they gave was that they'd put money into it before each holiday, for Jeannie to buy Eliza any special items of clothing needed for the different destinations. They hoped it would be easier for her to accept their help that way.

They left early on the final morning, driving back towards the city together to catch their planes. They talked for the entire car journey. About Eliza, first. They'd both felt such a bond with her. They tried to imagine what her father might have looked like.

Who he might have been. They talked about all they'd done with her over that long weekend, as well as the concert. They'd read with her, cooked, walked around the small town. They'd felt how proud she was to be walking down the main street with her godmothers, especially one who was a little bit famous. They hugged her tightly as they left and received big hugs back. 'I'm so glad you're my godmothers,' she'd said.

Then they talked about Jeannie. With affection. Concern. About her restless energy. Her unpredictability. The elaborate stories. They tried convincing themselves that she was fine, that she was living life the way she wanted to live it. It was so clear how much she adored Eliza. How much Eliza adored her back. They were such a team. And no, it wasn't a conventional life, but Jeannie had never wanted a conventional life, had she? And yes, she had drunk too much over the weekend, but if she couldn't let her hair down with her two oldest friends, when could she? They'd drunk a lot while they were there, too.

The years had passed. They continued to salve their consciences with those bank deposits and the twice-yearly trips for Eliza. They had been no hardship at all. They'd both begun to earn more money than they needed. They also truly loved Eliza. That little earnest girl had grown into a lovely, clever, shy but curious teenager. She was so polite. Helpful. Eager to please. Too eager, sometimes.

Sometimes it worried them that she was so much Jeannie's opposite. But they were always reassured by the obvious love between mother and daughter. They always got Eliza to ring

Jeannie as soon as she arrived at her holiday destination, and to ring her the night before she left. Never in between. Jeannie insisted. She wanted to hear all the trip details when Eliza was home again, not drip-fed in daily phone calls. But even so, if they were staying somewhere with a fax machine or, later, a computer, Eliza would receive surprise messages from her mother.

*Dearest Best Daughter in the Entire World,* she'd write. *I hope you are having the holiday of a lifetime. Don't forget me, will you? Your adoring mother xxxxxxxxxxxxxxxxxxxxxxxxx xxxxxxxx* one of them read. The kisses covered two pages.

Maxie had often been reminded of something they'd said to Jeannie all those years before, when they first proposed the annual godmother holidays. That Jeannie was so lucky to have a daughter, that perhaps they might not ever be so lucky. That Eliza might be the closest thing they'd ever have to a daughter. It had come true.

Maxie would have gone down the IVF route if she had met Hazel ten years earlier, when she was in her forties, but it was too late now. She knew Olivia would love to have had a daughter of her own too. That hadn't proved possible for her and Edgar. Eliza had filled such a big space in their lives. What would they have done without her all these years? What would Eliza have done without them?

She heard the sound of a car. Hazel had returned. Maxie stepped outside, smiling, glad that she was no longer alone with her thoughts.

Hazel didn't smile back. 'I checked my emails.'

'You've been nominated for a BAFTA?'

Hazel shook her head and told her what the email said. It wasn't good news.

# CHAPTER NINETEEN

By Friday night, Eliza had realised something surprising. She was enjoying working with Celine.

If she'd been back with Gillian, trying to satisfy a client as tricky as Celine, she'd have been starting early, finishing very late. Making long lists. Spending any free time worrying. Not here. It was unpaid work, yes, but she was making progress. The two rooms were definitely getting tidier. She was standing up to Celine more and more. Yesterday, Celine had even begrudgingly thanked her.

Her life felt different in other ways too. There was no going home to a quiet, solitary apartment. No searching for films or books to fill her hours. She didn't seem to have spare hours. Sullivan messaged constantly. Whenever Alex or Rory visited Celine's suite to deliver room service, they stayed to chat. Maxie sent a photo each day of the Highland walks she and Hazel were doing.

Rose had noticed a change in her when they spoke that morning. Eliza almost sounded relaxed, she said. It was doing her good to be away. They swapped stories, Eliza about Celine, Rose about Harry and their kids. They talked about Eliza's god-mothers. How every day she was thinking of new questions to ask them.

Each night Eliza met Olivia for a drink, followed by dinner. Tonight, rather than eat in the hotel restaurant, they were dining in an Italian trattoria three streets away. Olivia had arranged to meet her there at eight, after she'd been to visit Edgar.

The air was cool as Eliza set off from the hotel, along Haymarket Terrace. The restaurant was lively. As she took her seat at their reserved table, her phone beeped. Sullivan, of course. She played a word. He played one back. The winning one. He won most of their games. A message appeared. *Commiserations again, FF! Better luck next time*. Moments later, he'd started a new game.

Olivia had asked her if she was finding his constant messaging too much. No, she'd said truthfully.

She checked her watch now. Five to eight. The restaurant door opened, a cold breeze eddying in. It wasn't Olivia. It was Lawrence. He didn't see her. She watched as the maître d' gave him a warm welcome. He was obviously a regular. As they stood talking, she had the chance to study him.

She'd described Alex and Rory to Rose. Alex, with his charm, good looks, styled hair and tailored suits, clearly spent time on his appearance. Rory was the opposite. His clothes never quite seemed to fit. His hair defied gravity. How would she describe Lawrence? The word 'solemn' came to mind. He was about her height, with that greying but still dark hair. A solid build. There was something old-fashioned about him, she decided, even though he was only a few years older than Alex and Rory. As if he'd stepped out of a black-and-white film.

He took a seat on the other side of the restaurant. She waited for him to notice her but his attention was on a folder of paperwork. He was interrupted by an older woman. The owner's wife, Eliza guessed. As she told a story, he laughed. It completely changed his face. He looked quite —

'Eliza, darling, I'm sorry. The traffic was terrible.' It was Olivia, taking off her coat, waving across to the head waiter, who clearly knew her. 'Have you got a drink? Paolo, sparkling water for my goddaughter and a glass of red for me, please.' She spotted Lawrence. 'Look who's here.' She went across to him. They exchanged a few words, then looked over at Eliza. She raised a hand in greeting.

Olivia returned. 'He might join us for coffee later. He insisted he's having a working dinner. If I didn't benefit so much from his dedication, I'd worry he was a workaholic. Now, let me order for us.'

The waiter was solicitous. The chef himself came out after their starters. Eliza found herself enjoying the attention that came with being in Olivia's orbit. It had been like this when she was younger too.

As they waited for their main course, Olivia raised her glass. 'I'm sorry, I neglected the toast. To you, Eliza. For saving our bacon when it came to Celine. I don't even care if it's temporary.'

Over their main course, Eliza asked after Edgar.

'Just the same,' Olivia said, her tone deceptively cheery.

'What is the same?' Eliza asked.

'Oh, I sit down beside him, and we chat, and I fill him in on everything that has been happening with the hotel, and the boys, and Celine, and our occupancy rates, and —' Her voice broke. 'And my poor darling Edgar doesn't take in a word. I don't even know if he hears me any more.'

Eliza reached for her godmother's hand. 'I'm so sorry.'

Olivia's usual poise seemed to falter. 'I miss him so much, Eliza. He's there, he still looks like himself, but it's not him. And I try to pretend, and keep talking to him, but sometimes it's so hard.' A pause, as if Olivia was deciding whether to be truthful or not. 'I know you never saw the best of him. But he was such a wonderful husband. He built the hotel into the place it is today. It's his legacy. But I don't know if either of his sons are ready to take over as general manager. Or if either of them should.'

Eliza was unused to Olivia being so open. 'But they're both good workers, aren't they?'

'They do the bare minimum. Enough to be paid. Sometimes it's a blessing that Edgar doesn't know what's going on with them both. He'd have never understood Rory's business idea. Jigsaw puzzles, of all things. As for Alex and his hostel, if Edgar knew even half of what he's up to —'

'What is he up to?'

Olivia hesitated, then told her about Alex stealing from the Montgomery to stock the hostel's bar. 'I'm sorry, Eliza. It's not fair to download on you like this. But I keep dreading that Lawrence will give Deirdre his notice and we'll be forced to decide between Alex and Rory. His contract ended four months ago.' She sighed. 'Perhaps I should just ask him outright tonight what his plans are. Except I don't want to hear what —'

Her phone rang, interrupting the conversation. 'Hazel?' Her expression grew serious. 'Oh my God. Poor Maxie. I know, plaster for weeks. Yes, talk to the doctor. I'll wait.'

Maxie was in hospital in Glasgow with a broken ankle. She and Hazel had been hill-walking when she slipped and fell. She'd been flown to hospital in Glasgow in the rescue helicopter. She was just out of the operating theatre now.

Hazel came back on. Olivia sympathised again. 'Give her our love. We'll be there first thing tomorrow.'

Hazel met them in the hospital reception early the next morning. It was only an hour's drive from Edinburgh. Hazel looked exhausted but relieved to see them. She led them up to Maxie's private room on the fourth floor.

Maxie attempted a smile as they came in. 'Nothing like a memorable honeymoon to kickstart a marriage,' she said. There was a bandage on her forehead, bruising visible too.

They both leaned in and hugged her, careful to avoid the protective frame over her right leg.

'You look terrible,' Olivia said.

'I know,' Maxie said. 'Married life suits me.'

She and Hazel described the fall, Maxie's foot wedged between two rocks, the bad cut to her head. There had been a lot of blood.

'We were so lucky, though,' Hazel said. 'The hill rescue team was on a training run nearby. They were packing up when they got the call. Got to us within half an hour.'

'Another fifty metres up and we mightn't have had phone reception,' Maxie said. 'It was my own stupid fault. I'm too old to be leaping from rock to rock. Without proper walking boots too.'

'On the bright side, not every honeymooning couple gets a trip in a rescue helicopter,' Hazel said.

Maxie squeezed her hand. 'We'd had other bad news too. Hazel's been called to New York early. She has to leave tomorrow. But what do I do now?'

'You come to me, of course,' Olivia said. 'The Montgomery convalescent home. For as long as you need, until you're fit enough to fly to New York.'

'Oh, Liv, I was going to ask if —'

'You don't have to ask. Of course you can.'

Hazel spoke then. 'And I keep telling her she has to stop worrying about packing up the flat. I'm going to call New York today to delay my trip. Go down and start packing tomorrow.'

'You can't, Hazel,' Maxie said. 'You have to be in New York tomorrow.'

'I'll have to tell them I can't. Our only other option is a moving firm and I know you hate that idea —'

'I really hate that idea. The flat's not even half-organised. I can't let complete strangers do it, going through our photos, our clothes —'

'I can do it,' Eliza said.

Maxie turned. 'Sorry?'

'I'll go to London and pack it up for you. I can arrange the shipping too.'

'Eliza, you can't,' Maxie said. 'It's in such a mess.'

'I love messes. Cleaning them up, at least. I could send you photos of everything and you could tell me what stays in the flat and what belongs to you both. I'd bring back anything you need now, and ship the rest to New York.'

'Eliza, that's a brainwave!' Olivia said. 'Hazel, Maxie, what do you think?'

Hazel agreed instantly and gratefully. Maxie burst into tears. For real, again.

# CHAPTER TWENTY

By the time Olivia was driving back into Edinburgh, Eliza had already researched removal companies and was waiting on three quotes for shipping household effects to New York. She'd booked the sleeper train from Edinburgh to London that night. Maxie had insisted on paying for it.

'How great to see Eliza-in-Action,' Olivia said, glancing over with a smile. 'I'll break the news to Celine later. After your train has left, so you don't have to hear the screeching.'

Eliza's phone rang. It was Rory, inviting her to visit his workshop that afternoon if she was free. Olivia urged her to go. The train didn't leave until nearly midnight.

Moments after she'd made the arrangements with Rory, her phone pinged. It was Sullivan, playing a word. She played one back. A message from him appeared.

*Excellent word placement, Eliza! What are your plans for today?*

*I'm going to see a jigsaw puzzle workshop. It belongs to Olivia's stepson Rory.*

*You lucky thing! I LOVE jigsaw puzzles! Is there any possibility I could come too??? Please??*

Eliza rang Rory. He was more than happy for Sullivan to join them. She messaged Ann-Marie and got the go-ahead from her too. She'd just started to message Sullivan when her phone pinged.

*Thank you so much, Eliza!! (I'm sitting beside Ann-Marie.) See you soon!*

Eliza met Rory in front of the hotel. He was wearing paint-spattered jeans and a baggy jumper, his fair hair in tufts. He led her over to a small van. They collected Sullivan on the way. His father and stepmother Sophie's house was in an exclusive part of Edinburgh.

Eliza pressed the polished brass doorbell. Sullivan opened it instantly, Ann-Marie behind him.

'Ready when you are, Eliza. See you later, Ann-Marie!'

Eliza promised Ann-Marie that Sullivan would be home by six.

'Teatime,' Sullivan said. 'Perhaps I could have a bite to eat with you and Rory before you drop me home? I'm sure Dad won't mind. Ann-Marie, could you please ring him and check?'

'He's operating this afternoon, Sullivan,' she said.

'But not until later. Please, Ann-Marie?'

She phoned, spoke, then held out the phone. 'Eliza, would you mind?'

Sullivan's father introduced himself in a cultured Australian accent. He sounded distracted. 'My son isn't annoying you, I hope?'

Eliza assured him Sullivan was great company.

'Good to hear, thank you, Eliza,' Sullivan's father said. He hung up first.

As they drove away, Eliza didn't think she'd imagined the look of relief on Ann-Marie's face.

Sullivan peppered Rory with questions throughout the short journey. Eliza learned that Rory had got the idea for his hand-made jigsaws three years earlier, after shopping with his girlfriend, Milly, for a birthday present for her young nephew. She'd wanted something colourful, sturdy. Locally made. Unsuccessful, they stopped for lunch at a pub. On the napkin, he'd sketched exactly what she wanted – colourful animals, one for each letter of the alphabet, all interlinked. He spent the next week finding the materials. Asked around and found a retired carpenter to help him. A fortnight later, he'd presented Milly with a handpainted wooden jigsaw puzzle. She loved it. Her nephew adored it. Within days, Rory was asked to make more – for sale – for their friends and families too. That led to craft markets in Edinburgh,

Glasgow and beyond. He'd even sold some of his puzzles in Berlin, he told them, when he was visiting Milly.

'And is it financially viable, Rory?' Sullivan asked as they drove into a small industrial estate. 'You don't need to divulge figures. I'm just curious about such a labour-intensive enterprise.'

Rory exchanged an amused glance with Eliza. 'Not yet, Sullivan. But one day, I hope.'

'All the best with it,' Sullivan said as he hopped out of the van.

The workshop was at the back of the estate. Eliza's first impression was the smell – a combination of sawdust, paint and thinners. The unit was divided into different 'zones', Rory explained. The cutting area, painting area, drying racks and packing area. After the artwork was painted, each piece was cut into puzzle shapes with the fretsaw. Each puzzle was presented in a calico bag.

Rory told them he sometimes used a computer to do his designs, or if he was trying out colour combinations. But most of his work involved paint and pencils. He found that the most satisfying.

'Give it a try, Sullivan.' He handed him an A4 piece of plywood. 'Draw your favourite animal.'

As Sullivan drew, Rory and Eliza tried to guess it. A monkey? A squirrel? Finally, after Sullivan drew black lines on a long bushy tail, Eliza got it. A ring-tailed lemur.

'My lifelong ambition is to go to Madagascar and see one in the wild,' Sullivan said. 'In the meantime, I visit them in zoos.

Edinburgh Zoo has a particularly lovely group. Or a particularly lovely *conspiracy* of lemurs, I should say, to use the correct and marvellous collective term. Eliza, would you like to visit them with me? Perhaps we could go there tomorrow?'

'Sullivan, I'm sorry, but I have to go to London for a few days.'

'When you get back? We could take a picnic and make a day of it?'

It was very hard to say no to Sullivan, she was discovering. Yes, when she got back, she promised.

'Now, the painting,' Rory said, handing Sullivan a tray of paints. 'There's plenty of spare wood if you'd like to do one too, Eliza?'

'Please, Eliza!' Sullivan said. 'You too, Rory. Not to be competitive – to share in the fun of working on a creative project together.'

'Well, Eliza?' Rory said. 'Shall we share in the fun of working on a creative project together?'

Several minutes later, they were painting side-by-side at the table. The workshop fell quiet. Sullivan was busy adding golden eyes to his lemur. Rory was drawing a boat in full sail on a blue sea.

Eliza had thought about it, then begun to draw the tall green vase that had belonged to her mother. She didn't need to have it in front of her, she realised. She had drawn it so many times over the past thirteen years. She used a mixture of light and dark shades of green paint to give it shape and definition. She added a quartet of red roses in full bloom, mixing deep crimson with lighter pinks for the petal detail, more shades of green for the leaves. The feeling of total absorption in her work was as familiar and comforting as ever.

His lemur done, Sullivan looked over at her painting. 'Eliza, that's wonderful! You're an actual artist!'

Rory agreed. 'You've got a real gift. I should hire you to do a whole flower range.'

They helped Rory lay their paintings onto the trays to dry. He'd do the next steps – the cutting and varnishing – later that week, he said, and give them to Eliza when they were ready. He showed them some of his other finished puzzles. An ocean scene, with the pieces cut into the shape of fish. A city scene, the pieces in car shapes. They were about to leave when Rory took an uncut puzzle from the drying rack, set the fretsaw working and slowly, methodically, cut it into pieces. It was the letter S.

'There you are, Sullivan,' he said, giving it to him. 'Your own S-for-Sullivan jigsaw puzzle.'

Sullivan's smile lit up the workshop.

An hour later, they were in a nearby café. They'd just had fish and chips. Sullivan was now scraping at the last mouthfuls of a bowl of ice cream. He finished and sighed happily.

'I always wanted days like this with my parents. You two are more fun. You haven't fought once.'

'It probably helps that we're not married,' Eliza said.

'Or your parents,' Rory added.

'Tell me about your parents, Rory?' Sullivan asked.

'Well, my dad's name is Edgar Montgomery. My mother was called Ruth but sadly she died when I was younger than you. Since I was eleven, I've had a stepmother called Olivia.'

'My godmother,' Eliza added. 'The lady you met the other day.'

'Two mothers in one lifetime,' Sullivan said. 'Which was your favourite?'

'Sullivan!' Eliza admonished.

Rory didn't seem to mind. 'I loved my mother because she's my mother, Sullivan. I was very sad when she died. But Olivia's always been kind to me. I love her too in a different way.'

'And which of your mothers did your father love the most?'

'Sullivan!' Eliza said. 'Rory, I'm sorry.'

'It's fine, Eliza. He loved them both, Sullivan. I don't remember him fighting with either of them.'

'He wouldn't remember now either, would he? I heard about his dementia. I'm very sorry.'

Eliza gave up trying to step in. Rory seemed comfortable enough answering any questions.

'I'm actually not sure he even knows who I am any more. Or what's happening around him.'

'So you could do whatever you like and he wouldn't know?' Sullivan said.

'Well, I suppose that's one way of looking at it.'

Eliza got up to pay the bill, before Sullivan turned his laser questioning on her. On her return, she gathered up her coat. 'Time we got you home, Sullivan.'

'But we're getting on so well,' he said.

'If we want to have that zoo trip together, we need to stay in your father's good books.'

He stood up immediately. 'Good thinking, Eliza,' he said.

Eliza walked him up to the front door at seven p.m. He rang the bell once. Twice.

The door was opened by a woman in her thirties, pretty, with long dark hair. 'Sullivan, you're back.' She had an English accent. 'I wasn't expecting you this early.'

'We're right on time as it happens, Sophie.' He introduced Eliza to his stepmother. 'Eliza has offered to take me to the zoo next week. As long as she gets permission, of course.'

Sophie ignored that. 'I hope he was good today?' she asked Eliza.

'The epitome of good behaviour,' Eliza said, smiling. 'Sorry, his great vocabulary is catching.'

Sophie didn't react. 'Sullivan, go and get ready for bed. One hour on screens. No more.'

He gave a boyish whoop and ran towards the stairs, stopped, then ran back. He flung his arms around Eliza with sudden force.

'That was a fantastic outing, Eliza, thank you. I can't wait for our zoo visit. Enjoy London.'

He ran past her again, up the stairs and out of sight. Sophie waited, then lowered her voice.

'Thank you. I can't tell you how much I needed a break.' She rolled her eyes. 'All those questions! You do know he's obsessed with lemurs? Dean had to take him to the zoo three times last year.'

Eliza found herself feeling defensive. 'I've never met a kid like him. He's great fun.'

'He's unique, all right.' Her tone wasn't complimentary. There was a sudden sound of a whimpering baby behind her. She reached into her pocket and took out a business card. 'My mobile's on that. If you can't get hold of Dean to organise anything with Sullivan any time, ring me instead. I'll always say yes, believe me.'

'But you don't even know me.'

'Dean and I googled you. You were a conference organiser in Melbourne. You graduated with honours from Melbourne University. You're also Olivia Montgomery's goddaughter. Everyone in Edinburgh knows Edgar Montgomery. It's sad, isn't it? Such a cruel disease.' The baby started wailing. Sophie winced at the sound. 'Feeding time. Again. It's always feeding time.'

She shut the door in Eliza's face.

Eliza returned to the van where Rory was waiting. She thanked him for being so kind to Sullivan. Then she said something that she'd wanted to say to him since she arrived.

'I'm sorry about your mother, Rory.'

'I'm sorry about your mother too, Eliza.'

They drove for a few minutes in silence, then he turned to her again.

'Do you remember much about her?' he asked.

A lot, she told him. She had seventeen years' worth of memories. She hesitated, then asked him the same question.

'Hardly anything,' he said. 'I was only six when she died. Alex remembers her much more clearly. I think that's why he was always angrier at Olivia than I was. He saw her as an imposter. I was happy to have a kind lady in the house who liked making me meals and reading to me.'

The mental picture of two little motherless boys, sad Rory and angry Alex, had her blinking away sudden tears. 'It must have been so hard for you both.'

He gave her that sweet, sad smile. 'It was hard for us all, Eliza,' he said.

# CHAPTER TWENTY-ONE

Eliza's overnight train to London was leaving at 11.40 p.m. Olivia drove her to Waverley Station. They took a seat in the waiting area, under the ornate glass dome. On the walls were hanging flower baskets. The station had a feel of old-fashioned adventure. They could hear a mixture of accents and languages around them: Scottish, English, American, German.

'Promise me you won't spend all the time packing?' Olivia said. 'I know you've got a tight deadline to clear the flat, but please try to do some sightseeing, won't you?'

Eliza nodded. 'And Maxie will definitely be here when I get back?'

'All going well with her recovery, yes. Her surgeon sounds happy.' She reached for Eliza's hand and squeezed it. 'I know this waiting is hard. But we'll give you all the answers we can soon, I promise.'

Olivia spent a few minutes with her on the train, admiring

the luxurious cabin, the tiny bathroom, the comfortable bed and crisp linen. She only admitted then that Celine hadn't taken the news of Eliza's London trip well.

'Put it this way. She said she hopes you choke on the London smog. She also didn't like it when I reminded her that London hadn't had serious smog for decades.'

A whistle blew. Olivia waited on the platform until the train left.

Minutes later, she was getting into her car again when her phone rang. It was Maxie.

'Liv, I've just remembered something! The postcards are still in the study. What if Eliza finds them?'

'Of course she'll find them, Maxie. She's doing your packing. But it doesn't matter, does it? Don't we want her to read them?'

'Yes, but not yet. I didn't get the chance to go through them all first.'

'Maxie, we can't know if anything on them is true anyway. And Eliza grew up with Jeannie, remember. She knows more about her habit of exaggeration than anyone.'

'But these aren't only tall tales about possible fathers. Would you want Alex or Rory knowing what you got up to in your twenties?'

Olivia's answer was instant. 'Not in a million years.'

'Should we at least warn her they're there? I think we should. Though I'm not sure I can do it. I think I'd only get upset.'

Olivia bit her tongue. Maxie managed to get out of doing a lot of things for fear of getting upset.

'I'll phone her tomorrow,' she said.

*

Eliza's train arrived on time into Euston Station. There was a touch of mist outside but already the promise of a bright spring day.

She'd been to London once before on holiday with Olivia. They'd had ten days of tourist sights – Madame Tussauds, a London bus tour, a West End musical. Even a trip on the muddy Thames. As she stepped out of the station, it felt exotic and familiar at once.

Maxie had given her directions, instructions and an envelope of money. 'Take cabs if you want, darling,' she'd insisted. 'Hang the expense.' Eliza had liked hearing that phrase from her too.

She decided to take the Tube. She'd mapped out her route. Hazel and Maxie's flat was near Hyde Park, off Park Lane. Such a wonderful location, Maxie had told her. Hazel walked to work most nights. Maxie had run around Hyde Park most mornings. Some mornings. 'Well, once,' she said.

Eliza emerged at Green Park Station. Rather than use Google Maps, she followed Maxie's written directions. Walk along Piccadilly, then up Down Street. Follow the roads around to Shepherd Street. It was a quiet pocket of shops and restaurants, a cobbled street, half sun-lit, half in shade on this spring morning.

Their flat was on the third floor of a narrow terrace with a bright blue front door. She let herself in and took the steps to their level. She opened the door, deactivated the alarm and looked around.

It was compact but light-filled, with a galley kitchen, living room and bathroom with a big bath. One double bedroom, another small room being used as a study. An extremely messy study. There were bright paintings on every wall. Framed photographs too. Dozens showing Hazel and Maxie in different places – in restaurants, on beaches, in cities. The photo Eliza had sent Maxie, the one taken after her school concert. Every shelf was crammed. Every cupboard full.

A lot of work needed to be done. It would take her two full days at least. She couldn't wait to get started.

By lunchtime, she'd already made good progress. She'd begun in the kitchen, photographing items for Maxie, sending them and getting swift replies about what belonged to her and Hazel and what needed to stay in the flat. Crockery. Glassware. Vases. *Yes. No. Yes. Yes. No. No.* She stopped for a quick lunch, before taking down the paintings in the living room then starting to pack the books.

Sunshine was streaming through the windows, shaped into slices of light by the wooden shutters. She'd turned the radio to a classical station, enjoying the gentle music and smooth-voiced presenters. It was only when she checked the time on her phone that she saw she'd missed two calls from Olivia. She phoned her back, apologising.

'Is everything okay? Is Maxie all right?'

'She's fine. I'm at the hospital with her now. She's waiting to see her surgeon.' She hesitated. 'Eliza, when you start packing up Maxie's study, you'll come across something. And Maxie and I both want to . . . not warn you, but prepare you. It's to do with Jeannie. Something Maxie was putting together for you. As an eighteenth birthday present.'

Eliza remained quiet.

'Photos of the three of us. School reports, that kind of thing.' A pause. 'Eliza, you know your mother wasn't like everyone else. She really was one in a million.'

'Yes,' Eliza said.

'She loved socialising. Flirting. Men loved her too. It was a bit of a game for her, I think, when she was travelling. She loved writing to us about them all. Look, for all we know Jeannie was making it all up, to amuse us. She loved telling stories. You know that better than anyone. She used to send us postcards about her adventures. A few every week. She must have sent dozens —'

'Dozens of postcards?' Eliza interrupted. 'You've had them all this time? And not shown me?'

Olivia hadn't expected that reaction. 'We were waiting for the right time, Eliza. We wanted to —'

In the background came Maxie's voice. There was a brief exchange between them, then Olivia put the call on speakerphone.

'Eliza, I was the censor,' Maxie said. 'I'm sorry. I wanted to make sure you were old enough.'

'I'm thirty, Maxie.'

'I know. What Olivia's trying to tell you is that Jeannie told us she'd made a bet with herself to see how many men of different nationalities she could sleep with during her travels. That's what some of the postcards are about. I wasn't ever going to include those in your present. Just the general ones about her travels.'

'Eliza, you don't have to read any of them yet if you don't want to,' Olivia said. 'Bring them back to Edinburgh with you. We can read them together. When we sit down to answer your questions.'

There was a long pause before Eliza spoke again. 'Thank you. Maxie, the red cushions on the sofa – do they belong to you and Hazel or should they stay in the flat?'

'She's upset with us, isn't she?' Maxie said as soon as Olivia hung up. 'Angry. You heard her. She reacted as if we'd deliberately been keeping them from her.'

'We had been.'

'We *hadn't*, Liv. It was just never the right time to show her. This is all my fault. I should have thrown them out years ago. Or brought them up here like you asked. Oh, why didn't I remember!'

Olivia wasn't in the mood for Maxie's dramatics. 'We've taken her by surprise, that's all. She was about to find them anyway, remember. Of course she'll want to read them. We just needed to warn her they were there.'

'But I didn't get to re-read them all. What if there's something in them we don't want her to know?'

Olivia didn't reply. She was asking herself the same question.

Eliza was no longer near the sofa. She'd gone looking for the postcards as soon as the call with her godmothers ended. She found them in the back of a cupboard in the study. Dozens of them. The bundle was held together by an old shoelace.

She sat on the floor, slowly untied the shoelace, picked up the first postcard and began to read.

At first she was cautious. Then confused. As she kept reading, eventually a new feeling started to bubble up. It felt strangely like excitement. Hardly any of the tales on the postcards matched the travel stories her mother had told her. But the more she read, the more she was realising something. She hadn't heard all her mother's stories after all.

It was like unexpectedly finding a treasure chest of memories. It meant so much to see Jeannie's handwriting again, too. Yes, some of the postcards were scandalous, but they were so over-the-top that Eliza suspected her mother had invented details purely to amuse or startle Olivia and Maxie. Jeannie had never been coy about discussing sex with her, either, had she? She'd loved to shock.

Her mother hadn't just written about her various male conquests. Eliza found out exactly where Jeannie had travelled during that year in Europe. Where she'd stayed. The different people she'd met. The many adventures she'd had. Eliza had also read more than she could have hoped about someone else.

The man who might be her father.

Why had Maxie and Olivia been so worried about her reading the postcards? They were wonderful! Who to ring first? To thank first? She called Olivia.

'I've read them all,' she said as soon as her godmother answered.

'Are you okay?'

She laughed. 'I'm better than okay. Olivia, it was like she was back with me, beside me. Telling me new story after story about her time here, all of her travels. I can't believe it. Her best friend wasn't a girl called Emma, was it? It was Emmet. An Irishman called Emmet. She mentions him in loads of the postcards. She says she was going to try to talk him into coming to Australia. Olivia, it's Emmet, isn't it? Emmet is my father.'

'I don't know, Eliza.'

'But you must know. She must have told you.'

'She didn't. She always told us she would tell you everything first.'

'I'm going to get the sleeper train back to Edinburgh tomorrow night. I'll be back at the hotel by eight-thirty the next morning. We can talk about it all together then. Thank you both so much. I can't wait!'

There was only a brief hesitation. 'Neither can we,' Olivia said.

*

Eliza was too distracted now to keep packing up the flat. She'd already made a good start. It was time for a break. Olivia had told her to be sure to do some sightseeing while she was here. As she carefully tied the shoelace around the precious bundle of postcards again, she knew exactly where she would go.

She borrowed a paper map she'd found in Maxie's kitchen. She liked how old-fashioned it felt. Perhaps her mother had used maps like this too. She took the long way, across Green Park, past Buckingham Palace, along Birdcage Walk. The gardens were unfurling into colour, the long rows of flower beds being admired by dozens of tourists like her. Squirrels darted in and out of the foliage, posing perfectly for photos. A haze of the brightest green was appearing on the trees.

She kept walking, soon reaching the Houses of Parliament and Big Ben, hidden behind scaffolding. She passed several red phone boxes being used as background props for selfies. She stood on Westminster Bridge, looking across at the London Eye, slowly turning in the spring sunshine. There was a scattering of boats on the river, the water a dull blue-brown, as muddy as the Yarra in Melbourne.

At every step, she pictured her mother here. More than that. She imagined the two of them here together, retracing Jeannie's steps. They'd talked about doing it. After Eliza finished uni, they'd decided. They'd both save up and do a big trip together. 'Hang the expense,' Jeannie had said.

Eliza took a seat on a bench in the park beyond the Houses of Parliament. She needed to be still. Close her eyes. Think of good memories to replace sudden sad ones. Today it was harder than usual.

She'd always hoped the day might come when she could think about her mother and feel a gentle warmth. Acceptance. It still hadn't happened. Even now, thirteen years later, there were so many moments she wanted to share with her. Talk about with her. Not just landmark events like her graduation, or getting the job with Gillian. She kept longing for ordinary times. Normal times. She'd love to have invited her to dinner in her flat in Melbourne. Gone away for weekends with her. Had theatre outings. Seen films together. Spoiled her on Mother's Day. Travelled with her.

She'd love to have been sitting here with Jeannie right now.

A young couple sat down beside her. Spanish or Italian, looking into the woman's phone, at a map or at the selfies they'd taken that day. Eliza stood up and kept walking.

Ten minutes later, she was in front of the Tate gallery. It was smaller than she'd expected. A flight of stone steps, six tall columns, long banners announcing the current exhibition.

Jeannie had told her more than once about her first visit to the Tate. About a game she'd played there. She'd visited on a freezing winter's day, she said. As she walked in, she'd given herself a million pounds to buy whatever painting she wanted. She saw the perfect one within minutes. But she didn't want to make a snap decision. She kept exploring the gallery. Until she was drawn back to the first painting.

She told Eliza she had stood gazing at it for hours. That it made her heart glow. She went to the front desk, took out her cheque book and bought it. They took it off the wall, parcelled it up, and asked, 'By air or sea, madam?' And to that day, she told Eliza, she'd regretted her answer. By sea, she'd said. It was still sailing the seas somewhere. Thank God she'd bought a postcard of it too.

Eliza had grown up with that postcard. It had been displayed on the fridge of every house they'd lived in. On the fridge of her own flat in Melbourne. Before she left, she'd packed it away safely in the box of books Rose was storing for her.

The gallery was crowded, despite the good weather. Eliza didn't ask for directions. She did what her mother had done. She walked through one large room into the next. Down a hallway to another. Through an archway into another. Then she stopped and abruptly turned around. There it was.

*Carnation, Lily, Lily, Rose* by John Singer Sargent.

It was in an ornate golden frame. An early summer garden, alive with masses of flowers: white lilies, blush-pink roses, deep-red and butter-yellow carnations. Amid them, two young girls in long white frilled dresses holding a paper lantern each, engrossed in setting the candles inside alight, the dull white paper transforming into an apricot glow. Tucked here and there among the flowers around them were other lanterns, already glowing apricot-pink. The two girls looked as though they were lit from the inside too, their white dresses bright against the green foliage.

Eliza felt her heart beat faster. She stepped nearer. It was so familiar to her. Yet the postcard hadn't come close to captur-ing the lantern light, the skin tones, the detail of the grass, the flowers. The secret world of the children, lighting candles with no adult in sight, bewitched by the magic they were creating.

Eliza had been prepared to be moved by seeing the painting. What she hadn't expected was what she realised now. Her mother had once stood here, in this room, in this art gallery. On this same spot.

The grief came like a wave. *Oh, Mum.* She was suddenly crying. In public, in the most famous gallery in London, attracting attention. She could feel it, but she couldn't seem to move.

She wanted to be here with her mother. She wanted to be looking up at the painting with her. Hear her whispering, *'Isn't it beautiful, Eliza? Isn't it the most glorious piece of art in the world? See the lanterns, that glow the artist somehow created with paint? Wouldn't you swear it was all real?'*

Finally she turned, wiping her eyes, ignoring a curious glance from an elderly couple. She took a seat on the bench in front of the painting. She didn't know how long she stayed there. Ten minutes, twenty?

Each time they'd gazed at the postcard together, Eliza and her mother had concocted a story about it. The girls were sisters, they'd decided. Close in age. Their parents were wealthy. Every summer, they invited friends to their mansion. At dusk on the first day, the two sisters – Lily? Rose? – would be in charge of lighting the lanterns before everyone went for a long garden walk, listening to birds calling as the light faded. Afterwards, a ball, an orchestra, everyone in gowns and suits, waiters with trays.

Outside, the Australian sun would be blasting their scrubby

backyard, the concrete, the clothes line. It wouldn't matter. In those moments, Eliza and her mother would be far away, inside the painting.

Eliza had to shut her eyes tight and will the tears not to come again. In her pocket, her phone pinged. She ignored it. It pinged again. She had to check. Sullivan, playing a word. No message this time.

She turned off her phone. All around her, people were walking in, taking out their phones, photographing one or two paintings without even looking at them properly, then walking out again.

She stayed for another fifteen minutes, gazing at the painting, thinking about her mother.

On the way out, she walked through the gift shop. It was as crowded as the galleries themselves, people browsing through items featuring the Tate's paintings. Not only books, prints and postcards. Umbrellas, tote bags, cups, scarves. An entire section was devoted to *Carnation, Lily, Lily, Rose.*

'*I suppose we have to share it with other people,*' she imagined her mother saying. '*But you and I both know it really belongs to us.*'

Eliza bought one of the postcards and tucked it into her bag.

# CHAPTER TWENTY-TWO

It was nearly six p.m. in Edinburgh. Olivia was on her way back to the Montgomery after an afternoon with Edgar. She'd run into roadworks. She called Lawrence to check all was fine.

'Two minor issues with guests, both sorted,' he said.

'And Celine?'

'Let's just say, the sooner Eliza's back from London, the better.'

Olivia wanted to swear. Not only at the roadworks. Or her fellow drivers, beeping their horns impatiently around her. She wanted to shout at Celine, order her to get out. Shout at Alex to stop stealing. At Rory to be more interested in the hotel. Instead, she breathed deeply. 'Thanks, Lawrence.'

She knew why her mood felt fragile. It had been a difficult visit with Edgar. More difficult than usual.

'How is he today, Lyn?' she'd asked the head nurse as she came in.

'No change, Olivia.'

How she longed for a different answer one day. 'He's back to his old self.' Or even, 'He's different.' Something new, something better than this awful limbo.

'Hello, darling.' She went across, sat down beside him and took his hand.

He didn't look at her. He was staring, unseeing, out of the window, his face turned from her.

She still talked to him, of course. Told him about Maxie in hospital, about Hazel going to New York early. She shifted in her seat and talked instead to the photos of him she'd displayed on the wall above his bed. For her, yes, but also for the nurses. Photos of Edgar as a young man. At the Montgomery. On their wedding day. On holiday together. With Rory and Alex as boys, teenagers, adults. Images to remind them that this man, this silent patient, who was drifting further away, becoming physically smaller every day too, had once been someone wonderful, clever, successful. Loved. Still loved.

She told him about Eliza in London. Packing up Maxie's flat. She told him what had happened with Jeannie's postcards. How they had been worried about what she might read in them.

Edgar had never met Jeannie, though he'd heard so much about her over the years. He'd always been understanding too, about why Olivia needed to go to Australia every year, not only to see her family but also Eliza. He'd sometimes helped her decide where to take Eliza on their godmother holidays.

He had occasionally spoken to Jeannie on the phone.

Sometimes when she was sober. More often, when she was drunk. Late in Australia, after Eliza was asleep. It seemed to be Jeannie's time to open a bottle of wine or more. To think. Remember. Sometimes get angry. Then make her phone calls.

The timing was always bad. Late evening in Australia was often lunchtime in Edinburgh. Jeannie would call the main Montgomery number. It would be put through to Olivia's office, or sometimes to their private wing. Olivia would know by Edgar's tone if Jeannie was sober or not.

'She's right here, Jeannie. Let me put her on.'

Sometimes, Jeannie would still be mimicking Edgar's Scottish accent when Olivia took the receiver. She seemed to find it funny. It never was. Olivia would do her best to stay calm, to be patient, to talk to Jeannie, of course, but then gently suggest she call back another time.

'Why? There's no time like the present. This is my present to you. My time. A wee bit of my time.' The bad Scottish accent again.

A day or two later, there'd be another call, or sometimes a fax. Full of apologies. 'Sorry, darling. I swear there's a poltergeist in this house that fills up my glass when I'm not looking.'

A few weeks would go by. Then another call.

'She needs help,' Edgar said once.

'I know,' Olivia said.

'How old is Eliza now? It can't be good for her to see that, her mother drunk —'

'I know, Edgar. I do what I can.'

'Don't answer her every time,' Edgar said once, when she was complaining. 'Wait until she's sober.'

His words still haunted her now.

The blare of a car horn behind her made her jump. She took her foot off the brake and accelerated. Another loud horn blared. She slammed on her brakes. She'd nearly collided with a car coming from the left. Her phone rang again, startling her. She answered using the hands-free. It was Maxie.

'Hi, Liv. How was Edgar? Was it a good visit?'

'Oh, it was great. Wonderful. We had such a laugh together. Talked about the old times. How do you think it was, Maxie? Edgar doesn't know what day it is, let alone what time it is. Two weeks could go by without me visiting him and he wouldn't even miss me.'

There was a long pause. 'Liv? Are you okay?'

'I'm sorry.' Another breath. 'It was the same as it always is. I go to see him for me, not him. I talk to him as if he is well. I even leave pauses for him to answer.'

'I wish you'd let me visit him too.'

'I told you. I don't want you to see him. Not like this.'

'Have the boys been in recently?'

'Rory was in last week. I don't know about Alex. He always says he finds it "troubling" to go there.' She said the words in a sarcastic tone.

'Maybe it is.'

'He's their father, Maxie. Too bad if it's troubling. It's troubling for me. They're both happy to reap the rewards of being

Edgar's sons, but without any of the work. Alex is stealing again. Not only alcohol. Paintings now too, I think. Rory only ever wants to be in his workshop. Sometimes I wonder if I'm the only one who cares about the hotel any more. Or if I'm making a mess of it all myself.'

'Of course you're not, Liv. You've done wonderful work there. I think you just need to talk about it all with someone.'

'You think I should go and see a therapist?'

'No, I think you should drive to Glasgow tomorrow to pick me up. My surgeon said I'm ready to be discharged. You can talk to me as much as you need.'

# CHAPTER TWENTY-THREE

Eliza arrived back into Edinburgh on the overnight train. It was barely eight a.m. as she walked out into Waverley Station again.

She'd finished packing up Maxie and Hazel's flat in record time, working with new energy after her visit to the Tate. After two full days of efficient sorting, packing and labelling, all their belongings were now with the removal company, ready for shipping to New York.

She caught a taxi outside the station. Her mother's postcards were tucked safely in her handbag. She'd read them all again during the train journey, enjoying them even more the second time round.

Back at the Montgomery, on her way to Maxie's suite, she made a detour to her own bedroom to collect the folder of paperwork she'd brought from Melbourne.

Her godmothers gave her the warmest of welcomes. Maxie thanked her again for all she'd done at the flat. She looked settled into her temporary home, her plastered foot up on a stool.

Eliza took a seat by the bay window. She couldn't stop smiling. 'I've got so many questions. I was going to start by asking you to tell me everything you know about my father. But it's all in the postcards, isn't it? That's why you wanted me to read them. To work it out myself. All Mum ever told me was that she first met my father overseas, then he came to Australia. It has to be her Irish friend Emmet, doesn't it?'

'We really don't know, Eliza,' Maxie said. 'I'm sorry, but we don't.'

'She never told us either,' Olivia reminded her.

'But isn't it like Mum to leave all these clues? It was like she was speaking to me, like she was back with me. She hadn't been able to tell me on my eighteenth, but she was somehow telling me another way. Did you ever meet him? When he was in Australia? Do you know his surname, anything else about him? Could you help me find him?'

Olivia seemed taken aback at the sudden onslaught. 'We'll help as much as we can, of course. But are you sure now is the right time? Have you had breakfast? Do you need to freshen up?'

Eliza laughed. 'Olivia, I've been waiting for years to talk about this. I've got so many questions, I hardly know where to start. Not just about Emmet. About Mum. Her family.' She noticed an exchange of glances. 'What is it? Is something wrong?'

'Eliza —' Maxie began, before Olivia interrupted.

'Eliza, we need to start with one story first. It might help other things we tell you make sense.'

'About my father?'

'About Jeannie. Something that happened before she went travelling.'

'Something bad?'

Olivia stood up and put the *Do Not Disturb* sign on Maxie's door.

Olivia did most of the talking, with Maxie adding occasional extra detail. Eliza sat still, listening intently.

Their boarding school was an hour outside Melbourne, Olivia began. On rare occasions, the senior girls were allowed to catch a train into the city, as long as they were back in their dorms by ten. It had been Olivia's idea for the three of them to have an outing.

'I seconded it,' Maxie said. 'I'd had enough of school food. I was desperate for a pizza.'

They decided to go to Carlton, the city's Italian quarter. They pooled their pocket money and bought two pizzas to share. Afterwards, they went strolling up and down Lygon Street. It was a hot night. Young – and handsome – Italian boys were doing laps in their cars. They were three seventeen-year-olds, giddy with freedom, alone in the city.

'Jeannie asked us to dare her to do something,' Olivia said. 'She was in a wild kind of mood. Like she was fizzing with electricity. I dared her to ask at a café for a free slice of pizza. She asked for three, and got them. Then she dared us to ask her to do something more exciting. Something dramatic.'

'But before we could think of anything, she ran off from us,' Maxie said.

Jeannie had spotted a delivery van parked outside one of the pizza restaurants. The engine was still running. The driver's door was open. She got in and she took off.

'She only had her learner's permit,' Olivia said.

'And this was in the middle of Melbourne,' Maxie said. 'On a Saturday night. It was so busy.'

'And she started driving around the block, like the Italian boys were doing. Twice. Each time she honked the horn and waved at us. We were so shocked. We kept calling to her to stop it, to come back. And then the driver came out and he was —'

'Shocked and angry. And he said, "Where's my van?" And we said, "Our friend's taken it, don't worry, she'll bring it back."'

'And he said, "But what about my little brother?"'

'The next time she drove past we saw him,' Maxie said. 'A kid aged about nine in the passenger seat. He looked terrified, or maybe he was excited. It happened too fast to be able to tell. Because she was so busy waving and shouting out to us that she didn't see the car pull out in front of her.'

'And she crashed into it.'

Eliza's eyes were huge in her pale face. 'Was he killed?'

Olivia shook her head. 'He wasn't even injured. Somehow, miraculously, neither of them were. But the car was a write-off.'

The police were called. An ambulance. The boy was in tears. The driver and the owner of the restaurant, his cousin, were enraged. Threatening Jeannie, shouting at her. She was shouting back at them. Then the police arrested her.

'Arrested her?'

'She'd stolen a van, Eliza. They thought she was drunk or on drugs.'

Olivia remembered their awful panic. Who should they call? They had to use the phone in the restaurant, the owner glaring at them, the patrons whispering and staring. They decided not to ring their parents. They rang the school instead. Olivia made the call. She hoped for kind Sister Frances. She got fierce Sister Roberta. She started crying on the phone. Sister Roberta snapped at her. 'Speak clearly. Is anyone injured? Thank God. Stay where you are.'

Forty minutes later a woman in her fifties came to the restaurant. 'Sister Roberta sent me.'

'Are you a nun too?' Maxie dared to ask.

'I'm Roberta's sister. I'm a lawyer.'

She drove them to the police station. She told them to stay in the car. She was in the station for nearly an hour. Outside, they had no idea what was going on.

It was now as if Eliza wasn't there. Olivia and Maxie were telling each other the story again.

The lawyer finally came back out. With Jeannie. She was lucky. All she had was a small cut on her cheek. They were driven back to school to an icy welcome. Sent to their dorm. No talking allowed.

The following days were tense and terrible. They were separated, moved into different dormitories. Their parents were notified. They were given warnings. Grounded. Jeannie's parents arrived the next morning. There was a long meeting with the principal.

'We never found out exactly what happened. We think her parents paid the restaurant off. Paid for the repairs to the van. Paid compensation. Paid the sisters.'

Jeannie did let them know about the telling-off she'd received from her parents. It lasted for hours, she said.

That was the last time Olivia and Maxie ever spoke to Jeannie on the school grounds.

'What about at your graduation? You didn't talk to Jeannie that day?' Eliza asked.

Olivia and Maxie exchanged glances. Eliza noticed. 'What?'

Silence.

'What? What aren't you telling me now?'

'Your mum didn't finish school, Eliza. She dropped out. About a month after the crash.'

'She'd gone home to see her parents.'

'Summoned home, we think.'

'And on the Monday afterwards, she didn't come back.'

'We tried ringing, left messages, but they were never returned. Jeannie didn't reply to our letters.'

'The nuns said there were family issues.'

'That's why Mum didn't go to university?' Eliza said. 'Because she hadn't finished high school?'

'It's part of it.'

'Part of it? What's the rest of it?' Her voice was quiet.

'Eliza —'

'Tell me everything. Please.'

'She ran away from home. And we don't know for sure, but we think she must have taken either jewellery or money from her parents. Because she suddenly had a lot of money.'

Olivia took over. 'We didn't hear from her for weeks. This was before social media, or mobiles, remember. The only way we could send her messages was through her parents and they still weren't answering. We wrote, but the letters always came back. The nuns couldn't help. They said they were doing what they could to mediate, but they admitted they didn't know where Jeannie was either.'

'Then I got a letter,' Maxie said. 'A week before we finished school.'

'It was written with cut-out newspaper letters, like a joke ransom letter.'

'The name of a hotel in Melbourne, a date, a time. We knew it was her.'

'So we turned up. It was a good hotel. Not a dive. She was sitting in the foyer waiting for us.'

'Where had she been?'

'She didn't tell us. Ever. But she'd booked a room in the hotel. She smuggled us in, and we stayed the night. We watched movies. She ordered room service.'

'How was she paying for it?'

'She wouldn't tell us.'

'We tried, Eliza. We spoke to her all night. We asked about her parents, about finishing school —'

'She was —'

'Manic. High.'

'Was she taking drugs?'

'I don't know. I don't think so.'

'We were never sure.'

'She told us she'd gone home that weekend and there'd been another enormous fight with her parents. Her father's mother was staying then, too. They read her the riot act. Told her how disappointed they were. How she'd let herself down again. Let them down. That she was fooling herself if she thought her stupid behaviour would ever get her anywhere. Her father was in a rage. She'd told us before about what a bad temper he had.'

'And she told us she said to them, "Well, it sounds to me as though you don't like me very much, do you? So let me fix this situation as best I can, for all our sakes." She packed a suitcase. And she left.'

'They let her walk out? A seventeen-year-old?'

'She'd just turned eighteen.'

'We also think that's when she stole something. Maybe a few things. We never knew for sure. But she made a joke about a necklace she was wearing when we met her. It looked expensive.'

'That's how she could afford to go travelling overseas?'

'We think so.'

'She told me she'd received an inheritance.'

They both stayed silent.

'Why didn't you tell me any of this before now?'

'Jeannie told us she'd tell you everything herself.'

'We had to promise not to tell you.'

Eliza had gone still. 'Are my grandparents alive?'

'We don't know.'

'Do they even know Mum died?'

'We don't know, Eliza. I'm sorry.'

'You didn't try to contact them back then?

Olivia and Maxie's silence was their answer.

'What are their names?' Eliza asked.

'We never knew their first names,' Olivia said. 'We only knew them as Mr and Mrs Miller.'

'What was their address?'

'We don't know. We wrote via the school. Eliza, we met them so briefly. We were kids. And after – after Jeannie died, we didn't even know how to contact them.'

'Why didn't you tell me any of this back then?'

'You'd just lost your mother. We had no way of knowing how they'd react if we did find them, put you in touch with them. They might have sent you away. That's what Jeannie always feared, that —'

'I've always had grandparents. Grandparents I might have met.' Again, she looked from one to the other. 'Did they even know about me?'

'We don't know.'

'You never asked Mum?'

'Yes, but Eliza, it was sometimes hard to know if Jeannie was telling the truth.'

'But they were the family I could have had. And you still didn't tell me about them.'

Olivia tried to explain again. 'We had no choice, Eliza.'

'Your mother made us promise not to say anything to you,' Maxie said.

'My mother is dead.' The words tore out of her. She'd shocked them. Shocked herself. 'How could you have visited me, year after year, spoken to me every week, and lied to me? When I could have had a family? When I could have had people who loved me, looked after me. My mother's parents. How could you have done this?'

'Eliza —'

Olivia stepped forward. 'Eliza, please, I know it's a shock, but we need to explain —'

Eliza was trembling. 'There's nothing to explain. I had a family and you didn't tell me.'

Maxie tried. 'Eliza, Jeannie and her parents hadn't spoken in years. Even before you were born.'

'That was their business. Between them. They were still my grandparents. I could have tried to have a relationship with them. Do I have aunts? Uncles?'

'We don't think so.'

'As far as we know, Jeannie was an only child.'

'As far as you know.' She stood up. 'I have to go home. I have to find them.'

'Eliza —'

'Can't you see that? Can't you understand how this might feel for me?'

'We've worried about it all your life, darling.'

Eliza flinched at the darling.

Olivia noticed. 'Eliza, we did what Jeannie asked us to do,' she said.

'No,' Eliza said. 'You made a decision not to tell me, even after Mum died.'

'We promised her.'

'She died, Maxie. The promise should have died with her.'

'Please, Eliza. Please try to stay calm.'

She stood up. 'I've done nothing but try to stay calm for thirteen years. I've done nothing but try to be the best-behaved person I can, to try to keep everything bad at bay, stop anything else terrible happening to me. But it was pointless, wasn't it? Because I was in the dark all that time. My life could have been so different. But you both chose —' She shook her head. She stared at them, as if she was seeing them for the first time. As if she was shocked at what she could see. 'I have to go. I can't stay here.'

'Eliza —'

Olivia stepped forward again, but she was too late.

Eliza had run out of the room.

# CHAPTER TWENTY-FOUR

Eliza found her way back to her bedroom. Her hands shook as she opened the door. She locked it behind her, leaned against it. She felt the beginnings of a panic attack. A tightness in her chest.

What should she do? Fly home? No. Not that long flight again. Not yet.

She needed to talk to someone.

She needed to talk to Rose.

Her phone pinged. Rose. Mind-reader Rose. She clicked it open.

*We did it! We escaped!* A photo of Rose's and Harry's feet at a poolside.

Eliza remembered. They were on a weekend away for their ninth wedding anniversary. Their first break in years. She wouldn't ring her now. She also needed to let everything settle. Get away from here, too.

She sent Rose the cheeriest message she could, wishing them a happy anniversary and a wonderful time away. Then she packed.

She only had one case. It didn't take long. She went down to the foyer and stopped. Where could she go?

Alex was taking a break from the reception desk. 'Leaving so soon, Eliza? You will give us a good review on TripAdvisor, I hope?' He stopped. 'Are you okay?'

She shook her head.

'Has something happened?'

She nodded. She couldn't seem to find the words.

'Do you want me to get Olivia?'

'No!' She said it too forcefully. 'No, I don't.'

'Have you had a fight? Are you running away?'

All she could do was nod.

'Well, good for you. I've wanted to run away from here for years.'

'I don't know where to go.' She was saying it to herself as much as to him.

'Where would you like to go? Back to Australia?'

'Not yet.' She didn't have a job there. A home. 'I need to be on my own for a while.'

'May I suggest a place?'

Less than ten minutes later she was unpacking in a single room in Alex's hostel. It was so close to the Montgomery but she might have been in a different city. The hostel was all bright colours, music, chatter. On their way to her room, he'd pointed out the communal kitchen and living room. Both were filled with people, mostly young, but some older travellers too. Talking, reading, on their phones, playing pool.

She'd offered to pay but Alex refused.

'We're practically family, after all. Though count your blessings you're not a Montgomery. Stay as long as you like. I don't mean that literally. One Celine in the family is enough.'

She thanked him, touched by the unexpected kindness. As he left her to settle in, she sat on the bed. Her phone beeped. Sullivan.

*Hi Eliza! Are you back from London yet?*

*Yes, I just got back.*

*Welcome! I'm ready to go to the zoo anytime you want, all you have to do is say the word!*

It wasn't even lunchtime yet. Her overnight train journey already felt like it had been days ago. Her mind felt like it was on fire. She needed any distraction she could get.

*How about now?*

*Really?? THANK YOU!!! I'll ask Ann-Marie to ring you right now!!!*

Five minutes later it was all arranged.

Alex was behind the hostel reception desk as she came down.

'I'm heading out for a few hours,' she said.

'It's a hostel, Eliza. Not a Boarding House for Respectable

Young Ladies. You can do whatever you want and not tell anyone.'

He was right, she realised. For the first time in her life, she really could.

Back at the Montgomery, Maxie was in tears.

'I knew it would be bad. I never thought it would be that bad.'

'Stop crying, Maxie. It's not helping. We have to do something to fix it. We shouldn't have let her go.'

'We? What could I have done? Tried to run after her with my crutches?' Maxie became more upset. 'You were right. We should have told her everything years ago. After Jeannie died.'

'We couldn't. Don't you remember what Eliza was like then? She was in pieces, Maxie. She was so fragile. I was always worried she'd have a complete breakdown. All that kept her going back then were the good stories, the funny stories, remember? The madcap Jeannie tales over and again, like bedtime stories. We couldn't have told her the truth. Not even some of it.'

'Then we should have found out if her grandparents were alive or dead before we told her.'

'We didn't know it was going to come up so soon today. And how could we have found out, anyway? It's more than thirty years since we were at school. We don't know anyone there any more.'

'I do.' Maxie took out her phone and scrolled through her emails. 'The alumni and fundraising manager at the school was in touch with me last month. About a new drama wing they're opening.'

'And you didn't tell me?'

'There's been a fair bit going on, Liv.' She called out a name and the phone number. 'Can you please ring them? You're better at these kinds of things than I am.'

Olivia began to say something, then changed her mind. 'The office would be shut.'

'You could leave a message. Tell them what we're looking for. Say we'll ring back tomorrow.'

Olivia called and left a message. She'd just hung up when her phone rang again. It was Alex.

'Yes?' she said.

'No need to sound quite so delighted to hear from me, Olivia.'

'Sorry, I'm in the middle of something.'

'Yes, sending poor Eliza out into the cold streets of Edinburgh.'

'You saw her?'

'She was standing like a waif in the foyer, lost and with nowhere to go —'

'Where is she now?'

'In the hostel. In my last spare room. And now surely I've atoned for my sins of fourteen years ago —'

'Thank you, Alex.' She hung up and turned to Maxie. 'She's at Alex's hostel.'

'Let's go over there. Talk to her.'

'No. She needs to be on her own. To cool down.' She sat down. 'What have we done, Maxie? Have we wrecked everything?'

Maxie's eyes filled with tears again. 'I think we have.'

Sullivan was waiting on the front steps with his backpack when Eliza arrived in a taxi. He was excited to see her. She helped him with his pack. It was surprisingly heavy.

By the time they reached Edinburgh Zoo, her anger had subsided to a low glow. Her mind kept turning over all she'd learned, even as she tried to listen to Sullivan, chattering beside her.

At the entrance, Sullivan undid his pack and arranged the contents on the ground. Two apples, two sandwiches, two juices, a novel and what looked like several hundred pounds in cash.

Eliza was taken aback. 'Sullivan, where did you get that?'

'It's my allowance from Dad. I've been saving it. You can't be expected to pay all the time, Eliza. You've already given up your leisure time. And got me out from under Sophie's feet, as she put it.'

'This is my treat. I'm shouting you.'

'Next time's on me, then,' he said, as he tucked everything away safely again.

They joined the queue. Two school groups were ahead of them. Eliza tried to push her own complicated thoughts away and focus on Sullivan instead.

'Is it okay at home for you, Sullivan? When your dad's at work?'

He shrugged. 'It's probably easier then. I don't have to try to make him like me. I've given up trying to make Sophie like me. She's always busy with The Baby now, anyway. But Dad said he might take me somewhere tomorrow. If he doesn't get called in to do some more operations.'

Again, Eliza tried to find the right words. 'Does your mum know what it's like here in Edinburgh for you?'

'Of course. We Skype three times a week, even now when she's on her American lecture tour. She got a bit teary last time. She misses me a lot.'

'But she still sends you here?'

He shrugged again. 'It's a legal arrangement. She doesn't want to but the lawyers said she has to. It's not always bad. Sometimes after dinner Dad plays Monopoly with me. Well, he did once. You can say hello to my mother if you like. She's Skyping me in' – he checked his watch – 'eight minutes.'

At his suggestion, they set themselves up in front of the meerkats. 'My favourites are the ring-tailed lemurs, as you know, but Mum loves these fellows.'

Right on time, his phone chimed. 'Mum!' he said happily.

It was a relief to hear him sounding so cheery. To hear the warm tones of his mother in return. The phone was thrust in her direction. Sullivan's mother appeared to be in a hotel room. Eliza instantly saw the likeness. They had the same thick dark hair, the same large dark eyes.

'Eliza, hello! I'm Lisa. Thank you so much. You must think we're an odd family, sending our son off with strangers. Except you're not, of course. Everyone seems to know your godmother.'

'You've got a great son,' she said.

'He's the best,' Lisa said, smiling that same big Sullivan smile. 'You've made quite a fan, too.'

Sullivan looked pleased with himself as she handed the phone back. He pointed the phone in the meerkats' direction, then blew a series of goodbye kisses at the lens.

'A great start to my day,' he said after hanging up. 'Now, lemur time!'

As they followed the path, she spotted a bright-yellow sign pointing to a koala enclosure.

'We're not the only Australians in Scotland,' she said. 'Shall we go and say hello to them first?'

'They don't do anything,' Sullivan said. 'They just sit on tree stumps and look doleful.'

They went in, all the same. There was a female koala with a baby on her back, barely visible through an arrangement of eucalyptus leaves. Eliza and Sullivan waited for them to move. They didn't.

'Did you ever want to ride around on your mother's back, Eliza?' Sullivan asked after a while.

'No, to Mum's relief, I'd say. I was taller than her by the time I was your age.'

'I'd like to be as tall as you. Where does your mother live, Eliza? Is she in Melbourne too?'

'She's not, Sullivan, no.' It was still so hard to say it. 'My mum died when I was seventeen.'

His eyes widened. 'I'm so sorry. Why didn't you tell me before now? So you've lived with your father since then?'

'No.' Another pause. 'I've never met my father.'

'Who looked after you?'

She explained that she was nearly an adult when it happened. That her godmothers had helped her.

'Helped you? In what ways?'

How did she answer that? The holidays when she was a child. Financially, when she was at uni. The phone calls. Visits. Unexpected gifts. The constant support. Not only when Jeannie died. Ever since.

'Lots of different ways,' she said.

'I can share my mother with you if you'd like. She's very nice.'

'That's kind of you, Sullivan. But I'd say she's got her hands full with you.'

He gave his funny bark of laughter. 'She says that herself. Can we please go to the lemurs now?'

They were walking along the path to the lemur enclosure when Sullivan's phone rang again.

He answered. 'Hello, Dad! Yes, I'm with Eliza at the zoo. Yes, we're on our way to see them now. Thanks, yes, you have a good day too. Happy operating!'

After he'd hung up, he reached into his backpack, took out a piece of paper and made a note.

'Do you keep a record of all your conversations?' Eliza asked, puzzled.

'Only Dad's,' he said, matter-of-factly. 'Mum asked me to log any one-on-one time with him here, on the phone or in person. I think she's planning a legal challenge regarding the access arrangements. I once overheard her tell a friend that Ann-Marie spends more time with me here than he ever does.'

'Sullivan, I'm so sorry.'

'No need to apologise, Eliza. One, it's not your fault. Two, it's true.'

She followed as he led the way to the lemurs. It was a large, leafy enclosure. There were two separate groups of them, their orange and black-ringed eyes so bright. Their distinctive upright striped tails made Eliza think of bumper cars. Sullivan was smiling as if he'd run into old and dear friends. Several groups of people came in, took a photo, then walked out again.

'How can they leave so soon?' Sullivan asked. 'I could watch them tumble and play all day long.'

After their picnic lunch, Eliza offered to buy him a lemur souvenir. He inspected the gift-shop shelves with a forensic eye.

'Nothing I don't have,' he said. 'I bought up big last year. A key ring, a notebook, even a lemur cup. It's time they expanded their range. I'll email them tomorrow to suggest it.'

'I'm sure they'll enjoy hearing from you, Sullivan,' she said, as they walked to the exit together.

*

Back at the Montgomery, Olivia and Maxie were both in Olivia's office, at her computer. It hadn't been easy for Maxie to get up the stairs but they'd managed. They'd been at their task for five hours.

They were writing down everything they remembered about Jeannie. Even if Eliza didn't want to talk to them yet, they hoped she'd read their words. They would email it all to her in the morning. Then leave it up to her to decide what would happen next.

Olivia's computer screen was covered in dates and names. Together they'd put down all they could remember about the times they'd met Jeannie after they left school, the conversations, when and how they'd heard she was pregnant. They'd counted back to when it was most likely that Eliza was conceived. It had to have been in Melbourne, when she was working in that Collingwood pub. They wrote down everything they remembered about meeting Emmet. All Jeannie had said about him and his cousin. Her other housemates. The details they remembered about Emmet's accident. They re-read every word of Jeannie's postcards, thankful that Eliza had left them behind. Made a note of as many facts as possible, leaving out the more outlandish stories.

Maxie was now googling 'Melbourne bashing Irishman', trying to find Emmet's surname. Nothing matching the dates came up. Either the incident was too long ago or it hadn't been reported.

Olivia was going through the folder of paperwork Eliza

had brought from Melbourne. They'd both looked at it earlier, hoping it might yield something helpful. Eliza's school report had been on top. They had read it together, amused and moved by it. The rest of the paperwork appeared to be bundles of bills and old bank statements clipped together. Other odds and ends too – a takeaway menu from their local café, a shopping list in Jeannie's familiar handwriting.

As Olivia leafed through it, she thought of all she'd leave behind if she was to die suddenly. Emails she'd written to Maxie over the years, expressing frustration with Rory and Alex. The many love notes Edgar had given her. He'd often left them tucked away for her to find, under her pillow, or in the pocket of her favourite coat. She didn't want anyone else to ever read them.

All she had learned so far in this second read-through was that Jeannie was a serial late payer of bills. All the invoices were red-topped. She looked at the bank statements again. Jeannie's various wage payments appeared once a month, all so low. Sometimes there had been as little as twenty dollars in her account. How had she and Eliza lived on this? Olivia saw payments she had made to Jeannie for Eliza's annual holidays. There were similar deposits around the time of Maxie's holidays too.

She was about to put the bank statements back in the folder when she noticed something. She leafed forward through the pages, then back. She did a quick calculation, using Eliza's age as her guide. From the time Eliza was born up until she was about twelve, there had been one or two large deposits a year. Sometimes as much as two thousand dollars, but usually less.

After Eliza turned thirteen, however, they stopped. She checked through them again. No, she hadn't missed any.

'Maxie, did you ever deposit money into Jeannie's account when Eliza was little? Before the holidays started?'

Maxie looked up from her googling and shook her head. 'No. She'd never take any, remember?'

Olivia passed her the statements. 'So what were these? Who was this?'

'Mr and Mrs Quaker?' Maxie suggested.

'The dates don't match. They died before Eliza was two.'

Olivia noticed a code beside those deposits. As Maxie went back to her own research, Olivia googled the code. It took some digging, but she discovered it signified that the deposit had arrived into Jeannie's Australian account in a foreign currency.

'I think I've found something,' she said.

# CHAPTER TWENTY-FIVE

The hostel was buzzing when Eliza returned after dropping Sullivan home from the zoo. She was glad she'd taken him. It had made him happy. It had temporarily stopped her troubled thoughts. But now, alone in her room, back came her anger and confusion towards Olivia and Maxie.

She'd had grandparents. She'd had a family. How could they not have told her that, in thirteen years? All those lonely days and nights and weekends she'd had. All the Christmases with Rose and her family, grateful to be there while quietly wishing she didn't have to be. She might have been with her own family. It was suddenly unfathomable again.

She couldn't stay in her room on her own. There was no radio or TV to distract her. Outside, she could hear voices, laughter, chat from the common room. She'd go out there. Pretend to be as carefree as all the other travellers had appeared to be as she'd walked past. The bar had been busy. Groups of travellers had been taking turns sharing songs via their phones. There even appeared to be an impromptu hairdressing salon operating in a corner of the café area.

She was about to leave her room when her phone pinged. It was Rory.

*Alex told me you're at the hostel. Hope you're okay? Are you doing anything tonight? Milly is over from Berlin. Want to join us for dinner?*

Company. An escape from her own thoughts. She wrote back immediately. *Yes please.*

*Great!* He sent through the details of the restaurant. *See you at 8* ☺

Outside, she found a spare seat at the edge of the common room. She pretended to be looking at her phone, even as she listened to everything around her. Again, so many different accents and languages. Flirting and conversation and music. She heard snatches of travel stories and travel plans. Talk of Interrail passes. Pickpocketing mishaps. Attempts at scams. Bursts of laughter from the bar.

She turned as one of the staff came in with a box of wine and started to restock the shelves. A memory flash of that dinner with Olivia. The news that Alex was stealing from the Montgomery, taking their alcohol to stock his own hostel bar.

As if she had conjured him out of nowhere, he was suddenly there beside her.

'I do hope everything is to your satisfaction, madam,' he said, taking a seat beside her, stretching out his lanky frame.

She sensed admiring glances from some of the travellers around them. She felt a dart of gratitude that her attraction to him had been years ago and short-lived.

She thanked him again. Told him she was very happy.

'You're dining with Rory and Milly tonight, I hear? Sorry I can't join you.' He laughed at the expression on her face. 'The Montgomery jungle drums beat loud and clear. I always know what Rory's doing. He always knows what I'm doing. He might not always approve, but I tell him anyway.'

She couldn't stop a glance at the bar. He noticed and raised an eyebrow. 'Don't tell me, Olivia has shared that particular jewel from the family treasure chest of secrets with you, has she?'

Eliza didn't want to get involved. 'It's nothing to do with me, Alex. It's your family's business.'

'But you're almost family.' Alex was relaxed. 'Did she complain to you about my unlicensed borrowing of artwork as well?'

Eliza didn't know what he meant. He pointed to the wall beside the bar, then to the wall behind the reception desk. There were paintings on each. One was of an Australian country road, purple shadows in a deep green valley, in a golden frame. She remembered seeing it on her first day here. Hanging in one of the hallways of the Montgomery.

She couldn't hide her surprise. 'You've been taking paintings from the hotel too?'

'Taking? I was worried you'd say stealing. They're my inheritance. All I'm doing is accessing them a little earlier than legally expected.' He leaned in as the music around them grew louder. She could smell alcohol on his breath. 'Look, I can imagine what Olivia's been saying. That I'm a thief. That I'm lazy. That I don't care about my father. Far be it from me to defend myself, Eliza, but please remember there are always two sides to every story.'

She felt the need to defend Olivia. 'She hasn't said much. She's just worried about the future of the hotel. About Edgar.'

'Olivia worries too much about that hotel. She needs to realise there's more to life than that place. Not just her life. My life. Rory's life. And while we're on the subject, she's not the only person who worries about my father, even if she thinks she is. I don't visit him as often as she does. But I do visit him. Care about him. He's been my father longer than he's been her husband. I wish she'd let me love him in my own way.'

Eliza didn't get the chance to reply. Alex was called over to the reception desk by a trio of disgruntled-looking backpackers. She saw him instantly switch into his most charming persona.

'So, any more takers?' an American voice called out from the corner. 'Have scissors, will travel! Ten years' salon experience, here at your fingertips!'

It was the impromptu hairdresser. A young woman, dressed in a bright-red jumpsuit, her own hair wound into a loose bun, a fifties-style scarf wrapped around it. She looked so carefree, so stylish.

'Only twenty pounds for a whole new look!' she called out again. When it seemed as though she had no takers, she began to fold up the plastic cape she was holding.

Eliza stood up. 'Wait. Please.'

The young woman turned to her with a smile. 'Hi, I'm Becky. Please, take a seat.'

Eliza had worn her hair long since she was a child. She knew her mother had liked it that way. Her godmothers, too. Olivia had often told her how much she liked seeing it in the long plait. Gillian had always insisted she wear it in a low bun. Rose had never voiced a preference either way. She'd only expressed jealousy at how dark and glossy Eliza's hair was. Rose had fought her grey hairs for years.

Eliza had never even considered changing her hair. But here, tonight, a feeling like recklessness was coursing through her. Before she could change her mind, she pulled her hair out of the plait and ran her fingers through it, loosening it around her shoulders.

Behind her, Becky lifted up the strands, complimenting her on how healthy it was. How shiny. How long. 'So, what would you like me to do with it?' she asked.

'Cut it off, please,' Eliza said.

An hour later she was back in her room, sitting on her bed, staring at herself in the mirror.

What on earth had she done? What had she been thinking? Where there had once been a long black plait, there was now a short dark pixie cut. She looked completely different. She felt completely different. She kept waiting for the rush of regret. There was nothing.

She stared at it some more. She moved her head from side to side. It actually looked okay. It actually seemed to suit her. Becky had taken her time. It was obvious within minutes how skilled she was. It wasn't an ordinary crop. She had shaped, thinned and feathered Eliza's hair until it was a stylish, glossy cap.

'Not to blow my own trumpet, but that's one awesome haircut,' she'd said.

Alex had come over and wolf-whistled. 'Eliza! If I hadn't already behaved like a cad all those years ago, I'd be making another pitch for your affections right now.'

Rory was as admiring when she met him at the restaurant at eight. He didn't wolf-whistle, as Alex had. He just told her he thought she looked lovely. Then he smiled at someone behind her. Eliza turned. It was his girlfriend. She was petite, curvy and bright-eyed.

Rory made the introductions. 'Eliza, my almost cousin, please meet the marvellous Milly.'

Conversation was instantly easy. Milly was over from Berlin for three nights, she said. One night in Edinburgh with Rory, then to Bristol for two nights for her mother's birthday. It was obvious to Eliza how strong the relationship between Milly and Rory was.

As the evening went on, Milly kept reminding Eliza of Rose. They shared the same warmth and curiosity. Strong opinions. It also became clear that Milly had heard a lot about Eliza. But it wasn't until Rory was greeted enthusiastically by a man in his thirties, an old school friend, and beckoned over to his table to catch up over a quick drink, that Milly turned her full attention on to Eliza.

'So, what do you think of the Montgomery?' Milly asked.

'It's a beautiful hotel,' she said.

'It is, I agree. But it's suffocating Rory. Silver spoons can be handy, but they can also choke you.'

Eliza blinked. It seemed Milly wasn't one for polite chitchat.

'I've always liked Edgar,' Milly continued, 'but he wouldn't have been an easy father.'

'You met him before the dementia?'

She nodded. 'Rory and I have been together for six years. It's been so sad. For Edgar, for Rory and Alex. Olivia too, of course. I like her a lot. She was so kind to Rory, I know. I'm sorry about your mother, Eliza. Rory told me about her. And about the fight with your godmothers.'

Eliza's surprise at all Milly knew must have shown.

'He didn't go into detail,' Milly said. 'And you don't need to tell me any more if you don't want to.'

Eliza realised she did want to talk about it. Here, unexpectedly, with this kind-eyed, curious stranger.

Afterwards, Milly was sympathetic. Not to Eliza. To her godmothers.

'The poor things. It must have been so difficult for them not to tell you the truth all these years. I can only imagine how guilty they've felt.'

'You think my godmothers felt guilty about me? Or about breaking the promise to my mother?'

'Both, perhaps. I don't know Olivia very well, but I know from Rory she's a good person. Perhaps she and your other god-mother have wanted to tell you everything, but felt they couldn't. You were so young when it happened, Eliza. They must have been in an impossible position.'

Eliza wasn't ready to be sympathetic to them yet.

'It's not that simple,' she said. 'There was so much they could have told me. They chose not to. Not just about my grandparents. About my mother. My father too.'

'Why didn't you ask them yourself before now?'

'I didn't feel ready. I was waiting for the right time. The right circumstances.'

Milly gazed at her, then raised an eyebrow.

'It's not that simple,' Eliza said again.

'Isn't it? Rory tells me off for being an amateur psychologist, Eliza. He's right. I don't have any qualifications. But sometimes I can't stop myself from saying what I see. Especially when there are two sides to a story, but no one will talk about them. Look, I can shut up if you want me to.'

Eliza hesitated, then shook her head. 'Please say it.'

'Take Rory and Alex. Their father always wanted them to love the hotel as much as he did. All they've ever wanted to do was other things. Perhaps one day they'd have told him that. But three years ago, the same day he told them about his diagnosis, he asked them both to stay on at the hotel. Of course his news was tragic. But it was also textbook emotional blackmail, don't you think? Even so, they both obeyed him. They're still obeying him. Out of love. Respect. Perhaps even some guilt. Even though it's the last place either of them wants to be.'

Eliza was taken aback at all Milly was telling her. 'Does Olivia know that?'

'I don't know how much Olivia knows,' Milly said.

'She knows Alex is stealing alcohol from the Montgomery. She knows Rory really only wants to be doing his jigsaw puzzles.'

'Rory and I think Alex is actually trying to get sacked. So that the decision can be taken out of his hands entirely.'

'What decision?'

'About staying at the Montgomery. Working there, let alone managing it one day. I know Rory wishes it was all out of his hands too. The puzzles aren't just a hobby for him, Eliza. It could be a full-time business. A successful one.'

'But what about the hotel? Olivia said either Rory or Alex will be the next general manager.'

'Perhaps she should ask them first if either of them actually want the job.'

'They don't? Neither of them?'

'Why not ask Rory yourself?'

Eliza turned. Rory was joining them again.

'I was boasting about you, telling Eliza how successful your puzzles are,' Milly said, as he took his seat beside her. 'And she's just asked me if you want to manage the hotel.'

'Rory, I'm sorry,' Eliza said. 'What happens there is none of my business.'

'I wish it wasn't mine, either.'

'But the hotel's been in your family for generations, hasn't it?'

He shook his head. 'My father bought it at auction after the previous owners went bust. The first thing he did was rename it the Montgomery.'

'But the website, your brochures – they all say it's been family-run for four generations.'

'It has,' he said. 'Just not by our family. It's called marketing, Eliza. Don't believe all you read.'

'Then why have you stayed there so long?'

'Because Dad asked me to and I promised him I would. Even though he doesn't know who I am any more.'

'You visit him?'

'Of course. Twice a week. Alex goes once a week. He's our father, Eliza. We love him.'

'But what will you do if you are asked to be general manager?'

'Milly and I talked about it today. I'll say no. I'm not right for the job. Not only because I'd be useless at it, or because I'd rather be in my workshop.' He glanced at Milly. She gave a subtle nod. 'Milly and I are going to be pretty busy elsewhere soon.'

'We're having a baby, Eliza,' Milly said, smiling. 'I'm nearly three months pregnant. It wasn't entirely planned, but now we can't wait.'

'We're still deciding what to do next,' Rory said after Eliza had congratulated them both. 'Milly says she's ready to move back here. I don't want to be too far from Dad. But whatever happens, I don't ever want to manage the hotel.'

'So Alex will become the next general manager by default?'

'Over his dead body. I doubt he could fit it in between all his other projects, anyway. It's a full-time job running that hostel of his. Not to mention the unorthodox way he stocks and decorates it.'

'Eliza happened to mention that she knows all about that,' Milly said.

'Olivia told you?' Rory asked.

Eliza nodded. It seemed there were no secrets tonight. 'You don't mind what Alex is doing?'

He shrugged. 'I'm his brother, not his conscience. I can't tell him how to live his life.'

Eliza woke at the hostel the next morning to an email from Olivia.

*Maxie and I are so sorry, Eliza. We're doing all we can to make amends. Talking to each other, swapping stories, reading everything we ever received from Jeannie to give you as much information about her, her parents and your father as we can. We've attached some of it here. You were right. We should have done this years ago. Please contact us if and when you feel ready to talk. O & M xx*

Eliza had had a restless night. She'd woken often, lying in the darkness, listening to the sounds of the hostel outside.

She'd thought about her mother. Her godmothers. All they had done for her over the years. About Rory and Alex. About all that Milly had said to her.

She wrote straight back. *I'm so sorry too. Thank you for writing everything down. I'm ready to talk again whenever you both are.*

# CHAPTER TWENTY-SIX

Olivia and Maxie were seated at the round table by the bay window when Eliza came in. The table was covered in piles of paperwork. They hugged her and she hugged them back. They loved her new haircut, they told her. She knew they meant it.

'Are you happy if we get right to it?' Olivia asked. At Eliza's nod, Maxie took over.

'We're so sorry to start with bad news,' she said. 'We found out more about Jeannie's parents.'

Eliza tried to ignore a sharp jolt of something that felt like disappointment. A staff member at their old school had put them in touch with a retired nun. She'd given them Jeannie's parents' full names. They'd gone in search online. Jeannie's mother had died ten years earlier. Her death notice had asked for donations to be made to the Stroke Foundation. Her father had died the following year, cause unknown. They were both buried in Melbourne.

'Was Mum mentioned in the death notices?' Eliza asked.

They had checked for exactly that.

'I'm sorry, Eliza. No,' Olivia said.

Eliza let that settle too. She had never met her grandparents. But there was still a ripple of hurt.

'Did I have aunts or uncles?'

Olivia shook her head. 'Jeannie was definitely an only child.'

Maxie took over. 'We read through all the postcards again too, Eliza. Made notes of any facts and dates we thought might help us.' She handed Eliza a printout of all they'd emailed her that morning.

'We also read through the paperwork you brought from Melbourne,' Olivia said. 'There were years of bank statements. Someone was sending your mum money. A lump sum once or twice a year, until the year you turned thirteen.' She paused. 'We think it might have been your father.'

'His name was on the statements? It's been there all this time?'

Olivia shook her head. 'All we could find out was that the deposits were made from overseas. We don't know who by. But we pooled everything else we remembered. All the relevant dates. Anyone she ever spoke about from that time. You were right. It does all point to her friend Emmet.'

'We actually met him once. Very briefly. He was living in Melbourne when we visited Jeannie. He'd travelled out to Australia with his cousin.'

'You met him?' She looked from one to the other. 'Do I look like him?'

'It was thirty-one years ago, Eliza, we're sorry,' Maxie said. 'We don't remember much beyond him having darkish hair and a nice accent.'

'Was he tall?'

'We think so,' Olivia said. 'But we don't remember for sure. We do know he was in an accident soon after. A bad one. He went back home to Ireland after he recovered.'

'He's definitely the most likely candidate. If not him, his cousin. Jeannie mentioned him too.'

'The only problem is we can't find Emmet's surname anywhere. Or the cousin's name.'

Eliza glanced down at the pages Maxie had given her. 'So we're trying to find an Irishman or his Irish cousin who lived in Australia for a few months thirty-one years ago.' She looked up. 'There must have been thousands of them.'

'We've got a few extra details that might help us. We know his family ran a pub in Ireland. Jeannie worked in it for a month, before she came back to Australia.' Olivia picked up the postcard in question. 'That narrows it down. She said she could see a castle from it.'

'I know it seems worse than finding a needle in a haystack,' Maxie said, 'but I'll keep looking until we find him. I've got all the time in the world at the moment. I've already googled "Irish castles". And "Irish castle ruins". There are only thirty thousand of them.'

'Thirty *thousand*?' Olivia said.

'And only seven thousand pubs,' Maxie added.

'That's if the one we're looking for is even still open,' Eliza said. 'Maxie, please, let me help.'

'You can't,' Olivia said. 'You're coming for a walk with me. I need to tell you something else.'

Edinburgh's Royal Botanic Garden was a short car journey from the hotel. The day was warm with a soft breeze. The spring sun shone on the new green growth on the trees. The paths were lined with flowerbeds already filled with early blooms opening up.

Olivia and Eliza began talking as soon as they began walking.

'Eliza, while you were away, Maxie and I didn't only go through Jeannie's paperwork. We also argued about her. About something we've been arguing about for years. What we should tell you. What we can tell you. You're thirty years old. Do you truly want to hear everything we know?'

'Is it bad?'

'It's complicated. Because your mother was complicated. But you knew that. Know that.'

Eliza nodded.

Gently, carefully, Olivia shared more stories about Jeannie. About her phone call telling them she was pregnant. About Mr and Mrs Quaker. Their accident. Her and Maxie's visits to Jeannie and Eliza over the years. The arguments. The conversation about the items in the house that may or may not have been stolen. She told Eliza about the late-night calls they'd receive from Jeannie. How angry she was sometimes. How drunk sometimes. How up and down she often was.

They took a seat on one of the benches. A cool wind had started up.

'We can go into the café if you like?' Olivia asked, noticing Eliza shiver.

She shook her head. 'Not yet. Please, keep talking.' She paused. 'Olivia, I know Mum wasn't always well. Mentally. I didn't have a name for it when I was young, but since then, looking back —'

Olivia reached for her hand. 'I know, Eliza. We tried talking about it with her. She didn't like it. She wouldn't discuss it. We don't know if she was ever diagnosed as bipolar, or anything else. If she had any treatment. When we were at school we just thought it was Jeannie being Jeannie. It kept happening after we left school, too. The mood changes. The stories. If you were ready for mischief, there was no one better. If you weren't,' she paused, 'sometimes it was trickier.'

Eliza fell silent for a moment, then turned to Olivia.

'Why did she have me? She didn't have to.'

'She never spoke about the alternative. When she rang to tell us, she was five months pregnant with you and so excited about it. She always said you were the best thing that ever happened to her.'

'She always said that to me too.' Eliza's voice was quiet.

'Was it terrible for you, Eliza? Those up and down times. All those moves to the different towns?'

'It was mostly wonderful. She was so different from any other mothers that I knew. She was fun. She was moody, but I could see the change in moods coming. She'd get really busy, change the décor in our house, or even cook a lot. Other times she'd just want to lie in bed. And I would lie beside her and read, or bring my painting things into the room. She named her moods after the seasons. Sometimes she said she was in summer, or if she was low, it was winter. Sometimes it was a very cold, dark winter.' She took a deep breath. 'I don't know what you and Maxie think, but I know she didn't mean to do it, Olivia. Even before I read the coroner's report. She would never have left me alone like that by choice. I know she wouldn't.'

'I know the police asked you this, Eliza. And I promise I'll never ask you again.' She hesitated. 'Did Jeannie leave any kind of note at all?'

Eliza's eyes widened. 'All this time, you thought she had? That I'd destroyed it? Not told anyone?'

'We're trying to be as honest with you as we can. We hope you'll be the same.'

Eliza was silent for a time. 'I remember getting out of the taxi. Walking up to the house. I could hear music playing. The house was full of music. And light. Every light in the house was on. The doors were open. Every dish had been used. Every glass. As if she had been having the time of her life while I was gone, eating everything, drinking everything. It was usually spotless when I got back from any trip. As if she'd done nothing but clean while I was away. All the cleaning things were out in the kitchen. Cloths and sprays, the mop, the broom. She must have been about to get stuck in, clean it up for me, but then she must have decided to have that bath first and that's, that's when —'

Olivia put her arm around Eliza. She could see her goddaughter was trying to hold back tears. She waited quietly until Eliza was ready to speak again.

'She rang you five times that night, didn't she?' Eliza asked eventually. 'Why so many times?'

'You know why, sweetheart. I told you, and I told the coroner too. To say how excited she was that you were coming home. To laugh at how much cleaning she was about to do. She said that you were like the Queen, thinking the world smells like fresh paint. Because whenever you arrived home after one of your holidays with us, your house always smelt like cleaning products. She told me she would always associate you with the smell of lemon bleach, that she loved the smell too, because it meant you weren't far away. She'd been counting down the hours till you came home. She was so excited about you going to uni, too. She was already planning her first visit to you there.'

'And she wouldn't have said any of that if she was —' She stopped there.

'No, Eliza, she wouldn't have.'

'I've read the coroner's report so many times, Olivia. I know it off by heart. He must have seen so many situations like that. All those different factors. The alcohol. The bath. The sleeping pill. Sometimes it would have been suicide, wouldn't it? But not with Mum. I knew she couldn't wait to see me again. She'd said it in that email. And she'd only taken one pill, the coroner said. Two at the most. She'd told me she got them from a friend at work. I know that was a mistake – they weren't prescribed for her – but it wasn't an overdose. She just had too much wine. Got in the bath. Fell asleep. It was an accident. A terrible accident.'

'I know, darling. I know it was,' Olivia said. 'Maxie knows that too.'

Eliza turned to her. This time she didn't fight the tears. Olivia held her close.

'What would I have done without you both?' Eliza said, her voice muffled. 'Not just then. Ever since.'

'You don't have to ask. Because we're not going anywhere. You're stuck with us.'

Minutes passed, Olivia holding Eliza tight, gently stroking her dark cap of hair, soothing her.

It was Eliza who eventually suggested a cup of tea. They walked, arms linked, to the café. Eliza offered to fetch their drinks.

While she was at the counter, Olivia rang Maxie.

'Any luck with Emmet?'

'Nothing. All I've managed to do so far is rack up a big phone bill. Is she okay?'

Olivia told her about their conversation, keeping an eye on Eliza across the café. Maxie made her repeat the last exchange with Eliza. About Jeannie's final moments.

'You didn't say anything else, did you?'

'I told you I wouldn't.'

'She can't ever know, Olivia.'

'She never will, Maxie. I won't ever tell her.'

As Eliza approached with their tea, Olivia abruptly hung up.

On the way back to the car, Eliza asked if Olivia would mind if she walked back to the hotel. She needed the fresh air, the exercise, to clear her head.

'Of course I don't mind,' Olivia said. 'Come home whenever you're ready.'

As she sat in the car and watched Eliza walk away, she tried to fight a feeling of self-loathing. She'd promised Eliza they would tell her the truth from now on. She'd already lied.

# CHAPTER TWENTY-SEVEN

Two hours after her walk, Eliza was back in Celine's suite again. Sullivan was working beside her.

He'd messaged as she was walking back to the Montgomery. His father had been called into work. Was there any possibility that he could drop by for a visit? Yes, she'd messaged back. Ann-Marie had dropped him off. He'd extravagantly complimented Eliza's haircut. He'd cheered when she'd asked if he wanted to help her do an hour's sorting for Celine.

She'd agreed to do that too, as a favour to Olivia. Her godmother had been very apologetic when she rang and asked her.

'She's been in bed for the past two days with a cold. We were revelling in the peace. But the rest seems to have supercharged her. She's ringing reception every five minutes. We just need to calm her down even a bit. Are you sure you don't mind?'

Eliza was sure. She knew Maxie was doing all she could to

find Emmet's pub. Olivia had been very grateful in regard to Celine. She'd also promised to send up afternoon tea for three.

'What an awful haircut,' Celine said as soon as she saw Eliza. 'You look like a man.'

'No, she doesn't,' Sullivan said. 'It really suits her. Doesn't it, Lawrence?'

He'd arrived at the door, carrying a tray of coffee and biscuits. 'It looks great, Eliza.'

'I think it really shows off her lovely eyes,' Sullivan said.

Lawrence agreed with that, too.

'Stop fawning over her, the pair of you,' Celine snapped. 'You're making me feel sick again.'

'If you need me to take you to the nearest hospital, just say the word, Celine,' Lawrence said.

She glared at him suspiciously, then suddenly spoke in a fast stream of French. 'T'as un tête a faire sauter les plaques d'égouts.'

Lawrence replied as swiftly. 'Une faute de grammaire, comme d'habitude, Celine. *Une* tête. Feminin.'

Sullivan listened, wide-eyed. 'How amazing! What did you both say?'

Lawrence calmly explained. 'Celine told me I have a head that would blow the manhole covers off sewers. I replied that she'd made a grammatical mistake as usual. A head is feminine in French.'

Celine retaliated by turning up the volume of the TV extra loud. Any more conversation was impossible. Lawrence left, winking at Eliza and Sullivan on his way out.

*

Their sorting was interrupted soon after by the constant ringing of Celine's mobile phone. She didn't pick it up.

'Do you need to get that?' Eliza asked after the third unanswered call.

Celine replied without taking her eyes off the TV screen. 'No. It's only my husband. He rings all the time. He wants me back. Let him wait. Treat 'em mean, keep 'em keen.' She cackled alarmingly.

An hour later, Eliza excused herself to go and visit Maxie and Olivia. She made Celine promise not to swear at Sullivan. She checked that he was all right to be left sorting Celine's photos on his own for ten minutes. He told her he couldn't be happier.

Her godmothers didn't have any news for her. Maxie had been googling more Irish pubs, more Irish castles. It was becoming worse than finding a needle in a haystack.

'Eliza, did Jeannie ever say anything else to you about her time in Ireland?' Olivia asked. 'A place she visited a lot, the name of a river, anything that might help us narrow it down?'

'Not that I remember. I know she learned some folk songs there. She liked singing them. She also told me she was an expert at pouring Guinness. But that's no help. An Irish pub serving Guinness?'

'Don't worry,' Maxie said, turning back to her laptop. 'If he's out there, we'll find him.'

\*

When Eliza returned to Celine's room, Sullivan wasn't sorting photos. Celine wasn't shouting at him. They were sitting in front of the television, in an armchair each, a bowl of popcorn between them.

'Sullivan? Are you oka—'

'Shut up,' Celine said. 'They're getting to the juicy stuff.'

They were watching a programme on a cable channel. Eliza stood behind them and watched for a few minutes. It was a Top 10 countdown of celebrity downfalls, with regular recaps. Images of Hugh Grant, Robert Downey Jr, Lindsay Lohan and Charlie Sheen flashed by. The American narrator bellowed highlights of their careers, as snippets of red carpet strolls, award ceremonies and scenes from their best-known films were interwoven with police line-up photos, paparazzi shots and slinking court appearances.

'Sullivan, I'm not sure it's good for you to watch this,' Eliza said.

'It's warning me about all the pitfalls that might lie ahead.'

'Would your father let you watch it?'

'Over his dead body.'

'I think it's time I took you home.'

'I haven't finished Celine's photos yet. We're only up to the 1960s.'

'Shut up, you two,' Celine snapped. 'I'm trying to listen.'

Beside her, her mobile phone rang. She ignored it. Her husband again, Eliza guessed.

An ad break came on, but not before the breathless presenter told them who was next. Mel Gibson.

Celine rubbed her hands together. 'Couldn't leave him out. I saw him in Nice once. Good-looking. Tiny though. They're all tiny. Tom Cruise is only two-foot high in real life.'

'Really?' Sullivan said.

'Yes. Pocket-sized. It's all done with trick photography.'

As a quick series of ads flashed by, Eliza tried again to convince Sullivan to leave with her.

'No, it looks like it might rain. I didn't bring a raincoat.'

'It's a sunny day, Sullivan.'

'We'll just watch to the end. Please, Eliza. I never get to watch things like this at home.'

'That's what's worrying me.'

'Leave him alone, you nag,' Celine said. 'Let the kid have some fun.'

'It's not fun. It's celebrity gossip.'

'Shut up, would you?' Celine said. 'It's back on.'

Sullivan sat back happily. 'Mel Gibson's Australian like Eliza and me,' he said, as snippets of the actor's films flashed on to the screen – *Mad Max*, *Gallipoli*, *What Women Want* – interspersed with shots of award ceremonies and photos of him over the years.

'He doesn't sound it,' Celine said.

'He's an actor. He can do all sorts of accents,' Eliza said, drawn in now despite herself.

Celine scoffed. 'A terrible Scottish one, though. There, look, in that one.' On screen, the actor was now on a horse, blue paint covering most of his face, shouting in a Scottish accent. '*Braveheart*? Rubbishheart, more like it. Such liberties with Scottish history. Garbage from start to finish.'

'Did you ever see that film, Eliza?' Sullivan asked.

'Count your blessings if you didn't,' Celine said.

There was no answer.

They turned around.

Eliza was gone.

Olivia was still with Maxie when Eliza came bursting in.

'*Braveheart*! Mum and I saw *Braveheart* on video one night. I remember she got really excited about it! She said it was filmed in Ireland. That she worked near the castle they used. That she wished she'd been living there when it was filmed, maybe she could have been an extra.'

'But it's a Scottish story, Eliza,' Olivia said. 'She must have been mistaken.'

'Please, Maxie, google it.'

Seconds later, Maxie looked up from her laptop, eyes wide. 'Eliza's right. It was filmed in Ireland. In a town called Trim, in County Meath.' She googled again. 'There are only fifteen pubs in Trim.'

*

Olivia printed out a list of the pubs and their phone numbers. They decided on a cover story. Maxie would speak in her native Australian accent. Say she was calling from Melbourne. Putting together a surprise for her brother's fiftieth. Tracking down his old friends, getting them to record video messages. Did anyone from the pub have a relative called Emmet who'd lived in Australia thirty or so years ago? Her brother had shared a house with him.

She had no luck with the first five calls. The sixth rang out unanswered. She hit the jackpot on the seventh. A young man, relaxed, cheerful, happy to listen and ready for a chat.

'Aye, the fella who owns the pub is Emmet. Emmet Foley. He went out to Melbourne when he was my age. I'm going there myself at the end of the year. He's been giving me some tips. Where to go, where not to go. I didn't want to break the news to him that it might have changed in three decades.'

'Could I speak to him?'

'Sorry, no. He and his wife and kids are away on holiday. Back the day after tomorrow. I'm holding the fort. Doing a mighty job of it if I do say so myself. Do you want to leave a message? You're calling from Australia, you said?'

Maxie couldn't leave an Edinburgh number. Her mobile was a UK one too.

'No. I don't want to put him to any expense. I'll call back. Before I go, can I please ask a strange question? If you're not too busy?'

'Ask away.'

'Can you see the castle from the pub? Trim Castle? The one used in that Mel Gibson film?'

'I'm looking at it right now,' the young man said.

# CHAPTER TWENTY-EIGHT

'Do you want us to be there with you?' Olivia asked Eliza.

Her answer was immediate. Yes. Both of them.

Emmet wasn't due back in Trim for two days. They'd take the car ferry, Olivia decided. Better for Eliza, more room for Maxie and her plastered foot. Within an hour, it was organised. They'd drive the three hours from Edinburgh to Cairnryan Port. Get the ferry to Belfast, a two and a half hour trip. Drive for less than two hours to Trim. Olivia booked them into a hotel there, right next to the castle. Google Maps told them it was minutes from Emmet's pub.

It only took a day for their plans to unravel.

Hazel was given an unexpected two days off from the New York production. She was flying back to Edinburgh to see Maxie for a brief reunion. Eliza assured Maxie she understood: of course she couldn't go to Ireland now.

Olivia received a different kind of phone call. The matron in charge of Edgar's care rang, asking for an urgent meeting. Edgar appeared to be entering a new phase of his illness. Agitation. Fear. He was constantly asking for Olivia. When she went to see him, he wouldn't stop weeping.

On her return, tearful herself, Olivia called Maxie. 'I can't leave him. What if something worse happens while I'm away?'

'We'll postpone the Irish trip. Eliza will understand.'

'We can't. She's waited years for this.'

'Could she go alone?'

'She doesn't drive.'

'She could fly. We could arrange a driver from the airport.'

'I don't think she should be on her own.'

'Who, then?'

'I'll ask Lawrence.'

'You'd send her away with a stranger? On a trip like this?'

'He's a good man. Reliable. Calm. That's what she needs. The bookings are all in place. Lawrence can take my car.'

'Have you asked him yet?'

'I'll do it right now.'

Forty minutes later, it was organised. He'd come to Maxie's suite, listened quietly as Olivia explained the situation, asked several questions and then agreed.

Maxie waited until he'd left before turning to Olivia. 'I know this is inappropriate, given the circumstances, but he's handsome, isn't he? Smart too. Is he single?'

Olivia rubbed her eyes. 'I don't know. But you're right. That is inappropriate.'

*

Eliza was taken aback at the news. 'Lawrence? But I hardly know him.'

'Just think of him as your chauffeur,' Olivia said. 'He'll follow your lead the whole time.'

'So he knows everything about me now? All my family secrets?'

'We told him the bare minimum. That you were going to look for your father, or to talk to someone who might have known him. It's up to you if you want to tell him anything else.'

Eliza thought about it. Perhaps it was the best possible arrangement. Someone professional, distant and responsible, acting as, yes, her chauffeur. She'd only had brief exchanges with Lawrence since she'd been at the Montgomery, but he had always been kind, courteous. There'd even been glints of humour when Celine was involved. She agreed.

On the way back to her room, she saw him working at the front desk and walked over.

'I'm sure it's not in your job description,' she said quietly, 'but I really appreciate it.'

'You're welcome, Eliza,' he said.

She noticed again how his smile transformed his face.

She told Celine that afternoon that she wouldn't be able to work with her again that week. Celine insisted on knowing why.

Eliza said she needed to go to Ireland. That Lawrence was taking her.

'Well, well, isn't he the dark horse?' she said. 'Sucking up to the boss's goddaughter. Whisking her off for some Celtic sightseeing. And a bit more than that too, I bet.'

'It's nothing like that, Celine.'

'I suppose you're taking Sullivan too? Your little crony.'

'No, I'm not,' Eliza said. He had asked if he could come, when Eliza messaged him that afternoon. She'd promised him an Irish souvenir instead.

'I hope your plane crashes,' Celine said, turning back to the TV.

'We're going by ferry.'

'I hope it sinks,' Celine said. She pointed the remote control and turned up the volume.

Eliza spent the evening before the Irish trip with her godmothers. Hazel was due to arrive from New York in the morning. Maxie was trying hard to play down how excited she was. Olivia seemed calmer about Edgar. His doctor was trialling a new medication. It had stopped some of his anxiety.

All three of them had been doing more online research now that they knew Emmet's surname. The local newspaper was online. He'd featured in it a lot over the years. He seemed to be from a well-known family in the area. His pub had sponsored local football teams, fundraisers. It had live music on the weekends.

A quiz every week. His father had run it before him. They'd found articles about his retirement party, including photos of the whole Foley family. Emmet, his parents and three dark-haired men who had to be Emmet's brothers. Olivia found an obituary about his father. He'd died three years earlier. A GAA man to his fingertips, the opening paragraph read. They'd had to google that. It stood for Gaelic Athletic Association.

They'd all closely inspected the different photos of Emmet.

'Do you think I look like him?' Eliza asked.

'You're both tall,' Olivia said. 'Dark hair. But I'm sorry, all I ever see in you is Jeannie.'

They'd learned he was married, with two daughters in their late teens. Maxie had discovered they were both athletes. Long-distance runners. She'd printed out stories about them for Eliza.

She read the articles. There were photos of them too.

'Is his wife Asian?'

'I don't think so,' Olivia said. She showed Eliza another printout. Emmet with his wife, Dervla, at an athletics association award ceremony. *Proud parents Emmet and Dervla Foley*, the caption read. Dervla was pale-skinned, blonde-haired, smiling. 'His daughters might be adopted, or perhaps they're from an earlier marriage.'

Eliza studied the two young women. 'They could be my half-sisters?'

They might be, Olivia and Maxie agreed.

Back in her room, unable to sleep, Eliza found herself googling all the photographs again.

The idea of her father had always been like a shadow hovering on the edges of her life. But now, here she was, so close to learning more. She might not only have a father alive and well. She might have a stepmother. Half-sisters. Grandparents. Uncles. Cousins.

A whole family in Ireland. Waiting for her.

# CHAPTER TWENTY-NINE

Olivia and Maxie gathered in front of the Montgomery to see her off. Maxie was on crutches, but in cheerful form. Hazel was arriving in two hours. Olivia was going to see Edgar after Eliza's departure.

Eliza hugged them both.

'We're with you in spirit,' Olivia said.

'We're at the end of a phone if you need us,' Maxie said.

Olivia's car pulled up in front of the Montgomery. Lawrence got out, took Eliza's bag, stowed it in the boot, and stood back.

She hugged them again. 'I hope Edgar will be okay. That Hazel has a great stay. That Celine behaves herself. That —'

'Eliza, go, darling. Think about yourself, not us.'

She waved until they were out of sight.

*

As they made their way through the outskirts of Edinburgh, Lawrence asked if she'd like to listen to the radio. She accepted, glad when he chose Classic FM and soothing music filled the car. She was so nervous. She needed to stay as peaceful as possible, she realised, to think ahead to —

Her phone pinged. Sullivan.

*Safe travels, FF. I'll miss you.*

*I'll miss you too*, she said. *Have you got any plans today?*

*Dad's trying to take the day off! We might go on the open-top bus tour together!*

The thought of it made Eliza happy.

They soon left the city behind. Green hills started to appear.

'Thank you again for this,' she said to Lawrence. 'I know I should be able to drive at my age.'

'I like driving. I also like ferries. And Ireland. I should be thanking you for the two days off work.'

'But you're the boss. You can give yourself days off whenever you want.'

'Only on paper. Olivia's the real boss.'

'Lawrence, I don't know exactly what Olivia told you —'

'It's your business, Eliza. You don't have to tell me anything. I'm here as your chauffeur. You can even sit in the back if you want.'

'I'm fine here, but thank you.'

She gazed out the window as they took the road to Cairnryan Port, the music gently filling the car. Lawrence was peaceful company, happy with silence between them.

The only interruptions were the messages coming in on her phone.

Olivia first. *All ok?*

Then Maxie. *Everything ok? Mxx*

Rose. *Thinking of you, my friend. R xx*

Eliza had phoned her the evening before and told her all that was happening. She was grateful again for the feeling of being surrounded, watched over.

She sent back brief replies, then switched her phone to vibrate only and closed her eyes. In came thoughts of her mother. Would Jeannie have wanted her to be making this trip? Wanted her to be meeting Emmet after all these years? There was no way of knowing. Her anxiety started to rise again.

She sought distraction in conversation. 'Where did you grow up, Lawrence?'

If he was startled by the sudden personal question, he didn't show it.

'We moved around a lot. My father was English, but my mother was French. We went back and forth between their two countries for a lot of my childhood. We had a few years in Germany too.'

'That's why you're fluent in so many languages?'

'It helped. My father had his own export business.'

'Have you got brothers and sisters?'

'One half-sister, Annick. My mother was married before she met my father. Annick's about to turn forty. We've been summoned to France next week to help her forget it. A three-day family gathering in a villa near Bordeaux.'

'And did you always want to work in hospitality?' Her questions sounded so formal, she realised. As if she was interviewing him.

'I always wanted to travel. It's a good career for that.'

She asked more questions. He briefly described his career path, from studying in London to hotel management work in Europe and New York. Before she could ask more, he changed the subject.

'And you, Eliza? What's next? Apart from setting up a service to tame difficult guests.'

She knew Olivia had told him about her previous job. She told him the truth. She had no idea yet.

'If you could do anything, though?'

An image appeared in her mind. Paints. Paper. Children. 'I think I'd like to be an art teacher.'

'You're an artist?'

No, she told him. But she loved how it felt when she painted. She'd had a great art teacher at school. It would mean going back to university but perhaps she would, one day. She was surprised to hear herself saying all of this. She'd never put it into words before.

'Have you ever wanted a different career?' she asked.

'Don't tell Olivia, but I'm already doing it.'

'You're moonlighting?'

'Only in my spare time, I promise. It's a hobby more than a second career. Photography.'

He did some portraits, he told her, but mostly landscapes. The more remote, the better, at different times of the day, in different types of weather. It was one of the reasons he'd taken the job at the Montgomery – its proximity to the wild landscapes of the Highlands. He'd taken hundreds of photographs in the past three years, he said.

'I have an exhibition in Edinburgh in the summer. During the Festival.'

'You do?'

'Please don't be impressed. I'm not the only one. There are dozens on at Festival time.'

'I don't know if I'll still be here. Could I see your photos anywhere else?'

'I have a website.'

'You do? I'm sorry to keep sounding so surprised. I assumed —'

'I work in the hotel six days a week? Hang upside down like a bat in the cloakroom on the seventh?'

The mental image made her laugh. 'Yes.'

'No. I spend my days off sheltering from the rain in the Highlands, trying not to ruin my camera.'

'What's your website called?'

He told her. She took out her phone and scrolled through the photo gallery. He'd captured the wild Scottish landscape in image after image of mountains and lakes, tumbling streams and stormy skies. There were striking shots taken in summer too, vividly coloured wildflowers and heather appearing to glow against moss-green backdrops.

'They're stunning,' she said truthfully.

He thanked her. He gave her that lovely smile again, too.

*

Olivia had booked them into the first-class lounge area of the ferry. They took their seats, looking over the water, the land beyond. He took out a book. A spy story. She was restless now. Growing more nervous. She explored the ferry. Responded to Sullivan's Scrabble moves. Sent back a row of happy emojis when she received a selfie of him and his father on the tour bus.

She did another circuit of the ferry. It was like a luxury hotel. People talking, relaxing. One area featured a fake fireplace, the flames flickering, creating an oddly cosy atmosphere. There were couples, families, single people.

She returned to her seat as one of the staff was taking lunch orders. A middle-aged woman, jolly, chatty. Eliza was too nervous for a big meal. She ordered a sandwich. Lawrence had gone for a walk too, taking his camera with him, she noticed.

'So are yourself and your husband off on a holiday?' the waitress asked.

'He's not my husband.'

'Sorry, your partner.'

'He's not my partner either.'

She lowered her voice. 'He's not abducting you, is he?'

'It's kind of a work trip.'

'Ooh, lucky you,' she said with a wink. 'I do like good-looking workmates.'

*

The crossing was smooth. They were back in the car and driving out of Belfast by two p.m. An hour into their journey, Lawrence pointed out a sign. They'd crossed the border into the Republic of Ireland. The road signs were now in English and Irish, the distances in kilometres, not miles.

Her heart gave a little jolt when she saw the first sign for Trim.

'Do you need to be there by any particular time?' he asked.

It seemed strange that he didn't know their plans. 'I'm not sure how much Olivia told you —'

'She gave me the basic details. That it's something of a family reunion.'

It was, in some ways, she realised.

'I've never met my father.' She tried again. 'I don't know who my father is.' She tried once more. 'My mother had me when she was twenty-two. She always made it a kind of game about who my father was. She promised to tell me when I was eighteen. And . . .' She faltered. 'And unfortunately she died not long before my birthday.'

'I'm very sorry.'

She couldn't seem to stop talking now. She told him Olivia and Maxie had been helping her to find him. 'The man in Trim I'm going to see – we know he knew Mum. He was living in Melbourne around the time she got pregnant and we think it could be him. But he was there with his cousin. It might be him too.' She finally stopped. 'Sorry. I'm a bit nervous.'

'I'm not surprised.' A pause. 'You were very young to lose your mother.'

She stopped herself from going into detail again. It was an accident, she said simply. He sympathised again.

He asked her what she wanted to do when they got to Trim. She'd check into their hotel first, she said. Then she would go to Emmet's pub. And then —

Her phone vibrated. Olivia.

*Hope all is ok, dear E? Are you in Trim yet? Hazel's arrived, and we're all thinking of you. Hope everything's ok with Lawrence too? xxx*

Eliza replied with a brief, truthful message. She was extremely nervous. Lawrence was being very kind.

As they continued driving, she remembered all Olivia had told her about his reasons for coming to Edinburgh. About his wife's death nearly four years earlier. It seemed important to acknowledge it.

She tried to find the right words. 'Lawrence, Olivia shared some of your story with me.' It sounded so clumsy. 'About your wife. I'm so sorry.'

A moment passed, then he glanced across at her. 'Thank you, Eliza.'

There was more she could have said. But it seemed right to leave it there, like that, between them.

They passed another sign for Trim, this time directing them to a motorway exit. She knew from her research that it was only a small town. A population of nine thousand. As they came in on a side road, the light changed, as if before a storm, the sky glowing and dark at once. They came around a bend and there was the castle, rising high above the town. It was so unexpected. So majestic.

Lawrence pulled onto the side of the road so there was more time to look at it.

She had researched Trim Castle too. She'd read it was the largest Anglo-Norman castle in Ireland, built over thirty years, from 1176. The facts hadn't prepared her for its size or beauty.

He asked her what she wanted him to do next.

'I can drive through the town first, if you want. Help you find the pub you're looking for?'

She thanked him, but said she thought it might be better if she found it on foot. She knew she needed to be on her own.

Their hotel was across the road from the castle. At reception, she exchanged numbers with Lawrence.

'What will you do now?' she asked.

'Read. Walk. Explore.' He indicated a black bag over his shoulder. 'Maybe take some photos.'

'Lawrence, I don't know what will happen, how long I'll be. Whether I'll —'

'Eliza, don't worry about me. Do whatever you need to do. If you need me, message.'

Upstairs, Eliza discovered Olivia had booked her into a room with a striking view of the castle. She unpacked, then flicked through the information folder. Alongside a history of the castle was a page on the filming of *Braveheart*. There was a map of the town, with a list of pubs and restaurants. Emmet's pub was included. She noticed something else. An Emmet Street. It almost felt like a sign.

She couldn't go straight to his pub. Not yet. She'd go across to the castle first. Get some fresh air.

She walked the short distance to the entrance, on the way passing an information board about *Braveheart*. Near the castle gate was a sign about guided tours. She didn't go in. She followed a path around the castle walls instead, then across a footbridge. She stopped and looked down at the fast-flowing river tumbling over the rocks. The castle formed a dramatic backdrop. Another tower was visible on a higher field. A sign told her it was called the Yellow Steeple. She took the path up to it. She could see someone was already there, taking photos. Lawrence. He saw her and waited.

'Did you find the pub okay?' he asked as she reached him.

She admitted that she hadn't been there yet.

'I passed it earlier, when I walked around the town. You can see the roof of it from here.' He lifted his camera, focused, then held it in front of her. Standing close, she was aware of the piney scent of his aftershave. She could clearly see the pub's roof through the viewfinder. She had a sudden longing to stay here, watching from afar. To see Emmet for the first time from this safe distance.

*Go now, Eliza.*

She didn't know if the voice in her head was her own, or someone else's. Her mother's?

She thanked Lawrence, then walked back down the hill into the town.

It was nearly four. A good time, she hoped. After the lunch trade, before any evening rush. It was a day of grey skies interrupted by sudden cloud clearances, sending shafts of bright light across the sky. Emmet's pub was brightly coloured. Window boxes planted with red geraniums. Stained glass above the door. It only took her a moment to adjust from the daylight to the pub's dim interior.

It smelt of coffee. Of toasted sandwiches. An underlying smell – smoky, from a fireplace, not cigarettes. A yeasty smell of alcohol. It was warm. A fire had been lit in the corner, the source of the smoke as well as the warmth. There was music playing on a radio. Fleetwood Mac's 'Landslide'. The DJ back-announced it, before passing over to the newsroom. Eliza listened to a solemn Irish accent detailing several news items.

The bar was quiet, empty tables on either side of her. A group of four were in a far corner, playing cards, serious about it. Americans, or perhaps Canadians. Then a cheery voice sounded, coming from a man appearing from a room to the side of the bar.

'Here you are, folks. Toasted sandwiches for four. More pints on the way.'

She'd studied the newspaper photos closely. There was no mistaking him. He was taller than her. He had dark curly hair. A friendly face. He was stockily built, wearing a checked shirt, jeans.

She stayed near the doorway as he chatted to the foursome, laughed at a remark, something about the weather, about Irish people always being happy to talk about it, their national pastime.

He noticed her in the doorway and called over a cheery greeting. Then he was behind the bar, loading four dark creamy pints of Guinness onto a tray, back to the group, carefully placing a glass in front of each with sure practised movements. He went behind the bar again, then disappeared, to a kitchen, she assumed.

She couldn't stand there all day. She moved to the bar. Felt the beating of her heart. Clenched her hands to stop them trembling. She wanted to be able to press pause, or to ask him to stand still, let her stare at him, this man in his fifties. To try to imagine him as her mother would have known him, a man in his early twenties. She wanted to search for a sign of that accident he'd had, a scar, a mark. Olivia and Maxie hadn't remembered all the details. Just that he'd been knocked out in a fight, been in a coma for weeks before waking, seemingly without any repercussions. A lucky man.

'Now, what can I get you?' He was back, standing in front of her.

Did she introduce herself now? Or order a drink first? Wait until the four people had gone? She didn't know what she wanted to do, how to do this. Even after imagining it for so many years.

He was waiting.

'A sparkling water, please.'

'Ice and lemon?'

'Yes. Yes please.'

He was back with it in moments. She took the coward's way out again. She took her drink to a table in the corner, under some posters advertising a pub quiz taking place that evening, a forthcoming GAA fundraiser. Other flyers advertised local services, babysitting, interior design. He came over and she thought he was going to talk to her. Instead, he cleared the table behind her. Glasses, two plates. It must have been busy here at lunchtime. She'd chosen the time well.

The other four people were barely making a start on their pints, more interested in their card game.

He came past again. *Now. Do it, now.*

'Excuse me.' Louder. 'Excuse me, sir.' Sir? She felt a wave of embarrassment. She was doing it wrong.

'Yes?'

'Are you Emmet?'

'I am indeed.'

'My name is Eliza. Eliza Miller. I'm from Australia.' Her accent had already told him that. She waited, embarrassed again, hoping his barman had told him an Australian was dropping in today.

'So you are,' he said, smiling now. 'You're a long way from home.'

'My godmother spoke to your barman. She said I might be visiting.'

'She spoke to Liam? Sorry, what about? He's been off sick. I haven't seen him since I got back from holidays myself.'

This was worse. She was starting from scratch. About to explain, she was saved again. The door opened. A local called over to Emmet. A pint was poured and delivered. Then he was back to her.

'Sorry about that. Not that we're exactly rushed off our feet yet. You were talking to Liam?'

'My godmother was. About a video message.' She couldn't go ahead with that cover story. She dived in instead. 'My mother was Jeannie Miller. In Melbourne. Thirty-one years ago.'

His reaction was instantaneous. 'You're Jeannie's daughter! Jeannie! Jesus, why didn't you say?' She was shocked, nearly spilt her drink, when he leaned down, pulled her to her feet and hugged her. Hugged her tightly. 'I see it in you now. I wouldn't have if you hadn't told me. God, now I can't unsee it! What did you say your name was? Eliza? How is Jeannie? Is she here in Ireland too? Has she sent you in here first as a joke? I wouldn't put it past her!'

'You remember her?'

'Of course I remember Jeannie! She kept me sane in London and here for a month one summer. Apart from nearly helping me lose my life, she also saved me in Melbourne.' He laughed again. 'She sent you to Trim to surprise me? Why didn't she contact me herself? How long has it been? Thirty years? More. Jesus, Jeannie Miller's daughter! How fantastic. Hold on, stay there, would you?'

He went over to the group of four. Asked if they were all right for everything? They were, great, good. He checked with the other customer. 'Tom, you're all right for now? Good man.'

He came back, pulled up the stool across from her, sat down, shaking his head. 'I can't believe it. She always threatened to visit again but she never did. We lost touch. Nothing like Facebook for us back then. How is she? God, I see her in you now, clear as day.'

There was no way to sugar-coat it. She blurted it out. 'I'm sorry, but she died.'

'She *died*. What? When? Oh, God, I'm sorry. Jeannie dead. It doesn't seem possible. When?'

'Thirteen years ago. She was about to turn forty.'

'Dear God, so young. Too young. I'm so sorry. Was it cancer?'

She told him the truth. Something made her feel her mother would want Emmet to know. She kept it brief, but she explained the circumstances. The bath. Alcohol and medication. The coroner's involvement. The ruling that it was a tragic accident.

She could see shock in his eyes. He told her again how sorry he was. 'What age were you?'

'Seventeen.'

'Ah, you poor kid. You poor thing.' He frowned then. 'So what year were you born?'

She told him.

'My own pretty eventful year. So she had you not long —'

The door opened. A couple, tourists. She knew he'd have to get up any moment to serve them.

She'd waited for this meeting for so long. Imagined it so many times. She had wanted her father to be a nice man. Better than nice. A good man. A kind man. A man who'd loved her mother even for a little while. She'd seen, so quickly, so clearly, Emmet's affection for Jeannie. She'd planned to slowly raise the subject. To tell him about the games her mother used to play about her possible different fathers. She'd planned to be tactful. Diplomatic. To tread so carefully.

She forgot all of that. She asked him now, quickly, before he left again and she lost her nerve.

'Emmet, I'm sorry, but I need to know. Are you my father?'

# CHAPTER THIRTY

Emmet burst out laughing.

'Jesus,' he said. 'I'd forgotten how direct you Aussies are. Listen, can you hold on? I'll be right back.'

She wanted to run. Start again. Come back and do it in a dignified way. She wouldn't have been surprised if he'd asked her to leave. A stranger, asking that.

After serving the new arrivals, he returned with his phone. 'Are you in Trim long? My wife would love to meet you. She met Jeannie too. That month we were here, working together, before she went back to Australia. Hold on.' He dialled. 'Love, it's me. You won't believe it. We've an Aussie in the bar. A young Aussie. You'll never guess whose daughter she is. Jeannie Miller. Yes, I'm serious. No. No, sad news there. You will. Grand, yes, see you soon.'

He still hadn't answered her question. He was smiling, shaking his head in amazement. 'Jeannie's daughter. Here in my pub. It's incredible.'

She was puzzled. Had she even asked the question out loud? She tried again. 'Emmet, I don't know if you heard me.'

'I did indeed. I don't get asked a question like that every day of the week. Eliza, much as I'd be proud to claim you, I can categorically assure you I'm not your father.'

It couldn't end like this. 'Are you sure?'

'I couldn't be surer.' His expression was kind. 'Look, much as I love living in a small town, not everyone needs to hear everyone's business. My wife's on her way. She runs the pharmacy down the road. We've a room out the back here. It's a bit more private. Come there with me. I'll join you as soon as I can, when Dervla arrives.'

She was embarrassed now. 'If it's bad, if it's too awkward, I can leave.'

'No. You're not going anywhere. I want to hear everything. Your mother was a great friend to me. You have a fair old lot of questions yourself, I can see. Dervla might do better than me at answering some of them. She remembers that time better than me in some ways. Come with me.'

She followed. He lifted a latched shelf and they stepped behind the wooden counter of the bar.

'Your mother worked behind here,' he said. 'She was terrible at pulling pints of Guinness, mind you.'

'Terrible?' Eliza remembered her mother saying she was an expert Guinness pourer.

'Shocking,' Emmet said with a laugh. 'She was always too impatient. Wouldn't let it settle. Now, take a seat in here and I'll be back as soon as I can.'

Her phone was pinging. She didn't need to look to know it would be Olivia. Maxie. Perhaps even Rose, up in the middle of the night, anxious to hear what was happening.

She was in what looked like a private lounge room for friends or special guests. The walls were covered in framed photos and newspaper articles. Family photos, sports photos, photos of the local community. Emmet with the three men who had to be his brothers. An older couple – Emmet's parents, she assumed – standing in front of the pub, holding up a trophy, the wall behind them painted in what must be the Meath colours, green and gold. Australia's colours too.

She was reading one of the articles when Emmet returned. A smiling blonde woman was with him.

'The local paper wouldn't have a thing to write about it if wasn't for us. Eliza, this is my wife, Dervla. Dervla, this is Eliza. Jeannie's daughter.'

'God, I can see it in her. You're right. She's the image.' Eliza was shocked again to be hugged by a stranger. 'I'm so sorry. Emmet told me the sad news about Jeannie. I can't believe it. I'd never met anyone so fearless. So ready for adventure.'

'And trouble,' Emmet added.

'And yes, trouble,' Dervla said, smiling. 'You're what age, love?'

'Thirty.'

'She had you young. Smart woman. We're what's called geriatric parents. I wish I'd got my two when I was in my twenties. That's them there.' She pointed to another framed photo.

The two teenage athletes. 'Ursula and Ava. Emmet and I adopted them from Vietnam. It's a long process here, so much red tape. It's survival of the fittest. But we were determined. If we couldn't have children of our own, we'd find ourselves a family some other way.'

Eliza looked from one to the other. 'That's what you meant?' she said to Emmet.

He nodded. 'I knew Dervla would be able to tell you more easily than I could. She's much happier discussing my reproductive system than I am. Though I'm sure the locals have guessed that Ursula and Ava aren't my biological children. How, I don't know.'

Dervla rolled her eyes. 'He always thinks that's funny.'

'It is,' he said. 'But yes, Eliza. When I said I was sure I'm not your father, that's what I meant.'

'Is that what Jeannie told you, Eliza?' Dervla asked. 'That Emmet was your father?'

'Not exactly,' she said. Where did she start? She had that urge again, to pause everything. Or to go back in time and still have that hope that it was him. Because if it wasn't, who —

A bell sounded from the bar. A group of people, by the sound of the voices.

'I'll go,' Emmet and Dervla said as one.

'You go,' Dervla said. She waited until he'd left, then spoke. 'Eliza, why didn't you let us know you were coming? We were away last week. You could have turned up like this and we wouldn't have been here. Are you in Ireland on holiday?'

Eliza explained about being in Edinburgh. Her godmothers helping her piece it together.

'They were never a couple, Eliza. Your mum and Emmet. Believe me, I wondered as much at the time. Especially when she came back from London with him, and he followed her out to Australia. Not that I could say anything. I'd asked him for a break. I thought we were too young. But he told me – and I've always believed him – that they really were the best of friends. She was the big sister he'd never had, he said. I think she felt the same. I spoke to her once after he had his accident. She was so devastated, she blamed herself – I'm sorry, do you even know about his accident?'

'Not everything. I only heard about it this week, from my godmothers. My mother's best friends. It's a long story but —'

There was a sudden burst of laughter from outside. More voices. Another group had arrived.

'I'd like to hear it,' Dervla said. 'Emmet would too, I'm sure. And I know it's him you'd like to speak to the most. He knew your mother much better than I did. Are you staying in Trim tonight?'

Yes, she said. In the hotel by the castle. She was here with a friend from Edinburgh.

'You Aussies are amazing, the way you travel. That's grand you're sorted in the hotel. We've got an Airbnb apartment above the pub here. I was going to offer you that. We used to live here, but when the girls came, I put my foot down. It's hard enough being a publican's wife sometimes without living on the premises too. My mother-in-law said she wished she'd been as firm. Emmet and his brothers were all raised here. Sheila's in a lovely apartment at the other end of town now. She'd love to meet you too, I'm sure. It would do her good to see a new face. She's had a tough time of it since Hugh died three years ago. My father-in-law. Sheila met Jeannie too, of course, the summer she was here.'

Eliza was doing her best to keep up with everything Dervla was saying. She spoke very quickly.

'They talked on the phone a lot too, I know,' Dervla said. 'After Emmet had that accident. It was such a terrible time. I was travelling myself by then. South America. Out of contact for a month. No social media in those days. I didn't even know about his accident until I got to my hotel in Santiago to find dozens of messages waiting. Thank God he and his father were already on their way back home by then, or I'd have flown out to Australia myself. Ah, here's Emmet back now.'

He was smiling. 'Sorry to be so long. That castle brings in the tourist buses. Not that I'm complaining. Eliza, I'm sorry again – you've come all this way, hoping I was who you were looking for. I'm trying to think if she was seeing anyone else around that time. But I'm the wrong person to ask. You know about my accident? When we were working in that pub in Australia together?'

She nodded. 'My godmothers met you. Mum's two best friends from school. They'd gone to Melbourne to visit her. You dropped off a key. You all lived in a share house, apparently. Do you remember them?'

'I'm sorry, but no. I lost about a month of memories from around that time.'

'You're lucky that's all you lost,' Dervla said. She took over again, telling Eliza that Emmet was nearly blind in one eye, that his hearing wasn't great in his left ear. That it could have been so much worse, though. People had died in fights like that. No one had ever been charged in his case, but —

Emmet interrupted, saying that Eliza wasn't here to hear any of that. 'But I still remember Jeannie clearly, of course. From our time in London. The month she spent here. And I remember her talking about her two friends from school a lot. The Successful Ones, she called them. But I'm sorry, I don't remember meeting them in Australia. I've only got a few fragments from my entire time there.'

Eliza felt hope slip away. There was one more possibility. She had to ask. 'They thought of someone else. Mum told them you'd travelled to Australia with your cousin. I'm sorry to ask – you might not remember, but did anything happen between them? Could it have been him?'

He frowned. 'The cousin I went to Australia with?'

She knew she was grasping at straws. 'Could they have got together without you knowing? Maybe even when you were in hospital? The timing's right, isn't it?'

'The timing, yes, but the rest, no. Eliza, I'm sorry. I went to Australia with my cousin Orla.'

Dervla clarified it. 'His female cousin Orla.'

Eliza felt winded. She hadn't realised she'd been holding

out such hope. It hadn't occurred to her that his cousin might be female. She tried to show as much interest as possible when Emmet reached for his phone and showed her photos of Orla, now in her fifties, living in America, working as a doctor. He offered to put them in touch. Perhaps Orla might remember someone else from that time that Jeannie may have known.

Eliza nodded, thanked him. She rubbed her eyes, suddenly overwhelmed.

'Are you okay?' Dervla asked.

'I'm fine, thanks. Just tired. We had an early start.'

'Of course.' The bell at the bar sounded again. 'Look, I'm sorry, I need to get back to work. Dervla does too. Can you come back later? Maybe I can tell you some tales about Jeannie that you haven't heard before.'

'Your mother might like to meet Eliza too, Emmet. She and Jeannie got on well that summer, didn't they?'

He nodded. 'She always said she'd never met anyone like Jeannie. The wild colonial girl, she called her.' He smiled. 'Ma will be in here tonight too. Pub quiz night. She's on the winning team. Undisputed champions for the past year. It's not a fix, either. Want to join us, Eliza? To be honest, there's not much else going on in Trim on a weeknight.'

Could she sit in a pub, take part in a quiz, as if everything was somehow normal? Nothing felt normal any more. 'Yes. Please. Put me down for two.' She hoped Lawrence wouldn't mind.

On her way back to the hotel, she texted him. Not about her conversation with Emmet and Dervla. About the quiz. *Sounds good*, he answered immediately. It started at nine. They agreed to meet at 8.45 p.m.

Back in her room, she sat at the window, gazing out at the castle. She tried again to imagine her mother here. Walking the streets of this town. Staying in one of the rooms above the pub. Working behind the bar, pouring bad pints of Guinness, joking with Emmet's parents, their customers. She could picture it so clearly that it hurt.

What did she do now?

She took out her phone. Read her messages. Olivia, Maxie and Rose, all waiting to hear her news.

She kept it brief. *It's not Emmet. Or his cousin. I'll explain more soon. We'll be back on the ferry tomorrow. xxx*

Their replies were swift. Sympathetic. Loving. She held the phone tightly, and tried not to cry.

Lawrence was already waiting in the foyer when Eliza came downstairs. She'd ordered room-service dinner, had a shower and changed into a simple blue shift dress. He was wearing a dark suit jacket over a white shirt. Dark jeans.

She thanked him, then apologised. 'I know it's beyond the call of duty. We don't have to stay long.'

'I'll be there to the bitter end. I should warn you, I'm very competitive.'

'I mean it, Lawrence.' She explained what had happened that

afternoon. 'I'll just say hello to Emmet and his wife again. Meet his mother. We can leave before the quiz starts if you want.'

'Let's see what the prizes are first.'

The pub was now crowded, every table taken. There was music playing, lively conversation, three staff behind the bar, including Emmet. She waved but he didn't see her. She felt a tap on her shoulder.

'Eliza, you made it!' It was Dervla. Eliza introduced Lawrence.

'A pleasure to meet you,' Dervla said, all efficient organisation. 'Now, it's ten euro each, all for charity. I'll take that now. Remember you're in the running for a great cash prize and consolation prizes too.' She pointed to a table covered in bottles of wine and green-and-yellow baseball caps. 'Those Meath caps are sought after, let me tell you.'

She led them to a table and introduced their teammates. It was the four tourists Eliza had seen in the bar earlier. Two couples from Vancouver, in the middle of a road trip around Ireland.

'Emmet's the MC and quizmaster,' Dervla said, coming back with sheets of paper and pencils. 'One of the barmen too. You've got a few minutes before we start if you want to get a drink. His mother Sheila's just arrived. We haven't told her you'll be here. It'll be a great surprise.' She gestured towards a woman at the bar, talking to a group of people. She was in her seventies, grey-haired, well-dressed.

Eliza insisted on getting the drinks for Lawrence and herself. The noise increased as she followed Dervla to the bar. She stood back as Dervla tapped Emmet's mother on the shoulder.

'Sheila, let me introduce someone to you. A surprise visitor.'

Sheila turned and smiled at Eliza, waiting.

'Do you remember that Australian barmaid from all those years ago?' Dervla said, speaking over the hubbub. 'Emmet's friend from London? The one he stayed with when he went over to Australia?'

Sheila frowned as if she was trying hard to hear. She nodded, still looking at Eliza.

'This is her daughter,' Dervla was now nearly shouting. 'She's come all this way to meet us.'

Sheila's expression changed. Behind them, Emmet was tapping a glass, bending down to a microphone, calling for quiet. Dervla turned and began calling for quiet too, cheerful, clapping her hands. 'Quiz time, everyone!'

Eliza realised Sheila was saying something to her. She had to lean in close to hear.

'You can't be,' the older woman was saying. There was a brief lull in the noise of the room. Long enough for Eliza to clearly hear Sheila's next words, spoken in a whisper. 'Jeannie said you'd died.'

# CHAPTER THIRTY-ONE

She must have misheard. It was the only explanation, Eliza thought. The microphone squealed again. There wasn't a chance to ask Sheila to repeat it. Dervla had taken her mother-in-law by the arm, escorting her to her table, calling 'Good luck' over to Eliza.

She brought their drinks back, a pint of Guinness for Lawrence, Coke for herself. In the few minutes before the questions began, she learned the Canadians were relaxed, witty company. Full of stories about their Irish travels. Lawrence was equally relaxed. As the quiz got underway, she also discovered he was very smart. Their teammates soon bowed to his knowledge.

Eliza found herself taking it seriously. All the nights alone in her Melbourne apartment watching documentaries on world politics, current affairs, geography and geology began to pay off. Between her and Lawrence, with only occasional help from their quizmates, they were winning rounds.

'We struck it lucky,' one of the Canadians said. 'You two do the work, we'll get the spoils.'

Emmet was an entertaining quizmaster. Confident, funny, with Dervla as his sidekick, the relationship between them clearly affectionate. The bar staff were kept busy between rounds. Eliza tried to imagine the pub more than thirty years earlier, her mother serving, collecting glasses, joking with a younger Emmet. Sheila was on the other side of the room. Every time Eliza looked across, she felt her scrutiny.

After a final round devoted to Irish sporting heroes, they lost their lead. Not to Sheila's team. To a different table, vocal in victory, accepting the weekly trophy like a conquering football team. Eliza checked the time. It was past eleven.

Lawrence must have been waiting for her cue. He stood up. 'Ready when you are,' he said.

She saw that he still had half a pint in front of him. 'You're welcome to stay.'

He shook his head. 'Chauffeur rule number seven. Escort home is mandatory.'

She tried to get to Emmet and Dervla to say goodbye, but they were too busy. She'd come back in the morning before they left, she decided. There was no sign of Sheila. Perhaps she could talk to her again in the morning too.

It was a short walk in the cool air to their hotel. She thanked Lawrence as they stepped into the foyer.

'I still think we were robbed,' he said. 'Your knowledge of volcanoes in the Asia-Pacific region was truly impressive.'

She smiled. 'As was yours on the Spanish Civil War.'

They had a brief exchange regarding the morning's arrangements. They'd leave for the ferry at ten. Back in her room, she checked her messages. Rose again. Her godmothers. All asking if she wanted to talk. She felt too tired. Overwhelmed, again. She texted, thanking them, saying she'd call in the morning. She checked Scrabble. Sullivan had played a word. She played one back, then waited. No reply. She hoped he was tucked up at home, asleep after a great day out with his dad.

As she got into bed, she hoped sleep would be possible for her too.

She woke at seven-thirty to a loud ringing sound. She hadn't set her alarm. It was the bedside phone. She reached up and answered. It was the hotel receptionist.

'Good morning, Ms Miller. Mrs Foley is downstairs to see you.'

She was still half-asleep. 'Mrs Foley?' Did she mean Dervla?

'I'll put her on. One moment.'

She sat upright, trying to wake up.

'Eliza.' An elderly woman. An Irish accent. 'I presumed you were staying here.'

Emmet's mother, Eliza realised. 'Mrs Foley? Is everything all right?'

'You can call me Sheila. I need to talk to you before you leave. Please. As soon as possible.'

Eliza began to explain that she was still in bed. She was interrupted.

'I'll wait downstairs. Thank you.'

Eliza quickly showered and dressed. She came down the stairs. Sheila was sitting on one side of the foyer. Straight-backed, her handbag on her lap.

As they greeted one another, Eliza felt the scrutiny again. As if the older woman was trying to memorise her appearance.

'We need to talk privately,' Sheila said. 'It won't take long.'

Emmet must have told her why Eliza was here, the question she'd come to ask him. His mother obviously wasn't impressed. Her mood was almost hostile. Eliza glanced around. The foyer was crowded. There seemed to be coachloads of people staying, all down early, ready for sightseeing.

'I don't know where we could go, I'm sorry. Perhaps a café in town?'

'No. We can't be seen publicly. Your room would be best. Quickly, before anyone sees us.'

'My room? Sheila, I'm sorry, I don't understand. Is everything —'

'I'll explain when we're alone.'

Eliza led the way, confused and tense. She went in first, hurriedly tidying her bed. 'Please, sit down. Can I make you a tea? Coffee?'

Sheila stayed standing. 'How old are you, Eliza?'

'I'm thirty.'

'When did you get here? To Ireland?'

'Yesterday. I've been in Edinburgh.'

'Is it the first time you've been to Trim?'

'Yes.'

'And your mother, she's still in Australia?'

'No.' A pause. 'Emmet didn't tell you?'

'We haven't spoken properly yet. He was too busy last night.'

'My mother died. Thirteen years ago. When I was seventeen.'

'How?'

'Mrs —'

'Please, Eliza, tell me how she died.'

'It was an accident.' She left it at that. 'You met her? When she was here with Emmet that summer?'

'Of course. My husband ran the bar, I looked after the food, the rosters. Tried to keep the peace between Emmet and his father.'

'They didn't get on?'

'Not for years. That's one of the reasons he went to London. Eliza, why are you here?'

Eliza was taken aback at the question. At the whole situation. She didn't know how much Emmet might want his mother to know. 'I'm not sure if I can say. It's personal.'

'Please. It's important I know.' She seemed agitated.

Eliza carefully chose her words. 'My mother never told me who my father was. She was going to, but she died before she could. It's only now that I've started looking for him.'

Sheila didn't speak. She just waited.

Eliza continued. 'My godmothers have been helping me. We hoped it was Emmet. But yesterday,' she paused, 'I learned that wasn't possible, for the reasons you know.' She didn't mention his cousin.

'I see. So now you'll leave again?'

She nodded. 'We're getting the ferry back to Scotland today.'

'We?'

'I'm travelling with a friend.' The simplest way to describe Lawrence.

Sheila walked to the window and stared out at the castle. Eliza watched her, puzzled.

'It was used in a film, you know,' Sheila said. Her tone was strangely casual.

'Yes, I know. *Braveheart*. I've seen it.'

'I was an extra. My husband Hugh and I both were. Alongside hundreds of Irish Army Reserve volunteers. That's how they got it made here. Promised the filmmakers all the extras they'd need. One day the volunteers were dressed as English soldiers. The next they were in different costumes, dressed as Scottish ones. I read an interview with Mel Gibson. He said it was quite an editing feat, but he had a suspicion there was a scene in which the same extra killed himself. Such a funny story.'

Neither of them laughed. Eliza still had no idea why Sheila was there.

'I will sit down, Eliza, if you don't mind. And I'll have that cup of tea, if you're still offering.'

As Sheila took a seat in the armchair by the window, Eliza put on the kettle and prepared two cups.

Sheila continued to talk as if Eliza had asked a question.

'They were great friends, my husband and son, until Emmet became a teenager. Looking back, of course, they were normal father–son arguments. A clashing of wills. Hugh wanted him to study PE. Emmet wanted to travel first, then study. A waste of money, Hugh thought. Get a career on track first. It built up over months, until one terrible big row. Emmet was gone the next day. It didn't help that Dervla had called that break the same week. Nothing to keep him here.

'He got the ferry to London. We didn't know where he was for days. Then he rang. I'd never been so glad to hear his voice. He was in a squat, with a load of other young ones. In Kilburn. Little Ireland. That's where he met your mother, as far as I know. He loved it. Loved London, the freedom. This is a small town. He couldn't even sleep in of a morning here without someone passing a remark about it.

'I begged him to ring me once a week. Begged him to come home even for a month in the summer. He could work hard, all the shifts he wanted. Earn enough money to go travelling again. That's what sold it, of course. They arrived together. Emmet and Jeannie. I remember it so clearly.'

It was Eliza's turn to listen intently. Was this why Sheila was here? To share her own memories of Jeannie?

'It's a cliché, but she was a breath of fresh air. So full of life. Cheeky. We gave her a trial shift, and she was so hardworking, we took her on behind the bar as well. She'd been backpacking around Europe, staying in hostels. I never knew if I should believe her stories, but they were always entertaining.

'We missed her when she left after a month. She said it was time to go home. We didn't know then that Emmet would be following after her. It set off the rows with his father again. They were like two stags, fighting and clashing antlers. It was affecting his little brothers too. The tension was too much for us all. Dervla had gone travelling by then too, of course.

'I didn't blame him for going. At the last minute his cousin Orla decided she'd go too. It was catching, this idea of Australia being the Promised Land. It went great at first. Jeannie got him work in the bar with her. I'm sure I didn't hear the half of what they got up to. But then he had that accident, Eliza. That fight. The worst phone call I've ever received. Every parent's worst nightmare. I would have driven straight to the airport myself. But Hugh insisted it had to be him. He'd had an awful argument with him before he left. He was inconsolable. "What if Emmet dies? What if that argument is the last time we ever speak?" We could only afford to have one of us go. We had the other boys to look after. The pub.

'So Hugh went. Jeannie collected him at the airport. They went straight to the hospital. Hugh phoned me after he'd seen him. He was crying. He barely recognised his own son, he said. Emmet's face and his whole head was so swollen. His eyes just slits. His ear, the left side of his face. I never saw it, but I could imagine it. Every day, Hugh, Orla and Jeannie were taking turns to be with him, keeping vigil. Jeannie blamed herself. She'd sparked the row, she told Hugh. She had to make amends. She did everything she could. She even offered Hugh Emmet's room in their share house. So he could save on hotel rooms. We didn't know how long it would go on, you see.'

It was as if Sheila wasn't talking to her any more.

'Hugh sat there beside his son for hours every day. Telling him how much he loved him. Telling him all the things they used to do together when he was little. Treating the castle as if it was their own playground. All the matches he took him to. He told him that of course it didn't matter if he never wanted to teach PE. If he wanted to do something else, he would support him, whatever he wanted to do, he just had to wake up, come back to us.

'I don't know when it happened. I don't know if it happened more than once. If she started it or if he started it. If it was only the night that Emmet finally woke up, if there was a kind of crazy intense relief involved. I can imagine that. That big intense rush of feeling. It was that night, he told me. But perhaps it had been building between them both before then.'

Eliza had gone still. Her mind couldn't take in what she was hearing.

Sheila was gazing out of the window as if she was simply reminiscing. 'They came back to Ireland a fortnight after Emmet woke up. The three of them, Emmet, Orla and Hugh. It really was a miracle. I'd expected a wheelchair. But he walked out smiling. As if nothing had happened.'

She turned. Finally looked at Eliza. 'But I was wrong. Something had happened. You had happened.'

Her words were like a punch. Eliza stared at her.

Sheila continued. 'I don't know exactly when she told Hugh. I don't know how much he sent her either. Whether it was thousands, or a few hundred. Everything got back to normal, so quickly it was almost strange. Dervla and Emmet got engaged. Emmet started working full-time in the pub. Hugh agreed to any changes he suggested. They worked side by side. Sponsorships, fundraising. Hugh went back to coaching. He was only in his early forties. Fit. He got so involved in the GAA. Coaching and county politics. He loved it. We were so happy. So lucky.'

Eliza now felt as if she was in a strange dream. None of this seemed real.

'Then one night,' Sheila said, 'about eleven years after Emmet's accident, Hugh came home with big news. He was off to Australia at the end of the year. All expenses paid. They were setting up a tournament, Australia and Ireland, compromise rules. He'd be representing Meath's interests. That's when he contacted your mother, Eliza. He contacted Jeannie and said, "I'm coming to Australia in a few months. I'd like to see you. I want to meet our daughter." Oh, not that I knew any of this. Not then. I was still in the dark, you see. I thought I had a good marriage. An honest marriage.

'But it was all arranged. A date, a time. A place. Then about a month before his trip, he got a phone call. Jeannie. Hysterical. There'd been a terrible accident. An accident outside a school. An elderly man had lost control of his car. Three girls killed. Her daughter, their daughter, among them. She'd clung to life for two days but her injuries were too catastrophic. She had died.'

Eliza spoke then. Finally. 'No,' she said. 'No.'

It was as if Sheila hadn't heard her. 'And of course he believed her. Why wouldn't he? Perhaps he was even relieved. Perhaps it was for the best. Jeannie told him she wanted no more contact. That she was too heartbroken. He was surely relieved about that, too. He would never have to tell his wife about any of it, would he? The wife that he'd told, every single day of their marriage, that he loved.

'But guilt is the strongest of emotions, isn't it, Eliza? You might be too young to realise that yet. Guilt and love. Because Hugh did love me. I know it. And I loved him. The day we heard he had stage-four cancer was one of the worst days of my life. But we had warning, at least. Time to talk. To grow even closer. Look back over our lives together. Talk so honestly. He needed to salve his conscience, I suppose. Seek forgiveness. That's the only reason I can think of to explain why he did what he did. Why he decided one night, a month before he died, that I needed to hear everything. All of it.'

Eliza could barely breathe.

Sheila was looking right at her now. 'So you can see why I might have been surprised to meet you last night. Why I might have appeared shocked. Why would someone turn up here all these years later, impersonating a dead child? But then I couldn't take my eyes off you. Because I recognised you. Not just your height, but your gestures. The way you smiled. I could see instantly you were Hugh's daughter. I can see it even more clearly now.'

Eliza's hands were now trembling. She couldn't seem to stop it.

'He asked me to forgive him. Over and again. He cried in my arms. He said he couldn't go to his grave keeping so huge a secret from me. That the guilt was killing him as much as the cancer. And I told him I forgave him, because how could I not? My darling husband, who was dying, who was already skin and bones. He told me it had tormented him for years. That he knew it would hurt me, and oh, he was right: it hurt so much. So I lied, Eliza. I lied, there by his deathbed. I told him that of course I forgave him. I lied, and I lied and I lied.

'And it helped him. He changed instantly, I could see that. He became' – she searched for the words – 'lighter of spirit. As if some grace had come over him. Relief. As if there were no barriers any more, as if we now knew each other inside out, right to the end. As if he hadn't just ruined my life.'

'When did he die?' Eliza spoke, finally. She couldn't say his name.

'Three years ago. We were all with him. Emmet, his brothers.' She was silent for a moment, then she looked up. Her voice was steady, her eyes shards of ice. 'You must have known some of this. Enough for you to come here.'

Eliza found her voice again. Explained, as briefly as possible, what had led her to Trim. Heard herself talk about her godmothers, Edinburgh, the ferry trip.

Abruptly, Sheila stood up. 'Have you been to the castle?'

'I walked around it yesterday.'

'Have you been inside?'

She shook her head.

'Come with me now. You haven't had breakfast, have you? Do you need something first? Coffee?'

'I'm fine.' How could she answer in such an ordinary way?

'It's chilly enough outside. Drizzling too. Bring a raincoat if you have one. It can also be muddy there. Have you got any boots, or just those runners?'

The change of subject was unsettling. The apparent concern. Eliza put on her boots and picked up her raincoat. They were about to leave the room when Sheila spoke again.

'You have his eyes. He had beautiful eyes. Emmet didn't notice? Didn't say anything?'

Eliza shook her head. Unsure of why they were leaving, why she was obeying her, Eliza followed the older woman downstairs, outside and across the road in the cool misty air to the castle.

# CHAPTER THIRTY-TWO

It was eight a.m. in Edinburgh. Olivia had slept badly. She was still on edge, waiting for Eliza's call. Last night's visit with Edgar had been one of the hardest ever. Sitting beside his bed, watching him sleeping, finally peaceful after so much distress. He'd seesawed between severe tremors and bouts of weeping. She'd sat there holding his hand, stroking it for nearly an hour before she realised something.

This was it. This was how it was going to be. He was never going to get better.

It didn't matter how many times she visited. How many reports she read out to him. How many one-sided discussions she had about his sons or stock-control issues or staffing difficulties. Reminiscences about their first meeting or their favourite paintings. All they'd done together, the trips they'd taken, the hotel they'd built up together. He was not coming back to her.

She'd cried all night. As if the tears she had kept at bay over the past few years had been waiting for their moment. So many times she'd answered questions about him. 'Just the same,' she'd say, attempting to be as cheerful as possible. Who had she been fooling? Only herself.

She was so tired. But, for once, she thanked her workload. Deirdre, Lawrence and his team managed the day-to-day operations, but there were always emails for her to answer, online reviews to respond to. She checked the different portals every day. They were usually ninety per cent positive. She publicly replied to each of them. A standard response. *Thank you so much. We aim to make each guest's experience at the Montgomery memorable and special. We look forward to welcoming you again.*

Occasionally there were critical ones. Last week someone had complained about the view. *Only boring rooftops,* the young woman wrote. Olivia knew how she'd have liked to reply. *It's Edinburgh, not the Bahamas. What did you expect, coral reefs?* She kept it polite. *Thank you for taking the time to comment. We hope to welcome you back another time.* Blandly professional.

She opened up the main review sites now. Clicked, refreshed. Frowned. There were thirty new reviews. All one star. *I'd have given it no stars if that was an option,* one said. Many were in capitals. It felt like someone was shouting at her.

She read each one. *Promises but doesn't deliver. UNACCEPT- ABLE wait for room service. Rude UGLY staff. Tired décor. Boring menu. Staff cut corners. Stains EVERYWHERE. Room smells like rats.*

She stood up, fury washing over her. 'I'll give you rats, you evil cow.'

She printed the reviews. Fetched the master key. Made her way to the right floor. She didn't care if Celine was midway through putting on her ridiculous make-up, showering that crinkled, starved body of hers or whatever else she might be doing. She inserted the key and flung open the door.

'I've had enough of you. Get out.'

Celine was in her dressing gown. 'You get out! How dare you burst in like this!'

'How dare *you*! After living here free for weeks, because you're family? What family member does this?' She held up the printouts. 'You're venomous, Celine, like your reviews. And I've had enough.'

'Edgar said I can stay. He's still the boss. Even if he has lost his marbles.'

A new rage sliced through Olivia. 'I'm not asking you, Celine. I'm telling you. You have twenty-four hours to pack, get out of my hotel and out of my sight.'

'You have no right. Pass me my phone.'

'So you can ring for help? Who? Edgar? Your grandsons? Lawrence is out of the country. Deirdre is investigating legal loopholes to evict you. Who does that leave, Celine? Me. Do you think I care? When you repay my patience and indulgence of you and your vileness by doing this, not just to me but to our hotel?' She threw the reviews onto the floor.

Celine lifted her chin. 'Don't blame me if you can't face facts.'

'Get out.'

'Where will I go?'

'I don't care.'

'I'll sue you.'

'Please do.'

'I'll bring this rat-infested hotel to its knees.'

'Go ahead.'

'You'll never welcome another guest.'

'Fine.'

'I'll end up homeless. You could live with that, could you?'

'I'd celebrate it.'

'Well, too bad. I'm not going anywhere. I'm the grandmother of two Montgomerys. I'm legally entitled to be here. Edgar said so.'

Olivia walked out, slamming the door behind her.

Five minutes later, she was back at her desk, adrenaline still racing through her body. She couldn't even ring Maxie. She didn't want to interrupt her time with Hazel. Her phone rang. She snatched it up, hoping it was Eliza.

It was Alex, asking if he could come to her office. There was something he wanted to talk to her about. He was the last person she wanted to see. But it was a distraction, at least.

'Yes, of course,' she said.

# CHAPTER THIRTY-THREE

The castle wasn't officially open so early, but the gate was ajar. Sheila knew someone in the office.

'Just showing a visitor around,' she called. They received a wave to go ahead.

Sheila hadn't stopped talking since they'd left the hotel. All about the filming of *Braveheart*. Sheila hadn't met Mel Gibson, but she'd seen him from afar, she told Eliza. The filmmakers had built onto the castle ruin, to make it look whole again —

Eliza stayed silent, waiting, until Sheila finally ran out of *Braveheart* facts. They kept walking until they reached the centre of the castle, out of sight of the entrance. They were surrounded by tall walls, broken by gaps. Eliza could see the fast-flowing river. The Yellow Steeple. Beyond that, the town itself.

Sheila stopped, her arms around her body as if she was cold, despite her coat. 'My husband was one of the pillars of this town, Eliza. Everyone knew him. He was a good man. A family man.

A sporting man. The whole town turned out for his funeral. There were so many people outside, they had to broadcast on loudspeakers. Everyone was so kind to me afterwards. To the boys too. We were married more than fifty years. We had such a big celebration for our fiftieth. In that hotel you're staying in. It was controversial at the time, so close to the castle, but we all go there now. It's brought a lot of business to the town, and —'

'Sheila, please —'

'I'm from here. Born and bred. My parents owned a shop in town. Everyone knows me here. Hugh was from Meath too, but the other side of the county. My uncle had the pub – he was the one who offered it to us as a business. No kids of his own, no one to hand it on to. Because it's all about family, in business and in life, isn't it?

'I always thought the worst day of my life was when I heard about Emmet's accident. When Hugh had to rush to Australia to be with him, in case he died. I spoke to Hugh in Melbourne every day. He'd ring from the hospital and tell me how our son was, every detail. I'd ask him what he thought would happen. I'd be crying, and he'd console me and say, "Please don't cry, Sheila. Everything will be all right." But I've always wondered, Eliza, was he sleeping with Jeannie even at that stage? He said he wasn't. That it was just that one night. But he had years to come up with that story, didn't he?'

Eliza couldn't speak.

'Why did he have to tell me, Eliza? Was it because your mother had told him you'd died? That there was no chance of you turning up? But you hadn't died, had you? I've been up all night trying to make sense of it. Have you any idea how hard this is for me? How hard you've made my life? All the years Hugh and I had together, so many special family moments and all the time, across the world, he had this dirty secret. A ticking time bomb waiting to ruin my life. You, Eliza. You and your mother.'

Eliza found her voice. 'Stop it. Please. Stop talking about us like that.'

'But it's the truth. Oh, it's not your fault. I can see that. It's your mother who's to blame, can't you see? For everything. Emmet going to Australia. His accident. Luring my husband, the little sl—'

'*No.*' The anger came over Eliza suddenly. 'You can't talk about my mother like that. I loved her so much. She and Emmet were the best of friends. He told me. She was so good to him. If he was to hear any of this, to hear what you —'

Sheila moved quickly, grabbing Eliza's arm so tightly she felt her skin pinch. 'You'll not tell him, or Dervla or anyone in this town any of this, do you hear me? You will not make my family a laughing stock. Waltz into my life and ruin my reputation and have people gossiping as I walk down the street. You get out of this town. Right now. And don't come back.'

'No. I need to talk to Emmet again.'

'I'm his mother and I forbid you. Hugh is dead, God rest his soul. He and I were the only ones here who knew what happened between him and your mother, and I will deny it with my last breath. Even though he betrayed me. With your mother. With you. The biggest mistake of his life.'

'I am not a mistake.' Eliza's voice was clear and loud. Sheila shushed her, pulled at her arm again. She shook it off. 'My mother told me all my life how loved I was. How much she wanted me. How much better her life was because of me. She never said my father ruined her life. She always said she was glad she met him, otherwise she wouldn't have had me. She didn't tell me who he was, but she was going to. When I was old enough to understand.'

'And then what? What would you have done?'

'What I've done now. I'd have come to Ireland and tried to meet him.'

'I wouldn't have let it happen. If you'd turned up when he was still alive —'

'He wanted to meet me. It was my mother who stopped that from happening.' Eliza was still trying to make sense of it. Out of nowhere, a memory of something her mother had once said flashed into her mind. '*I never wanted to share you.*'

'You have to leave, Eliza.' Tears had appeared in Sheila's eyes. 'I'm not an evil woman. I'm not. I've been the best mother I could. Tried to be the best wife. But for what? Hugh dead. Three of my four boys away. Emmet's here but Dervla can't stand me. And I can't stand her. I think she's spoilt and selfish. If she hadn't broken it off with Emmet, none of this would have happened. She's as much to blame as your mother.'

'No. You can't blame her. Or me. Or my mother. If anyone

is to blame, it's your husband, Sheila. My father.' The words felt like ice in her mouth. 'He was the adult. My mother was only twenty-one.'

It was as if she hadn't spoken. Sheila gazed around as if she was astonished to find them where they were. She looked old. Exhausted. Eliza felt something tilt. As if the energy around them had been sucked out of the air. She was exhausted too. But she needed to say something else.

'I'm going to talk to Emmet again, Sheila. Hear his memories of my mother. I need —'

'Not yet. Please. Let me tell him first. Tell him everything. You owe me that.'

'No, I don't. I don't owe you anything.'

'Please, Eliza. Give me until tomorrow to tell him. Then you can talk to us together. At my apartment. In private.'

Eliza turned around. A group of people was coming in, led by a guide. The castle must have opened. 'I'm going back to Scotland today.'

'Can't you stay one more night? Please. I need time with Emmet.'

Eliza thought about it. She nodded.

Sheila asked for her phone number. 'I'll send you a message. After I've told him.'

There was nothing else to say for now. No farewell. Eliza stayed where she was until Sheila had walked out of sight.

*

Lawrence was waiting in the hotel foyer at ten a.m., as they'd arranged. When she walked in from outside, her hair and clothes damp from the mist, his expression changed. 'Is everything okay?'

She shook her head. She told him something unexpected had happened. That she needed to stay an extra night. 'I know you need to be back in Edinburgh. Please, go ahead. I'll get back another way.'

'If you need to change our plans, we can change them.'

'Lawrence, it's not part of your job. You can't miss another day.'

'Eliza, I'm here on behalf of Olivia. We'll do whatever you need to do.'

She didn't go to her room. She needed people around her, the bustle of a hotel foyer. She took out her phone to ring Olivia, Maxie or even Rose. She put it away again. She couldn't talk about it yet.

Across the foyer, she saw Lawrence with the receptionist, changing their room bookings. He'd said he'd take care of the ferry booking too.

What did she do now? There was a whole day to fill. She couldn't stay here. Where could she go?

\*

Lawrence came back over to her. Everything was organised, he said. It had been no problem.

She began to apologise again.

'Please, Eliza. You don't need to say sorry.'

'But what will you do now?' she asked. 'With an unexpected day here?'

'I asked the receptionist for some tips. Where the nearest, wildest scenery is.' He'd already taken plenty of photos of the castle and tower the day before, he told her. The receptionist had recommended a trip to the Wicklow Mountains. Lakes, streams and forests, just over an hour away.

She asked even before he could offer. 'Can I please come?'

They drove in silence at first. Her thoughts were anything but quiet. She couldn't seem to take it all in yet. She was still too shocked.

She was grateful again for Lawrence's peaceful company. For the radio playing at low volume. An Irish classical station, gentle piano music. Her eyes kept filling with tears. She stared out of the window, trying to hide them from Lawrence.

She had never thought the truth would be anything like this. Her father had been a married man. A father of four. He had wanted to meet her. She thought of the lies her mother had told to stop it from happening. *Why, Mum? Why?* She thought of the look in Sheila's eyes. It had felt like hatred.

She was struck by another thought. Her mother had told Hugh that Eliza had been killed in an accident. What would Jeannie have told her on her eighteenth birthday? Would she have given her false information about her father, to stop her from going in search of him? To stop exactly what had just happened with Sheila? Or would Jeannie have told the truth, told her exactly who her father was? That his name was Hugh Foley. That he was her friend Emmet's father. That she had told him Eliza was dead so she would never have to share her with him.

Eliza had come to Ireland hoping for answers. She now had more questions than ever before.

They were coming closer to the mountains now. The road began to rise ahead of them. They seemed to pass quickly from suburbia, from occasional large houses to this wild scenery. All around them were the Wicklow Mountains, bare at first sighting, but then their colours and textures became obvious. It was wild heather, she realised. In colours that reminded her of tweed, mossy greens, browns, flashes of yellow, even red.

The road was like a mountain track. No lines. No kerbs. It felt like they had it to themselves. They'd passed just one other car. She saw a lake, down deep in a valley, silver-blue in the light. The sky around them was filled with clouds, but patches of blue were appearing. Those shafts of light again. In the distance, darker areas of the deepest green. Forests. Further in the distance, more mountains, including a small triangular one, distinctive among the smoother waves of the others.

She'd never pictured herself in Ireland. Never imagined anything like this happening. She wanted her mother. She wanted Jeannie to explain everything to her. She needed to hear it. All of it.

Her father was a married man. A married Irish man. He had wanted to meet her.

The tears returned suddenly. The tears, the sorrow, the shock and the grief again. That grief that would never ever go away. All of it rose up inside her. She started sobbing, there in the car beside Lawrence. Crying so hard that it felt like she would never be able to stop.

'Eliza?'

She couldn't answer him. She didn't know what to say. She didn't trust herself to speak.

She felt the car stop. Felt the buffeting wind. She undid her seatbelt. She would get out. Walk. Try to stop these tears, that seemed to be coming from deep inside her —

The cold outside took her by surprise. The wind felt like ice. She leaned against the car, trying to catch her breath now, feeling her chest tighten. Her coat was on the back seat, but she couldn't reach in and get it. She didn't know what to do. She had no idea what she should do any more.

All her life she'd secretly hoped that somewhere, somehow, there might be a family waiting for her. She was wrong. There was nothing. Her mother was dead. Her father was dead. She was on her own.

'Eliza?'

He had got out of the car too. He was standing beside her. There was a moment, a long, still moment, and then she turned into him. He was broad, warm, solid. His arms came around her, gently holding her. She pressed her face against his shoulder. The tears were unstoppable. She lifted her head to try to speak but couldn't.

He said her name again. He told her not to worry, not to speak. He kept holding her, solid, gentle.

Finally, she felt able to lift her head, wipe her eyes. 'I'm so sorry —'

'You don't have to be.'

'I need to explain.'

'No, you don't need to. Only if you want to.'

She was shivering. He noticed. He opened the car door for her. Helped her in. He took his seat again too. He turned on the heater. The car slowly warmed. As her shivering stilled, as her tears finally stopped, she started to tell him. She kept her voice low. She told him what had happened with Sheila. He let her talk, as he had let her cry outside.

When she had finished, Lawrence quietly asked her if she'd told Olivia yet. Did she want him to ring her? No, she said. She needed to know more before she could tell her and Maxie. She needed to talk to Emmet again. With or without Sheila's approval. She was waiting to hear from Sheila, she said. She'd been checking her phone throughout the journey. There'd been no word.

'We can drive back there now,' he said. 'You can go to her house. Or we can go to Emmet's pub.'

She thought about going back to Trim now. Walking the streets of the town. Feeling like – what? A pariah? Waiting for someone to look at her, see her father in her? She couldn't do that. Not yet.

'What were you going to do up here?' she asked.

'Walk. Take photos.'

She asked him the question she'd asked him back at the hotel. Could she please come?

He drove on for another few minutes. In the distance, he'd seen a path leading across the boglands. He parked to the side of the mountain road. It was still so quiet. Only an occasional car had passed by. She felt safe. There was something decent about Lawrence. She knew Olivia wouldn't have asked him to make this journey with her if she didn't feel the same way.

They began walking along the stony path. She had been hill-walking before, in Australia, on holidays with her god-mothers. She'd seen wild scenery in New Zealand, in the Scottish Highlands. This wasn't as dramatic. The mountains were more like hills. But as they walked, the wind rising and falling around them, the light changing dramatically, sunshine replaced by silver light, then dark clouds, a constant moving display, she felt herself awed by the beauty of it.

The path led down to a stream, water turned orange-brown by the heather, tumbling into foam as it passed over grey rocks.

There were ferns on either side, so many different greens, their fronds unfurling into spring. As Lawrence moved to different locations with his camera, she put her hands into the water. It was icy cold. So clear.

They walked for two hours. He produced chocolate from his coat pocket. Apologised that he hadn't packed sandwiches, coffee. Told her he was usually more organised on photography trips like this.

It had become darker, the clouds fully covering the sky, blocking the sun. A wind was rising again. There were spatterings of rain. They returned to the car. She only had the weakest signal but she could see she'd had no message from Sheila yet.

He kept driving, over the mountain. Houses began to appear again. They came into a village. A pub was open. Flowers on the windowsills, as there had been at Emmet's pub. He parked and they went inside. There was a fire crackling in the corner. They ordered hot soup and sandwiches. Again, Lawrence made conversation easy. They didn't talk about her, or that morning. They talked about travel. She told him about her godmother holidays. He asked her to tell him some of the favourite places she'd visited with them. Remembering those trips, the special times she'd had with Olivia and Maxie, soothed her.

On their journey home, the car was warm, the sky growing dark. Somehow, she slept. They were not far from Trim when something woke her. Her phone. Messages from her godmothers, Rose, Sullivan. And one other. A message from Sheila.

*Please come to my apartment at nine a.m. tomorrow. Sheila.*
An address followed. So businesslike. As if she was confirming a
dental appointment.

She read it to Lawrence.

His expression was serious. 'That's good news, isn't it?'

Eliza didn't know any more. She hoped it was. There had
been no mention of Emmet.

They parked at the back of their hotel. Moments before they
walked into the bright busy foyer, she stopped, searching for the
words. Where could she begin, to acknowledge all he'd done
that day?

'Thank you, Lawrence. For being so kind.'

His smile was gentle. 'Any time, Eliza,' he said.

She couldn't go up to her room yet. The room where she and
Sheila had been, just hours earlier.

'Would you have dinner with me?' It sounded too abrupt.
'Please. Only if you want to. You might prefer room service.
Some time alone. After all that driving.'

'I'd like that very much. Here, at eight?' He gestured to the
restaurant behind them.

'Here at eight. I'll book it.'

'See you then,' he said. Another smile and he was gone.

She made herself go upstairs. She turned on all the lights in
her room. She turned on the TV, needing background sound.

She took out her phone, hesitating again about calling Olivia or Maxie. It was still too early to message Rose. She knew Lawrence had let Olivia know they were staying the extra night. She sent a group message to her godmothers: *I'm sorry not to have called yet. I will as soon as I can. Love to Hazel. I hope Edgar is as well as possible. E xx.*

She took a seat in the armchair by the big window. The same chair Sheila had sat in that morning. The sky was dark now. The castle loomed large across from her. Lights illuminated the stonework, making it appear mysterious. Again, she imagined her mother looking up at this castle too.

She took out the folder of printouts Maxie had given her. She found a photo of Hugh, from his retirement party. Sheila and his four sons beside him. *Legendary Publican Retires*, the headline read.

She looked at his image for a long time.

When she came downstairs again, Lawrence was waiting for her. At the restaurant entrance, a young waitress introduced herself, brought them water, took their orders, offered her the wine list. She declined, but offered it in turn to Lawrence.

'Water's fine for me too,' he said.

Eliza had worried it would feel awkward, after all that had happened between them that day. It didn't. They talked about their impressions of Ireland. His time in Scotland. He asked about her work with Gillian. Celine, too. He laughed when she shared some of the insults. He shared some in return. As the evening progressed, she started noticing more about him. The unusual colour of his eyes: not blue, not green, something in between. His voice: an English accent, yes, but with touches of something else too. Some Scottish, perhaps. Or something from his French mother? He had a great laugh too. She noticed again how soothing it was being in his presence. His calmness.

Afterwards, did she or was it Lawrence who suggested a walk? It was dark, but there were other people out. The spotlit castle was the centrepiece of the town. They decided to walk around the perimeter walls. Halfway around, they stopped abruptly at the sight and sound of a flock of black birds, rooks or ravens, flitting in and out from one of the towers. They were standing close. They were alone. He turned. She turned. It felt like the most natural thing to lean into him, to kiss him, feel the gentle pressure of his lips in return. For that kiss to go on, as his arms came around her, pulled her in closer. To give herself over entirely to touch. To feel a rising desire, his lips on hers, on her neck, her lips again, as his arms tightened, a building sensation —

'Lovely night for it,' a voice said behind them.

An elderly woman, walking a small white dog.

'Yes,' they agreed.

They walked back to the hotel. Not holding hands, but close. In the foyer, there was a moment, but it passed, without words. She thanked him again for everything. He wished her well with the meeting the next morning. They went to their separate rooms.

She tried to sleep, tossing and turning, before giving up and opening the curtains, watching the sky slowly lighten above the castle. Waiting until it was time to go to Sheila's apartment.

# CHAPTER THIRTY-FOUR

In Edinburgh, Olivia was still wide awake. She hadn't been able to stop thinking about Alex's unexpected visit to her office that morning. His unexpected offer.

He'd come in and taken a seat across from her. 'Rory told me you were in with Dad for hours last night. How is he?'

That surprised her. They rarely spoke about Edgar. Olivia didn't like getting upset in front of Alex or Rory. She wasn't even sure how often they visited their father these days. 'He's fine,' she said. Then a wave of tiredness hit her. She was fighting a headache. She massaged her temples.

'Is he? Are you?' Alex said.

She started to say, 'Yes, everything's fine.' But it wasn't. To her own surprise, and Alex's, her voice caught. She had to reach for a tissue, hide her eyes.

'Olivia?'

'Just a second,' she said, her voice muffled.

'Do you want to be alone?'

'Alone?' She dropped her hands. 'More alone? I can't do this any more, Alex. I've tried so hard to do what your father would want, but I'm failing, aren't I? I know you and Rory are unhappy here, but I don't know how to fix it. I've tried with Celine, but —' Her voice caught. What had happened to her? Was it hormones? Exhaustion? She was falling apart. In front of Alex, of all people.

'Let me go and talk to Celine,' he said. 'I've had an idea. That's why I asked to see you.'

She shook her head. 'There's no point. She'll only abuse you.'

'You've checked out Dad's promise legally?'

'Yes. Twice. Edgar's letter is tantamount to a legal promise. She's allowed to stay here for as long as she wants.'

'Specifically here? Specifically the Montgomery hotel? Or with the Montgomery family?'

'What's the difference?'

'Can I see the letter?'

Olivia didn't need to get it. She'd read it so often, hoping for a loophole. She knew it off by heart. 'It says she is welcome to stay with us, Alex. Us meaning the Montgomerys. Here, in the hotel.'

'Could I still see it?'

She stood, unlocked the filing cabinet, found it and gave it to him.

He read it carefully, then looked up. 'Olivia, have you seen the occupancy rates for my hostel? It's nearly full. Every night.'

She was in no mood to praise him, if that's what he was wanting.

'Nearly full,' he repeated. 'But there's always a vacant room. In my hostel, Olivia. I am a Montgomery. It's a Montgomery property.'

She stared at him. 'Are you suggesting what I think you're suggesting? That we move Celine into your hostel?'

'Yes.'

'Have you gone mad?'

'Not yet.'

'Alex, you and I don't always see eye to eye, but I wouldn't wish her on my worst enemy. You've seen her. Heard her. How rude she is. How noisy she is.'

'I can be rude. Hostels are noisier.'

'She does nothing but complain.'

'We have a good complaints system. It's called "Like it or lump it". In any case, I'll ask my staff to give her so much attention she won't have time to post any bad reviews.'

'But even if you could get her to move, where would you put her? A dorm full of twenty-year-olds?'

'That would be too mean. To them. Olivia, I think Celine's bored senseless. If you ask me, that's why she keeps demanding those temps or Eliza and that weird kid. For company. She wants people around her.'

'Yes, to bully them. Insult them. I can't see her happily relaxing in a hostel common room, can you? Exchanging travel tales? Giving tips?'

'I can, actually. She travelled all her life, remember. She must be full of stories. I have a vacant room at the back of the hostel. Ground floor. Close to the common room. She could come in and out as she pleased. Hold court.'

'A woman of her age?'

'We have lots of older travellers staying. Olivia, why not give it a week's trial? Run it past Deirdre legally. Tell Celine there are rats in her room. Bed bugs. That you need to fumigate her entire floor. Or tell her I came begging. That I'm hoping to attract an older demographic. Well-heeled, well-travelled, sophisticated but also budget-conscious men and women. I need a trial guest. A discerning elderly guinea pig. Now I say it, that's exactly what I do want.'

'She'll insist on room service.'

'She can have it. In our case it's called Deliveroo. All she eats is burgers anyway. There's a good chipper down the road. I'll fetch it myself. It'd be cheaper than the prices here, anyway.'

'Are you serious about this?'

'Deadly serious,' he said.

It just might work, she realised. Even temporarily. 'Thank you, Alex. Thank you very much.'

'You don't want to ask me about the gin I've taken? The wine? The paintings?'

'Is there any point?'

'Not really.'

'Are you taking care of the paintings?'

'Yes.'

'Then our meeting is concluded. And frankly, the way I'm feeling, if you manage to lure Celine into your hostel long enough to give me even a short break, you can drain our liquor store dry.'

'Are you serious?'

'Deadly serious,' she echoed.

'So we'll give it a try?' he said.

'We'll give it a try,' Olivia replied.

He stood up. He was smiling. 'It's a pleasure doing business with you, Olivia.'

'And you, Alex.'

It truly had been. As she'd walked up the stairs to face Celine, she'd almost had a spring in her step.

# CHAPTER THIRTY-FIVE

In Trim, Emmet was having difficulty concentrating on his usual morning bar tasks. He'd barely slept the previous two nights. He checked his watch again. Not even eight a.m. yet. Another hour before it was time to go to his mother's house. Not only to see her. To see Eliza again too.

He made himself a coffee and sat at one of the tables in the empty pub, trying to put his thoughts into some kind of order. He'd been trying, and failing, ever since the conversation he'd had with Dervla when they got home after the pub quiz.

They'd lain in bed talking until the early hours, as they often did. This time only about Eliza, of course. As Dervla said, it wasn't every day a random Australian woman turned up asking if you were her father.

'Let's meet Eliza for a coffee before she heads back to Scotland,' he'd said to Dervla. 'I was no help on the father front, but she might like to hear more stories about Jeannie.'

'I'll call the hotel first thing and invite her,' Dervla said. 'And, who knows, you might still help her find her father. You or Orla. You were both around at the right time. Maybe Jeannie met him at the pub you both worked in? Or he was a friend of a friend in that share house you lived in?'

'Maybe. It was open house, as much as I can remember.'

'Shame you can't ask your dad. He was there then too, of course. Maybe he noticed her flirting with someone.' She turned over, switched off her light and was asleep in minutes.

Her last words had stayed like neon letters above his head.

*Shame you can't ask your dad. He was there then too, of course.*

The next morning he'd come into the bar early, as usual. His barman Liam was there, taking in deliveries, chatty as ever. Emmet barely listened. He was too preoccupied, trying to summon up even some small memory from those weeks in Melbourne. But it was as if they'd been wiped out by a blackboard duster, just traces left behind, the odd word here or there. He recalled moods rather than details, of fun nights and lazy mornings in their share house, for example. Nights out after their shifts in the pub. But no facts.

It had only been much later, when he was back home in Ireland, that he'd learned his father had stayed in his bedroom the entire time he was in that coma, of which he also had no memory. Jeannie had insisted a hotel was too expensive. Orla had been living there too, working as a temp, taking it easy before she started her medical studies. They'd had two other flatmates.

A Dutch girl, or was she German? And a girl from New Zealand. Or was it Canada?

His father and Jeannie.

In the same house for those weeks.

Could they —

No. Of course not. Of course they couldn't have. Jeannie was only twenty-one years old, for God's sake. His father would have been . . . Emmet did the maths. Thirty-one years ago. His father would have been forty-three, forty-four. He had seemed so old back then. Now, at the age of fifty-two himself, it seemed young.

His father and Jeannie?

No, it couldn't have happened.

It was his *father* he was thinking about. And he would have noticed something, surely? Flirting between them? Something?

Except no, he wouldn't have. Because he'd been in hospital then, hadn't he? Lost to the world.

But it wasn't the first time they met, a voice inside him was saying. They'd met before. Here in Trim.

Emmet still had good memories of the summer he'd brought Jeannie home with him. She'd leapt at the chance. She loved the idea of staying in a family pub beside an actual castle. They'd decided to surprise his parents. They got a bus from London to Holyhead in Wales, the ferry to Dún Laoghaire, caught a bus to Trim. The whole journey from London took three days. There'd been no way of affording to fly back then.

His parents liked her. He remembered that. His mother had said she was 'refreshing'. Jeannie was a hard worker, enough to endear anyone to his father. He'd been obsessed with hard work, as Emmet learned to his cost. But Jeannie had also made Hugh laugh, with her irreverence, her cheekiness. 'Tell me every single thing I should know about Ireland, Mr Foley,' she'd said. 'From A to Z.' His father took it seriously, Emmet remembered. Each day of that month, he'd given Jeannie a new fact.

She'd wanted information about the castle, especially. Emmet remembered something else then. His father taking Jeannie on a tour of the castle. Emmet was invited but didn't join them. He'd been on enough castle tours, thank you. They'd come back laughing. Was his memory playing tricks, or had Jeannie been arm-in-arm with him when they came into the pub again?

Possibly. Jeannie had always been so tactile. She'd hugged him often during their friendship. She flirted with every man she met. It was her way. Teasing them. Complimenting them. She got plenty of male attention in return.

But Jeannie and his father?

Together?

It suddenly seemed important to talk to Eliza again. He'd stepped away from Liam, taken out his phone and called the hotel. The receptionist put him through to her room. It rang out.

He was relieved, he realised. What on earth had he been going to say? 'Eliza, I've been giving it some thought. I don't know for sure, but there's a faint possibility you could be my father's daughter.'

He thought of her height. Her colouring. Her eyes.

He wished he and Dervla had taken a photo of Eliza. At first meeting, he'd only seen Jeannie in her. But that's who he'd been looking for. Not every child resembled their mother and father in equal amounts, after all. He and his brothers looked more like their mother's father than their own father.

He left Liam to finish the deliveries alone. He went to the room at the back of the pub, over to the wall of photos he'd looked at so many times. He stood in front of the one taken at his father's retirement party. Emmet's three brothers had flown in from Canada and the US. There they were, the four of them, either side of their parents. That same photo had appeared in the local paper. He looked at each of them in turn. If Eliza was there too, would she look like the missing part of a set? Like their long-lost sister? Half-sister technically, but still.

It couldn't be true. It couldn't. His parents had the strongest, longest marriage he'd known.

After that, he'd tried to get back to work, but the idea wouldn't leave his head. He couldn't talk about it with Dervla. Not yet. He told Liam that his mother had called. She needed an urgent handyman job done. He'd be back soon. Liam happily waved him off, turning the radio up even before he'd left the pub.

He rang the bell at his mother's apartment. No answer. He phoned her. No answer again. He had a key but he'd left it back at his house. About to go and get it, he heard his name being called. His mother's neighbour. A nosy woman in her sixties. She had a yappy white dog at the end of a leash.

'Your mam was out and about early this morning,' she said cheerily. 'I was out walking Pumpkin, saw her go into the castle hotel. It's well for some, I thought. Breakfast out on a weekday.'

He tried ringing her doorbell again. This time she answered. She was immaculately dressed and groomed, as always.

'Emmet! Is everything okay?'

She must have asked him that question thousands of times in his life. 'I'm grand. Can I come in?'

'Of course. You're sure everything's okay? You look a bit flushed. Tea? Coffee?'

'Neither thanks.' He took a seat in her spotless living room. He recalled his father sitting in these chairs, standing against that fireplace, watching TV in this living room. It had never suited Hugh. He'd always been much more at home in the rooms above the pub. If it had been his choice, that's where he would have liked to die too, Emmet felt sure. Instead of in that hospital room, machines beeping, all of them gathered around him —

'Has something happened?' Sheila asked, sitting down.

He couldn't put it off. 'Ma, we had a visitor to the pub yesterday. Dervla introduced you at the quiz, I think? Eliza, from Australia. Jeannie's daughter. You remember Jeannie?'

A reaction, a subtle one, but he saw it, even as she frowned, put her head on one side. 'Eliza? Yes, Dervla briefly introduced us. Though we didn't get to talk. Such a long way to come. Australians are such good travellers, aren't they?'

'Did Dervla tell you why she was here? What she came here to ask me?'

'No, she didn't.'

Emmet knew his mother well. He knew women well, after thirty years with Dervla, after being the father to his two girls, watching them grow from innocent, open toddlers to the darling but sometimes cunning young women they were today. He always knew when they were lying or hiding something. He'd honed that skill over years of bartending too. His mother did know something.

'She was looking for her father, Ma. I think she had an idea that it might have been me. I had to explain that wouldn't have been possible. I was thinking of emailing Orla, though, to see if she remembered anyone else from that time.'

His mother nodded, her expression neutral, as if this didn't matter to her one way or the other. It was out of character. She would normally have been far more curious. She had met Jeannie, after all. He continued, choosing his words carefully.

'Then I got an idea in my head after Dervla and I were talking. And it's madness' – he tried to laugh, make light of this strange conversation, this question he was still framing – 'but the only other person I really remember being around Jeannie at that time was Dad. It's ridiculous, but you know those middle of the night thoughts. I kept thinking about Eliza's height, and how tall Dad is. Dad was.'

He had said it. The words were released.

Across the room, his mother hadn't moved. She looked at him for a long moment. Then, as he watched, tears began rolling down her cheeks.

He went straight over. 'Ma?'

'I can't talk about it, Emmet.'

He knelt on the floor beside her. 'Talk about what?'

'This. All of this.'

'Jeannie and Dad? You know all of this already?' As she looked down at her hands, twined on her lap, he said it again. This time it was a statement. 'You know.'

She didn't reply.

He had to ask it. 'Ma, is Dad Eliza's father?'

A long pause. Then, finally, a nod.

'Did he tell you?'

Another nod.

'When?'

There was a long silence and then she spoke. 'A month before he died.'

'You've known for three years that Dad had a daughter and you didn't say anything?'

There was a sudden flare of temper. 'How could I, Emmet? How could I possibly begin to bring that up? Over Sunday lunch?'

So many questions were crowding his mind. 'How long did it go on between them?'

'It's none of your business.'

'It's absolutely my business. Jeannie was my friend. Jesus, Ma. When did it start? When she was here in Trim with me that summer?'

There was a long pause. She wouldn't look at him.

'I need to know,' he said quietly.

'He said it happened once. In Melbourne. After you woke up. When you came out of the coma.'

'Did he always know about Eliza? From the start? Were he and Jeannie in contact?'

'Yes.'

'I need to know more than that.'

'No, you don't.'

'Ma, please, tell me.'

'I don't want to tell you. It was hard enough to hear your father telling me. I thought it had all gone away. Where it belonged. But then there she was at the quiz. In our pub. Like a ghost, risen from the dead.'

'From the dead?' He thought she was talking about Jeannie. 'You knew that Jeannie had died?'

She shook her head. Impatiently. 'Jeannie told him Eliza had died. That she'd been killed in an accident outside her school. Not long before your father was due to go to Australia. When he was offered that trip, do you remember, the GAA one?'

Of course he remembered. There had been such a fuss about it. All for nothing. His father hadn't even gone in the end. He'd said one of the younger fellows should have his place.

'When the trip was first announced, he contacted Jeannie. Said he was coming to Australia. He wanted to meet his daughter. Jeannie agreed. Then a month before the visit, she rang him and said her daughter had been killed. Jeannie told him she was too devastated, she couldn't meet him herself, ever again. It was too painful.'

'He believed her?'

'Of course he believed her. Why wouldn't he believe her? A mother telling someone her daughter was dead? What kind of sick person would make up something like that?'

Her words settled around Emmet, sparking more memories of Jeannie. Her wildness. Her exaggeration. Her fearlessness. Her lows, other times. Deep lows. Had she been sick? Mentally sick?

'Why did Dad tell you?'

Her hands were still twisted in her lap. 'He said he couldn't go to his grave carrying that secret. That he knew it might ruin everything between us but he had to tell me.'

'Jesus.' He stood up. 'Jesus, Ma.'

'Stop blaspheming.'

He'd heard that thousands of times over the years.

'Is Jeannie dead?' she asked. 'Is that true?'

He nodded. He had no reason to believe Eliza hadn't been telling him the truth. He told his mother as much as he knew.

'Was it suicide?'

'A coroner's report said no.'

He sat down again. His head felt too full of images. His father. His mother, hearing that news, a month before he died. Jeannie, in a bath, drunk. Dead. Jeannie and his father —

'I talked to Eliza again myself,' his mother said. 'I went to the hotel to see her this morning. We went for a walk around the castle.'

'And?'

'And what?'

'Did you tell her?'

A nod.

'Ma, what did you tell her? What did she say?'

'I told her what I've just told you.' A pause. 'She said she'd like to talk to you. I said I needed to tell you first. I hadn't planned on actually doing it, but here we are.'

He wanted to swear again. 'You wouldn't have told me, if I hadn't come to you today? You lied to Eliza?'

Sheila didn't answer.

'What about the others?' He meant his three younger brothers. 'Will you tell them?'

'Of course not.'

'They need to know too. Eliza is our sister. Our half-sister. Jeannie was my friend.'

'Some friend.'

'You're blaming her?' He stared at his mother. 'What are you saying? That she seduced him? She was twenty-one years old. Oh, Jesus,' he said again. 'Was it —' He couldn't say the word. His mother could.

'Rape? Hugh said it wasn't. I believe him. He said it started in the most innocent way.' She wasn't looking at him now. 'He said that none of them had been sleeping. Him. Jeannie. Orla. Taking turns at the hospital, being by your bed. Reading to you. Talking to you. He'd been with you the night you woke. He said it was the most incredible relief, like being pulled back from the depths of hell. He'd stayed by your side, hardly believing it could be possible. You talking. Awake. Alive. Orla had been due to take over from him. He met her at the front of the hospital. "Go home and sleep," she'd said. "Go home. It's such wonderful news." He'd gone home. Jeannie had been alone in the house. The others were at work. She opened a bottle of champagne. Real champagne.'

'Dad didn't drink champagne.'

'He did that night. He said he felt like a different person that night. That he'd never felt anything like the sense of relief when, out of the blue, completely out of the blue, after all those days of you being unconscious, you opened your eyes, and said, clear as day, as if it was the most ordinary thing in the world . . .'

Emmet had heard the story of his awakening so many times. He didn't need to hear it now.

'They were euphoric,' Sheila continued. 'I remember Hugh using that exact word. He and Jeannie drank all the champagne. She had some dope. He said he'd have done anything, taken anything, that night, the relief was so incredible.'

'I don't need to hear any more.'

It was too late. She was going to tell him whether he wanted to hear it or not. 'He said he never meant it to happen. He would never have done it sober. They'd been on the sofa together, laughing, talking, such relief. Feeling so euphoric together.'

Emmet never wanted to hear the word euphoric again either.

'And then they kissed.'

Emmet was suddenly nauseous. He wanted to know who kissed who first, but he didn't want to know. His mother was talking about his father and Jeannie. His dad and Jeannie, together, on that sofa he had sat on in Melbourne. Or in the room he had slept in? His bed?

His mother was still talking. 'He said they both regretted it in the morning. Said it would never happen again. He swore to me that it didn't. I believed him.'

'When did he find out about the baby?'

'He didn't tell me all the details. Just that she'd let him know. She'd moved from Melbourne. Was in a country town, with a couple who took her in. She'd fallen out with her own parents years before, apparently. The couple told her that every baby had a mother and a father, and that they both deserved to know about each other. They urged her to at least let Hugh know. And when the time was right, to make sure her baby knew who her father was too.' She took a breath. 'He told me she rang the pub one night.'

'He got a call like that and he didn't tell you about it? You didn't notice anything?'

'I tried to remember if he'd ever come home in a state of shock. If he did, I don't remember it. I think he only told me in the end because he believed she had died.'

'Did he know Jeannie was dead?'

'I don't know. He said after he had the call about Eliza being killed, they never spoke again.'

There was a long silence in the room.

He broke it. 'What are we going to do?'

'What do you mean? We do nothing, of course.'

'Nothing?'

'Eliza will go away and we go on as before.'

'We can't unknow this, Ma. We can't forget the fact we've discovered I have a sister. Dad had a daughter. Has a daughter. You have a stepdaughter.'

'She's nothing to me.'

'She was Dad's daughter.'

Sheila said nothing.

'Did he have other affairs?'

'This wasn't an affair.'

'Did he have other one-night stands?' It sounded cruel, that term, but he needed to use it.

'I don't think so.'

'You don't think so?'

'We were married for more than fifty years, Emmet. You think it was sunshine and roses every day? You're married yourself. You know it's not. Five years before you went to Australia, there was another woman. A local woman. I'm not going to name her; you'd recognise her. I was wary of her. She liked Hugh. Too much. We fought about it. I asked him after he told me about Eliza. He swore that nothing ever happened between them. That he'd only been unfaithful to me once. With Jeannie.'

'And you believed him?'

'I had to.' She nearly whispered the words. 'I wanted to. Because he told me when he was dying, when he had only weeks to live. You think I wanted to spend those last days with him talking about all the times our marriage had gone off the rails?

You think I was glad he told me? I wish he had never opened his mouth. I wish he had gone to his grave with that secret. I wish you had never gone to Australia, or London, never met that, that —'

He knew the word she was searching for. Whore. Tramp. 'You can't blame Jeannie, Ma. There were two of them.' The image was still making him sick, but he had to say it. 'Dad and Jeannie.'

'I know that. I know what happened. And I know he must have kissed her first, he must have. He was a man in his forties, beside a pretty, sexy young woman. Of course it wouldn't have been the other way around. Or maybe she had a crush on him, or maybe she thought it was fun, or maybe they were both so delirious on their euphoria, the champagne, the dope, I don't know. But here we are, thirty-one years later, and the fruit of that union is here too. Aren't we lucky?'

He reacted to the tone of her voice. 'It's not Eliza's fault.'

'It was Eliza's decision to come looking for him.'

'She wanted to know who her father was. She needed to know.'

'She didn't need to know. What difference does it make now she's an adult?'

'Every difference. It would always matter. I wanted to be a father, Ma. I wanted it badly. Dervla and I longed to be parents. And when I found out we couldn't, because of me, that I was the reason we couldn't have children of our own, you think I was only upset about that for a couple of days and then got over it?

It's one of the reasons we're all here, isn't it? To have families, bring up children, love them? And when it doesn't happen, for whatever reason, it's not easy. You have to mourn it, think about it, look at it for —'

'It's nothing like your situation. And you have Ursula and Ava. You are a father.'

'Yes, thankfully. And I love them as much as I'd have loved our own sons and daughters. Which makes me realise even more strongly why Eliza is here. She needs to know who she is, where she came from, who she came from.'

'And now she does. Job done. And no one else needs to know.'

'Yes, they do. My brothers need to know. I'm not going to be the only son who knows this.'

'They do not need to know. You live here. You found out by accident. It stops at you.'

'I'm telling them. I'm also telling Dervla.'

'She especially doesn't need to know. She couldn't keep a secret if her life depended on it.'

'She's my wife.'

'Where do we stop then, Emmet? Do we hold another party in the pub? I could walk the streets of Trim, couldn't I? In and out of the shops, saying Hugh died three years ago but look who just turned up – his Australian daughter, imagine that!'

'Why not? Why not do exactly that? Once and for all.'

She ignored him. 'Would I then ring Hugh's family? His sisters? Give them a brand new niece? Then what, Emmet? Would we take out an ad in the *Irish Times*? Spread the word that way too?'

'Ma —'

'And for the rest of my life, everywhere I went, I'd hear it, wouldn't I? There's Sheila Foley. Couldn't keep her husband happy. He went off to Australia and got some young one half his age pregnant. Isn't it disgusting?'

'You're talking about real people, Ma. My friend Jeannie. Her daughter, Eliza. She's not disgusting.'

'Well, I am disgusted. How dare Hugh do this to me? How dare he tell me? How dare Jeannie tell him their child was dead? Why didn't she let him meet her, let him keep sending that guilt money and then go to his grave, holding his secret to his chest. Why did he have to tell me? Why, Emmet?'

She was sobbing now. He watched, stricken. He didn't know what to do. Console her? Leave her alone? She stood before he had a chance to decide.

'I was going to contact Eliza. Whether I'd told you or not. But I've changed my mind. There's nothing more to say to her.'

'There's so much more to say to her,' Emmet said. 'I want to talk to her about Jeannie. I want to hear about her own life too. Eliza's. Who she is, what her life has been like.'

'There's no point.'

'There is every point. Jeannie was my friend. Eliza is my sister.'

'She is not your sister.'

'She is my half-sister. Half is better than none. I always wanted a sister.'

'How dare you say that? Do you know how much I always wanted a daughter?'

'Yes, I do. You never stopped going on about it when you were giving out to us about our muddy football boots or our smelly, messy rooms. "If I had a daughter, I wouldn't have this mess." You would, you know. I have two daughters and I have never seen such mess.'

'Your daughters are wonderful.'

'I agree. And they love you, their grandmother. You found it in you to love them, didn't you? Even though they're not our flesh and blood? Can't you find some feeling for Eliza? Even sympathy?'

'Don't you even begin to compare her to them. It's a completely different situation. This Eliza could destroy our family forever. Ruin everything.'

'This Eliza is a person, Ma. If you don't contact her, then I will. I'm going to talk to her again, whether you like it or not.'

He had walked out on his mother then. Something he had never done before. He hadn't told Dervla any of it, either. That was also a first. Later that evening, he'd received a text message from his mother.

*She will be at my apartment at 9 a.m. tomorrow.*

Sheila hadn't named Eliza. She hadn't invited him. But they both knew without saying that he was going to be there too.

He checked his watch once more. Eight-forty. He couldn't wait any longer. He'd go to his mother's apartment now.

# CHAPTER THIRTY-SIX

Eliza was at Sheila's front door at five minutes to nine. Sheila opened it before Eliza had a chance to ring the bell. Eliza was surprised to see Emmet in the hallway behind his mother.

Sheila looked tired. Her eyes were red-rimmed.

'Emmet knows everything now too,' Sheila said flatly. 'I didn't want him here, but he insisted.'

'Good morning, Eliza,' he said. He smiled. She could see he was trying to make it easier for her. She said good morning in return.

'Follow me,' Sheila said. Her back was ramrod straight. They went into the living room. It was a dull morning. The standard lamp was on.

'Please, sit down,' Sheila said.

Emmet sat too. 'Eliza, I can only imagine —'

'I'll handle this, Emmet, thank you.' Sheila said with a sharp glance. 'This has come as a shock to me, Eliza, as you know.'

'Ma, in fairness, I think it's Eliza who's had the biggest shock.'

'I asked you to be quiet, Emmet.'

Eliza stood. 'If this is a bad time, if you both need to talk more —'

'I've nothing more to say to Emmet, Eliza. And it won't take me long to say what I need to say to you.' She paused. 'I appreciate this is difficult. That you had no idea what you'd discover when you came here. Emmet explained that you thought it might have been him that your mother —' She stopped. 'Which would have been preferable, of course.'

'Ma, please —'

Sheila ignored her son. 'Your mother was a troubled young woman, Eliza. You might not have known how troubled, but I certainly noticed it when she stayed here that summer. And of course, it was her idea to get Emmet to Australia, and because of her he had that acci—'

'Stop it.'

Eliza still hadn't spoken. It was Emmet again.

'Stop talking about Jeannie like that. Please,' he said. 'As if this was her fault somehow. Dad was responsible. He was the adult in that relationship, if you can call it that. And Jeannie didn't lure me to Australia. I always wanted to go there. She just made it possible. She found me a place to stay. She got me work.'

'She nearly got you killed.'

'That fight was my fault. I was the one who'd drunk too much. I was the one who threw the first punch. Yes, I missed and the fellow who hit me had better aim, but I had that accident because of my own actions.'

'You can't remember it. You told us that.'

'I can't remember lots from that time. But there's something memorable about being hit in the head that's stayed with me. Jeannie was a good person, Ma. A great person. Loyal. Fun. Smart.'

Sheila made a scoffing noise.

Emmet turned to Eliza. 'I'm having a lot of trouble with this myself. I can't begin to imagine how you're feeling. I'm sorry for how my mother has talked to you. I'm sure you didn't expect any of it.'

'She must have known she'd stir up trouble.' Sheila didn't say Eliza's name. She was looking at Emmet. 'What did she think would happen? That we would say, "Oh, hello, here you are, proof of Hugh's biggest mistake"?'

Eliza spoke then. Loudly. 'I told you, Sheila, I'm not a mistake.' At their shocked expressions, she lowered her voice. 'I'm sorry for your hurt, Sheila, and I'm sorry to cause problems between you both, Emmet, but I am not a mistake. I was loved. I loved my mother very much. I miss her every minute of every day.'

Sheila made a dismissive noise.

Eliza stood up. She kept her head high. 'No, Emmet, I didn't know what to expect coming here. If I would get to meet my father, or only hear stories about him. Nothing happened as I hoped. I know you can't wait for me to go, Sheila. So I will.'

She turned to Emmet. 'Thank you. For being my mother's friend. And for being so kind to me.'

She walked down the hall and let herself out. She didn't look back. As she reached the centre of town, she rang Lawrence. She asked if they could leave now.

It took her only minutes to pack once she got back to the hotel. He'd checked them both out by the time she came downstairs. They were on the road to Belfast and the ferry port before ten. He'd changed their ferry booking again. They'd be back in Edinburgh by the afternoon.

She felt his concern, but this time she couldn't talk about it. It was as if the dinner, the kiss, hadn't happened. He put on the radio. Once again, classical music filled the silence.

She turned to him as they were arriving into Edinburgh.

'Thank you for everything, Lawrence.' A pause. 'For being such a good chauffeur.'

'You're very welcome, Eliza,' he said. They fell back into silence again.

Eliza texted Olivia as they were approaching the Montgomery. She heard straight back. She was with Maxie, in her room. *We can't wait to see you. To hear everything.*

They sat around the table by the bay window. Eliza shared all that had happened in Trim. Her godmothers moved rapidly between shock at the truth about her father, curiosity about

Emmet, anger towards Sheila. They asked many questions, wanting details she was still digesting herself. It wasn't a story to tell in one neat package. She was still feeling the shockwaves.

By the time she finished, it was twilight outside. Olivia turned on the lamps. Their questions were slowly coming to an end. They knew she had told them everything she could. As much as she knew herself.

Olivia reached over and squeezed her hands again. 'I'm so sorry, Eliza. I know it wasn't what you hoped. It isn't what we wanted for you either. Was it okay with Lawrence, at least?'

'He was very kind.' She didn't say any more.

She needed to change the subject. She asked if anything had happened at the Montgomery while she was away.

Her godmothers exchanged a glance.

'What?' Eliza said. 'Tell me, please.'

It was only then that Olivia told her what had happened with Celine.

# CHAPTER THIRTY-SEVEN

To begin, Olivia explained about Alex's offer to move Celine temporarily into the hostel.

'The *hostel*?' Eliza said. 'Celine? How did she take that?'

'Put it this way,' Olivia said. 'I learned lots of new swear-words from her.'

She had gone to Celine's room, prepared for the worst, she explained. As expected, there had been another shouting match. Celine refused to believe Olivia's story about her room needing urgent redecoration. More insults followed. Swearing, in English and French. The letter from Edgar was brandished again. Then, midway through their argument, Celine's mobile phone had rung. Olivia quickly gathered it was her estranged husband calling from France.

'He rang her all the time when I was with her,' Eliza said. 'She never answered.'

'This time she did,' Olivia said.

Maxie sat back, smiling, clearly waiting to enjoy hearing this story again.

'I've never seen anything like it,' Olivia said. 'Celine turned from a wild tiger into a purring kitten. She started speaking to him in a kind of creepy little-girl voice.' She shuddered. '"Is my *chouchou* ringing to say a big sorry to his little baby at last?" Then she switched to French. I could only understand some of it, but it was bad, believe me.'

Eliza found herself suppressing a shudder too.

'She was making him promise all sorts of things. Expensive gifts, mostly. I wanted to stay and eavesdrop, but she shooed me out. Literally. Waved her hands at me.'

'As if Olivia was a fly!' Maxie said. 'So rude!'

'So I waited outside until I couldn't hear them talking any more —'

'Fighting the nausea,' Maxie said.

'Then I came back in, fully expecting another fight about the hostel. Instead she was at her wardrobe, pulling all her clothes out. Flinging them everywhere. She ordered me to "fetch" you, Eliza. She'd clearly forgotten you were in Ireland. She said she had "decided" to go home to France. That it had nothing to do with my "nonsense" about the hostel. That she'd never have moved there, in any case. She was leaving only because it suited her, now that her husband had come to his senses. Then she insisted that as she was being so accommodating by vacating the room for refurbishment, it was only fair, as she was an esteemed family member —'

Maxie laughed.

'That we cover her travel costs back to France. A business-class flight that evening. The shipping costs of all her research material too. Every last page and photo of it.'

'And you agreed?'

'I'd have paid her costs to the moon if I had to. I not only agreed, I helped her pack.'

'The two of you, working side by side?'

'Not in a pink fit. It was a truce, not a reconciliation. She booked herself in for a facial at the spa down the road and left me to it. I called on four of the housekeeping staff to help me while she was gone.'

'And that's it? She's actually gone? For good?'

Olivia nodded. 'She flew out that same evening. Ordered herself a chauffeured limousine to the airport. I checked the airline website. Her flight to Nice landed safely. All we can do now is hope she didn't parachute out on the way over.'

'Tell Eliza about the lovely thankyou note she left,' Maxie said.

Olivia was also smiling now. 'We found an envelope addressed to me, after she and the driver had gone. Thrown onto the front steps. It was the receipt for her facial. She'd charged it back to the Montgomery. She did the same with the driver's invoice. I didn't care. I'd have paid him triple if I had to.'

Eliza could see the relief on her godmother's face.

Olivia checked her watch then and apologised. She had to leave. 'One problem goes, another arrives. Deirdre's called an urgent meeting with Alex and Rory. She wants me there as well. Lawrence, too.'

'Alex is up to his old tricks?' Maxie asked. 'Or don't tell me, Rory's been turning your paintings into jigsaw puzzles?'

'I don't know what it's about.' Olivia suddenly looked tired again. 'All Deirdre would say is that she wants the four of us there.'

Olivia stood up. Before she left, she hugged Eliza again. Maxie reached for her hand and squeezed it. They didn't need to say anything more. She could feel their love and understanding.

Eliza excused herself then too. She needed to go for a walk, she realised. A long walk, on her own.

She met Rory on her way out. He had something for her. Two calico bags: the jigsaw puzzles she and Sullivan had painted. She thanked him, promising to give Sullivan's to him as soon as she could.

Alex was behind the reception desk. 'Eliza! How was Ireland? Please don't say green. Why Olivia gave our saintly general manager the privilege of your company there rather than me, I can't imagine.'

'Can't you?' Olivia appeared behind him. 'The meeting's in ten minutes, Alex. Be on time, please.'

'Deirdre's here for it too?' he said as their lawyer came through the front door. 'This *is* serious.'

Deirdre gave a curt nod. 'See you upstairs, Alexander.'

As Eliza stepped outside, Lawrence was coming up the stairs. Less than forty-eight hours ago she'd been in his arms, crying. Kissing him. Now, here they were, greeting each other so formally.

He hesitated, as if he was about to say something.

Deirdre spoke from the front door. 'Lawrence, a private word before the meeting, please?'

Eliza said goodnight and kept walking.


There was a small park four blocks from the Montgomery. She had just reached it when her phone sounded with a text message. It was Rose.

*Up in middle of the night here. (Child with nightmares. Fast asleep now. Mother wide awake & making school lunches.) Feel like a chat in 30 mins or so??*

Eliza replied immediately. *Yes please.*

In the meantime, she began walking along the tree-lined path. Rows of Edinburgh's distinctive stone buildings were visible through the branches. The air was cool, her coat warm. She passed dog-walkers, two joggers. She did one full circuit of the park, the movement helping her thoughts to settle. As she began a second circuit, she allowed herself to think about her mother again. To think about all the questions she wanted to ask her. There would always be so many.

A list appeared in her head. A long list.

*Can you please tell me about that night, Mum? Tell me why you wanted to sleep with him?*

*How did you feel the next day?*

*How did it feel when you found out you were pregnant?*

*Were you scared? Did you think even for a minute about not going ahead with it?*

*Did you ever wish afterwards that he had met me?*

*What was he actually like?*

*What were his favourite bands, books?*

*Could he sing?*

*Was he funny?*

*Did you have any good conversations with him?*

*I don't think you had time to love him, and it doesn't matter if you didn't, but did you* like *him?*

*Would I have liked him?*

So many questions. No chance of answers. She kept walking. A minute later, she abruptly stopped.

Yes, she knew Sheila would never speak to her about Hugh again. But perhaps someone else would.

She took out her phone and dialled. It rang once, twice, three times. As he answered, she could hear the sounds of his pub in the background.

One hour later, she was on her way back to the Montgomery. She'd spoken to Emmet for less than five minutes. It was all the time they'd needed to make the arrangements. She'd spoken to Rose for much longer.

By the time she said goodbye to Rose, she felt calmer. She had also made a decision. She knew that Olivia would ask her to stay longer in Edinburgh. That Maxie would ask her to come to New York soon. She knew it would be hard to say no to them both, but she'd done all she'd come here to do. It was time to go home.

Her phone rang as she reached the steps of the hotel. It was Olivia. She had more big news to share.

# CHAPTER THIRTY-EIGHT

Once again, the three of them sat around the table in Maxie's room. Olivia shared every detail of the meeting with Deirdre, Lawrence, Alex and Rory. She didn't seem tired any more. She was almost exhilarated.

It had been an hour of bombshell news, she told them. She shared it in the order she'd heard it.

Firstly, Lawrence had resigned.

'He emailed Deirdre from Ireland. Giving her the exact one month's notice they'd legally agreed to after his initial three-year contract had expired. He's been offered a job in Spain. Managing a boutique hotel in San Sebastián.'

As Maxie began firing questions at Olivia, Eliza stayed silent. Lawrence hadn't said anything about this to her. He'd had no reason to, of course.

'But what will you do without him?' Maxie asked. 'And what does that mean for the Montgomery? Who takes over as general manager, Alex or Rory?'

'I had the same questions,' Olivia said. 'Deirdre asked Alex and Rory if either of them felt ready to take over. She asked them to be honest. They made it clear that neither of them want the job. Not now. Not ever. They've stayed for the past three years only because they promised their father they would. They can't wait to leave.'

'Good heavens,' Maxie said.

Olivia explained that she'd expected Deirdre to say she would now advertise for a new general manager. Instead, she surprised them again. She'd prefaced her announcement by confirming she was following Edgar's explicit instructions, as outlined when he appointed her as his power of attorney.

'It was like being in a courtroom. All delivered in crisp legal language. Basically saying that in the event of neither Montgomery son wishing to take up the role as general manager, a vote was to be called between the brothers and me as to the future of the hotel. The question was simple. Did we want to keep it running, or did we want to sell it?'

Maxie and Eliza stayed silent, wide-eyed, as Olivia continued.

Deirdre had spoken over their shocked questions, she told them. She explained that in the past year there had been three approaches from different multinational hotel chains, enquiring if the Montgomery was for sale. Each time, she had advised that it wasn't, at this point in time. If their vote tonight was a unanimous yes, she would go back to all three potential buyers and ask for their offers in writing.

'And?' Maxie asked.

'It was a unanimous yes,' Olivia said.

Maxie and Eliza were taken aback. Olivia seemed unable to stop smiling.

'It's what Edgar wanted. It's what we all want. It's the best thing for all of us. We have Lawrence to thank. If he hadn't resigned, we might have kept going as we were, none of us wanting to be here.'

She'd loved being at the hotel when she was there with Edgar, she told them. But for the past three years, it had just made her sad. Alex and Rory felt the same way. Alex wanted to concentrate on the hostel. Deirdre's initial legal advice was that the hostel could be separate to any sale of the main hotel. Rory wanted to do his puzzles full-time. He had shared some other big news too: he and Milly were having a baby.

'I'm going to be a grandmother!' Olivia said. She started crying. Maxie did too.

Eliza did her best to pretend that this was news to her too.

She shared her own news after that. Firstly, that she had decided to go home to Australia at the end of the week. Her godmothers reacted exactly as she expected. They didn't want her to leave yet. They put up persuasive arguments for her to stay. Listened to her good reasons for going home. Finally, they told her that they understood.

They were more surprised by her second piece of news. That she had phoned Emmet in Ireland again. That he had offered to come to Edinburgh to see her before she left. Just for the day.

'I'd like you both to meet him again one day. I really hope you will. But I think it's better if it's just him and me for now. There's so much we need to talk about. I hope you understand.'

She was relieved when they told her they did.

Two days later, Eliza was at Edinburgh Airport, waiting for the midday flight from Dublin to arrive.

She gazed around her, at the bright lights, the shops, the cafés. She'd be back here again in three days, trying to prepare herself for that journey home. It felt like a long way off yet.

Her phone beeped. Sullivan playing a new word in their latest Scrabble game. She'd told him she was going home soon. He'd instantly replied.

*Hurrah, I'll be home soon too!!! See you in Melbourne! (We will keep in touch, won't we???????)*

*Of course!* she'd written back.

Since then, he'd been sending suggestions for their outings. The Lemur Island exhibit at Melbourne Zoo. The cinema. He also had a growing interest in leafy sea dragons, he'd told her. There were apparently some excellent specimens at the Melbourne Aquarium.

Passengers started to emerge from the Dublin flight. Emmet appeared. At first, they smiled at each other. Then he stepped forward and hugged her.

'Thank you for coming,' she said.

'Thank you for phoning me,' he said.

When she had rung him two nights earlier, she'd offered to return to Ireland. To meet him in Dublin somewhere, if Trim was too difficult. No, he'd said. She'd already come all the way from Australia. The least he could do was fly to Scotland. They talked about meeting in a hotel or a café in the city centre. It was Emmet who suggested they stay in the airport. All they needed was a table, chairs and coffee, after all.

Eliza led the way to the nearest café. They found a spare table at the back. She offered to get the drinks. He began talking as soon as she returned with their coffee.

'My mother still isn't taking it well, Eliza, I'm sorry. I spent two hours with her yesterday and . . .' He hesitated. 'She's very angry. With you. My father. Jeannie. Me. Especially me. She says it's my fault for introducing Jeannie into our family.'

'I know I'm biased, but I'm glad you did,' Eliza said.

A flash of a smile. A slight ebbing in the tension.

'I'm not too sure where to start,' he said. 'I don't know what you'd like to know about him.'

Eliza wanted to know everything. She began with the simplest of questions. 'What was he like?'

Emmet gave it some thought. 'When I was young? Tough. Ambitious for me. Disappointed in me.' A pause. 'We didn't have an easy relationship for years. I was the oldest son. He wanted me to be a particular person. Sporty. Community-minded. A copy of him. He didn't leave a lot of space for me to decide what I wanted for myself. Not until after Australia. Everything changed after that. A near-death experience is vastly underrated by family counsellors.' Another quick smile.

'Did you always feel loved?' She'd never have imagined asking such a personal question. But this wasn't a normal conversation.

'Before the accident, it didn't occur to me whether I was loved or not. All I felt was stifled. Afterwards . . .' Another pause. 'Afterwards, I knew it because he'd tell me, all the time. Not just in Australia. When I was back home, recovering. He drove me to every rehab appointment. He was different with my brothers from then on too. More affectionate. Less strict. He encouraged them to leave Ireland, spread their wings. We never doubted his love. He told us all, right until the day he died.'

'You didn't have any idea about him and my mother? Until this week?'

'It was as big a shock to me as it was to you, I'm sure. I'm still trying to take it in. Trying to imagine how it happened, even though that's the last thing I want to do.'

She felt the same.

'Eliza, your mother really was a one-off. Charismatic. My dad was amused by her, I know. She was a great storyteller too. That counted for a lot with him.'

'Did anything happen between them when she was here?'

'I don't think so. She was flirty, but to be honest, she was flirty with everyone. Always full of tales of this or that fling. She was going for some kind of United Nations record, she said. I took it all with a pinch of salt. You had to with Jeannie. Not that she didn't get plenty of offers. She was gorgeous, so full of life —' He stopped. 'I'm sorry, Eliza. That she and I lost contact. I still can't believe she's gone.'

It was his turn to ask personal questions. He asked about Eliza's childhood. Where they had lived. What sort of work Jeannie had done. He asked her again about Jeannie's death. She told him more than she'd told anyone since the night it happened, even Rose. Every detail was still so vivid in her mind. She told him about her godmothers arriving. The autopsy. The funeral. The aftermath, the coroner's report, the paperwork, so much of it handled by Olivia and Maxie. Packing up their house.

'You still went to university? So soon afterwards?'

'I had to do something. I had to keep going.'

'You must miss her so much.'

'Every single day.'

'And she had really never told you anything about your father?'

Eliza shared some of her mother's stories, choosing the more outlandish ones. The Hollywood stunt double. The spy. The mood lightened again. She could see he was trying not to smile.

'I know it isn't funny,' he said. 'But —'

'She found it very funny, I know that.'

'Do you think she would have told you the truth when you turned eighteen?'

Eliza nodded. 'She'd promised. She was always good at keeping promises.'

'Eliza, I'm sorry to ask this.' He was fidgeting with a sugar packet. 'Was her death an accident?'

Such a direct question, but they had gone far beyond diplomacy.

'Yes, it was. I know she would never have wanted to hurt me. She was a wonderful mother.'

'I can imagine,' Emmet said. 'She was a wonderful friend.'

'Mum talked a lot about you, Emmet. About what a good friend you were to her.' She'd brought the school project to show him. She handed it over, apologising for mishearing his name.

He read aloud from it. '*She got a job in a bar and lived in a big house called a squat and made a good friend who lived there too. The friend's name was Emma. Emma was funny and kind and Irish.*'

He looked up and thanked her for bringing it. She could see a glint of tears in his eyes.

'Eliza, when I was at my mother's house yesterday, I told her I was coming here. I asked her if I could show you some photos of Dad. She wasn't happy, but she agreed. At least, she went out for a walk and left me with the albums so I could borrow what I wanted. I can make copies to send you if you want. Or you can take photos of them now.' He reached down to a bag at his feet and took out a large envelope. 'How about I leave you with them for a while? I'll go and count planes or something. Just text me when you're done.'

He was making it as easy as possible for her. She was touched and grateful.

For the next thirty minutes, she pored over each photograph. They weren't in any order. Emmet must have taken them

397

from the albums at random. There was a photo of Hugh in his seventies behind the bar, then one of him as a child. A wedding photo. At various sporting matches. She began to see some likenesses. Not just her height. Was it in the shape of their faces? Their eyes?

She spent the longest time looking at a photo of Hugh with Emmet. From the date on the back, she guessed it had been taken shortly after they returned from Australia. Emmet with his hair cut short, one patch shaven, but smiling. Beside him, arm around his son, was Hugh, aged in his early forties.

He was good-looking. Tall. Dark-haired. He had a great smile. She'd seen photos of her mother at twenty-one. So pretty, so vivacious. She didn't want to imagine any more, but her mind still took her there. She could picture two people, alone in a house late at night. All the factors at play. So much tension, then relief. Alcohol. Drugs. All the elements making something happen. Making her happen.

'*I will always be grateful to him.*' Her mother's words were seared in Eliza's memory. '*If it wasn't for him, I wouldn't have you. And you are the best thing that ever happened to me.*'

She texted Emmet. He was back within minutes. He was on the phone. His mother?

'My head barman. Problems with a delivery.'

He finished his call and sat down. She gave him back the photos, thanking him. She asked more questions. The names of his brothers. Where one of the photos had been taken. More about where his father had come from.

He answered everything, sharing family stories. She would never know what Hugh might have been like as her father, but she was slowly getting an idea of him as a man.

'Have you told your brothers about me?' she asked.

He hesitated before answering. 'Not yet. Or my daughters. My mother doesn't want me to. She said it would ruin every future family gathering.' He saw her reaction to the word 'ruin'. 'I'm sorry. It was a bad choice of words. I want them all to know, when the time feels right. You deserve it and they deserve to know. I'd rather tell my brothers face-to-face, though. And we're not together very often. I can call them if you want me to, or I can wait.'

She thought about it. More questions flooded her mind. What if they didn't react as well as Emmet had? As kindly? What if the news caused real tension in the family, with Sheila especially? Yes, one day she would like to meet them all. She hoped that one day she would. But perhaps it didn't all have to happen right now. She'd waited thirty years to meet Emmet, after all. 'I'm happy for you to do whatever feels right,' she said.

'I'll tell them everything, one day, I promise. When —'

He didn't need to finish the sentence. She knew he meant after Sheila was gone.

'And Dervla?' Eliza asked.

'I've already told her. We tell each other everything.'

'Was she shocked?'

'She was, yes.' He left it at that. He asked Eliza who she had told. Her godmothers and her best friend, she said. One other person too. Lawrence. She didn't know how to describe him.

He asked when she was going back to Australia. At the end of the week, she told him. He asked who she had waiting for her there. Her best friend Rose and her family, she said.

'You have no other family in Australia?' he asked.

'I had grandparents, but I never met them. My mother told me they'd died in an accident.'

'As she told my father you had?' He hesitated. 'Eliza, Jeannie wasn't always well, was she?'

It was thoughtfully put. 'No. I didn't always realise it at the time. My godmothers have told me more stories. She was in trouble a lot.' She told him about the car theft, about Jeannie leaving school early. He didn't look surprised. 'You knew about that?'

'She told me about it in London. But she told me so many stories, I was never sure which were true. They were always entertaining, though, I'll give her that.'

Out of nowhere, Eliza felt like laughing. Yes, her mother's stories had always been entertaining. It seemed extraordinary to be talking to someone who'd known that too. Who'd heard her stories. Been amused by them. Who had cared about her too; she could tell.

She saw Emmet glance at his watch. They'd been talking for two hours. It felt like only minutes had passed.

'Eliza, I know my mother wasn't welcoming. That she wanted you gone. I'm sorry. She has a particular life in our town, a social standing. I wish she'd been different to you. But she's an elderly woman. She's still grieving, still missing my father so much —' He stopped. 'If you ever have any other questions, about the photos, about my father, please ring me any time. Text. Write to me at the pub, even. I'll always get back to you.'

She told him she understood about Sheila. Part of her did. It was enough for her now that Emmet would keep in contact. She thanked him for that. She had one more question.

'Are you ashamed of me, Emmet? Of my mother? Of what happened?'

He gave it thought. 'No. I was shocked at first, I can't lie. But I've had time to think about it. The accident in Australia changed things between me and my dad. It changed me too. Not just physically. That one stupid drunken fight could have been the end of my life, before it had really started. If you ask me, any of us are lucky to be here and all of us make errors of judgement. I run a pub. I've seen and heard more life stories than I'd have imagined. Some sober, most not. Some good, many not. Who am I to tell people how they should or shouldn't behave?'

'Have I ruined your family?'

He briefly smiled. 'That would suggest it was perfect to begin with. Mine isn't what you'd call a "normal" family, Eliza, let alone a perfect one. Two of my brothers don't get on. I also know my mother and Dervla don't like each other. They try to hide it but . . .' He shrugged. 'If you ask me, family life is sometimes more about pretending to get on than actually getting on.'

She had more questions now, but it was time for him to go. She stood up. So did he.

She walked with him to the departures area, to as far as she could go with him. She thanked him again. 'Not just for coming to see me today. For all you did for my mother.'

'I'm very glad we met, Eliza.'

'I am too,' she said.

She saw tears in his eyes again. She felt like crying too.

'And we'll meet again,' he said.

'Yes, please,' she answered.

They hugged goodbye. She stood waiting and watching until he was out of sight.

# CHAPTER THIRTY-NINE

She was in a taxi on her way back to the Montgomery when Lawrence rang. She hadn't seen him or spoken to him since their brief exchange on the steps two nights earlier.

'Is everything okay?'

Everything was fine, he said. 'There was something I wanted to ask you the other night.'

He was flying to France the next day, for his sister's birthday gathering. He'd be away for four days. He'd heard from Olivia that Eliza would be gone by the time he returned. He asked if she was free for dinner that night. Just the two of them. Yes, she told him. She was.

They'd arranged to meet in the hotel foyer at seven. Just as she'd finished putting on her make-up, her phone rang.

It was Sullivan's mother Lisa, calling from Melbourne. She'd arrived home from her American trip. She was ringing to ask a favour. She understood of course if Eliza didn't want to do it, but Sullivan had still begged her to ask. He wanted to change his flight back to Australia so he could not only leave early, but also be on the same plane as Eliza. So he could accompany her, help her cope with the flight, rather than be an unaccompanied minor himself in a week. His father's permission had been sought, and granted. Too swiftly granted, according to Lisa. But the final decision was Eliza's.

She didn't need to think about it. That would be great, she said.

Lawrence was waiting in the foyer when she came down the stairs.

'You look beautiful,' he said.

She felt a blush rise.

She was nervous, she realised as they stepped outside. A mixture of self-consciousness and over-consciousness. Of Lawrence walking close beside her. The smell of his aftershave. The feel of his hand, a gentle touch on her back as they turned a corner. The memory of their kiss in Ireland.

He'd chosen a restaurant within walking distance of the Montgomery, on the edge of the city centre. They were given a warm welcome, seated at a table that seemed to be reserved for special guests.

She'd been anxious that there might be silences, awkwardness. But once again there was so much to talk about. They spoke about his new job. The possible sale of the Montgomery. His sister's birthday. She told him all that had happened with Emmet.

'Are you okay?' he said.

'Yes, I am,' she said. It was the truth.

During their meal, the manager came over to greet Lawrence.

'Have you seen his work?' he asked Eliza. 'He's wasted in that hotel. That's one of his, you know.'

The manager gestured towards a portrait of himself and his wife, laughing in front of the restaurant. It was full of life and personality. They'd walked past it on the way in.

'He didn't mention it was his,' she said.

'Lawrence, my friend. Here with a beautiful woman. What better time to boast?'

After the manager left, they exchanged stories from their working lives. They talked about books. Films. As the minutes passed, she grew more aware of him physically. His kind eyes. The way he listened closely as she spoke. His curiosity. She liked the way he seemed to laugh easily. That he found her funny. She told more stories from her work with Gillian. He shared stories of badly behaved guests. Now and then, they talked over each other, as if there wasn't enough time for all they wanted to say.

She asked him about his family. She learned that a childhood that had sounded so cosmopolitan, moving from European city to city, speaking several languages, had been difficult. His father had been declared bankrupt twice. His mother left several times. His father would promise to change; she would go back to him. He'd start a business, it would fail, he'd start another.

She asked him about his late wife. She didn't know her name. Lawrence thanked her and spoke softly about her. Her name was Sara. They had been married for two years, living in New York, when she fell ill. They had eight months together before she died. 'I needed to change everything afterwards. My life. My job. Where I lived, especially.' He had contacted Edgar. They'd met years before at an industry event, when Lawrence was beginning his career. Edgar had asked Lawrence to get in touch if he ever felt like working in, as he put it, 'the wilds of Scotland'. Lawrence didn't go into more detail, but he told Eliza that his time there walking, photographing, grieving and remembering had helped him more than Edgar could have known.

They were interrupted by a waiter, asking if they needed anything. They assured him they were fine. When they were alone again, Eliza asked when he was leaving for France. First thing the next morning, he said. She was leaving in three days.

There was a subtle shift in the mood between them. As if they were now on borrowed time.

They talked about the art on display at the Montgomery. Of his favourite painting. Hers. Other artists they liked. He'd been inspired by Olivia's collection, he told her. In his three years in Edinburgh, he'd gone to student shows, begun his own collection.

'I'd love to see them,' she said.

'They're in my flat,' he said.

They could walk there now, he said. That would be lovely, she said.

He insisted on paying. She protested, but there was no dissuading him. She watched as he talked to the manager, settling their bill at the counter.

What would the Eliza in Melbourne have done in this situation? She probably wouldn't have even been out. She'd rarely socialised in all the years she worked with Gillian. What would Rose advise her to do now? What would her mother say? She began to imagine and then she stopped herself. She was thirty years old. She was a single woman. He was a single man. A single, attractive, kind, smart and sexy man.

They started kissing even before they stepped inside his flat. While his front door was still open.

He lived on the ground floor of a Georgian building. They'd made their way there in near-silence, the attraction between them growing with each step. His hand once again a gentle touch on her back as they walked. It felt like a promise.

At the doorway, he put the key in the lock, turned to her to say something. But then he didn't speak. He leaned down towards her and she tilted her chin and they met halfway, a soft touch of their lips that quickly became more. He drew back first, opening the door, his arm around her waist, the two of them in his hallway now, no lights on, the front door shut, the street light sending a glow through the front window, shadows and light. There in the semi-darkness, lips on lips again. She could feel his body against hers, her own hands now on his arms, his shoulders, each of her caresses matched by his.

They could have kept talking. He could have showed her his paintings. Made her coffee. But neither of them wanted that now. The apartment stayed dark. They moved from the hallway to the living room. She saw in the dim light a wide sofa, a lamp, walls with paintings in shadow, but she was too conscious of his hands on her, his lips on hers, her clothing being inched aside so his fingers could touch bare skin, her pulling at his shirt too, feeling the smooth warm skin of his back. Then they were on the sofa, more kisses, more skin against skin, clothing being removed even as their kisses became more urgent. He breathed her name. She said his in return, a question, an answer, that meant they stood again, barely clothed, and she followed him, his hand in hers, through the room, into his bedroom.

She'd never felt like this. Never wanted to lose herself so entirely in a man's embrace, kiss, body. There were murmured words, caresses, as his kisses left her lips and went lower, as he stopped to look at her, to admire her, to compliment her. She lay on his bed, now naked as he was, and closed her eyes and felt his fingertips and his lips trace her body, her breasts, lower, her body arching, reaching for him in turn. A whispered conversation, more kisses, yes to protection, yes to not stopping, yes, yes and yes, so many times, as she felt the weight of him on her and she shut her eyes and felt an explosion of pleasure like never before.

He held her tight afterwards. She felt him kiss her, felt his fingers trace patterns on her naked back. And then, moments or minutes later, movement against each other's bodies again, as slow kisses became faster kisses, as desire flared between them once more. The second time was even better.

She woke at four a.m. He was asleep, an arm across her. She gazed at him, so peaceful, dark lashes, dark eyebrows. She was thirsty. Carefully, trying not to disturb him, she reached down, put on a shirt she found on the floor beside the bed and tiptoed out. She was standing in the kitchen, sipping the water, when she heard a noise behind her.

It was Lawrence. Smiling. 'That shirt suits you. You can have it if you like.'

She gazed down at herself in his shirt. Knowing his eyes were on her, she walked over to him through the dark room, slowly slipping the shirt off as she reached him. Their kisses replaced words.

They woke again at six. More quiet conversation, bodies entwined. She felt sated, cherished.

'Thank you,' she said, kissing him again.

He laughed softly. 'You're welcome.'

'You're good at this.'

'I was about to say the same thing to you.'

He needed to leave for the airport, she knew.

'I'll walk you home,' he said.

He made her a coffee as she showered and dressed. In the dawn light, she joined him in the kitchen. Cups in hands, he did show her his paintings. They looked even better in the light.

Edinburgh was barely awake as they walked back to the

Montgomery. This time they did hold hands. It felt good. As they reached the hotel's street, he stopped, touched her cheek.

'I hope you can find your way from here?'

They were less than two metres from the hotel. 'I think so,' she said.

The briefest of kisses. A beautiful kiss.

'Have a great time in France,' she said to him. 'I hope the new job goes well, too.'

'Safe travels back to Australia,' he said.

He asked if they could keep in touch at the same moment she asked him. A laugh, another kiss. She looked back as she reached the front steps. He was still there. Smiling at her. A final wave, one from her in return, and she went inside.

# CHAPTER FORTY

Three days later, Eliza was sitting in the middle seat of a row at the back of a plane soon to take off on an eight-hour flight to Dubai.

'Don't be too sad, Eliza,' Sullivan said beside her from his window seat. 'Remember, Olivia said she's hoping to get to Australia again soon, even for a quick visit. And Maxie said if you don't come to New York, she'll just have to go to Melbourne herself.'

Her godmothers had indeed said those things. But it was always hard to say farewell. They'd hugged her as tightly as she hugged them. Maxie would be leaving for New York herself in a few days.

Eliza had thanked them for more than usual this time. She thanked them for being so honest with her. For telling her the truth. For answering all her questions. For being there for her once again, as they always had been.

'I hope it wasn't too sad saying goodbye to your father?' Eliza asked Sullivan. 'Or your little sister?'

He shrugged. 'Dad and I get on better on Skype than in person. I'm hoping me and The Baby will too.'

Eliza wouldn't have been surprised if it had been Ann-Marie who took Sullivan to the airport. Instead, it was his father, Dean. He was in a suit, well-groomed, businesslike, harried. It was clear he had other places to be. He'd thanked Eliza as if she was the airport's hired representative. He'd barely acknowledged Olivia or Maxie. He'd left before Eliza and Sullivan had gone into the departures area. Olivia and Maxie stayed waving until they were both out of view.

They'd had time to look around the duty-free shops and to have a snack in one of the airside cafés. It was while they were there that Eliza's phone had rung.

'Olivia?' Eliza said, answering immediately. 'Is everything okay?'

'Better than I could have hoped,' Olivia said. Eliza could hear Maxie laughing in the background. 'I'm sending you a photo I've just received.'

It arrived seconds later. Celine, in a gold bikini beside a pool, under a blue sky and bright sunshine. She was holding up a cocktail. That was it. No message. No caption. No thankyou.

Eliza's phone pinged four more times before they boarded. Rose, once, confirming Eliza's arrival time. She'd be there to meet her. Their guestroom was already made up. The other three messages were from Lawrence in France. Wishing her bon voyage. Sharing a quick and funny story from his sister's birthday party, along with a photograph of a stunning French scene, curving vineyards and a setting sun.

As the plane began to taxi, Eliza felt the familiar jolt, the quickening of her heart. She closed her eyes, tried not to clench her fists, kept her breathing steady.

'We can hold hands if you want to, Fearless Flyer?' Sullivan said.

'I think I'll be fine, Navillus, but thank you very much anyway.'

'I'm right here if you need me,' he said.

Four days after she arrived back in Australia, Eliza took a bus from Rose's home town of Colac to Melbourne. Another bus to Maryborough, the country town in which her mother was buried.

Jetlag had helped ease her back into Australian life. So had three nights with Rose and her family. She'd played with the kids, sat up late talking, helped Harry do their traditional Sunday barbecue. Every moment made her realise how well she knew them. How welcome they made her feel.

Each evening, once they had the kitchen to themselves, Rose asked her many questions. About her godmothers. About Emmet. About Eliza's father. About Lawrence too.

'What will happen next?'

'I don't know,' Eliza said.

As she walked down the quiet road towards the cemetery, she pulled her coat in around her. There was an autumnal bite in the May air. She hadn't brought flowers. After the first year, she never had. It had made her too sad to see the bouquet leaning against the stone, the flowers long dead, the wrapping paper warped by summer sun and winter rain.

It was a small graveyard, at the back of a church built from golden stone. In the days following her mother's death, there was no way she could have made decisions about where Jeannie should be buried, what should be on her gravestone. Maxie had remembered a conversation from years earlier. Over wine, during one of Maxie's annual visits. Jeannie had been talking about Mr and Mrs Quaker, the couple who had taken her in when she was pregnant with Eliza. They'd been laid to rest in what Jeannie had said was 'the most beautiful cemetery I've ever seen, as far as cemeteries go'. She'd declared that, when the time came, she'd 'like to be cremated, thank you'.

Afterwards, Olivia and Maxie had asked Eliza if she wanted to keep her mother's ashes. That had felt impossible. Her mother, in that urn? It was Olivia who came up with a solution. Maxie made the phone calls, spoke to the stonemason, got contact details for Mr and Mrs Quaker's distant niece. She gave her permission. Jeannie's ashes were put inside a brass urn and secured to the side of Mr and Mrs Quaker's headstone. Her name and dates were engraved on a plaque, with two extra lines underneath. *Beloved and loving mother of Eliza. Beloved and loving friend of Maxie and Olivia.* It felt right to them all. Jeannie sheltered by the Quakers, even all these years later.

Eliza had the cemetery to herself. She sat on the edge of the grave, close to her mother's urn. She touched it often as she spoke to her. She told her everything that had happened during her trip. About the flight. Maxie's wedding. Olivia, Celine and the Montgomerys. Sullivan. Lawrence.

She told her everything that had happened in Ireland.

'I didn't meet Hugh, Mum. I was three years too late. But I found out all about him. And I met Emmet. I liked him so much. My half-brother Emmet.'

She spoke about it all, about Sheila and her other sons too. How she had felt learning the truth at last. She told Jeannie everything, as if her mother were sitting across a table from her, eyes alight, asking for more stories, delighting in her, as she'd done so often in the seventeen years they'd had together.

# CHAPTER FORTY-ONE

Maxie and Olivia were at a café in Edinburgh Airport. Maxie's flight to New York was leaving soon.

They were talking, as they so often were, about Eliza. Remembering her heartfelt farewell words to them four days earlier: 'I feel like I know everything about Mum now. It helps so much. Thank you for finally telling me the truth.'

They'd both hugged her tightly. They told her they were so glad everything was now out in the open. So glad there were no more secrets between them. They'd stood at the departures gate, waving until she and Sullivan were out of sight. It was only then that they'd allowed themselves to cry.

They were trying not to cry again now.

'It still hurts so much,' Maxie said. 'I hate lying to her.'

'I know you do,' Olivia said, reaching for her friend's hand across the table. 'So do I, Maxie. But we told her everything we could. As much as we could.'

There was silence between them for a few moments.

'Liv, I'm going to talk to that therapist again. Next time I'm in London.'

'The one who asked you to write everything down?'

Maxie nodded. 'It helped me back then. For a while. I'm hoping it might help again.'

Olivia's eyes filled. 'I think I'd like to talk to her too.'

Soon after, Maxie was staring out of the plane window. It had been so hard to say goodbye to Olivia, after so recently farewelling Eliza. She knew they had made the right decision thirteen years ago. But it was still so hard to live with the guilt. Their guilt.

The therapist had urged her to be honest with herself. To keep talking about it with Olivia.

She and Olivia had done nothing for months but talk about it. They'd told each other the truth from the start. It hadn't helped either of them. It was still the first thing they both thought about each morning. The last thing each night. Guilt was eating them both up.

'You need to try to get it out of yourself some other way,' the therapist had suggested. 'Bring it out into the light somehow. Use all the tools you have. You're an actress. You told me you've been trying your hand at playwriting too. Imagine seeing it unfold on stage. Imagine yourself, Olivia and Jeannie, having a chance to talk about it. Explaining it all to each other. Why you did what you did. Said what you said.'

'I can't. Jeannie's dead.' It physically hurt to say it.

'Imagine that she's still able to hear. Able to respond to you both. Imagine what she would say.'

As her plane started to taxi, Maxie shut her eyes, picturing all she'd written. The words were still strong in her memory. She'd included everything she remembered. Everything Olivia had told her.

Everything they could never, ever tell Eliza.

# CHAPTER FORTY-TWO

SETTING: A BARE STAGE. OLIVIA IS SEATED AT STAGE LEFT. MAXIE IS SEATED AT STAGE RIGHT. ABOVE, ON A SWING, THE GHOST OF JEANNIE, SLOWLY MOVING BACK AND FORTH.

THE THREE WOMEN SPEAK ONLY TO THE AUDIENCE, NOT TO EACH OTHER.

SPOTLIGHT FALLS ON OLIVIA.

OLIVIA: *Jeannie rang me five times the night she died. She was drunk. She was hysterical. She was dramatic. She often was all three of those things.*

JEANNIE, SLOWLY MOVING IN SWING ABOVE: *You're right. I was.*

OLIVIA: *She was threatening to kill herself. She kept saying that she'd made such a mess of her life. How worthless she was. How Eliza would be better off without her. That she had realised Eliza was ashamed of her for drinking too much, not having a proper job or a degree, for not giving her a proper childhood, with a father, a steady home life.*

JEANNIE: *I did feel like that sometimes.*

OLIVIA: *I'd been having a bad day myself. I didn't know it at the time but Edgar, my husband, was in the early stages of dementia. Soon I would understand his mood changes, but that day it felt like our marriage was falling apart. That we didn't know how to talk to each other any more. That I was a bad wife, a bad step-mother. I'd spent all those years learning about art, for what? To curate a display in a hotel, that people barely glanced at as they walked by with their suitcases? I wasn't in the right mood to talk, but Jeannie kept phoning. She sounded drunker each time. Angry one moment, tearful the next, accusing me of being a bad friend, then weeping and saying she couldn't do without me.*

JEANNIE: *I always did like to keep an open mind.*

OLIVIA: *At first I tried to placate her. I told her Eliza would be home soon from her holiday with Maxie in New Zealand. That she needed to get ready, go and collect her, but only if she was sober enough to drive. She lost her temper. Told me to keep my* nose out of her life and her business. *That it was all right for me there on the other side of the world, the queen of the castle, surrounded by comfort and riches, with an adoring husband. What did I know about hardship or loneliness? What need did I have for an occasional drink? I hadn't even had to go to the trouble of having my own children, had I? I'd got two ready-made ones, two spoilt boys, shipped off out of the way to boarding school. I had no idea how hard it was to raise a child from babyhood, let alone on my own.* [PAUSE]

*It was that last accusation that did it. Jeannie knew I'd longed for a baby of my own. That Edgar and I had tried from the start of our marriage. That I would have done anything to have a daughter. And yet she had taken that knowledge and turned it back on me.* [PAUSE] *I hung up on her. But not before I called her a bitch. A selfish bitch. And told her she didn't deserve Eliza.*

JEANNIE CONTINUES SILENTLY SWINGING BACK AND FORTH.

OLIVIA: *She rang again. Twice. I didn't answer. She left a message. I played it back. She was weeping, but she was still angry at me. She said I was right. That she was a bitch. A selfish bitch. That she didn't deserve Eliza. That maybe it would be better for everyone if she took herself out of Eliza's life. That she would do it as gently as possible. Not make a mess. A bath. A pill. Lots of wine. She even laughed. 'I'm making it sound* quite idyllic, aren't I?' That was the last thing she said to me. Perhaps the last thing she ever said to anyone.

LONG PAUSE.

JEANNIE CONTINUES SWINGING.

OLIVIA: *When Eliza rang me five hours later, I was in the office at work. Her name came up on my phone, and somehow I knew. I knew in that moment what had happened. I don't know how. In that moment, before I answered, before I'd had it confirmed, I knew I would have to lie.*

JEANNIE, SOFTLY, SING-SONG, STILL SWINGING: *Liar, liar, pants on fire.*

OLIVIA: *The only person who ever heard the truth about those conversations is Maxie. I lied about them to Eliza. I lied to the police. The coroner. I lied to Edgar when I told him about it. I told everyone who asked me that yes, Jeannie had rung me five times that day, but I said it was because she was so excited Eliza was coming home again. That she had come up with all sorts of plans for us to get together at Christmas. That she wanted to ask my advice about Eliza's uni accommodation. I lied when I told everyone that she had sounded so happy. So full of plans for the future, for herself and for Eliza. I lied and I lied and I lied.*

STAGE FADES TO BLACK. TEN SECONDS LATER, A SPOT-
LIGHT APPEARS ON MAXIE AT STAGE RIGHT. JEANNIE
IS STILL VISIBLE, GENTLY SWINGING BACK AND FORTH.

MAXIE: *Olivia rang me in New Zealand that night as soon as
she could. Not immediately. After she'd hung up from Eliza, she
rang the emergency services. She wasn't sure if Eliza was able to
do it, after what she'd seen, the shock she was in. I can remember
exactly what she said to me. 'Jeannie's dead, Maxie. She's killed
herself. In the bath. Pills and wine. Oh Jesus, Maxie, oh Jesus.
It's my fault.' I didn't reply to that. I was too busy thinking, 'No,
it's my fault. Olivia, it's my fault, not yours.'* [PAUSE]

*I wasn't surprised at the news. That was the strangest thing.
I should have been, but I wasn't. We'd been worried about
Jeannie for so long. Her mood swings. Her drinking. Her erratic
behaviour. We were even more worried about Eliza. We kept
encouraging her to go to uni. We offered to pay her tuition fees,
cover her living expenses. We thought it would be good to get
Eliza away from her mother for a while. We hoped that having
space to herself would help Jeannie find some peace, to stop
drinking, to maybe seek treatment for her anguished mind.*

*I knew Jeannie hadn't been sleeping properly for months.
She'd rung me, four weeks before she died. We were arranging
Eliza's trip to New Zealand, that was why I rang her, but we were
soon talking about her, not Eliza. She hated her local doctor.
'Suspicious eel-faced bat of a woman' was how she described
her. I remember it because I remember thinking 'eel-faced bat'*

*was a wonderful insult. Jeannie was always able to come up with great insults.*

JEANNIE, SWINGING ABOVE: *Thank you. I liked that one too.*

MAXIE: *Jeannie had been to see her about her insomnia. She told me she'd begged for help. Explained she'd been worrying about Eliza's exam results, about her leaving to go to uni. Said she just needed a bit of help to get through this bump, then she'd be back sleeping naturally again in no time. But the doctor was no fan of sleeping pills. She thought they were addictive. Dangerous. Jeannie couldn't afford to go to Melbourne to find another doctor. She knew there were alerts about doctor shopping, anyway. If she could just get a few good nights' sleep, though, she'd be a different woman, she told me. Had I ever experienced the horror of long-term insomnia? she asked me.*

*She knew I had. I'd told her about it the year before. During a tense time at work, I'd had terrible sleep problems. One of the producers had come to my rescue. She'd been prescribed very strong sleeping pills and still had some left. They worked wonders, she said. She gave me her leftovers. Use them sparingly, she warned me. I'd only needed three of them. So when Jeannie told me she needed help, I was able to say, 'Let me send you something. These are fantastic. But be careful with them.'*

*Of course I knew posting unprescribed medication was illegal. Of course I knew it was dangerous. But I was thinking of*

*Eliza. I wanted her to be able to get ready for her New Zealand trip without worrying about her mother. I decided all Jeannie really needed was a good sleep. So I posted her the pills. I put them between two bars of chocolate and a tea towel showing Oxford Street at Christmas. I packaged it all up and said on a card, 'Enjoy the chocolate. A little is a lot, remember!' I thought Jeannie would enjoy that, pretending that it was the chocolate, when I was talking about the pills.*

JEANNIE, STILL SWINGING: *I did enjoy it. Very witty.*

MAXIE: *Olivia kept saying to me on the phone, 'Maxie, it's my fault. It's my fault.' I thought I was mishearing at first. That she was saying, 'It's your fault, it's your fault.' Then I remembered that I hadn't told her about the sleeping pills. Olivia could be so judgemental sometimes. I knew she wouldn't approve.*

SPOTLIGHT SHINES BRIEFLY ON OLIVIA LOOKING AT MAXIE. HURT EXPRESSION.

MAXIE: *But Olivia wasn't talking about me. She was confessing to me. Telling me about the phone arguments. That she had called Jeannie a bitch. That Jeannie had left a hysterical message saying she was going to take some pills and drink wine and get in the bath. That Olivia had decided to ignore it. But then Olivia suddenly said to me, 'What did you mean, Maxie. Just now. You said it was your fault. What did you mean?'*

425

I told her about the pills. I started crying. I hadn't only sent Jeannie the pills. I had taken Eliza away on holiday. Jeannie would never have done it if Eliza was there. It was all my fault. Mine, not hers.

For five minutes, for five terrible minutes when we should have been talking about how we could get to Eliza, be by her side as quickly as possible, we were talking about ourselves. Trying to absolve ourselves of guilt.

LONG PAUSE.

SPOTLIGHTS APPEAR ON MAXIE, OLIVIA AND JEANNIE, STILL SWINGING ABOVE. SHE LOOKS DOWN AT HER TWO FRIENDS. HER EXPRESSION IS SERIOUS.

OLIVIA: *I said we couldn't talk about it any more. I told Maxie to get on a plane from Auckland to Melbourne. Hire a car, drive to Eliza as quickly as possible. I'd get there from Edinburgh as soon as I could. It took me a day and a half. It's the worst flight I've ever taken in my life.*

MAXIE: *My flight that night was the worst one of my life too.*

OLIVIA: *When we both finally got to her, Eliza was —*

MAXIE: *When we both finally got to her, Eliza was —*

THE SPOTLIGHTS ON THEM GO OUT BRIEFLY. ONLY JEANNIE IS NOW VISIBLE. SHE STOPS SWINGING. SHE IS STARING AHEAD. SHE IS SILENT. THE SPOTLIGHTS APPEAR AGAIN ON MAXIE AND OLIVIA.

OLIVIA: *We knew then that we could never tell anyone what we'd done.*

MAXIE: *Not the police. Not the coroner. Not anyone.* [PAUSE] *Especially not Eliza.*

LONG PAUSE.

THEY SPEAK THE FOLLOWING LINE IN UNISON.

OLIVIA: *It had to be our secret. Eliza needed us.*

MAXIE: *It had to be our secret. Eliza needed us.*

# EPILOGUE

*One year later*

Eliza was in the small garden of the apartment she'd rented in Collingwood. She was watering her collection of pot plants and keeping a close eye on the time. It was a Sunday, so the traffic on the freeway to the airport wouldn't be as busy as on a weekday, but she couldn't be late.

It still felt like a novelty to have every weekend off. It was one of many things she loved about being a temp. Eleven months earlier, she'd signed up with an agency that specialised in placing executive assistants. She'd discovered she had a gift for walking into a busy, chaotic workplace, quickly evaluating what needed to be done and setting up systems to make it happen. Perhaps in the future she might go full-time again. For now, she was enjoying the feeling of freedom.

Not that she was doing nothing on those free weekends. A month after her return from Edinburgh, while settling in to her new suburb, she'd walked down Smith Street and seen a colourful sign in a shop window. 'Arty volunteers needed!' it said. 'All paints supplied!' It was for a drop-in arts centre for local kids. A Saturday art club. She'd phoned the number that afternoon. Since then, for the past ten months, she had spent three hours every Saturday dressed in her oldest, now paint-spattered clothes, alternating between trying to teach a rowdy group of eight- to twelve-year-olds how to draw and paint, and trying to stop those same kids from flinging paint and paper aeroplanes at each other. She loved every minute of it. So did Sullivan. He'd begged his mother to let him sign up for the class as soon as Eliza told him about it. His paintings of lemurs and leafy sea dragons had been a great hit with the other kids.

Rose was all for it, of course. She liked teasing Eliza about her perfect 'work–life balance'. It wasn't perfect, of course – her work still brought as much frustration and as many difficult bosses and clients as it ever had, but she had learned to leave it behind when she left the office at the end of each day.

For the past six weeks, she'd been working in the city centre, three streets away from Gillian's old office. Each morning she'd called into the café downstairs to buy a cup of tea and a ham-and-cheese croissant for Hector, the elderly homeless man. She'd been surprised when he'd recognised her. 'Where have you been, Lofty?' he had shouted the first morning. 'Who stole your hair?'

Her phone pinged. It was Sullivan, playing a word and sending a message. *Is Lawrence here yet??* he'd written. *Not yet but soon*, she replied. He sent back a row of smiley faces and a heart.

The previous week, at Sullivan's insistence, she'd taken him for tea at the boutique hotel Lawrence would soon be managing. It was in South Yarra, close to Melbourne's Botanic Gardens. Bigger than the Montgomery, but smaller than the hotel he'd been managing in San Sebastián. Sullivan had given the building and public areas a close inspection – after googling the hotel's website for photos of the bedrooms and suites – and announced his approval. 'Very nice. Elegant without being showy.'

It wouldn't be Lawrence's first trip to Melbourne. He had visited Eliza for a fortnight in October. They'd talked so much. Laughed often. Made love often. Gone on two weekends away, to a house on the Great Ocean Road and then a cottage in the goldfields of Castlemaine. They'd spent a Sunday at Rose's house, where he had put up with teasing from Rose's older children, some ribbing from Harry and an interrogation from Rose. She'd texted Eliza her glowing approval that same night. Eliza had read it to Lawrence as they lay talking in bed.

There was so much she still wanted to learn about him. He seemed to feel the same about her. He was still one of the kindest men she'd ever met. He made her laugh. He was so interested in the world. She'd enjoyed seeing Melbourne through his eyes.

She had been touched when he asked if she'd show him one of the towns she'd lived in with her mother. She could have taken him to ten towns, ten houses. She took him to the last one, in Heathcote, two hours away. He drove. She'd only just got her learner's permit.

They parked outside. The house still looked run-down. She told him about her life there. About that terrible last night. About the desolate days packing it up. Then she took him to a different town, to Maryborough. They walked down the country road to the cemetery, to Mr and Mrs Quaker's grave. She showed him where her mother's ashes lay. They stood there, arm-in-arm, as Eliza told him more about her mother. There were still so many stories.

The two of them were taking it slowly. Getting to know one another through emails, messages, calls and photographs. She'd asked him if she could enlarge and frame several of his photos. He'd be honoured, he said. They were displayed in her living room. One of the castle in Trim, the stonework glowing against a stormy sky. Another from San Sebastián, a row of palm trees and an azure bay. The third taken on his recent Australian trip, when they went walking in the fern-filled forests of the Grampians. She'd hung his photos beside the one from the school concert, of herself, her mother and her godmothers. Each time she looked at it, she wished it was possible to tell her mother all that was happening. She wished Jeannie could have met Lawrence. She hoped that she would have liked him.

Emmet was looking forward to meeting Lawrence, she knew. Only Dervla had spoken to him at the pub quiz. That morning, Eliza had received an email from Ireland, with the latest version of Emmet's proposed itinerary. He, Dervla and their girls were coming to Australia in three months' time. To visit her, under the guise of a last big family holiday before the girls went to college.

They didn't know yet that Eliza was their half-aunt. Emmet was honouring Sheila's wishes, not just with his daughters, but with his brothers too. They would all be told eventually, though. One day. Eliza knew that.

She and Emmet had discussed it again during a recent phone call. Sheila hadn't reacted well to the news of the Australian trip, Eliza learned. 'Ma's still a bit upset,' was how he put it. Eliza hadn't enquired further. She'd moved from hurt to a kind of acceptance. Emmet knew the workings of his family much better than she ever would. There was still much to be grateful for. A big brother she'd never expected to have, most of all.

She did one more check through her apartment. There wasn't much to tidy up. She still had very few belongings. Her linen, her clothes, the bowls, the vase. Her painting materials on the table by the window. The two postcards of *Carnation, Lily, Lily, Rose* on the fridge.

A ping on her phone alerted her that her taxi to the airport was waiting outside.

His flight was on time. As she waited in Arrivals for him to appear, her phone pinged twice. Her godmothers, of course. She read Olivia's first. *Happy reunion, darling xx*. Then Maxie's: *Welcome Lawrence from us too! xx*

She hadn't seen them since her time in Edinburgh, but they spoke often. Olivia was enjoying her retirement now the Montgomery was sold. She was a doting grandmother to Rory and Milly's baby son, Eddie. They lived around the corner from her new apartment. Olivia told Eliza she sometimes brought

Eddie in to visit Edgar. Maxie was still in New York, still doing her UK TV series work via voiceovers. Eliza had asked Maxie about her playwriting. She had told her that it was on hold for the time being. Mostly, she was enjoying being married to Hazel.

Eliza occasionally asked about Celine, but apart from the photo she'd sent, there'd been no more contact. It was as if she'd disappeared into thin air. 'Thank God,' Olivia said. 'And God help the people of France.'

Olivia sounded so much more relaxed these days. She even spoke warmly about Alex. He had asked her if she would help him choose art to display on the hostel walls. She was enjoying discovering lots of new contemporary Scottish artists, she'd told Eliza. She even joked that it was just as well Edgar couldn't see what she was buying on Alex's behalf. He'd be disgusted, she said.

Both of Eliza's godmothers had claimed credit for her relationship with Lawrence. Maxie insisted it wouldn't have happened if she hadn't proposed to Hazel. Olivia said she was the one who'd convinced Eliza to come to Edinburgh. Eliza told them she thanked them both equally, every day. Not only for bringing Lawrence into her life. For so much else.

The first of the passengers from the long-haul flight began to appear.

She remembered leaving this airport a year ago. How different her life was then. Before she'd learned all there was to know about her mother. Before her godmothers told her the truth.

She saw him the moment he came through the doors. He caught sight of her at the same time.

They were both smiling as she walked across the hall into his open arms.

# CONTINUE READING FOR AN EXTRACT FROM *THOSE FARADAY GIRLS*

## Hobart, Tasmania, Australia 1979

The day the Faraday family started to fall apart began normally enough.

Juliet, at twenty-three the oldest of the five Faraday sisters, was first into the kitchen, cooking breakfast for everyone as she liked to do. This morning it was scrambled eggs, served with small triangles of buttered toast. She added parsley, diced crispy bacon and a dash of cream to the eggs, with a sprinkle of paprika as a garnish. She also set the table with silver cutlery, white napkins, a small crystal vase with a late-blooming red rose from the bush by the front gate and a damp copy of the *Mercury*, which had been thrown over the fence before dawn. The big earthenware teapot that had once belonged to their grandmother had centre place on the table, resting on a Huon pine pot holder that sent out a warm timber smell as it heated up.

Juliet stepped back from the table, pleased with the general effect. She'd been asked by her new boss at the city-centre café where she worked to come up with ideas for menu items. She made a record of this morning's arrangement in her notebook under the title 'English-style Traditional Breakfast???' A smoked kipper or two would have been a nice touch, but they were hard to come by in Hobart. Too smelly, anyway, if her childhood memory served her well.

Twenty-one-year-old Miranda was next up and into the kitchen. She was already fully made-up – black eyeliner, false lashes and very red lipstick – and dressed in her white pharmacy assistant's uniform. She looked around the room.

'Juliet, you really are wasted with us. You'd make some lucky familya lovely maid.'

She absentmindedly pulled in her belt as she spoke. Two months earlier, a visiting perfume sales representative had flattered her by mentioning her slender waist. She'd been working vigorously to get it as thin as possible ever since. She worked in the local chemist, publicly expressing an interest in studying pharmacy, privately thrilled with the access to discount and sample cosmetics.

Juliet was also dressed for work, in a black skirt and white shirt, with a red dressing-gown on top for warmth. She ignored Miranda's remark. 'English-style traditional breakfast, madam?' she asked.

'I'd rather skin a cat,' Miranda answered, reaching for the newspaper.

Eliza, sister number three and nineteen years old, came in next, dressed in running gear. She did a four-kilometre run every morning before she went to university. 'That's not how you use that phrase, is it?'

'It is now. I'd rather skin a cat within an inch of my hen's teeth than put my eggs in Juliet's basket.'

Juliet looked pointedly at Eliza. 'Would you like an English-style traditional breakfast, madam? Toast? Coffee or tea?'

'I'd love everything, thanks. And tea, please. I've got a big day today.' Eliza was studying physical education at university. During the week she coached two junior netball teams. On weekends she ran in cross-country competitions. The only time any of her family saw her out of tracksuits was if she went to church on Sundays, and she rarely did that any more. She took up her usual seat at the wooden table. 'Why do you put yourself through this every morning, Juliet?'

'Practice. Research purposes. A strongly developed sense of familial responsibility. It's all good training for when I have my own café.'

'Really?' Miranda replied. 'So if you were training to be an undertaker you'd embalm us each morning?' She was now eating a grapefruit and ignored a yelp from Eliza as her jabbing spoon sent a dart of juice across the table.

'If you get any funnier, Miranda, I'm going to explode laughing.' Juliet put Eliza's toast on and stood by the window. She pulled her dressing-gown tighter around her body as a sharp breeze came in through a gap in the frame.

It was autumn in Hobart, getting colder each day. Their weatherboard house was heated by open fires in the living room and the kitchen, though they were never lit in the morning. Wood was too expensive. This morning was bright and crisp, at least, the sun strong enough to send gentle light through the red and orange leaves in the front hedge. A scattering of frost lay on the ground. There'd been warnings already that the winter would be a cold one. Possibly even snow, and not just on top of Mount Wellington.

Juliet touched the windowpane as she refilled the kettle. It was icy cold. Their North Hobart house was in the dip of a hilly street, but high enough to give them a view of the mountain, though the trees their father had planted years ago were now threatening to block it. If she stood on tiptoes, Juliet could see the glisten of frost on cars in the street and on the hedges of the houses opposite. She gave a fake little shiver. She liked telling her friends that this weather was nothing like the cold she remembered from her childhood in England. Not that her memories were all that strong any more. Like their English accents, they had nearly faded away.

The whole Faraday family had emigrated to Tasmania twelve years earlier. The girls' father, Leo, a botanist specialising in eucalypt plantations, had been headhunted by a Tasmanian forestry company. Juliet could still remember the excitement of packing everything up in preparation for the month-long sea journey from Southampton. None of them had even heard of Tasmania before then.

The toast popped. Juliet prepared Eliza's breakfast and passed it across. She refilled the teapot for the others. Sadie and Clementine's cups were already on the table. Juliet took down her father's cup and saucer from the shelf. It was a delicate blue colour, with a border of cheerful red blossom. Their mother had always had her morning tea in that cup. Juliet could remember her sipping it, closing her eyes and saying, 'Ah, that hits the spot.' Only Leo used her cup these days.

The kitchen door was pushed open with a bang. 'Bloody hell, Juliet. Look at the time.' Sadie was still dressing herself as she walked in, her head emerging from an orange and red striped poncho. Her hair, last night the model of current fashion with its teased perm, looked like a flattened haystack this morning. None of her sisters remarked on it. She threw her canvas bag and a pair of cork-heeled boots into the corner of the room with a clatter, then slumped into a chair. Sadie woke up grumpy every morning. 'Why didn't you wake me? I told you I have an early lecture.'

'You didn't ask me to wake you. Do you want some breakfast?'

'What is it?'

'Cat sick on toast if you keep talking to me like that.'

'Sorry, Juliet. I'd love some of your beautiful cuisine. Thank you for getting up early to prepare it for me.' Eighteen years old, Sadie was in her first year of an arts degree. One month earlier she'd been in her first year of a science degree. She'd also completed one week of a teaching degree, before changing her mind about that as well. 'Such a shame there's not a degree in dillydallying,' Miranda had remarked. 'You'd top the class in that.'

'Where's Leo?' Eliza asked, bringing her teacup over for a top-up.

'Shed Land. He's been there all morning.' Juliet had been up at seven and the light in the garden shed their father used as his inventing room was already shining. He was spending more time in there these days than out looking after his tree plantations. She decided to give him another ten minutes before checking on him.

Miranda pushed the newspaper away and gave a graceful stretch. Her glossy dark-red hair shimmered down her back as she flexed her arms above her head. 'If you ask me, we're being replaced in his affections by test tubes and soldering irons. Juliet, call the authorities when you've finished washing the dishes, will you? If it isn't bad enough that we're motherless, we're now heading towards fatherlessness.'

'You said you preferred it when he's busy out there.'

'Busy out there is one thing. Abandoning his daughters for days on end is another.'

Juliet secretly preferred it when Leo was in one of his inventing frenzies. Life was much quieter. He didn't care whether each of them had done their share of the housework, express dismay about Miranda's short skirts, tell Sadie off for playing her music too loudly, remind Eliza to mow the front lawn, tell Juliet to find more uses for mince or tell Clementine to get over her hatred of mince. He hadn't even noticed when Juliet served roast chicken midweek, instead of as a rare Sunday luxury. She'd done it as a test.

If things weren't going well in Shed Land, it was like having a bee in the house. He was always around, offering help that wasn't needed and getting in the way. A real sign of his frustration was when he shut the tin door of the shed loudly enough for them to hear over their pop music, strode into the kitchen, turned off the stove or the grill and declared that he was feeling housebound and was going to take the five of them out for dinner somewhere. They usually ended up at Bellerive beach, eating fish and chips at one of the wooden tables by the water. Money was always too tight for restaurants.

'Morning, everyone.' It was Clementine, still in her pyjamas, her school blazer over the top, her long, dark hair tied back into a ponytail.

Four voices answered her in a sing-song way. 'Morning, Clementine.'

Clementine had barely taken her seat when she stood up again, pushed back her chair and made a dash for the bathroom down the hallway. Eliza and Juliet looked at each other. Miranda kept reading. Sadie began to look ill herself.

Clementine came back, whitefaced, clutching a facecloth. 'Sorry about that.'

Juliet looked closely at her little sister. Clementine was always pale – all five of them were – so that was nothing new, but she did look especially peaky this morning. 'Were you sick?'

Clementine nodded.

Juliet guided her gently into a chair and rested a hand on her forehead. She could remember sitting in that chair and having their mother do the same thing to her. It had felt so cool and comforting. It always made her feel a little better, straightaway. 'You don't have a temperature, Clemmie. It must just be a bug.'

'Poor Clemmie,' Miranda said. As Sadie leaned past her to the sugar bowl, she made an exaggerated face, flapping her hands in front of her nose. 'Breathing in Sadie's alcoholic fumes would give anyone a bug. What time did you get in last night, Sadie? I really don't think you are taking your studies seriously, young lady.'

'You're just jealous because I have a good social life and you don't,' Sadie said, putting three spoons of sugar into her tea.

'I have an extraordinary social life. It's just that I also have an extraordinary working life, unlike you two layabouts. Thank God I decided against going to university. Look what it's doing to the two of you. Turning you into hippies in front of our eyes.'

'I'm not a hippy,' Sadie said.

'What's wrong with being a hippy anyway?' Eliza asked.

'Nothing's wrong with being a hippy in the same way that nothing's wrong with being a smelly old dog lying around in front of a fire. It's just not what I want to be.'

'You think you are so perfect, Miranda,' Sadie said. 'You're not. You're so superficial. All you care about is make-up and clothes —'

'And perfume,' Miranda said. 'Don't forget perfume. And I'm reasonably interested in magazines, fake compliments and men buying me drinks.'

Juliet stepped in. 'Do you want to try some tea and toast now, Clemmie?'

'No, thanks. I'll skip breakfast.'

'You're not on a diet again, are you, Clementine?' Miranda said. 'The pressures of impending fame getting to you?'

She managed a smile. 'Something like that.'

'Everything okay with the play?' Juliet asked. Clementine had been out late each night that week doing final rehearsals for her school play, on top of all the weekend run-throughs. She had a walk-on role as a pirate and a credit in the program as assistant set designer. Juliet had been very pleased to hear it. Clementine was usually more scientific than artistic and not usually this enthusiastic about after-school activities. Juliet had discovered the real reason two weeks earlier, when she spotted Clementine and David Simpson, the boy playing the lead role in the play, holding hands as they walked down Elizabeth Street.

'It's fine. Why?'

Juliet shrugged. 'You've seemed distracted the last couple of weeks.'

'It's all fine. Just busy. But there —'

'Juliet, are there any eggs left?' Sadie interrupted. She always went for seconds. Miranda called her the Human Scrap Bin to her face, Piggly-Wiggly behind her back.

'In the pan. Help yourself.'

'Would you serve it up for me? Please?'

'No bones in your arms?' Juliet asked.

Sadie waggled her arms in a floppy way.

'Fall for that and you're a fool, Juliet,' Miranda murmured, flicking the page of the paper.

Juliet served Sadie anyway.

'Where's Dad?' Clementine asked.

'Shed Land,' Juliet, Miranda, Sadie and Eliza said together.

'No, he's not, he's here. Morning, my lovelies.' Leo Faraday came through the side door, bringing a gust of the cool morning air with him. He was dressed in a wide-lapelled grey suit, a crisp white shirt and a blue patterned tie. His hair had been slicked back, the usual dark-red quiff smoothed over. 'And yes, before you feel duty-bound to point it out, I do look extremely smart today and yes, I do have a meeting. Juliet, breakfast smells delicious. Miranda, what is that black stuff around your eyes; you look like a lady of the night. Eliza, have you been for a run already? Sadie, pick up your boots, would you? What's up with you, Clementine? You look like a wet dishrag.'

'She's got a stomach bug,' Juliet said.

'Poor chicken.' His concerned words rang false. He was smiling from ear to ear.

Juliet passed across the blue cup and saucer. 'Everything all right, Dad? What's going on out there?'

'Good things, Juliet. Interesting things. Unusual things.'

'In your mind, or in reality?' Miranda asked.

'We hardly see you any more, Dad,' Sadie complained.

Leo put down his cup and rubbed his hands together. 'Something hot is a-cooking out there, my girls. Something is nearly at boiling point. This time I really think —'

'Good heavens, is that the time?' Miranda said in an overly dramatic tone. They'd all had too many years of his invention talk. The revolutionary motor oil that put their old car off the road for three months. The device designed to repel spiders that had done exactly the opposite. The electronic rain gauge that burst into flames on its first test run. 'I'd better finish getting ready or I'll be late.'

Clementine stood up, clutching the facecloth to her lips, and ran to the bathroom again. They all heard the door slam.

'My word, she's a sensitive soul,' Miranda remarked, looking after her. 'Clemmie, it's all right, I'll be back after work.'

Clementine returned a few minutes later, palefaced. 'Sorry.'

'Have you been sick again?' At Clementine's nod, Juliet felt her sister's forehead once more. 'Are you sure you're okay?'

Leo felt her forehead too. 'You're not hot, but you are a bit clammy.'

'Clemmie's clammy,' Sadie said.

Miranda gave a bark of laughter. Sadie looked pleased. She liked making Miranda laugh.

'Have you eaten anything unusual?' Leo asked. 'It's not food poisoning, is it?'

'No, I'm sure it's not.'

'Too many late nights, that's what it is,' Sadie said. 'The sooner that romance – oh, I'm sorry, Clementine – the sooner that *play* is over, the better.'

'What will I wear on opening night?' Miranda asked. 'My blue gown or that amusing little lace number my couturier sent over from Paris last week? What about you, Sadie? Will you wear that jumper made of yak hair or perhaps that simply darling little patchoulisteeped handweave I saw you prancing about in last week? How many small rodents died in the making of that, I wonder?'

Leo was still concerned. 'Clementine, I'm not sure you should go to school today. You really do look peaky.'

'I think she should go to the doctor. That's the third morning this week she's been sick,' Sadie said.

'Third time this week?' Miranda raised an eyebrow. 'Really? I didn't realise that. Uh oh. It's morning. She's sick. Put 'em together and what do we see? P-r-e-g-n-a-n-cee.'

There should have been a laugh from one of her sisters. There should have been a denial from Clementine. There should have been a rebuke from Leo, and a smart answer back from Miranda.

Instead there was silence.

## AVAILABLE NOW

# ACKNOWLEDGEMENTS

*The Godmothers* is dedicated to a dear friend in Dublin, John Neville, who not only handmade my beautiful writing desk, but built my writing attic too.

My fictional Montgomery family's surname is a tribute to the late, much-loved journalist Bruce Montgomery and his wife Vicki, special friends since we met in Tasmania in 1996. Sadly, Monty died of cancer in January 2020, and is greatly missed by his family and friends. It means so much to me that he was happy and amused about me borrowing his surname for this novel.

Many people helped me with all sorts of research for *The Godmothers*. My big thanks to Xavier McInerney, Ethan Miller, Ruby Clements, Mikaella Clements, Ulli Clements, Dominic McInerney, Ben Petit, Pavel Barter, Katie Farrell, Dr Louise Dodds, Alan Macfarlane, Melanie Scaife, Catherine Dunne and my early readers Mary, Marie and Lea McInerney.

*Acknowledgements*

Thanks to my friends in Ireland, Australia and the UK for their listening ears and bookish support, especially Sinéad Moriarty, Noëlle Harrison, Claudia Carroll, Liz Nugent, Brona Miller, Maria Dickenson, Steph Dickenson, Sarah Conroy, Louise Ní Chríodáin, Sarah Duffy, Clare Forster, Kristin and Graham Gill, Nicolás an Piscín, Joanna and Keith Troughton, Jane Melross, Karen O'Connor, Bart Meldau, Carol George, Noelene Turner, Helen Trinca, Janet Grecian, Christopher Pearce, Mandy and Bruce Macky, Margie and Mark Arnold and Rod Quinn of ABC Overnights.

I'm so grateful to have been edited and published for the past twenty years and thirteen books by the wonderful Ali Watts of Penguin Random House Australia. It's been a pleasure to work with her colleagues on *The Godmothers* too: Amanda Martin, Melissa Lane, Julie Burland, Justin Ractliffe, Nikki Christer, Lou Ryan, Gavin Schwarcz, Jo Baker, Janine Brown, Debbie McGowan, Alysha Farry, Karen Reid, Bella Arnott-Hoare, Emily Hindle, Radhiah Chowdhury, cover designer Alex Ross, illustrator Dean Proudfoot and Midland Typesetters. It's also great to be setting forth in the UK and Ireland with Jon Elek, Rosa Schierenberg and all the team at Welbeck Publishing in London.

Love and warmest thanks to my agents in Australia and the UK: Fiona Inglis, Benjamin Stevenson, Clair Roberts and all at Curtis Brown Australia, and Jonathan Lloyd, Lucy Morris, Hannah Beer, Kate Cooper and all at Curtis Brown UK. My thanks also to Frances Brennan and Alan Duffy in Dublin, and photographer Matt Turner in Adelaide.

# Acknowledgements

None of this would be possible without the constant support I receive from booksellers and readers. Thank you all so much.

As ever and always, much love and thanks to all the McInerneys and Drislanes in Australia, Ireland and Germany; Austin O'Neill for his expert IT help at home; my sister Maura McInerney, first reader and first editor extraordinaire; and my husband John, for everything.

# ABOUT THE AUTHOR

Monica McInerney is the author of 12 bestselling books, published internationally and in translation in 12 languages. Her most recent novel, *The Trip of a Lifetime*, went straight to number 1 in Australia and was a Top 10 bestseller in Ireland. She has been shortlisted in the Irish Book Awards and the UK's RNA Awards, and her novel *Those Faraday Girls* won the 2008 General Fiction Book of the Year in the Australian Book Industry Awards. She was shortlisted in the same category in subsequent years for her novels *The Trip of a Lifetime, At Home with the Templetons, Lola's Secret* and *All Together Now*.

In 2006, Monica was the main ambassador for the Australian Government's Books Alive national reading campaign, for which she wrote a limited edition novella called *Odd One Out*. In 2019, 2018, 2016 and 2014, Monica was voted in the Top 10 of *Booktopia's* annual poll naming Australia's Favourite Authors.

Monica grew up in a family of seven children in the Clare Valley of South Australia and has been living between Australia and Ireland for nearly thirty years. She and her Irish husband currently live in Dublin.

monicamcinerney.com
facebook.com/monicamcinerneyauthor
instagram.com/monicamcinerneyauthor

# WELBECK

PUBLISHING GROUP

## Love books? Join the club.

Sign-up and choose your preferred genres to receive tailored news, deals, extracts, author interviews and more about your next favourite read.

From heart-racing thrillers to award-winning historical fiction, through to must-read music tomes, beautiful picture books and delightful gift ideas, Welbeck is proud to publish titles that suit every taste.

## bit.ly/welbeckpublishing

WELBECK

ANDRE
DEUTSCH

MORTIMER

MORTIMER

WELBECK